Dukat snee[...]e now.
You've bec[...]e Bajo-
rans. What'[...]a hard
look. "*Tem[...]*

Kell came to his feet. [...]p! How
dare you stand before me and judge my orders! You will
respect my rank and do as I command you!"

"I understand these aliens. I've seen how they think,
how they feel and what they want." Unbidden, memories
surfaced in his thoughts. *On the battlements of the Naghai
Keep on the eve of the great feast. Dukat and the lawman,
Darrah, talking as two men, nothing more; then again, in the corridors of the castle, as hate filled him and the need to take Hadlo's
life burned in his skin.* The Bajoran's words came back to
in him a flash of insight. *We're a passionate people. We get so
angry about things we lose focus on everything else.* "The Bajorans hold grudges forever," he told them. "They nurture
them like their children. All we need to do to blindside
these people is to bring them to rage. You only made them
afraid. We need to make them furious." Dukat leaned forward and picked up a padd from the jagul's desk. On it was
a report of two Bajoran warships that had recently departed
the star system. The raw anger he had felt when he entered
the room waned, replaced by a colder, more controlled
resentment. They were forming a pact here, he realized.
Without open words or accords, Dukat, Ico, and Kell were
opening the way to the fall of an entire civilization. *For the
good of Cardassia. For Athra and my family.*

"I know exactly how to do it," he told them.

STAR TREK®
TEROK NOR

DAY OF THE VIPERS
2318-2328

James Swallow

Based upon STAR TREK created by
Gene Rodenberry,
and STAR TREK: DEEP SPACE NINE®,
created by Rick Berman and Michael Piller

POCKET BOOKS
New York   London   Toronto   Sydney   Korto

Pocket Books
A Division of Simon & Schuster, Inc.
1230 Avenue of the Americas
New York, NY 10020

This book is a work of fiction. Names, characters, places, and incidents either are products of the author's imagination or are used fictitiously. Any resemblance to actual events or locales or persons, living or dead, is entirely coincidental.

First Pocket Books paperback edition April 2008

POCKET and colophon are registered trademarks of Simon & Schuster, Inc.

For information about special discounts for bulk purchases, please contact Simon & Schuster Special Sales at 1-800-456-6798 or business@simonandschuster.com.

Cover art by John Picacio

Interior designed by Jill Putorti

Manufactured in the United States of America

10 9 8 7 6 5 4 3 2 1

ISBN-13: 978-1-4165-5093-8
ISBN-10:   1-4165-5093-3

For my parents,
who showed me the way to the stars

Dramatis Personae

Arin (Bajoran male) priest, aide to Kai Meressa

Bennek (Cardassian male) a priest of the Oralian Way

Coldri Senn (Bajoran male) a high-ranking Militia officer

Cotor (Bajoran male) a senior vedek at the Kendra Monastery

Darrah Mace (Bajoran male) officer of the Korto City Watch

Darrah Karys (Bajoran female) wife of Darrah Mace

Procal Dukat (Cardassian male) archon in the Cardassian military justice system and father of Skrain Dukat

Skrain Dukat (Cardassian male) officer in the Cardassian military

Els Renora (Bajoran female) public defender for the Korto Justice Department

Gar Osen (Bajoran male) priest, resident of Korto District

Hadlo (Cardassian male) senior priest of the Oralian Way

Rhan Ico (Cardassian female) non-military xenologist

Jaro Essa (Bajoran male) senior Militia officer

Jas Holza (Bajoran male) Korto District administrator and member of the Chamber of Ministers

Jekko Tybe (Bajoran male) adjutant for Minister Keeve Falor, former partner of Darrah Mace

Keeve Falor (Bajoran male) member of the Chamber of Ministers

Danig Kell (Cardassian male) high-ranking officer in the Cardassian military

Kubus Oak (Bajoran male) member of the Chamber of Ministers

Lale Usbor (Bajoran male) First Minister of Bajor, succeeding Verin Kolek

Pasir Letin (Cardassian male) a priest of the Oralian Way

Li Tarka (Bajoran male) colonel in the Militia Space Guard

Lonnic Tomo (Bajoran female) senior adjutant to Minister Jas Holza

Meressa (Bajoran female) kai of the Bajoran faith

Myda (Bajoran female) officer of the Korto City Watch

Kotan Pa'Dar (Cardassian male) non-military Cardassian xenologist

Proka Migdal (Bajoran male) officer of the Korto City Watch

Tima (Bajoran female) religious novice

Syjin (Bajoran male) freelance pilot and courier

Tunol (Cardassian female) officer in the Cardassian military under Skrain Dukat

Verin Kolek (Bajoran male) First Minister of Bajor during 2318

DAY OF THE VIPERS

OCCUPATION DAY ZERO

◆ ◆ ◆

2328 (Terran Calendar)

Prologue

The priest's hand rested on the small, carved handle that controlled the pitch of the window's nyawood shutters. A slight turn of the wrist would be all it required to close them firmly against the lessening day outside, but he hesitated, peering through the slits at the city streets ranged below. The smell of smoke was more pronounced now, and the faint acridity made his nostrils twitch. The scent was already in the room with him, different from the wisps that issued up from the cairn of glowing stones in the chamber's fire pit. Outside, the fires that raged were uncontrolled and full of lethality; in here, deep within the fusionstone halls of the Naghai Keep, he was safe.

The thought drew up the corners of his lips in a brief, bitter smile, his blandly handsome face turning away. *Safe.* The term was such a relative concept, a fragile construct stitched together by fearful men and women who marked out pieces of their world and declared them inviolate, as if they could wall off danger and forbid it to trespass. Gar Osen, vedek of the Prophets, could declare himself *safe* inside these walls, but he knew that the granite battlements and copper-studded gates were no more than paper to an aggressor who was determined to breach them. To think of oneself as safe from anything was foolish; a person could only truly exist in degrees of jeopardy, spending their life balancing the chances of death against moments of comparative peace. The bitter smile turned grim and stony.

Beneath the windows of the keep, far out past the ring wall and the ornamental public gardens beyond, into the city of Korto itself, Gar's gaze ranged over the shaded boulevards of the municipality. The fading day was prematurely dark with oily gray rain clouds rolling in from across the Sahving Valley, as if the weather itself were attempting to draw a veil over what was happening down on Korto's thoroughfares; but he had no doubts that the same sequence of events was taking place all over Bajor, in the cities of Ilvia, Jalanda, and Ashalla, across the spans of the planet from Musilla to Hedrikspool and every province in between.

He imagined he would see the same thing, hear the same sounds if he could stand at similar vantage points in those places. A woman's scream, sharp as the bark of a tyrfox; the long rumble of a building collapsing; air molecules shrieking as disruptors split them asunder; and the regular pulsing drum of gravity-resist motors. Gar saw a trio of shapes nosing slowly over the Edar Bridge, shield-shaped things that looked like legless beetles, shoving stalled skimmers out of their way with arcing force bumpers. Each had a spindly cannon on a pintle mount that tracked back and forth, tireless and robotic. For a moment, he wished for a monocular so that he might be able to get a better look at the armored vehicles, but there was little need. The priest knew exactly what they were.

If he looked hard enough, he could just about make out the insignia painted on the sloping, gunmetal-colored hulls: a scythe-edged fan, something like a spread flower. The sigil, just like the grav-tanks and the beings that crewed them, was unlike anything native to Bajor. And yet they moved, not with the wary pace of new invaders, but with the arrogant and stately menace of an occupying army. Gar had only to watch them, and now the lines of figures in black battle armor coming up behind the tanks, to know that the Bajorans had already lost. The arrival had come, silent and steady as the sunrise, and Bajor had been looking the other way.

The more Gar looked, the more he saw. Black-suited shapes here and there, in the marketplace and the City Oval. The blink of beam fire, followed seconds later by the noise of it reaching him high in the keep. He wondered idly where the citadel's defenders had gone. Were they still up above him on the ramparts, peering through their rifle scopes at the same sights, too afraid to do anything, too surprised to discover they were no longer *safe?* Or perhaps they had run, fled to the hills or back to their families in the low-caste quarters of the city. The priest doubted that anyone had been able to escape. Nothing but smoke was in the air now, and he hadn't seen anything lift off from the riverside port since the morning—and even that craft had been so small and so fast, it was impossible to know its design and origin.

He thought he heard a clattering from the gates, but Gar's chamber was on the far side of the keep from the main portcullis and the wind rose and fell, bringing only snatches of sound to his ears. Not for the first time that day, his thoughts drifted to the desk in the middle of the room where his effects lay in untidy profusion. Beside an open copy of Yalar's New Insights was a cloth bundle concealing a narrow-bore phaser pistol. There was plenty of room inside the vedek's voluminous robes to conceal the gun, but then what would that benefit him? To be an armed priest on today of all days—it invited trouble. And besides, he was quite capable of killing with his bare hands, if the matter pressed him to it. He looked down at his spread palms, at the thin and lightly tanned skin, the lengthy artisan's fingers. There was a moment of disconnection, as if the hands belonged to someone else.

Gar heard sounds out in the corridor beyond and the thread of his reverie snapped. Swift, frightened footfalls stumbled along the wooden floors, getting closer by the second. The vedek stepped to the table and laid a hand on the phaser, those long fingers slipping into the cloth to wrap around the weapon's knurled grip.

A hard report sounded on the chamber door. He could hear someone gasping in deep breaths on the other side. "Gar! Gar!" The words were high with effort and terror. "Are you in there? For Fate's sake, open the door!"

Gar knew the voice, and he schooled his face in the moment before he released the latch.

A hooded figure in pastel-colored robes fell in through the door and slammed it shut behind. The hood fell back to reveal slick, jet-black hair framing a pale gray face lined in ropelike ridges, sunken blue eyes darting back and forth across the chamber. The Cardassian held a leather carryall clutched to his chest, knuckles white where they held on to the strap with wild determination. He blinked and swallowed hard. "Brother," he began breathlessly, "you have no idea how glad I am to see you! I didn't dare to hope that you would still be here."

Gar opened his hands. "Where else would I be, Bennek, if not here? In times of crisis, the Prophets would not have us flee and leave our kindred alone."

Bennek hesitated at those words, as if he sensed something of an admonition in them. He worked visibly to calm himself and placed the bag upon the table, taking an empty seat. Gar offered him a flask of water, and the Cardassian drank greedily.

"Why are you here?" Gar asked carefully. "You must know the keep won't offer you any sanctuary."

Bennek's eyes widened. "You would turn me out?"

Gar shook his head. "I mean that this place won't protect you."

The other man sagged in the chair. "I . . . I know that. They're out there, sweeping the streets with bio-scanners. Looking for Cardassian life signs." He nodded bleakly. "Yes. They'll find me soon enough. It's inevitable."

"The others?" The vedek eyed the bag, wondering about its contents.

"Gone," Bennek said in a dead voice. "Scattered, murdered . . . I pray to Oralius that it is not so, but I have only seen bodies." He grabbed at Gar's wrist in sudden panic. "What if . . . what if I am the only one left? What if I am the last to walk the Way?"

Gently, the vedek peeled Bennek's fingers from his arm and pushed him away. "My friend," he said quietly, "I can only imagine what horrors you are facing at this moment, and I pray for you. I know the Prophets and your Oralius will watch over you. You must be strong, Bennek, for if indeed you *are* the last of your faith, then you alone must rise to bear the weight of it."

The Cardassian looked away. "I don't know if I can." He choked off a sob. "I . . . Tima, she . . ."

"Strength, Bennek," repeated Gar. "The time for more mortal concerns will come later." He glanced at the window. The thrumming of the tanks was closer. "But for now, you should get away. Go to ground."

"Can you hide me?" The words were plaintive, like a child's. This Bennek was a far cry from the one who had first arrived on Bajor so many years earlier, full of purpose and brimming with unshakable belief. All that had been slowly beaten from him, flensed away over time until he was little more than the pale echo sitting before Gar. These past days, the events unfolding across Bajor, Osen saw now how they were the last turns of the screw, the final pressures that broke the Cardassian priest's will. "Please?" Bennek asked.

Gar shook his head. "You ask too much, Bennek. You've

been out on the streets, you've seen what is happening in Korto. If they find you here, they'll burn the keep to the ground, and everyone in it. Would you want that?" He advanced a step. "Would Tima want that?"

"No," Bennek said quietly, and then with more conviction, "No." A measure of his former strength returned to the Cardassian. "You're right, of course. Forgive me for my weakness."

"I'm sure even Oralius knows that no man can be strong every day."

Bennek nodded. "But now I have to be." He opened the bag and removed an object hastily wrapped in a torn and scorched strip of prayer tapestry. Gar recognized the tightly lined forms of Hebitian script across the blackened cloth. Bennek unrolled the tapestry and revealed an ornate mask carved from milky gray wood. The features of it were unquestionably Cardassian, but strangely fluid as well, and bore odd striations that some observers might think mimicked the nasal ridges of a native Bajoran. Something about the mask unsettled the vedek, but he was careful not to let that emotion show on his face.

Bennek let out a small cry of despair as he took up the mask and a part of it came away in his hands, a piece from the orbit of the right eye, whorled with delicately worked filigree in latinum and jevonite. "It must have been damaged when I ran from the encampment."

"It's only a small impairment." Gar appraised the mask. "This is an impressive relic."

"It is one of the original Faces of the Fates, from the time of the First Hebitians on Cardassia," said the other priest. "I've kept it safe for years . . ." He blinked, shaking away a moment of distraction. Placing the mask on the table, Bennek delved into the bag again and brought out a nested set of tubes made from murky glass. More etchings in the careful Hebitian script covered the exterior. "The

Recitations," explained the Cardassian. "This is one of only a few complete copies of the Word of my faith. This, my Bajoran brother, is the holy text of the Oralian Way in its entirety." Bennek's hands were shaking as he touched it.

Gar was no stranger to the religion, having seen Bennek and the members of his congregation perform their rites on many occasions. They would don the masks, ceremonially assuming the role as the avatar of their god, before speaking the lessons of Oralius as read from their sacred scrolls. The vedek assumed that somewhere there had to be definitive originals of the text, but he had never dared to imagine that one of them might be here, on Bajor. Bennek's breathless awe in the face of these two objects was ample illustration of the incalculable value the Oralians placed on them. "Why do you show me these things?" he asked.

The Cardassian was on his feet, nodding to himself. "You cannot hide me, I was wrong to ask it of you. I will leave this place, but in the name of our twin faiths, I ask you to do this for me, Osen." He pointed at the relics. "Conceal them. Hide the mask and the scrolls from the soldiers and promise me you will never reveal their location as long as you live, not until the soul of Cardassia grows strong again, not until the Voice of Oralius is ready to be heard once more. Tell me you will do this." Bennek thrust the scrolls into Gar's hands, and the vedek rocked back. "Swear it!"

There were more footsteps out in the corridor: the heavy thud of armored boots matched with the splintering of doors being kicked open. Gar heard gruff voices shouting and calling out commands to one another.

Bennek's eyes were pleading, shining with fear. "In the name of your Prophets," he cried, *"swear it!"*

TEN YEARS AGO

◆ ◆ ◆

2318 (Terran Calendar)

1

He made his way along the gridded walkway across the central span of the mess hall, throwing curt juts of the chin to the other junior officers who saw him pass. Glinn Matrik gestured toward an empty chair at his table, but Skrain Dukat ignored him and passed on by, stepping down into the sunken level of the dining area, to a bench with only one occupant, the surface of the table a controlled mess of padds.

Kotan Pa'Dar glanced up from the bowl of *tefla* broth before him, and his eyes widened in mild surprise. The scientist toyed briefly with the spoon in his hand as Dukat sat down opposite him with his tray of edibles. Pa'Dar aimed his utensil at the other man's bowl. "The broth's quite horrible," he began. "I think the dried *rokat* might have been a better choice."

In spite of himself, the dalin's youthful face soured. "There's a saying in the Central Command," Dukat noted. "The Union Fleet runs on three things. Determination. Obedience. And salted dry *rokat* fillets. Serve a term or two aboard a starship, Kotan, and you'll come to hate that fish as much as any of us do."

Pa'Dar smiled slightly. "I've never really eaten it that much, I must say."

"It's a staple on every fleet ship and installation from

here to the Spinward Edge." Dukat sipped the broth; and it was horrible. "I imagine *rokat* doesn't appear on the plates of families from Culat that often. Perhaps you're used to the finer things in life."

The scientist's face darkened around his jaw ridges. "It isn't that."

"Oh?" Dukat broke off a piece of black bread and soaked it in his soup. "It's always been my understanding that your family is one of ... shall we say, one of those better equipped to deal with the hardships of life?" He snorted. "When I was a boy in Lakat, there were times when a meal of overcured *rokat* would have seemed like a feast. For many, that still holds true today, perhaps even more so." For an instant, Dukat felt the ghost of an empty stomach, the memory of tightness in his gut from malnutrition. Even now, with two full meals a day at his command as a serving Union officer, the echo of the hungry child he had been still shadowed him there at the edges of his thoughts. He shook the moment away.

"You're teasing me, Skrain," said Pa'Dar. "I can't help where I was born any more than you can."

He nodded after a moment. "Yes, I am teasing you. It's because you're such an easy target." He grinned, showing white teeth, and sucked at the bread, savoring the simplicity of it.

Pa'Dar relaxed a little. The stocky young civilian had a bright mind, but he was sometimes so very naïve for a Cardassian. In truth, Dukat felt a little sorry for him. A life growing up in a relatively wealthy councillor clan from a university city, and then nothing but service to the Ministry of Science ... Kotan Pa'Dar was a sheltered fellow, and the dalin felt obliged to repay him for his diverting—if sometimes rather bland—company by opening his eyes.

"Is that why you're eating with me?" Pa'Dar shot a look over at Matrik and the other glinns two tables away, making rough sport of some off-color joke. "Before I came aboard this ship, my experience of dealing with military officers was usually one of clipped orders and dour disdain. At the best, scornful looks and faint distrust."

Dukat gestured languidly. "That's the soldierly mind-set for you, my friend. We're trained to regard you civilians as a regrettable impediment to our endeavors."

Pa'Dar glanced at him, and Dukat could see once again that Pa'Dar wasn't really certain if his friend was being honest or mocking. "So, then. Why are you joining me here, instead of making fun of me at a distance?"

"Don't you like my company?" Dukat replied. "As dalin, I *am* a ranking junior officer aboard the *Kornaire.*" He spread his hands to take in the room, the starship. "I know this is hardly the gul's private dining chambers, but still . . ."

"I'm just trying to understand you a little better, Dukat. I'm a scientist, that's what I do. I see phenomena, I seek answers."

"Phenomena." Dukat repeated the word, amused by it. "I've never thought of myself in that fashion."

"Your behavior is rather atypical for a Union officer."

Dukat stroked his chin. "Quite correct. I am atypical, very much so." He leaned closer. "There's too much rigidity in our people, Kotan. Compartmentalization and stratification. It breeds stagnation. Why shouldn't a scientist and a soldier share a meal and speak plainly to one another? Narrow-mindedness won't serve Cardassia in the long term, and I aim to serve Cardassia for a very long term indeed."

The doors slid open to allow the priests to enter the dining chamber, and they swept in, in a rustle of azure and cream-colored robes, long lines of square metallic beads trailing away along the lengths of their arms and the layered wrappings across their torsos. The larger of the two scowled through the thick luster of his beard and aimed a narrow-eyed glare at Kell; the gul sat indolently at the end of his table, pouring himself a generous glass of *rokassa* juice.

In return Kell saluted with the jug and gestured to the room's other occupant, an austere female in the duty fatigues of the science ministry. "Forgive me, Hadlo, but Professor Ico and I were quite hungry and we started without you." He smiled, a smug expression with no real humor in it. "There's still a serving for you and your, uh, associate." Kell nodded to the younger of the priests, who hovered nervously at the older man's shoulder.

Hadlo took his seat at the gul's table and gestured for his aide to join him. "We were detained by matters of the Way," he explained. "The day-meal must be marked by a brief thanksgiving to Oralius. I have explained this to you before, Gul Kell."

Kell nodded. "Ah yes, of course. But the Central Command's military regulations are quite strict on the scheduling of refreshment periods during shipboard operations. I'm sorry, but I cannot delay a meal in order to accommodate your . . . unique requirements." He sniffed. "Perhaps you could arrange to have your ritual earlier?"

"Oralius does not follow a mortal clock," said the younger priest. "Her Way has remained unchanged for millennia."

"Bennek," said Hadlo, with a warning in his tone. He helped himself to a healthy serving of broth. "Perhaps, Gul, you might consider attending *us* at some point during our journey to Bajor. The space you graciously provided my group in the *Kornaire*'s cargo hold has proven most adequate to our needs. I would enjoy having you visit to hear a recitation."

Ico took a purse-lipped sip of the *rokassa* and watched the interaction, faintly amused. She'd seen the same thing play out a dozen times over the course of the journey

from Cardassia Prime, and the woman found herself wish-
ing she had kept track of the barbs that lanced back and
forth between the two men. It would be interesting to tally
a final score between priest and soldier by the time they
arrived at Bajor.

Kell's face was a barely concealed sneer. "As diverting as
your readings might be, I'm afraid the very real and pressing matters of commanding this starship occupy every
moment of my time. I have no opportunity, or indeed
motivation, to sit and listen to your scriptures." He grunted.
"Central Command would prefer me to attend to issues of
certainty, not ephemera."

Ico decided to press upon the sore spot, just for the sake
of alleviating her own boredom. "I wonder. Have your
recitations drawn the attendance of any members of the
Kornaire's crew?"

Bennek answered for his superior. "We have seen some
new faces, Professor, yes. Admittedly, less than I had hoped."

Kell colored. "I'll have the names of any of my men
who shirk their duties to hear you talk about phantom deities," he growled.

Hadlo chuckled dryly. "My esteemed Gul Danig Kell,
you remind me of Tethen, the proud man from the fourth
codex of the Recitations. Like you, he refused to open his
eyes, even when the Faces of the Fates spoke directly to
him—"

"Spare me," Kell broke in. "I thought we agreed last
time that you would leave your holy scrolls at the door."

"Just as you agreed not to mock our faith," Bennek said
hotly.

Kell eyed the youth. "Have a care, boy. Remember
whose starship you're standing on. Remember whose air
you're breathing."

Ico put down her glass with an audible *clack*. "This is
the Union's starship, is it not?" She took a deep breath.

"And this is the Union's air as well. As much the property of the Cardassian people as it is that of the Central Command." The woman nodded to Hadlo and Bennek. "And these men, as much as you or I might take issue with their beliefs, are still Cardassian."

"Correct, as ever, Rhan," Kell allowed silkily. "Sometimes it escapes me that we all have a function to perform in this endeavor."

"We would not be here if our presence was not vital to this delegation," Bennek continued, unwilling to be mollified. He took a terse sip of *rokassa*. "The Detapa Council asked us to attend this mission in order to open a dialogue with the Bajorans. I find it difficult to understand why they agreed to let a commander who so clearly finds our presence distasteful direct this formal contact!"

Ico studied the youth; he had fire, that was evident, but he was untrained, and he lacked the ability to focus his passion that Kell or his mentor possessed. She imagined that he would learn that lesson soon, or else he would find himself facing men who were less inclined to suffer his foolishness. "Gul Kell is one of the Second Order's most highly decorated officers," Ico offered. "I'm sure he would never let even the smallest of personal prejudices affect the performance of his duties."

"Quite so," Hadlo added, making an attempt to derail any further argument before it moved forward. He gestured to himself, then to Ico and Kell in order. "The Oralian Way, the Ministry of Science, and Central Command have all entrusted us with this important formal contact. Together, we will meet Bajor and show them the face of a unified Cardassia."

"Unified?" The youth wasn't willing to let the matter drop; and indeed, Ico could see a small quirk of pleasure on Kell's lips as well. The gul was in the mood to argue, she could see it in the tension around his eye ridges. "What unity is there in Cardassia these days, beyond the unity of suffering?" Bennek put down his glass and stared at Ico. "Have you seen the datastreams from the homeworld, Professor? The reports of the famine and the dissent among our people?"

"Our people?" Kell said quietly. "Some would say it is *your* people who have brought those things to pass, Oralian."

Bennek ignored the other man, his watery gaze still on the scientist. "The planets of our species are pushed ever closer to the edge of poverty, the forced austerity imposed by the military stretching our civilization to its limits. And for what? So that we can engage in pointless, unresolved conflicts with the Federation, and petty skirmishes with the Talarians?"

"I am not a soldier," Ico ventured in a mild tone, "but even as an academic I recognize the threat the Talarians pose to our borders, Bennek. Do you not agree that they are a warlike race, expansionist and violent? Have you not seen the records of the raids they made on our fringe colonies?"

The young priest swallowed. He had clearly expected Ico to support him in the face of Kell's bellicose manner, and now that she had not done so, he was floundering. "I . . . I have," he returned. "But I question the need for us to commit so much matériel and men to fighting them. We've warned them off. If they keep out of our space, shouldn't that be enough? Why do we have to invade their republic again and again when the effort of that war could sustain lives at home?"

Kell grunted with laughter. "Military doctrine by way of a priest. I never thought I'd see the like." The gul leaned forward. "Boy, all you have done is show your ignorance. For the record, the conflict with those Talarian savages is not a war. They don't deserve the honor of such a thing. It is a punitive engagement." He made loops in the air with his free hand. "They're like voles. Small, sharp teeth, quick, and numerous. Kept down, you understand, they are nothing but a minor impediment. But allow them to breed too much and you'll soon find an infestation on your doorstep. The Talarians dared to come into our space, the voles into our house." He grinned at his own analogy. "So we drove them out. And now we must cull their numbers. For their own good."

"And what about Cardassia's good?"

Ico sighed inwardly. The priest did not know when to be silent. Ignoring Hadlo's hand on his arm, he turned to face Kell, his cheeks darkening with anger. A more seasoned man might have known that this conversation was on a downward spiral, but Bennek was not a seasoned man. Ico knew that there was only one way this meal would end now, and it would not be quietly.

"Instead of sending ships to blockade Talaria, why not use the taxes paid to build them to construct hospitals and fabricators instead?" Bennek continued. "Then there would be no hungry millions, Gul Kell. If there were no great Cardassian war machine, there would be no need for the poor to starve! There would be no need for this mission, for us to seek aid from worlds like Bajor!"

"We do not seek aid from Bajor," Hadlo broke in, "only a partnership in kind that will—"

Kell glared over his glass at the young man, ignoring the old cleric's words. "Oh yes, there would be such peace and riches if only the Central Command did not squander our Union's scarcity of wealth on warships," he said in an arch voice. "How many times have I heard that from the lips of fools who have never left the homeworld, fools with their noses buried in scrolls full of dusty old legends!" He put down his drink hard and aimed a finger at the priest. "Oh, there would be such peace, Bennek, such peace indeed, and food aplenty for even the lowest commoner to gorge upon! Perhaps your utopia might last a week, a month at the most, before our worlds were crushed under the boot heels of invaders! Tholians, Breen, Tzenkethi, whichever ones got there first ... And the people would ask you 'Where are our defenders, Bennek? Where are our swords and shields?' And you would have to tell them that you traded their safety for a few full stomachs!" He drew himself up, his dark duty armor glinting dully in the dining chamber's muted orange lights. "You are right about one thing, boy. Cardassia *is* lean and hungry, and it must remain that way. A fat, content animal is a slow one, a victim in waiting. A hungry animal is a predator, feared by the herd."

Ico kept her face neutral, but beneath her placid expression she wanted to laugh at the man's retort. Kell's armor did only a passing job of hiding a well-fed girth that showed the gul's leanings toward indulgence and excess.

"You mistakenly believe that your participation in this mission allows you a degree of leeway, of input." Kell glared at Bennek and his master. "It does not. You Oralians, with your chanting and your ridiculous masks, you think your rituals have great majesty and import, but they are meaningless to me. You are aboard the *Kornaire* on my sufferance, because I have been ordered to take you to Bajor."

Hadlo gaped. It was clear to Ico that the cleric had never expected Kell to speak so bluntly in front of his aide. "This delegation ..." Hadlo said, struggling to recover some dignity. "The Detapa Council asked the Oralian Way to initiate this diplomatic mission! We are leading it!"

"As a way of building bridges between our two peoples," the gul said dismissively. "Yes, yes, I recall the words of the First Speaker. And as far as the Bajorans will know, that is the truth. But the reality—the Cardassian reality—is much different. This operation is wholly under the guidance of Central Command, not your Way, not the Detapa

Council. The military alone will decide how events will play out," he sniffed, leaning toward Bennek. "So remember that, boy. And remember your place."

With brittle grace, Hadlo used a napkin to wipe the corners of his lips and stood up, his meal completely untouched. Bennek followed suit, the young man wired with pent-up anger. "If it pleases the gul, we will take our leave of you," said the cleric tightly. "We must prepare for the evening's recitations."

Kell waved them away, his attention turning to the table to find a succulent seafruit.

Ico stared at the door after it closed on the priests' backs. She found herself wondering if Kell realized that he was as much wrong as he was right about who was really directing the mission to Bajor.

Pa'Dar blinked and ate some more of his broth, unsure of how to proceed. Finally, he changed the subject. "Any news from home? The communications feeds we receive on the lab decks are quite sparse."

"Censorship is commonplace in the military," Dukat replied. "You learn to read through it after a while." He toyed with the bread. "I know the question you really want to ask me, Kotan." He nodded. "This mission remains classified for the moment."

"Oh, no," said the scientist, lying poorly. "I was not concerned for myself. I was just wondering . . . what with the news of the famine in the southern territories just before we left home orbit. Have things improved at all?" He managed a weak smile. "Your family are there, isn't that so?"

Dukat's lips thinned, and without really being aware of it, the officer's hand strayed to the cuff of one of his sleeves. There was a small pocket there, and inside it a holograph rod. He didn't need to look at it to remember the images encoded there: a woman, his wife Athra, her amber eyes a mix of joy and concern; and the child, his son, swaddled in the birthing blanket that Skrain himself had once been carried in. He thought of the sallow cast to the baby's cheeks beneath the fine definition of the Dukat lineage's brow, and a sharp knife of worry lanced through him. It showed in the flicker of a nerve at his eye, and the dalin knew immediately that Pa'Dar had seen it.

In front of any other crewman, if he had been in the company of Gul Kell or any of the others, he would have hated himself for revealing such a moment of weakness, but Pa'Dar simply nodded, understanding. "Family is all that we are," intoned the scientist, the ancient Cardassian adage coming easily to his lips.

"Never a truer word spoken," agreed Dukat. "The famine continues," he went on. "The First Speaker has authorized the transfer of supplies from the stockpiles in Tellel Basin and Lakarian City. It is hoped that will lessen the problem. I admit I am not as convinced of that as the Council appears to be."

Pa'Dar seemed to sense the dark turn the conversation was taking and covered with a sip of water. "My family believe I am assisting the Central Command in a mapping exercise near the Amleth Nebula."

"As good a cover as any."

The scientist eyed him. "Amleth is perfectly well mapped as it is, Skrain. Such an assignment is an obvious fake, and if my family know that, they may believe the worst—that I am in harm's way, sent into Talarian space or off toward the Breen Arm on some secret errand." He blew out a breath. "I don't want them to be afraid."

"Then you should be glad. Bajor is hardly a conflict zone. I doubt we'll face anything more threatening there than the weather. I understand it's rather intemperate."

"For Cardassians," noted Pa'Dar. "Although apparently the coastal regions along the equator do have a tempera-

ture range we would consider more favorable." He nodded
toward one of the many padds on the table before them,
and Dukat noted the image of a green-white world turning slowly in a time-lapse simulation. "Your family is from
Lakat, yes? In the colder climes?" asked the scientist. "You'll
probably find Bajor not too dissimilar to your home in the
depths of the winter months. Our reports on their climate
show it's less arid than Cardassia, likely with an extended
growing season. It certainly appears more verdant."

"Indeed." Dukat studied the alien planet. It reminded
him of a ripe fruit on the vine, heavy with seeds and juice.
Absently, he licked his lips and looked away, returning to
his earlier point. "Think how pleased your family will be
when you return to Cardassia after this mission is complete," the dalin told the other man. "You'll be well, unhurt,
and more worldly from your travels, and with luck on our
side we will come home with the glory of a new ally for
the Cardassian Union."

"An ally," repeated Pa'Dar. " 'Cardassia always leads,
never walks in step.' Isn't that how the maxim goes? Do the
Bajorans know that? Do they even know we are coming?"
Doubt clouded the young man's face.

Dukat sensed the faint reproach in the civilian's words,
and for the first time he wondered if he might have been
in error befriending the scientist. Perhaps he had been too
open, perhaps he should have maintained the aloofness of
his fellow officers; but it was too late now to concern himself with such thoughts. "The Bajorans know us," he began
carefully. "We've crossed paths with their people on occasion, on their outer worlds, in the reaches of unclaimed
space. This will be a formal first contact, Kotan. An event of
great import for both races. And I'm sure the Bajorans will
immediately understand the enormous benefits that Cardassia's friendship can bring." The mere thought that any
other outcome was possible seemed so unlikely to Dukat

as to be hardly worth considering. He dismissed the dour look of doubt on Pa'Dar's face. "You'll see, Kotan. It will be a great opportunity for all of us. How often does someone of your status get the chance to take part in a delegation of this kind?"

"Yes," admitted the other man. "You are correct on that point. I admit, I am quite intrigued by the prospect of learning more about these aliens."

Dukat nodded again. "Just so." He felt a tension in his fingers and covered it by taking another spoonful of the broth. He did not doubt that Pa'Dar was a far more intelligent man than he, but for all his academic knowledge Pa'Dar lacked an understanding of the realities of things. Bajor would become an ally of the Cardassian Union, simply because Cardassia required it. The path that would bring them to that destination was unclear to the dalin for the moment, but he had no doubt that it would open to him as time went by. Dukat felt a certainty of purpose about the mission, a determination that coiled hard and cold in his chest; he thought of his wife and his child at home, of their modest accommodation in the extended family quarters of his father's house in Lakat, and that determination became firmer still. It was for them that they were doing this, it was for them that he would see the *Kornaire*'s mission a success.

Ico poured another glass of *rokassa* for herself and then one more for Kell. "Was that really necessary? You gain nothing by alienating the ecclesiasts."

The gul made a face. "Incorrect, my dear Rhan. I gain some entertainment for myself on this most ordinary of voyages. If I have no pirates or border violations to take my frustrations out on, then these Oralians will do just as well. I'm only sorry I'm not allowed to space the whole band of insufferable prigs."

She sighed. "At least promise me you will not antagonize Hadlo's aide any further. When we reach Bajor, it would not do for the first sight the aliens have to be Bennek's hands about your throat."

"Let him try. Soft little priest with his soft little hands. I'd soon teach him that blind zealotry is no substitute for focus of will." Kell took a gulp of the fluid.

"Like it or not, we need them. We need that zeal."

He nodded with a grimace. "Yes, I suppose so. And so I will tolerate them, for Cardassia." He saluted the name with his glass. "At least until this is over. Once they've served their purpose, the Union can go on about the business of erasing them from our society."

Ico paused as she ate and cocked her head. "You really do detest the Oralians, don't you, Danig?"

He stared into his drink, musing. "They're the worst of us. The very last vestiges of the old race we were before Cardassians came to understand their place in the universe. Throwbacks, Rhan, nothing but anachronisms." Kell's lip curled. "That arrogant young whelp, he's a perfect example. He has the nerve to accuse the military of impoverishing our nation, we who defend it!" The gul tapped a balled fist on his chest plate, touching the copper sigil of the Second Order affixed there. "But it's his religion that is to blame! They're the ones responsible for the state of Cardassia, not us!" He turned in his seat, his ire building again, and fixed her with a look. "How many centuries were our people forced to live under the yoke of the Oralian Way? With every measure of wealth, every stone and scrap of jevonite going to build towers of worship? Places where the people could huddle and listen to hollow promises of salvation and redemption, when there was nothing!" Kell waggled a finger at Ico. "They repressed us, kept Cardassia from advancing. If Hadlo and his kind had their way, we would still be living in crude huts, our learning stunted by their dogma.

You, Rhan, what would you be? Not a scientist! Some temple servant, perhaps, or a doting wife walking ten paces behind your husband!"

Ico said nothing. The years when the church had been the governing force behind Cardassian society were long gone, but there were many who still carried a strong resentment toward the customs of the old credo. It mattered nothing to Kell that Hadlo's faith was now only a pale shadow of the religion that had once dominated Cardassia's pre-spaceflight era. The gul's ignorance of the tenets of the Oralian Way was obvious by his words, but she knew that correcting him would gain her nothing. She simply nodded and let him continue.

"The future for Cardassia lies out here," he growled, jerking a thumb at the oval viewport high on the wall, at the stars outside turned to streaks of color by the ship's warp velocities. "Not in some ancient doctrine." He grimaced again. "Were I First Speaker, I'd have fed the lot of them to the Tzenkethi by now. They held us down, they wasted our resources. If not for the military, we would still be a downtrodden and backward people. Now every day we have to struggle to claw back the time those foolish priests cost us."

"And yet here they are, with us on this most sensitive of assignments. Do you find the irony in that as I do, Kell?"

The gul eyed her. "The Detapa Council believes those ridge-faced primitives on Bajor will be better disposed toward a Cardassia that exhibits some of the same childish fealty to religion that they do. Hadlo and his band of fools are only here to maintain that fiction. To mollify the aliens, nothing more."

She nodded. "From a certain point of view, such a tactic might be seen as a desperate one."

"What do you mean?"

Ico took another sip. "Has the Central Command grown

so unsure of itself that it must enlist priests to help it gain a foothold on Bajor? Are our proud warfleets spread so thin that we cannot simply take Bajor by force of arms?" She gestured around. "One ship, Danig. Is that all the Orders can spare from the wall of vessels protecting our space?" She knew the answer to those questions as well as Kell did, but neither of them would dare to say it aloud. Not here. Not yet.

His eyes narrowed. "I would advise you to watch your tone, Professor."

"Forgive me, Gul Kell," she replied. "In my line of work, it is the nature of a scientist to make suppositions and voice theories."

Kell looked away without even bothering to grace her with a response.

2

B'hava'el was low in the sky across the rooftops of the dockyards and the port hangars, throwing warm orange light through the clouds, but the chill of last night's storm down from the mountains was still hugging the ground. For most people in Korto, the day hadn't really begun. Trams on the main thoroughfare were filled with workers coming in from the habitat districts, the rail-riders passing equally full carriages going the other way packed with night servants, cleaners, and members of professions that shunned the light of morning. Darrah Mace walked the edge of the city's port field, occasionally glancing to his right to watch the highway traffic on the other side of the chain-link fence, but for the most part keeping his gaze northward, across the hangars and landing pads, over the grassy spaces around the runways. Ships clicked and ticked to themselves as he passed around them, some vessels dripping with runoff from the rain, others bleeding warmth from atmospheric reentry. He raised a hand and threw a wan salute at a group of laborers clustered around the impulse nacelle of a parked courier; they were using a crude steel plate to fry eggs on the ship's heat exchangers. One of them offered him a greasy slice, but Darrah shook his head good-naturedly and walked on. The scent of the makeshift cooking lingered in the air, following him on gusts of wind that made his over-coat twist and flap.

He'd heard there had been some trouble here last night, something about a fight interrupted, threats, and an issue or two unresolved. It was hardly atypical for the port. Darrah experienced a moment of memory from his child-hood, triggered by the cook-smell: walking along after his father to go see the big lifter ships where the old man had worked, the loaders and dockers all laughing against the grim exertion of their chores. Then an argument had broken out, and one man had beaten another with a bill-hook. His mother had been furious that the boy had been allowed to see that. She'd never let Mace follow his dad to work again. She'd never understood that the blood, the violence, hadn't frightened him. Mace had been with his father, who protected him. He thought about his own chil-dren for a moment, about *his* job; a bitter smirk formed on his lips as he imagined what Karys would say if Nell or little Bajin asked to follow *him* to work. "She'd pitch a fit," he said aloud.

Darrah hesitated at the edge of the landing apron, his chilly amusement turning swiftly into a frown. There was nothing here, and he'd done his part by just turning up, just taking a stroll around the port so people knew he was there. The laborers had seen him. They'd spread the word that Darrah had been around. That was probably enough. He pivoted on his heel, hesitating just for a moment as engine noise caught his ears. He stopped to watch as a slim, wire-framed freighter rose up on vertical thrusters from one of the elevated pads, turning a snake-head prow toward the sky. With a sharp report of ion ignition, gouts of smoky exhaust puffed from the ship's engine bells and it shot away like a loosed arrow, roaring right over his head toward the south and the ocean. He watched it go, reced-ing to a dot, for a moment being the young boy again; and then he realized that the noise of the liftoff had been hiding something else. Angry voices, from close by.

Darrah went quickly through the maze of alleyways between the day-rental hangars and forced himself to slow to a casual walk as he rounded the corner, bringing the site of the dispute into view. He took in the crescent-shaped ship sitting half in and half out of the hangar, and faltered. He recognized the craft instantly, and for a moment he considered just turning and walking away, leaving the situation to play out as the Prophets intended. But only for a moment. The vessel was an odd bird, the fuselage of a decommissioned Militia impulse raider married to a brace of refurbished warp drives off an Orion schooner. It had a mutant, misshapen air to it, as if the craft were the result of some unfortunate mechanical crossbreeding experiment. It didn't look like it should be flying, but Darrah knew full well that the pilot encouraged that appearance in a vain attempt to make it draw less attention. And the pilot in question, well, he was being pressed into the side of his ship by a man who had twice his mass, wearing dark clothes and a gaudy *Mi'tino* earring. Darrah frowned. In his experience, clans from the *Mi'tino* caste always had a sense of entitlement about them that made for poor relationships with anyone they considered a "lesser." Like, for example, a skinny shuttle jockey in an ill-fitting tunic.

Darrah cleared his throat, and the *Mi'tino* man paused with his fist cocked to punch his victim squarely in the gut. The pilot caught sight of Darrah for the first time, and his face flushed with relief, some color returning to his nasal ridges. "Ha!" The pilot managed. "You're gonna regret this now! Do you know who that is? He's only—"

"Syjin, shut up," snapped Darrah. "What are you doing?"

"What am *I* doing?" Syjin retorted, coughing because

the big guy had him by the throat. "What are *you* doing, standing there and watching this lugfish manhandle me?"

Darrah stroked the stubble on his chin thoughtfully. "I'm sure it isn't anything you don't deserve. Let me take a wild stab in the dark here and say that you're the person who was in danger of getting his head caved in here last night?"

"Yes," said the pilot. "Possibly. It's a big port."

"Hey," began the man in the dark jacket, angry at the new arrival. "Get lost!"

"Not that big." Darrah kept talking, ignoring Syjin's assailant. "I bet you deserve it. Can't you keep out of trouble for one single day? I mean, would that be too much to ask?" He was advancing as he spoke, letting his coat fall open a little. "Remember old Prylar Yilb at temple school? He was right about you. You're on a road straight to the Fire Caves, my friend. Damnation eternal."

"Hey," repeated the *Mi'tino*, but they weren't listening to him.

Syjin's eyes widened. "Yeah, right after you, Darrah Mace! I'm not the one who broke the icons in the vestry! I'm not the one he made write out all of Gaudaal's Lament a hundred times!"

Darrah threw up his hands. "Oh, this *again?* I was nine years old! Are you going to keep bringing up that story forever?"

Finally, the act of being ignored by the two men was too much for Syjin's attacker, and he turned on Darrah, still holding the pilot in place. "Hey!" he shouted. "I told you to get lost! Who the *kosst* do you think you are?"

Without moving too fast, Darrah pushed back his coat to reveal the earth-toned uniform he was wearing underneath it, the duty fatigues of a law enforcement officer in the Bajoran Militia. "I'm the police, friend. And that man, sadly, is a Korto citizen, and so I have to reluctantly consider him under my protection." He nodded at Syjin. "Why don't you stop choking him there and we'll try to settle this with some decorum?"

The man in the dark jacket swore a particularly choice curse that suggested Darrah's mother should take congress with farm animals, and what little of Darrah's good mood remained instantly evaporated. He lunged, quick enough to take the man off guard, and caught him in a viselike grip, his hand pulling hard on the assailant's right ear. Darrah twisted and pulled at the earring denoting the Bajoran's *D'jarra* caste, putting savage pressure on the lobe. The man howled and stumbled away, releasing Syjin and flailing.

"Something else Prylar Yilb used to say was, you could tell a lot about a man from the way his *pagh* flowed," Darrah growled. "Let's see what we can learn about you, huh?" He gave the ear a hard yank, and the man overbalanced and fell into a heap on the thermoconcrete landing pad. Darrah let him go and shot Syjin a look. "Hm. Not much. The ear of any good Bajoran is supposed to be the seat of their Prophet-given life force, but our friend here doesn't seem to have anything there but wax." He made a face and wiped his hand on his coat.

"Bloody *Mi'tino!*" wheezed the pilot. "You think you can push me around because your *D'jarra's* higher up the wheel than mine?" Syjin rocked back and forth on his heels, emboldened by Darrah's presence. "I might just be *Va'telo,* but I still deserve respect!" He nodded to himself and attempted to straighten his clothing.

"This isn't about that!" snarled the man, getting to his feet with one hand pressed to his pain-reddened ear. "This is about you sleeping with my wife!"

"I didn't sleep with her!" Syjin blurted. "It's your brother who's doing that! I just flew her out to meet him on Jeraddo!"

The redness unfolded across the man's entire face as

anger overwhelmed his reason. "You little maggot! I'll kill you!" Out of nowhere a glitter of silver slid from a pocket in the sleeve of the man's jacket, and suddenly he was holding a shimmerknife.

Darrah felt a familiar, icy calm wash over him, and by reflex his hand dropped to the holster on his belt. "Don't do this," he said.

"I'll kill you both!" roared the husband, blind fury propelling him forward. The knife came up in a line of bright metal; then the phaser pistol was in Darrah's hand and the short, sharp keening of an energy bolt crossed the distance between them. The man hit the deck for a second time, the small vibrating blade skittering away from his nerveless grip.

With a heavy sigh, Darrah reached inside his coat and tapped the oval communicator brooch on the right breast of his uniform tunic. "Precinct, this is Darrah. I need a catch wagon down at the port, hangar nineteen. Got a sleeper here, aggravated assault."

"Confirmed, Senior Constable Darrah," said the voice of the synthetic dispatcher. *"Unit responding. Remain on-site. Precinct out."*

"Wah," said Syjin, "you shot him. Thanks, brother. He would have murdered us both."

"Don't 'brother' me, you crafty son of a Ferengi. You're not family, you're my bloody penance."

Syjin pulled a hurt face and leaned down to examine the unconscious man. "Oh. Charming. Old Yilb used to say that all men are brothers in the Celestial Temple." He reached for a pocket on the other man's jacket, and Mace smacked his hand.

"Yeah, well, if you ever find it, you can start calling me brother then, not before." He blew out a breath, studying the man. "Poor idiot. His wife cuckolded him, no wonder he was furious."

"That's why I steer clear of the ladies," Syjin said sagely.

"Never let myself get tied down." He patted his ship. "This is the only mistress for me."

"Right," Darrah said dourly, "but you're more than happy to take a woman's money to fly her away for some offworld adultery. I'm sure if I looked hard enough I could find a law against that."

Syjin's smile froze. "Ha," he managed. "Oh, before I forget. I've got something for you and the children."

"Don't try and change the subject!" Darrah snapped, but the pilot was already inside his ship.

A moment later he returned with a hard-sided cargo container. "Here. This is for you and Karys and the little ones."

Darrah opened the box and inside he saw a few seal-packs of exotic alien foodstuffs. *Agnam* loaf and *methrin* eggs, a bottle of *tranya* and some hydronic mushies, the kind that Nell loved. "Where'd you get this? Is this a bribe?"

"No!" Syjin said hotly. "Can't a man give his old friend a gift? You're so suspicious!"

"Suspicion is what makes me a policeman. And, let's be honest, you have always had a rather elastic relationship with the law."

The pilot folded his arms. "It is the Gratitude Festival this week, isn't it? I thought I'd give you a small something to be grateful for. The Prophets smile on men who share their good fortune, right?"

Darrah felt slightly chagrined by his initial reaction. "Oh. Thank you." He looked up as a police flyer drifted in over the tops of the hangars and angled to land nearby. "As you're on-planet, are you going to come to the house? The kids would love to see you."

"I shouldn't," said Syjin. "You know Karys thinks I'm a bad influence on them." His expression turned more serious. "Besides, I think the little ones would rather spend the holiday with their mother and father than silly Uncle Syjin."

A frown crossed Darrah's face. "Festivals don't police themselves," he said defensively. "I have to keep on top of it. Besides, a wife, a home, and two growing cubs ... Constable's pay can only go so far. I need the extra duties." He nodded as Proka, one of the duty watchmen, climbed out of the flyer.

"There are other ways to earn latinum," said the pilot airily as Darrah walked away.

"That's true," Darrah said over his shoulder, "and if I catch you doing one of them, I'll put you in the blocks and grind up that tub of rust for spares."

"Thank you very little," Syjin snorted, and went back into his vessel.

The *Kornaire*'s hangar bay was one of the few areas on board the starship where the ceiling didn't hang low over the crew's heads. It was a peculiarity of this variety of vessel; unlike the newer *Galor*-class ships, the *Selek*-class heavy cruiser appeared to have been designed by a man of shorter stature. Dukat had heard the enlisted men making jokes when they thought he couldn't hear them, that Gul Kell kept his flag on the *Kornaire* not because he'd commanded the ship for so many years, but because striding the vessel's corridors made him feel taller. Dukat felt fairly indifferent about the ship himself; Kell's vessel had too many memories attached to it for the dalin, too many recollections of incidents and tours of duty that didn't sit well with him. Not for the first time, Dukat considered what kind of vessel he would take when his promotion to gul finally came. *Something more impressive than this old hulk,* he told himself.

Crossing behind one of the *Kornaire*'s space-to-surface cutters, he found Kotan Pa'Dar waving a tricorder over the drum-shaped shuttle on the tertiary pad. The tan-colored ship was a sorry sight, most of the forward quarter a mess of compacted metal and broken fuselage. The drop-ramp hatch at the rear was open, and inside Dukat could see the bodies wrapped in thick white cloths, piled against the bulkhead like stacked firewood.

Pa'Dar nodded to him. "Skrain," he said, by way of greeting. "Do you require something of me?"

Dukat shook his head. "Just making my rounds," he explained. The dalin gestured at the wreck. "All is well?"

The scientist peered at the tricorder's readout. "We made sure the drive cores were pulled before the craft was brought on board. There's no residual radiation or isolytic leakage, but it never hurts to check." He shrugged. "It is alien technology, after all. We can't be certain we've accounted for everything."

The officer walked to the hull of the ship and placed a hand on it. "Bajorans breathe the same sort of air as us. They have the same sort of gravity, eat compatible foodstuffs ... It's no surprise their ships are not that different from ours." His fingers found a fitting on the fuselage, a bolt and pinion connection that had been sheared off. Dukat frowned, unable to identify it.

"A servo-mast for the solar sails," said Pa'Dar, seeing the question before Dukat asked it. "Some of their smaller vessels appear to carry them as a redundant emergency propulsion system, in case impulse engines fail."

Dukat looked at his fingers and found a patina of grime there. He brushed the dust from his hands with quick, economical motions. "Quite primitive, really." He moved around to study the damaged section.

"That's one way to consider it," Pa'Dar conceded. "It does strike me as strange that the ship's systems are less advanced than our own."

"How so?"

"Their warp drive, their sensors, and other mechanisms, all of them are at least a century behind Cardassian technologies. I doubt this scout was even capable of making transluminal velocities beyond factor two, three at best. When one considers that the Bajorans are such an old culture, one would assume they would possess at least comparable if not superior technology."

Dukat gave a dry chuckle. "The age of the Bajoran civilization is a matter for debate, so I have been led to understand. After all, we have only their word that they are such an ancient and venerable species . . ." He glanced at the scientist. "And even if it is true, then what does this tell us?" He tap-tapped on the hull of the Bajoran ship. "They may be hundreds of thousands of years old, but they lag behind the rest of the galaxy, behind younger and more vital cultures like ours. Do you know what that tells me, Kotan?" Pa'Dar shook his head, and Dukat stepped on to the dropramp, peering inside. "They're stagnant. They lack the drive that Cardassia has in ample supply." He grinned to himself. "By the time the Union's a hundred thousand years old, we'll be the lords of the galaxy."

"Perhaps so," said the other man, although Dukat could tell he didn't share his confidence. "The ship's interior is off-limits," added Pa'Dar, as Dukat balanced on the edge of the ramp. "On Professor Ico's orders."

"I'm only taking an interest," Dukat replied. Inside, beyond the compartment where the corpses lay, he could see part of the command deck and the mess of shattered consoles up there. There was nothing recognizable as a helm or a navigation station; the impact that had killed the crew had ruined the vessel's internals completely.

"Do you know how the ship was damaged?" said Pa'Dar. "The data templates I was provided with are rather sparse. It looks like the result of a ground collision, or perhaps a partial failure of structural integrity fields . . ."

Dukat's smile thinned. "It's my understanding it was . . . an unlucky accident. Fortunate this craft was so near to a Union shipping channel. If not, these poor fools might have drifted about in the void for millennia. Their world would never have known their fate."

"The lost dead are never truly at rest," said a new voice, and the two men turned to see a robed figure approaching across the deck. He rolled back his hood, and Dukat found himself looking into an earnest, intense face. "It is a thing of great sadness."

"Bennek, isn't it?" Dukat said. "We have not met. I am Dalin Skrain Dukat, first officer of the *Kornaire*. This is Kotan Pa'Dar, of the Ministry of Science."

The priest gave them a shallow bow. "If you will pardon me, I have a duty to perform here."

Pa'Dar pocketed his tricorder, his expression taking on an irritable cast. "Duty? What duty?"

From a large drawstring pouch at his hip the young cleric removed an intricately carved mask of green wood studded with chips of white mica and flat blue stones. "A recitation." He nodded at the wreck and the corpses aboard it. "For the dead."

"I don't understand," said Dukat. "There are only Bajorans aboard that scoutship. No Cardassians."

"I know," Bennek replied, taking the mask and balancing it in his hands before raising it up to his chest in a gesture of benediction. "You may remain if you wish, gentlemen. I would ask only that you stay silent until the rite is concluded."

Pa'Dar's stout face quirked in the beginning of a sneer. "I have more important things to do, I believe." He made no attempt to hide a derisive snort and walked away, leaving Dukat and the priest at the foot of the drop-ramp.

Bennek whispered something under his breath and raised the mask slowly to his face, taking loops of metal from inside it to hook over his ears. Dukat found himself fascinated by the odd ritualistic motions of the young man. It was like some strange form of theater, a dance or a mime.

It was quite unreal. "Why do you do this?" he demanded, ignoring the priest's request for silence. "Why do you care about the bodies of aliens? They don't follow your creed."

"Oralius asks us to find paths for all the life we encounter on our journeys." Bennek's words had an odd hushed quality to them as they came from behind the mask. "Even if that life is not born of the same earth and sun as we are." He bowed and began to speak in a slow, rhythmic chant. "The power that moves through me, animates my life, animates the mask of Oralius. To speak her words with my voice, to think her thoughts with my mind, to feel her love with my heart. It is the song of morning, opening up to life, bringing the truth of her wisdom to those who live in the shadow of the night." The phrases that fell from the mask's unmoving lips had the steady pace of a reading performed hundreds of times, words known so well to the priest that he could speak them with perfect recall. "It is this selfsame power, turned against creation, turned against my friend, that can destroy his body with my hand, reduce his spirit with my hate, separate his presence from my home." The static aspect bobbed as Bennek nodded to himself. "To live without Oralius, lighting our way to the source, connecting us to the mystery, is to live without the tendrils of love." He made a gesture across his face. "Let the Way guide these souls to the place of their birth, and know her touch and her friendship." After a long moment, Bennek bowed to the ship and let the mask fall into his waiting hands.

And this is the Oralian Way? Dukat asked himself. *Is this all that they are, speakers of chants and rituals?* He studied Bennek and could not help but wonder why Central Command was so set against these religious throwbacks. If this boy was an example of them, then they were nothing to be concerned about. Dukat found it hard to reconcile the man who stood before him with the stories he had been taught in the academy, of Cardassia's harsh prehistory beneath the twin hammers of religious oppression and savage climate change. Was this open-faced cleric really the last remnant of a creed that had pushed his people to the brink of extinction? Dukat was almost amused by the idea. He studied the youth's skinny neck and the ridges of cartilage there, far thinner than Dukat's, without the muscles and ropelike strength born from hard training in the officer corps. He knew with utter certainty he could crush Bennek's life from him in a heartbeat.

The priest returned his precious mask to its bag, utterly unaware of Dukat's train of thought. "You have never seen a recitation before?"

"It was quite . . . diverting."

For the first time, Dukat saw something like intelligence behind the cleric's eyes. "I fear you may be patronizing me, Dalin."

"A fool is condescending to something he does not understand. I belittle only those whom I know to deserve it."

"And what do you know of the Oralian Way?"

Dukat folded his arms, countering the question with one of his own. "What was the purpose of that ritual? Do you think the Bajorans will thank you for it? Perhaps they may even be angered by your actions, if their dogma calls for some other pattern of behavior." He nodded to the bodies. "If this were a Bajoran ship and those were Cardassian dead, you would be dishonoring the deceased by speaking over their remains."

"Oralius sees only life," Bennek insisted. "Where it came from has no bearing on that fact. Oralius exists above us all. Those who find the path are welcome to walk it, regardless of their origin."

"That's no answer," Dukat replied. "Come, Bennek, I ask you. What value is there to what you have just done? What good are your words, your 'Way,' to these alien dead?" He was goading the youth now, interested in seeing what kind of reaction he would engender.

And there in Bennek's gaze was a flash of anger, a hardening of the jaw. "They are a doorway to the truth, Dalin Dukat. A manner in which we may all better ourselves and seek the common good. The words of Oralius, of the Way, they are a catalyst for the evolution of the living soul!"

At once Dukat saw the passion behind the words. Such a bearing he had often seen before, on the faces of his own men as they went into battle, in the eyes of the heartless tools of the Obsidian Order as they went about their grisly business; and there, in Bennek, was his answer. *That's why Central Command wants these people eradicated. It is their belief that makes them strong.* And belief in anything other than the supremacy of the Cardassian Union was not something the masters of Dukat's world would tolerate.

"I see," he said carefully.

"Do you?" Bennek said tightly. "I wonder."

Dukat raised an eyebrow at the temerity in the priest's tone; but any rejoinder he might have given was forgotten as *Kornaire*'s shipboard communications channel chimed into life.

"All division leaders and senior officers to operational alert stations," said the terse female voice of the ship's computer. *"Arrival in the Bajor system in eleven metrics, mark."*

Lonnic Tomo balled her fist and began slamming it on the door of her patron's chambers, fast and firm, over and over.

From inside she heard an annoyed grunt. "Enter! *Enter!*" The voice was clipped. "I know it's you, Tomo! Get in here!"

She ran an ebony hand over her scalp, the close-cut fuzz of her hair tickling her palm, and then she pushed open the heavy nyawood door and went inside.

Jas Holza was shrugging on a jacket and trying to hold on to a glass of water with his free hand. The minister's prematurely lined face was flushed with effort, his thinning hair unkempt. He had ordered Lonnic to let him rest until the afternoon, and this was barely the midday. His arrival back from Batal in the early hours of the morning had been a bad sign. The rain still coming down hard from the storm, his flyer had touched down in the courtyard of the Naghai Keep, engine noise echoing against the fusion-stone walls of the ancient citadel. But Jas hadn't debriefed his aide on his return as he usually did after such journeys, just barked at her to go away, telling her to come back the next day.

"What do you want?" he spat, and she knew it was bad. It took a lot to push Jas Holza into a bad mood, but when it did the storm that came after lasted for days. Lonnic wanted to ask about the events of the Batal trip, and she was sure that Jas thought that was why she had roused him; but those matters were of secondary importance now. The minister went to the window and turned the slats, letting in the air as he opened the doors to the balcony outside.

Beyond the narrow, tall windows of his chambers, the citadel gave him an unparalleled view of Korto's cityscape on the river plain below. The keep had been the ancestral home of the Jas clan since Bajor's Age of Enlightenment, and the minister's *D'jarra* ensured that it was his family who had held on to the reins of one of the most fertile and productive districts in all of Kendra Province. But owning land was not the same as managing land, and Jas had less of the required skill that his forefathers had shown.

"Well?" He rounded on her. "Talk to me, Tomo! You've dragged me to my feet, you may as well make it worth something!"

"Sir, I have Colonel Li Tarka of the Militia Space Guard and First Minister Verin Kolek waiting on comm channel nine for you. There's a matter of utmost importance that requires your immediate attention."

Jas's ire instantly dissipated. "Verin? Why is he contacting me? The next scheduled council meeting isn't for days yet." He blinked. "What do the Space Guard want?"

"It's about the *Eleda,* the scoutship?" she prompted. The minister's brow furrowed, and he orbited his desk, searching for something among the documents there.

"Eleda," he repeated, dragging the name from the depths of his memory. "One of ours, wasn't it?" Jas nodded to himself. "Yes. Old Rifin's son was the captain, wasn't he?" On Lonnic's look of agreement he tapped a finger on his lips. "Yes, I remember. Terrible business."

The Jas clan, in addition to owning land and mercantile concerns across Western Bajor, also ran a relatively successful asteroid prospecting business in the uninhabited systems throughout the sector. There was a small fleet of warp-capable survey ships that earned a decent turnover scanning for valuable ores that the larger belt-mining corporations could exploit. The *Eleda* was one of those ships, and it had gone missing a few months earlier out toward the Olmerak system. Bajor Traffic Control had declared it missing and presumed lost, and death benefit paperwork to pay off the crew's dependents was already in the works. The loss of the scout was unfortunate, but not uncommon; asteroid prospectors in the Bajor Sector regularly fell foul of pirates, belligerent Tzenkethi, or just plain bad luck.

The minister worked to make himself look more presentable, taking a seat behind his desk to face the oval wallscreen across the room. "Did someone find the ship? Are the crew still alive?"

He was doing a good job of moderating his earlier bad mood. Lonnic could see her patron was already thinking about rescinding the benefits. "Uh, yes and no, sir. The crew didn't survive, but *someone* found the ship."

Jas nodded. "I see, Li's people, was it?" He frowned again. "Olmerak is a bit of a way out for the defense fleet."

She shook her head. "The Cardassians found the *Eleda*, sir." The words sounded just as odd coming out of her mouth as they had when she'd first heard them herself, only a few minutes before she knocked on Jas's door. "They've . . . come to return it. And the bodies of the dead men."

The minister blinked, and for a moment his eyes went hazy as his vision turned inward. Lonnic knew that look; Jas Holza was a rather dogged political operator, and while his recent years had not been the most stellar part of his tenure as minister for Korto District, he still had the one skill that all politicians kept sharp—the ability to see an opportunity when it presented itself. He drew himself up and adjusted his collar one last time. "Tomo, put Verin and the colonel through, please. Let's see what these aliens want, shall we?"

His aide nodded and tapped a control on her belt.

Jas Holza settled on his default neutral expression as the screen activated. The display was split into two live feeds, with Verin on the left and Li on the right. The minister's eyes were drawn to Li Tarka first, the Militia officer all dark hair and intensity, his ghost-gray uniform stark against the command chair behind him. The colonel's broadcast was coming directly from the bridge of his flagship, one of the Space Guard's assault vessels that prowled the edges of the Bajor system. By contrast, Verin Kolek, representative for the Lonar Province and the current First Minister, was a careworn figure who appeared outwardly to resemble a kindly old grandfather. Verin's aspect, however, belied a sharp mind in a hard man.

The First Minister wasted no time on any preamble. "Holza, there's an issue at hand that requires your immediate involvement. This ship of yours . . ."

Jas nodded. "My adjutant has explained the situation to me."

"Did you have any involvement in this?" Verin demanded. "I know you're ambitious, but making overtures to an alien interstellar power on your own authority is unacceptable!"

Jas licked his lips. "First Minister, Colonel Li, please understand I'm as surprised by this turn of events as you are. Believe me, I've already listed the *Eleda* as lost, whereabouts unknown."

"You may wish to reopen that file," said Li gruffly. "As of this moment, my ship is shadowing a Cardassian battle cruiser at the edge of the system. They've transmitted detailed scans showing they have your scout and the remains of its crew on board."

"They want to return them," added Verin. "To you. Apparently, their technicians were able to recover part of the ship's database, and they learned you were the *Eleda*'s owner and patron of the dead men."

Jas found himself nodding. "That . . . that is correct."

Li's eyes narrowed. "The Cardassians have never done anything like this before, Minister Jas. They've always kept to their borders, stayed away from our core worlds. Any dealings we've had with them have always been through colonies on the fringes or third parties. The fact that a military starship from the Union has arrived in our home space is . . . unprecedented."

The politician smothered a twinge of surprise. He was hearing something in Li Tarka's voice that he had never heard before—*apprehension*. For most Bajorans, Jas Holza included, the Cardassians represented just one more aspect of the wide universe out beyond the edges of the Bajor Sector—unknown, alien, potentially dangerous. "Do you think it's the vanguard of an invasion force?"

Li's lips thinned. "One vessel wouldn't pose a threat to us. I have a flotilla of raiders standing off rimward of the Denorios Belt that could be here in moments. We could ash a single cruiser if they made any aggressive moves."

"And yet," said the old man, "the Cardassians aren't known for their spontaneous acts of diplomacy." He glared at Jas from the viewscreen. "The commander wants to speak with you, because the *Eleda* crew were your men."

Jas put his hands flat on the table in front of him and shot a look at Lonnic where the dark-skinned woman stood off to the side. Her face reflected the same concerns that he felt, but he schooled his expression carefully and did not show them. Taking a breath, the minister became aware of how delicate a circumstance he now found himself in. Verin's annoyance was clearly stemming from the need to bring him into this situation, and he knew that the old man would do whatever he could to discard Jas as soon as the Cardassians had been mollified. Jas's frequent opposition to Verin's policies of late and his thinly veiled suggestions that the aged politician should step down had isolated him in Bajor's political arena. If things had been different, he might have smiled at the discomfort the First Minister was exhibiting, but the matter was too serious to treat lightly.

If the Cardassians were here, coming as galactic neighbors and not at the head of a warfleet, then Jas was being presented with an opportunity that would never come again. With cold certainty, he knew that whatever choice he made in the next few minutes would alter the course of his political career forever. "I'll talk to them," he said with a nod.

"Holza," rumbled the old man, his eyes turning flinty, "be wary. Don't allow yourself to exceed your remit. Remember, your jurisdiction ends at the boundary of Korto District. Mine encompasses all of Bajor."

"As you say, First Minister."

Verin grunted and waved to someone off-screen. The view on Jas's display shifted to allow a new window to appear; and there were the aliens. "Do I address Minister Jas

Holza, patron of the scoutship *Eleda?*" There were three of them on the screen, the one in the center that spoke, another with a curiously slim face, and the last wearing what seemed like some colorful parody of a penitent's hooded robes.

Jas had never spoken to a Cardassian before, only seen them in holos or still images. He found he couldn't look away from the strange knotty lines of musculature around their necks and eyes. "I am he. I understand that I owe you gratitude for your recovery of my property and my employees. On behalf of Korto District and Bajor, I thank you. The families of the men lost aboard the *Eleda* appreciate your gesture."

The Cardassian inclined his head. "I am Gul Kell, commander of the starship *Kornaire.* This is Rhan Ico, of our science ministry, and Hadlo, a cleric of the Oralian Way. We represent a diplomatic initiative from our ruling body, the Detapa Council." Did he detect a slight air of disdain when Kell indicated the cleric? Jas filed that thought away for later consideration; at his leisure, he would go back over the recording of this conversation and sift it for subtle meaning. "We are returning your dead," continued Kell, "and with that act of compassion we wish to make formal contact with your world and your government."

"Then Bajor will welcome you," Jas answered, speaking quickly to cut off any reply that Verin would have made. *Now* was the moment; now was the chance to put himself in the middle of this before the First Minister forced him back on to the sidelines. "*I* will welcome you. I govern the city of Korto, on the northern continent of Bajor, from a seat of great honor known as the Naghai Keep. If you will agree to it, Gul Kell, I would gladly invite you and your party to accept my hospitality as a small measure of thanks for what you have done." He heard the sharp intake of breath from Verin's side of the screen, but did not spare the old man a look.

The Cardassian commander nodded. "That is acceptable. We will reach Bajor orbit in two of your rotations." The alien gave a curt nod. "Until then. *Kornaire* out."

The feed from the other ship blinked out and suddenly Verin's face was filling half the screen again. "Did I not make myself clear, Jas?" demanded the First Minister. "Your rank does not give you the right to set interplanetary policy for our world!"

"Forgive me, sir," Jas returned. "I did only what any man would—I offered gratitude to someone who had earned it—"

Verin's angry snort cut him off. "This matter goes far beyond your understanding! Don't try to build up your importance by blind opportunism!"

"My eyes are fully open," Jas retorted. He glanced at the Militia officer. "Colonel, I would ask that you have the aliens transport whatever remains of the *Eleda* and her crew to your vessel. Traffic Control will want to conduct a thorough investigation into the cause of the ship's loss."

Li nodded. "I concur, Minister. I'll see to it. In the meantime, we'll take the *Kornaire* on a slow, roundabout route in to the homeworld. That'll give us plenty of time to scan her and prepare our orbital posture. Just in case." He straightened in his chair. "Li out."

Now the screen showed only Verin's face. "You should have let me handle this, Holza," said the old man. "You don't have experience with aliens. I don't think for one moment that you understand what you've let yourself in for."

"You underestimate me, Kolek. You always have." Jas reached for the communicator control on the surface of his desk. "Think of this as a chance to learn how wrong you are about me." He tapped the keypad and the screen went dark.

Immediately, all the tension he had been holding in check flooded out of him, and Jas's face flushed with color.

Moderating the tremor in his hands, he snapped his fingers at Lonnic. "Fire's sake, I need a drink. Give me a glass of that Alvanian brandy." Tomo did as he asked, and he tossed back the contents of the tumbler with a single flick of the wrist. The smooth heat of the alcohol washed through him, smothering the churn of emotions. He eyed his assistant's distant expression. "Tomo? Don't drift off on me. This is important. I need you focused."

"Yes, sir," she said, with a wooden nod. "It's just . . . I hadn't expected . . ."

Jas helped himself to a refill and took his time with the second glass. "Neither did I. But then the hallmark of an intelligent man is the way in which he deals with the unexpected." He studied the glass. "I think I dealt with that to our advantage."

She nodded again. "It's strange," she began. "The one in charge, Kell. He introduced the one in the robes as a cleric." Lonnic's hand strayed to her face and touched the silver and gold links that hung from her right earlobe. "I've never heard of Cardassians having a religion before. I always thought they were . . . godless."

Jas turned to the open window, and a slow smile emerged on his lips. "It would seem otherwise. I wonder what else we'll learn about them?"

3

From the outside, the precinct house had the look of blunt, no-nonsense architecture. Compared to the other build-ings in this quarter of Korto, the majority of which were built from dark woods and sand-colored stone, the pre-cinct hunched low to the ground and peered out toward the highway like an angry face of rough granite. Prylar Gar Osen walked slowly toward it. It made him think of a pit wrestler, squat and unpleasant, while the rest of the build-ings around it were stately and elegant. In fact, the police compound was the newest construction, the original—and in Gar's opinion, far more graceful one—having been torn down and replaced when Jas Holza succeeded his father as minister of the district.

The priest crossed up the shallow steps and into the entrance hall. There were a few people spread out at the petitioning kiosks, but not enough to form a line. Gar threw a nod at the blond woman at the duty desk, and she beck-oned him through the security gate. She bobbed her head as he passed; he felt a twinge of guilt at not remembering her name, and he should have, because she was a regular at the temple. He covered his mild embarrassment by producing the padd he'd been given by Vedek Cotor. "I'm looking for someone," he began, offering her the device. "He was taken into custody this morning at the port."

"Hey, Myda," said a voice from behind him. "Don't worry. I'll look after this guy."

Myda. That was her name. She flashed Gar a smile and walked away. He turned and there was Darrah Mace, that usual crooked half-grin on his face. "Brother Darrah," he began in a mock-stern tone. "Have you deserted the Prophets? It's been so long since I saw you at services, I thought you might have been struck down by some ruffian."

Darrah cocked his head guiltily. "Sorry, Osen. I've been busy. If it makes you feel any better, I've been visiting the precinct shrine." He jerked a thumb at an alcove just inside the doorway where a small prayer banner was visible and candles burned slowly. "In this job, I need all the protection I can get, spiritual or otherwise."

Gar nodded, sensing the air of weariness in his friend's tone. "Have you thought about taking some time off?"

Darrah shot him an odd look. "Have you been talking to Karys and Syjin?"

The priest's thin eyebrows shot up. "Syjin's back on Bajor? I didn't know. Perhaps I'd better send a comm to the shrine, tell them to put an extra lock on the gate."

The constable frowned. "That's hardly very charitable of you, Prylar. I'm sure he'd never steal anything from a holy place. He does have some standards."

Gar smirked, following Darrah through the open space of the precinct's squad room. "True. Is he well?"

The other man mimicked a set of scales with his hands. "So-so. He nearly had the paste beaten out of him this morning down at the port. Some jilted husband went off the rails, and—"

"Oh dear," Gar's hand went to his ear. "The husband. A stocky fellow, a *Mi'tino?*"

"That's him. You know the man?"

The priest nodded. "He's the reason I'm here. His father

is a patron of the monastery, and we've been counseling the son about his, uh, relationship issues."

"Personal counseling?" Darrah repeated. "That's what hefty donations to the clergy get you, huh? Maybe I'll stick a little more in the collection box next time I visit."

"My door's always open, Mace, you know that." said Gar, with a rueful smile. "You stopped Tikka Rillio from beating me up when we were at school. The least I can do is watch over your spiritual well-being now that we're older."

"Tikka Rillio. Whatever happened to her?" The constable chewed his lip.

"She got herself a colonist husband and went off to Prophet's Landing, had a whole pack of children, I believe." He nodded to himself. "Easier to make something of yourself out there, where you don't have to pick and choose because of your caste."

Darrah smirked. "You should be glad you took to the church. She'd have carried you off with her given half the chance."

Gar returned a wan grin. "Yes. She was a big girl." He shook off the thought. "Anyway, Vedek Cotor asked me to come down and see about providing some spiritual comfort to our mutual friend in the cells." The priest's face fell as a thought occurred to him. "He didn't injure anyone, did he?"

Darrah shrugged. "He roughed up Syjin a little bit. Nobody of consequence."

"Now who's being uncharitable?"

"Hey, you know Syjin. He's never needed anybody's help attracting trouble."

Gar nodded. Darrah was right, as usual. Even when the three of them were boys at the temple school, it was Syjin who had demonstrated a knack for getting himself into all kinds of scrapes. Like Darrah, Gar's parents had both been around when he was a youth, but the pilot had been orphaned at an early age, and that manifested itself in a disorderly streak a mile wide. "You'll keep an eye on him?" said Gar.

"Don't I always?" Darrah replied. "Hey, he gave me something. You like *methrin* eggs?" The police officer motioned to a black box on his desk and then paused as a tall and athletic woman emerged through the doors from the precinct's upper levels.

"Don't the Militia codes prohibit serving law enforcers from accepting gifts from citizens?" she said, arching an eyebrow at the box's contents.

Gar felt a grin form on his face. "Hello, Tomo. You're looking well."

The minister's adjutant bobbed her head, her close-cut hair catching the light. "Thank you, Prylar."

Darrah was frowning as he turned the box to face Lonnic. "Okay then. Take what you want. Just save me some of the *agnam* loaf."

She waved him away. "Keep it, Mace. I'm not down here to hassle you."

Darrah shot the priest an arch look. "Huh. That's a rarity."

"Seriously," she continued, and she said the word in a tone that made both men pause. The easy air of friendship between them fell away. It was immediately clear to Darrah and Gar that Lonnic wasn't interested in their usual banter. "I've just been speaking to Colonel Coldri. He told me I should bring you in on this, seeing as the keep falls inside your patrol pattern."

"In on what?" Darrah demanded. For his part, Gar was already certain of what the next thing out of Lonnic's mouth would be.

"What do you know about the Cardassians?" she asked him.

Darrah shrugged. "Same as everyone else, I suppose.

Ugly and pasty-looking, no sense of humor, eat a lot of fish."

"That's not too far off the beam." She smiled without mirth. "They're coming here."

Gar saw Darrah go tense. "What, all of them?"

"It's a diplomatic mission," Gar offered. "A single ship, a formal first contact, that sort of thing."

Darrah shot him a look. "You knew about this?"

He nodded. "Just before I left the monastery, Vedek Cotor told me. The Kai is going to be part of the group that greets them, and I'll be serving as one of her pages."

"Meressa's going to meet the Cardassians?" The constable blinked. "Is that wise?"

"And not just her. Minister Jas is assembling a whole group of high-caste nobles to be at the keep when they land. Which brings me back to my original point."

Darrah's brow furrowed. "Why would aliens come to Korto? The capital's only just over the mountains, why not go there, or to Dahkur?"

Lonnic explained quickly about the conversation she'd been witness to that morning, and Gar took it in, filling in the gaps in the terse briefing that Cotor had given him.

His old friend's expression soured with each passing word. "Why am I always the last to hear about this sort of thing?" Darrah frowned. "Tomo, this is going to mean a lot more work for the both of us. I'm going to have to bring in more men to cover the additional security requirements, get Coldri to sign off on reinforcements . . ."

Lonnic handed him a padd. "Already done. The minister asked me who I'd recommend to handle the arrangements, and I told him you could do it." She eyed him. "You *can* handle it, Mace, can't you?"

Gar turned to the woman. "I think he was hoping to take some leave, spend some time at home . . ."

"Oh," said Lonnic, and she reached for the padd. "If

that's the case, I'll pass it to someone else. Proka Migdal, or one of the other district watch leaders."

Darrah shook his head and held the device away from her. *"No.* No, I'll deal with it. Nobody else knows Korto as well as I do. I'm the best person for the job."

Lonnic and Gar exchanged looks, and the priest saw a flicker of understanding on her face. "Mace, if you're due some downtime, take it. The precinct can run without you, you know."

He watched the other man study the padd. "I can take a retreat some other time, the kids won't mind. This is important. As much as I trust Proka, he's not up to managing something like this."

Lonnic nodded. "All right, then. The Cardassians will be here in two days, so I need a protocol for the arrival arrangements from you by tonight."

Gar frowned. "Couldn't you make it tomorrow? The Gratitude Festival starts tonight, at least let him have the evening off before you put a yoke on him."

"Very well. Tomorrow morning. You can start thinking about it on the way to the docks." She glanced at the chronograph display on her thumb-ring.

"Why am I going to the docks?" Darrah said warily.

Lonnic leaned over and tapped a panel on the padd, revealing a page of information. "The aliens have an on-planet liaison they've sent along as an advance representative. Minister Jas wants you to escort him up to the keep for a meeting at five-bells."

The constable's frown deepened, and he reached down to snap on his duty belt. "And I was kinda hoping today would be a slow day."

"Seems like the Prophets have other ideas," Gar offered.

"Isn't that always the way?" Darrah threw the comment over his shoulder as he made for the stairs leading to the basement parking garage.

✦   ✦   ✦

Darrah made good time from the precinct to the riverside docks, getting there just a little slower than he would have if he'd been coming in with a flyer instead of one of the Korto City Watch's courier sedans. The skimmer wasn't as fast as a flyer, that much was true, but it was a lot more well-appointed. There was a media suite and a wet bar in the back, so he understood, and the magnetodynamic suspension rode very smoothly. Darrah had never actually sat anywhere else but the driver's seat, though. He had a way to go before he got to a rank that came with this kind of benefit as standard.

Securing the car on the dock apron, he brushed a speck of lint off his tunic and looked up in time to see the sleek hydrofoil settling in to the pier on a stream of white breakers. The boat had come from the city of Janir in the north, racing down the old canals to reach the naturally cut channel of the River Tecyr. Korto sat on a bend in the Tecyr where it turned westward toward the ocean, the wide green waterway flowing fast and strong down from the Perikian Mountains. In Kendra Province and other parts of Bajor, people still used the rivers for travel and shipping cargo, and it was a common sight to see skiffs and packets rolling quietly along under solar-charged fansails; by contrast, the hydrofoil was a brash, noisy conveyance, all speed and angry buzzing aquajets. The boat bumped to a halt and settled into a wallow as crewmen scrambled to the pier to moor it securely.

Darrah saw the pennants flapping from the stern in the light breeze: two colored flags, one flying the city seal of Qui'al and the other the slightly gaudy clan sigil of the Kubus family. He had never dealt with anyone from that lineage before, but he knew the face of the man who stepped from the hydrofoil as well as any Bajoran who watched the newsfeeds. Kubus Oak, Minister for Qui'al and owner of one of the planet's largest offworld shipping firms, strode down the pier and across the docks as if he owned them. The man seemed little different in the flesh to how he looked on the feeds: a round face with deep-set eyes, short and nondescript hair, clothes that favored off-world styles.

Two of the minister's aides followed quickly behind. One was a mousy, slight man clutching a briefcase, the other a blunt-looking fellow who seemed to have been forced into a tunic a size too small for him. The second man had the unmistakable air of a soldier about him, and the constable could tell from his gait that he had a concealed holster in the small of his back.

Kubus stepped up, and Darrah opened the sedan's door for him. The minister scrutinized the vehicle. "This is a skimmer," he noted with a disdainful sniff.

"Your insight does you credit, Minister," Darrah replied, without a hint of sarcasm. The man had said four words, and already Darrah was taking a dislike to him.

"I'd expected Holza to lay on a flyer for me, at the very least." Kubus eyed the car, as if it were beneath him to climb inside.

"All on operational duty, sir," Darrah said smoothly, "and not a one of them is as comfortable as this vehicle." He gave a thin smile. "Don't worry, sir, I'll have you to the keep on time."

"See that you do, Constable," said Kubus, finally getting in, his assistants following suit.

Darrah pressed the accelerator and took the sedan out through the back streets, avoiding the main thoroughfares where traffic would be thick and hard to navigate. On the dashboard monitor, he saw the stocky man, the bodyguard, peering narrow-eyed out of the windows, frowning at the tight lanes as the car threaded through them.

He skirted the industrial districts and the housing projects beyond the City Oval, flashing past the great steps that led to Korto's *bantaca* spire and on to the loop roads up the hillside toward the Naghai Keep. Along the sides of the highway there was activity at every storefront, down every side road and boulevard. Banners and gales of flags were fluttering in place or being hoisted up for the start of the festival, and at every intersection there was a wide brazier. The better districts had ones plated in bronze or brass; the less moneyed wards of the city made do with simple iron cauldrons. Stalls selling scroll paper and quills were doing brisk business along with *jumja* kiosks and cook-wagons. Crossing over an intersection, Darrah caught a whiff of freshly made *hasperat* and his mouth watered.

He hadn't really thought that much about the Gratitude Festival this year, not really, only in terms of being a constable in the City Watch, in terms of work and not family. His entire consideration of the event revolved around the dispensation of officers for the duration, of what flyers to have on standby, which known bag-snatchers and pickpockets to keep an eye out for. The phantom taste of the *hasperat* soured on his tongue as he thought of Karys, of Bajin and Nell. Would this year's festival be like last year's, when he had pressed a handful of litas into his wife's fingers and went off to work after a few moments of standing with his children? Absently he remembered how Bajin had got sick last festival from eating too many toasted bean curd buns. He'd only found out about that after getting in as B'hava'el was rising, Karys making it clear in no uncertain terms that it was his fault it had happened.

Darrah pushed the thought away with a grimace and drove on. From behind him, he heard Kubus talking with the slight man. "What is that?" He was pointing at something out on the street. "A giant scroll?"

The minister's aide nodded. "Yes, sir. It's a quirk, a quaint tradition in some of the less sophisticated townships. Districts where the locals can't afford to purchase individual renewal scrolls for each person will often pool their money to buy one single scroll of great size; usually a prylar from the local temple will take on the responsibility of writing all the people's woes on the paper before it is burned in the brazier."

Kubus grunted. "The whole point of renewal is that the contents of the scrolls are private. What you write on them is between a man and the Prophets. Who would want some inexperienced cleric knowing your troubles?"

"Some of the people may not be able to write themselves," the aide demurred.

The minister's face soured. "Surely Korto is not so parochial that its citizens are illiterate? If that's true, then Holza is doing a poor job of stewarding the community."

In the driving seat, Darrah's grip tightened on the steering yoke. Perhaps when he put his troubles down on his renewal scroll tonight, there might be a space at the bottom to add the name Kubus Oak. Darrah deliberately let the skimmer jerk as he turned into the avenue through the ornamental gardens toward the high tower of the keep.

"Pardon me," he said, with mock sincerity, as Kubus's aide missed his mouth with a sip of water. Darrah had never been that fond of people from Qui'al, not since he was a teenager and the city's springball team had stolen the pennant from Korto by using decidedly unsportsmanlike conduct. Kubus Oak was doing little to improve the constable's opinion.

As he drew the sedan to a halt inside the ring wall, at the base of the portcullis, Darrah found himself wondering if there had been any point at all in dragging him off a vital assignment just to ferry this elitist out-of-towner up to meet Jas. It was a job any supernumerary could have done—perhaps not as swiftly as Darrah did it, thanks to his knowledge of the city streets, admittedly—not one for a senior constable.

He opened the door for Kubus, and the man exited the car without ever looking at him, moving off to be greeted by Lonnic, who threw Darrah a quick nod of the head. It was all about show, all about politics, and Darrah detested the cheap theater of it. Minister Jas wanted Minister Kubus to think he had great respect for him, so he arranged for a senior law officer to ferry him about like a common driver. *I've got more important things to do.*

He turned and found the slight man watching him, dabbing at the water mark on his tunic. "The minister will require transport back to the docks once his meeting is concluded," he was told.

"Really?" Darrah folded his arms. "How long will that take?"

"As long as it needs to."

"Is that right?" Darrah dipped into his pocket and took out the sedan's control key. "I'll tell you what. You tell Kubus, he wants to drive back, he can be my guest." Darrah tossed the key at the aide, who caught it badly, fumbling. "Just make sure he doesn't dent it."

The constable strode away, out through the gates of the keep. There was a tram stop just outside the ornamental gardens, and the route would take him straight back to his home. If he was lucky, he'd get back there before Karys and the kids left.

With a warmth that was utterly at odds with the misgivings he felt, Jas Holza greeted Kubus Oak with a smile and a nod. "Minister Kubus, it's a pleasure to have you in Korto. Welcome to the Naghai Keep."

"Thank you, Minister Jas," said the other man, "and let me be the first to wish you *Peldor Joi,*" he concluded, making the ritual greeting for the Gratitude Festival.

Jas showed him to a broad leather armchair. "Ah," he replied. "A little early, perhaps? The celebrations here will not formally commence until I make the Presider's address to the city tonight."

Kubus smiled. "On the contrary, my friend, I think you and I have plenty to be grateful for at this very moment." He nodded at his own statement. "Yes. The Prophets have favored us. They have handed us a great opportunity, perhaps even the greatest of our lives." The other man glanced at Lonnic as Jas's adjutant entered the room with a tray of *deka* tea and small refreshments. Jas took a cup, but Kubus waved her away, waiting until the woman had left them alone before he spoke again. "You understand my part in this?"

Jas sipped at his cup. "In the broadest of strokes." What he knew of Kubus seemed to be confirmed by his first impressions of the man; the minister for Qui'al District was direct and self-assured. He had a firm face, with short, spiky brown hair, but Kubus's eyes were sharp and watchful. Jas had expected no less. Although he had never dealt directly with the minister, he had often seen him in the council chambers and heard second- and thirdhand of the man's business. That Kubus Oak was a shrewd speculator was well-known. One did not become the head of Bajor's largest interstellar shipping agency without equal measures of cunning and intelligence. "Why don't you enlighten me?" he added.

Kubus spread his hands, taking in the room around them. "I've always felt that most of my kinsmen on Bajor are inward-looking," he began. "It's a failing of our nature, I think. Too much effort spent on matters of the spirit, on habit and tradition. We risk becoming parochial. Do you agree, Holza?" He leaned forward. "I may call you Holza?"

Jas nodded. "Of course. Oak." He licked his lips before replying. "In answer to your question, I suppose, yes, there is that possibility."

Kubus continued. "It's a big galaxy out there. Bajor's just a small part of it, and we have to come to terms with that if our species is to continue to thrive. In the thousands of years Bajorans have had civilization, we have only made the smallest of moves into the ocean of stars around us. In galactic terms, we're barely wading in the shallows, while other races we'd consider immature by our standards have great swaths of the quadrant under their aegis. We can't afford to be insular in the face of that." He smiled to himself. "I've made quite a good life for myself with this philosophy."

"So I understand." These sentiments were not anything that Jas hadn't heard before, either through Kubus's statements on the newsfeeds or from the mouths of other, less influential ministers who followed his lead.

"I'm not squeamish about dealing with aliens, Holza. Sometimes I think the First Minister and his cronies are afraid of the idea that there are other races out there."

Jas nodded again. While Verin preferred to keep contact with aliens at arm's length, maintaining that Bajor had always flourished without them, Kubus frequently agitated for more open relations with other worlds. As someone with interests both on Bajor and off it, Jas's own feelings fell between the two extremes.

The other man continued. "My people have been trading with the Xepolites, the Lissepians, the Cardassian Union—we've been at it for years. They trust my clan. My name is known offplanet. That's why the Cardassians have come to me with this."

"You've traded with them on some of the colony worlds, is that right?" Jas got a nod in return. "But they've never come into our space before."

"Not formally, not until today. It's a historic moment, Holza. In the future, you'll be telling your grandchildren about it." Kubus flashed a smile. "And I have to say, I admired the astute way you exploited the opportunity presented to you."

"Exploited?" Jas raised an eyebrow.

The other man's smile turned sly. "Come now, Holza, don't play the innocent. You could have stood by and let Verin take control of the situation, but you didn't. You saw a chance and you took it. That's the sign of a perceptive leader."

"I want what is best for Korto, and Bajor." Jas covered his frown with another sip of tea.

"As do I." Kubus sighed. "It's no secret that my views on openness have made me something of an outsider in the council—I freely admit that. Thanks to my previous dealings with the offworlders, the Cardassians are reaching out to me to act as their planetary liaison, and there are some who view me with suspicion. I am here today to ascertain if you are one of them, Minister Jas."

Jas shook his head slowly. "I may not have the reach of your ships and your organization, Oak, but I will admit I do hear some merit in your words. I don't see the harm in allowing these aliens to make formal contact with our world. As you say, this is a historic moment. The first time a Cardassian has set foot on Bajor."

"Yes," Kubus said, almost to himself.

Jas found himself warming to the subject. "Perhaps this is the time for Bajor to reconsider its place in galactic politics."

Kubus's smile widened. "I see that you and I drink from the same well, my friend! Indeed, a formal relationship with the Cardassian Union will be good for Bajor. It could usher in a new age of prosperity for our planet . . . and for the men who understand how to turn it to their advantage." His voice dropped to a conspiratorial hush. "After all, we outsiders should stick together, yes?"

"What do you mean?"

Kubus gave a dry chuckle. "I've heard of the issues that face Korto District. Your journey to Batal this week? I don't think it would be impolite of me to say that your standing with the council is not what it should be." He nodded to himself. "That will soon be a thing of the past."

Jas kept his expression unchanged, but inside he felt a flare of concern. That he had verbally crossed swords with Verin on the floor of the Chamber of Ministers was a matter of public record, but the business in Batal was supposed to have been a secret ... He stopped himself. There was nothing to say that Kubus knew the extent of Jas's problems, and he had to be careful not to give any more away. Still, the man was correct. Korto District and its leader had done very poorly in the political arena in recent months. Kubus was as perceptive as Jas had expected; he could understand how Jas had seen the arrival of the aliens as a chance to raise his profile once more, to put Korto back on the map. The other minister was right. Perhaps they did have more in common than either of them realized.

And yet ... There was something in Kubus's manner that did not sit well with Jas. As Kubus sat there, smiling thinly, Jas sensed that the politician was holding something back, that he had knowledge Jas simply wasn't privy to. His hands drew together across his desk and he studied the other man with fresh eyes. For the second time that day, Jas realized that he was on the verge of making a decision that would shift the course of his life. He narrowed his eyes and searched inside himself to find a focus. *I'm in a different arena now,* he told himself. *New rules to learn. New players to play against. New allies ... and enemies.*

"So," said Kubus, gesturing with one hand. "We should discuss the arrangements for the reception for our visitors."

Darrah Mace slid the door closed in time to hear his wife raise her voice from the landing upstairs. "If I have to tell you again," she was saying, "then everyone will stay home tonight and you'll have to keep your renewal scrolls until next year."

He frowned and made his way to the upper floor of the apartment, treading softly.

"You know what happens then?" Karys continued, her words filtering along from the master bedroom. "All the problems and bad things you wrote down on this year's scrolls won't go away and you'll be stuck with them for another year! So put on your good tunic, or we won't go to the festival!"

"I don't like that one," Bajin complained. Mace stifled a smirk. Karys's mother in Ashalla had bought the boy the tunic for his birthday in some fancy store in the capital, but the ten-year-old hated it. He was like his father that way, preferring the simple cut to anything extravagant.

"I don't—" Karys began as Mace entered the room.

Nell, sitting quietly on the bed in her sky-blue wrap, exploded into life and threw herself at him. "Daddy!" She was only six, but she moved like lightning, and grabbed on to the constable so hard he was almost winded.

"Hey, Dad." Bajin's face lit up as well.

"Peldor Joi, everybody," Mace returned, nodding to Karys. His wife refused to give him a smile in return.

"Constable Darrah," she began, "nice of you to join us. Could you help me here by telling your son to get properly dressed?"

Mace shot the boy a look. "Hey, 'Jin. Do what your mother tells you. Go get the tunic."

"I don't like it," he repeated.

"And I don't care," Mace said firmly. "Go on. You won't have to wear it again until next year, I promise. And at the rate you're growing, you'll be too big for it by then anyhow."

Dejected, the boy shuffled out of the room. Mace bent down to give Nell a peck on the cheek and then gave her a gentle shove. "Hey, go make sure your brother does what he's told, okay?"

The little girl's head bobbed in a nod and she ran out after her sibling, leaving the parents alone. Mace gave a weak smile and went to the closet, shrugging off his duty tunic along the way.

"You actually made it home before we left," said Karys, putting up her hair. "I suppose I should be thankful."

Mace leafed through his clean clothes. "Well, hold your applause. I may have just upset a member of the Chamber of Ministers to do it. Besides, I promised the kids." He found a clean Militia-brown tunic and pulled it out.

"You've promised a lot of things," she retorted. "A house instead of living in this stacker. Better prospects for us. No more long shifts."

"I can't earn enough for a better place by working less, Karys."

"Then just—" She turned to face him and stopped. "What are you putting on?"

"A clean uniform tunic." He ran his thumb up the seal tab and picked up his belt. "The other one's a little sweaty. I've had it on all day."

Karys's voice rose. "You said you'd quit early today, Mace. Quit. As in 'off-duty,' as in 'not a constable.' Why are you wearing your uniform?"

"It's a formal city function," he retorted. "I'm a law officer. People will expect it of me. I have to be seen."

"Oh, right," she snapped back. "And if there's some trouble, if someone gets rowdy, will you have to be a law officer then? Will you leave me and the children to go chasing some bag-snatcher? Can't you let go of that job for one single hour?" Karys fingered the *D'jarra* ornament on her earring, as she always did when she was annoyed with him.

"It's what I do!" Just like that, he was snarling at her, falling back into old patterns.

"You're arguing." The voice from the door made them

both stop dead. Bajin was there, the ugly tunic in his hand, frowning.

"We're not arguing," said Karys, abashed. "We're just talking loudly."

"That's what arguing *is,*" replied the boy, with a child's relentless logic. "I don't like it when you do that."

Mace gave a weak smile. "We're sorry, son." He paused for a moment, and then threw off his duty jacket, reaching for a clean-cut black shirt instead. "C'mon, everyone finish getting dressed. If we stay here talking all night, we'll miss the ceremony and all the toasted buns will be sold by the time we get there."

A grin emerged on Bajin's face. "Okay."

He glanced at Karys. "Okay?"

She stood and helped him button the shirt, the corners of her mouth quirking upward for the first time. "Okay."

Sunset had turned the sky a gorgeous burnt umber by the time they reached the City Oval. In every boulevard in every district of Korto, street parties were gearing up, and there was an atmosphere of infectious excitement that was hard to ignore. On the breeze there were the smells of cooking food, *bateret* incense, and hot, sugary snacks. Voices were raised in song, all of it good-natured if not always tuneful; here and there massive streetscreens were showing imagery from other festivals in other cities, with scenes from the Grand Avenue of Lights in Ashalla, the flame dancers on Tilar's beaches, even shots via subspace of celebrations on Prophet's Landing and Andros.

Here in Korto it seemed as if the entire population had emptied out of the tenements and come to fill the streets. They skirted past a group of performers who played out one of Lupar's Summer Tales, the one with the fisherman and the angry sea serpent.

The children laughed and danced around them, play-fighting and making faces. Darrah shooed them forward every time they tried to dawdle around the stalls selling *jumja* on sticks or trinkets for the festival. Nell had already made him buy her a glow-streamer, and the little girl cut outlines in the air with it.

Just watching her and Bajin brought him a good mood, and it eased the tension that Darrah had been feeling all week, but it was still difficult for him to ease back from being a police officer, and he felt a little foolish in the black shirt, as if he were making some halfhearted effort at going undercover. He was so used to prowling the festival and having the crowds part dutifully around the uniform he wore. It felt odd to go civilian, and he had to rein in his natural reflex to scrutinize the revelers, looking for shifty expressions and lawbreakers in the making. He tried to relax.

His work, his conflicts with Karys, and now this new thing about the aliens visiting—what he needed right now was a few hours to breathe, to get it out of his system. He glanced at his wife. She was right, really. She was right about most things, and despite how annoying that could be at times, it was one of the reasons why he loved her so much. Karys was right when she told him that the Militia was taking over his life.

But then there were the *other* things she said. She was always telling him that he was going nowhere. She wanted him to push for a promotion. She wanted him to do better so they could move from the apartment block near the canals and get a better place, a real home, in the hills. Darrah wanted those things just as much as Karys did, but she didn't seem to understand that advancements didn't happen overnight. Hard work brings rewards—that was the ethic he'd been brought up with as a *Ke'lora,* the *D'jarra* that encompassed the families of laborers, lawmen, and craftsmen. Unaware that he was watching her, his wife brushed her straight black hair over her shoulder, revealing her silver earring against the tawny skin of her face. Although they were married, one of the adornments on Karys's ear still reflected the *D'jarra* she had been born into, the artistic *Ih'valla*. She had never made an issue of it in all the years they had been together, but Karys had married below her station when she had accepted Darrah's proposal. Her clan had made it difficult for them at first; it was only with the birth of Bajin that Darrah had finally been considered an "acceptable" husband.

They crossed through a cordon outside the edge of the Oval, one of the watchmen on duty recognizing Darrah and raising an eyebrow at his choice of clothing, but saying nothing. Only the more moneyed clans and those of the upper tiers of the *D'jarra*s were allowed this far. In other circumstances, not even an *Ih'valla* and certainly not a *Ke'lora* would have been allowed inside the perimeter—but some things transcended the borders of caste, and being a senior law enforcer was one of them. As much as Karys might quietly dislike the commonplace life she led as a constable's wife, at times like this Darrah imagined she was quite happy with it.

They halted in front of the massive brass and iron brazier at the foot of the *bantaca* spire. Bajin kept playing with his hair, deliberately mussing it, so Darrah pressed a couple of litas into the lad's hand and sent him off to get buns. Nell trailed after him, singing a nursery rhyme about the Celestial Temple.

Karys took his hand. "What's on your scroll this year?" she asked him.

Mace fingered the ceremonial paper in his pocket. "Ah. The usual. I'm asking the Prophets to make sure my children don't age me too early, to see that anyone who shoots at me has lousy aim, to make my debts go away . . ."

She lowered her voice. "You know, Mother made the offer again."

He put a finger on her lips. "We're not taking her money, Karys. We've been through this. I don't care how many sculptures she's sold, I'm not going to owe her."

For a second, he thought she was going to argue, but then his wife sighed. "Let's not fight about this again. Not tonight. Can we talk about it some other time?"

"All right," Mace agreed, but even as he said it he resolved not to be shifted on the issue.

She tilted her head back to let her gaze range up the sides of the spire, and Mace did the same. Streamers in red and gold hung down from the stone obelisk and fluttered in the cool evening breeze. Carved from stone blocks that were so finely crafted that they locked together without need of cement or mortar, the *bantaca* was said to mark the place of a settlement in relationship to the rest of the universe. Darrah saw that the stars were coming out overhead, and he wondered if that could be true. If what Lonnic and Gar had told him about the Cardassians was accurate, then very soon Korto would indeed be marked as an important place, known out there as well as down here. The thought of the aliens coming to Bajor, of them standing where he stood now, sent a chill snaking down Mace's back. *Things will change,* he told himself, *but I'm not sure how.*

Karys squeezed his hand, sensing that something was troubling him. "I'm glad that you came tonight."

"Me too," he admitted, and kissed her gently on the cheek.

"Ah, young love," said Lonnic as she approached. "It's a delight to see."

Mace's wife broke into a grin and gave the other woman a brief hug of greeting. "Good to see you, Tomo." She gestured at her formal dress. "You're as elegant as ever."

"Too kind," Lonnic demurred.

"Thank you for letting my husband off his duties early," she added. "It's very generous of Minister Jas."

"Generous, yes." Tomo eyed Mace, who maintained an air of blank innocence. "That's one way to look at it." She leaned closer to Darrah and lowered her voice. "You owe Proka a drink, I would say. He covered for you at the keep."

Mace nodded slightly. "I appreciate it."

Tomo smiled thinly. "Don't worry. After spending thirty seconds in the same room as Kubus Oak, I don't think I would have wanted to ferry him around either. He's gone back to Qui'al, thank the Prophets."

"I don't think we've seen the last of him, though," Darrah opined. "Where's the minister?"

She pointed along the *bantaca*'s steps to where a temporary podium had been set up. Jas Holza was behind it, waving to the crowds and beaming into the lenses of a dozen camera drones. "Right there. If you'll excuse me, duty calls."

Mace turned back to his wife as the children came swarming around them, faces sticky with icing. "Did you bring us buns?" he asked Bajin.

Licking powdered sugar off his lips, the boy gave him the same innocent look Darrah had shown Lonnic only moments earlier. "Oh. Did you want some too?"

Jas Holza placed the padd containing his speech on the lectern in front of him and waved as the illuminators came up to full strength. A blink of indicators on the drifting orbs of the camera drones showed him that he was now being broadcast across the city and the district, and it pleased him to hear Korto quieted as he started his address. For all his problems in the greater political arena, at least in the city of his birth his people still respected him.

"*Peldor Joi,* my friends," he began. "It gives me great pleasure to stand before you today as Presider of Korto's Gratitude Festival. Ours is a city of proud and hardworking people, an example of Bajoran endeavor that shines like a jewel in Kendra's beautiful countryside." He smiled slightly. "But we all know, whatever circumstances our *D'jarras* saw us born to, from the lowliest man to the most noble, that no life goes on without regrets. No great city like ours is built without hardship." A swell of polite agreement crossed the crowd, and Jas scanned their faces, gauging their emotions. "All of us have worked hard this year, and tonight we come together to do two things." He took an ornate scroll trimmed with latinum leafing from his pocket. "We cast our troubles to the air by writing them upon our renewal scrolls and letting the fires consume them; and then we give thanks to the Prophets for watching over us for all the good fortune we have had in the year passed by, and in hopes for all the promise yet to come."

Jas stepped down from the podium and walked to the giant brazier, pausing to take a stone flask from Vedek Cotor. The camera drones moved with him in a slow, humming halo. He paused at the lip of the cauldron and spoke in a firm, confident voice, the sensor pickups in the drones amplifying his words for the whole city to hear. *"Tesra peldo, impatri bren,"* Jas began, speaking the words of the benediction in Old High Bajoran. *"Bentel vetan, ullon sten."* With a confident flick of his thumb, Jas popped open the stopper on the flask of consecrated oil and swirled the liquid around. Exposed to oxygen, it immediately puffed into smoky orange flame. Keeping his hand steady, the minister let the fluid stream out over the lip of the great brazier, and with a thump of displaced air the nyawood and straw inside caught alight. Sparks jumped and curled into the evening, and applause streamed behind it. All across Bajor, other Presiders in other cities would be doing the same thing—but now Jas did something different.

In previous years, the Presider would step forward and toss the first scroll into the fire to symbolize the proper start of the festivities; Jas did not. He hesitated, enjoying the moment of mild surprise he engendered. "My friends," he called out, "we write our dilemmas upon the scrolls and as they turn to ashes in these sanctified flames, so do our troubles. But tonight, before I throw my scroll into the fire, I have something important to add to it." From a pouch in his belt, Jas produced a stylus and unrolled his paper. The crowd was watching him intently now; this was a break with tradition, and to many it would be considered a breach of privacy. The words on each person's scroll were a personal thing, to be known only to the one who wrote them and the Prophets who looked on from the Celestial Temple. Yet, here was Korto's minister, openly showing what he was to write. With care, so that the camera drones could see what he was doing, Jas drew the character for "isolation" in thick, deliberate lines and presented it to the air. Then, with a twist of his wrist, he tossed the paper into the rumbling brazier, and the scroll was flashed into ashes.

"Tonight, I cast Bajor's isolation to the fires, and I urge you all to join me and do the same." He met the cameras with a strong smile. "In two days, Korto will take back some of her sons who were lost in the depths of space, and it will welcome those who bring their remains home to us. These people are not of our world. Some of us are afraid of them, of what they represent. Some feel they come with avarice." He shook his head. There was silence all around him now, save for the low crackle of the burning nyawood. The doubts Holza had felt speaking before Verin and again with Kubus were gone. His jaw stiffened. First it had been the old leader of the council attempting to push Holza from the center of these important events; and then Kubus, parlaying his business connections to the aliens in order to strengthen his own position. He had no doubt that each of them thought Jas to be unsuited to the challenges ahead, that they were the better men to take the helm. *That will not be allowed to happen.* Korto would be the fulcrum point for change on Bajor, he would see to it. The thought made Holza feel potent and strong, the certainty and confidence propelling him forward. "Some have nothing but distrust for outsiders. But I believe otherwise. I have seen that these visitors have their own path, just as we have ours granted by the Prophets. I believe that we can learn from them and forge a new friendship. I will welcome them. Korto will welcome them. And if the Prophets will it, then so Bajor will welcome the people of Cardassia to our shores."

The moment the alien name left his lips there was a ripple of astonishment that radiated out around him. Jas nodded as if to say, *Yes, you heard correctly.* "Mark this day well, my friends," he told them. "Bajor is about to enter a new era."

The applause began, and the minister stepped back as scroll after scroll fell into the brazier, lighting puffs of flame as they were consumed.

4

"Slow and steady, Dukat," said Kell from behind him. "We don't want to alarm the natives."

"As you wish, Gul." Dukat kept his expression neutral as he nodded to the young glinn in the pilot's couch. The junior officer eased back a little on the cutter's thrusters, dropping the slab-shaped vessel's airspeed. It wasn't as if they had been hurtling through the sky at any great speed, but Kell was the kind of commander who liked to micromanage his crew, to be seen to be doing something even when there was nothing to be done. The gul drew back into the main compartment of the *Kornaire*'s landing ship, to where the rest of the diplomatic party were seated. Dukat had a glimpse of the Oralians, Hadlo and Bennek and a couple more of their number with hooded heads bowed. *Are they praying for a safe landing? The flight isn't that bumpy.* Seated by Professor Ico's side, Pa'Dar caught Dukat's eye and threw him a nod before he went back to looking out through one of the armored portholes.

Dukat checked the glinn's course and saw she was keeping perfectly to the prescribed air corridor that the Bajorans had transmitted to them. Coming in over that curious blue-green ocean, they were now flying upriver toward their final destination. A flight of swift, needle-hulled aircraft were moving in echelon a few hundred *decas* above them, an escort of atmospheric fighters from the Militia's Aerial Guard. The shuttle's passive sensors showed him exactly where each flyer was, and he had no doubt that the men piloting those planes had one hand on their active scanner controls, ready to illuminate the ship with targeting systems if they diverged from their course by so much as a wing's span. The Cardassian smiled thinly. If the roles had been reversed, he would have done the same—then Dukat corrected himself. *No, I would never allow one of them to set foot on Cardassia. Not unless they were under guns or in chains.*

"Estimated time of arrival is seven metrics, Dalin," said the pilot.

Dukat nodded. "Look sharp. Your landing will be the first impression we make, so do it with skill."

"I will, sir."

Dukat peered out of the cutter's forward canopy and saw the Bajoran metropolis through the wisps of low-lying cloud. The colors, like the teal ocean, seemed peculiar to the eyes of a man used to the ashen gray and rusty umber of Cardassian cityscapes. Lush parkland of a kind that could never survive on Cardassia Prime's water-scarce continents was everywhere, each major artery lined with trees and great square commons laid out over the radial terraced districts. The buildings were largely of a uniform red-gold hue, most likely made from some kind of local stone, and there were spires and minarets on each intersection. Dukat saw nothing like the imposing towers and majestic arcs of his homeworld's architecture. Instead, the Bajorans favored domes that lay wide and low to the ground, or glassy orbs that seemed too fragile to be dwellings. With a practiced soldier's eye, the dalin examined the scope of Korto, thinking of the city in the guise of an invader. What forces would a commander need to commit to take a conurbation like this one? Where would he need to strike to cut off lines of supply, yet ensure that the prize remained intact?

Filing away his impressions for later deliberation, he shifted back in his acceleration chair as the shuttle turned gently into a banking maneuver, toward the towering castle on the hill overshadowing the city.

"Beginning final descent," said the pilot, and Dukat tapped the intercom and repeated the report to the rest of the passengers.

The shuttle slowed, coming over the walls of the Naghai Keep to stop in a hover above an open space in the broad inner courtyard. Dukat saw a pavilion down there, a small crowd of overdressed Bajorans looking up at them and shielding their eyes. To one side, beneath a set of ornamental arches, there was a raised dais and on it shrouded shapes that could only be the bodies of men. The white cloths that concealed the corpses fluttered as the shuttle dropped gently to the ground, the ship's repulsors casting up small cyclones of air and dust.

The crew of the Bajoran scoutship had been turned over to the locals so that they could prepare for whatever death rituals were needed. He wondered idly if the Bajorans had examined the bodies as thoroughly as the Cardassians had before returning them. He made a mental note to ask Pa'Dar later if they had gleaned anything interesting.

Settling on its landing struts with a hiss of hydraulics, the cutter touched down with barely a tremor of motion, and Dukat inclined his head at the glinn in a gesture of praise before rising from his station. He checked the hang of his duty armor and the flimsy peace-bond seal over the butt of the phaser pistol in his belt holster, then crossed to Kell's side.

The gul shot Hadlo a hard look as the elderly priest paused on the threshold of the hatchway. "I believe it would be best if I exited first, cleric."

Hadlo's lined face hardened. "What sort of message does that send to these people, Gul Kell?"

"Precisely the one I *want* to send," Kell replied, and thumbed the control that opened the wide gull-wing door.

Dukat was right behind him, and the rush of Bajoran atmosphere welled up and into the shuttle's interior, washing over the dalin's face. It was cool and sweet, lacking the dry edge of home.

Pa'Dar and Ico were the last to disembark, followed by two grim-faced glinns who wore the watchful look of men waiting in vain for a threat to emerge where none was lurking. Kell and Dukat, there in their black battle gear, next to the pastel robes of Hadlo, Bennek, and the other Oralians, and now the two scientists in the neutral blues and grays of their duty uniforms; Pa'Dar wondered what the natives would make of them, the three groups within the diplomatic mission all alien, all different.

The clothing worn by the Bajorans was a contrast as well. They seemed to favor earth tones, brown and ochre that reminded the scientist of the stonework of the city. *Perhaps the colors are supposed to represent some sort of metaphorical link between the people and their world?* It was an interesting hypothesis, and one that Pa'Dar might share with Ico when they returned to the *Kornaire,* if, of course, she could spare him the time. Of late, as the ship had come closer and closer to Bajor, his supervisor had been harder to pin down, always engaged in communications with the homeworld, distracted by assignments she was unwilling to discuss. Secrecy was part and parcel of life in service to the Cardassian government, but Ico's recent behavior had gone beyond that. He wondered idly if she were doing something illicit, perhaps engaging in a liaison with one of the ship's crew members.

Pa'Dar dismissed the thoughts and turned his attention back to the aliens. He was being provided with a unique opportunity here, and he would be remiss if he didn't make the most of it. His family were politicians and administrators back on the homeworld, and they had made no attempt to hide their disapproval of his choice of an academic career path. At best, his parents saw themselves as indulging a youthful caprice that they fully expected Kotan to grow out of in due course; the Bajor mission was a chance to prove them wrong, to show them that he could do something of value from the halls of the science ministry.

Pa'Dar studied the group of Bajorans who approached them from the larger group. At their head were a trio of males in ornate tunics of varying cut, one who clearly had assumed the mantle of command bearing a weathered face, the others following a step behind. Past them, there were three more in robes that shared some similarity to the dress of the Oralian clerics, although the Bajorans wore skullcaps or headgear that arched over their odd, wrinkled brows instead of hoods. And at the rear, a group of figures in what were unmistakably military uniforms. The sketchy cultural briefing Pa'Dar had absorbed before the mission's departure told him that much, but he was unsure how to interpret the colors of the tunics or the oval gold insignia on the collars. He elected to avoid addressing any of the Bajoran soldiers in the event he mistook a rank and offended one of them.

"Gul Kell, I am Verin Kolek, First Minister of Bajor," said the one with the heavily lined face. His voice had the timbre of age and acumen. Pa'Dar had watched the feed from the *Kornaire*'s communications a few days earlier, but until he stood here, staring at the alien, he had not truly understood how peculiar the Bajorans looked. Their flesh, with hues ranging from pinkish yellow to dark ebony, were nothing like the stony, harmonious gray of his own species; and the faces were so smooth and uncharacterful, with only a small patch of nasal ridges to suggest anything like the fine ropes of muscle and bone that adorned the Cardassian aspect. The one who called himself Verin was an elder, and Pa'Dar wondered how old he could be. Cardassians aged at a steady, stately pace, growing more regal as they did so—

but this alien seemed almost wizened by comparison. *And he is their ruler? Are all their leaders so decrepit?*

The minister was still speaking, indicating the younger men standing with him. "This is Kubus Oak, whom I believe your people have already met, and Jas Holza, whose hospitality we all share today." He gestured to the robed Bajorans, beginning with the lone female. "This is the honored Kai Meressa, and her adjutants Vedek Cotor and Prylar Gar." Finally, it was the turn of the soldiers. "Our Militia representatives, Jaro Essa and Coldri Senn."

The *Kornaire's* commander nodded with grave solemnity, and Pa'Dar wondered if the Bajorans detected the element of careful pretense beneath the motion. "I greet you in the name of the Cardassian Union and the Detapa Council. We regret that it must be under such circumstances as these"——he gestured toward the arched enclosure where the dead bodies were lying——"but it is Cardassia's fervent hope that on the foundation of such a tragedy our two peoples may come to better know each other as interstellar neighbors." He took a breath. "This is my first officer Dalin Dukat, and these are representatives of our Ministry of Science and the Oralian Way."

The woman Verin had called the kai stepped forward and bowed. "I welcome you to our world in the name of the Prophets," she began. Her voice was clear and melodic, and it carried across the courtyard. She looked to Hadlo and the other clerics. "Before we go any further, please let me express my personal delight in meeting a deputation from the followers of Oralius."

"You know of our faith?" said Bennek.

"Indeed," said the kai. "Our ecumenical scholars study the beliefs of many worlds, and we have come to understand that our faith can learn great lessons from those of other beings. I hope that during your visit here we will be able to speak of Oralius's teachings. We are interested to learn more of Cardassian spirituality."

Pa'Dar could see that Hadlo was surprised by the woman's openness. On Cardassia, matters of so-called *faith*—such as they were in these more enlightened times—did not usually find such a warm response from outsiders. The cleric nodded woodenly. "Of . . . of course. And I too would be fascinated to learn more about your Prophets."

Meressa glanced at Verin and Jas. "With the minister's permission, we will speak of them now."

Jas returned a nod. "Please, Kai, you may begin at your discretion."

The woman bowed slightly, and the troupe of alien priests moved to join several others of their number near the shrouded bodies.

The Bajorans made a sign over their chests. "Before we proceed, the kai will perform a blessing for the spirits of the *Eleda*'s crewmen," explained the younger minister.

Bennek craned forward to get a better look at the Bajorans, and Hadlo shot him a terse glance. "Show decorum," rumbled the old cleric.

"Of course," Bennek replied, but the priest's manner belied his statement. Bennek was fascinated by the aliens, and had been ever since the Oralians were approached to join the *Kornaire*'s mission. What he had seen of Bajor through glimpses of the wrecked ship and the dead men was compelling. Bennek had never set foot off Cardassia Prime in all his twenty-seven years, spending much of his life buried in Oralian scriptures and tomes from the ancient Hebitians. He had grown up steeped in the past of his planet, never once considering how life might exist in other places; but a chance moment, accompanying Hadlo when the cleric had been allowed to examine the *Eleda* crew's personal effects, had sparked something in him. Among the wreckage of the ship were the remains of a small alcove containing a portable shrine, and there he had come across fragments of a votive icon that resembled—albeit only slightly—a Face of the Fates. He remembered the physical shock at seeing it. Hadlo had dismissed the moment, describing it as a mere coincidence and nothing more, but Bennek couldn't shake the sense that there was something greater to the similarity. *Oralius lives above all,* he had reasoned. *Is it so strange to imagine she might have touched the souls of other beings as well as Cardassians?*

The daring thrill he felt at actually entertaining so radical a thought coursed through him once again. It was something he would never have dared to voice in the chapels of the Way—the conservative nature of his fellow believers was well known to him—but out here, far from home . . . Suddenly, the possibility seemed real. He watched Kai Meressa and the other Bajoran priests making patterns in the air with their hands. Bennek was energized by the idea of learning everything he could about these "Prophets," and perhaps taking the first step toward bringing these aliens to the light of the Way.

The youngest of the Bajoran clerics, the one the First Minister had introduced as Prylar Gar, saw Bennek watching him and inclined his head with a cautious smile. He wondered if Gar was thinking the same thoughts. The kai took lit tapers from two females in simple shift dresses and used them to light fat yellow candles on a portable altar, in front of the enclosure where the dead men had been placed. Bennek's gaze lingered on the women. The forms of the Bajoran females were so different from the women he had known on Cardassia; his culture favored wives and daughters to be muscular and athletic in build, mothers and elders to be robust and sturdy. These were willowy and lithe in comparison; they reminded Bennek of the desert nymphs from old fables. Their smooth, flawless skins made them seem ephemeral, almost angelic.

"The land and the people are as one," intoned Meressa. "This truth has been at the heart of us since the day the

Prophets first walked among us; but when our sons and our daughters venture far beyond the stars and dark fates come to claim them, they are no longer at one with the soil of their birth." The priestess bent down and scooped a handful of sandy dirt from the courtyard at her feet, then let it fall away through her fingers. She gestured to the corpses. "These shells are no more than the husks of what our kindred once were, the corporeal remains of friends, brothers, sisters, lovers." Bennek saw several of the Bajorans in the stands behind the dais nodding, some moved to tears. There were children among them, he noticed, realizing for the first time that those had to be the families of the *Eleda* dead.

Meressa continued. "Tomorrow, those shells will be taken from this place and committed to the land, buried to lie beside the shells of their ancestors. But what of their eternal souls? For those who perish in the void, uncountable distances from the land, what will befall their spirits?" She looked up into the sky and spread her hands. The Cardassian cleric felt the thrill of surprise once more; the kai's gesture mirrored the same ritual pattern that Bennek had performed aboard the *Kornaire*. All she lacked was a mask of recitation for the similarity to be complete. At his side, he heard Hadlo's sharp intake of breath, and from the corner of his eye he saw that Gul Kell's first officer was glancing his way. *Even Dukat sees the resemblance.*

"You need not fear for the souls of our brave friends," said the priestess, smiling warmly. "The faith that moves through us all, that brings life to our flesh and to our eternal spirit, is the faith of the Prophets. We feel their love and their wisdom, in life as we do in death, and in doing so we know that once our brief candle is extinguished"—the Kai paused, dousing one of the ceremonial tapers—"a new light will be illuminated. The light of the way toward the Celestial Temple, where all live anew in the bosom of the Prophets." She bowed her head for a moment, and all the Bajorans followed suit. "What remains after death is but a shell. A sign that the *pagh* has begun its final journey to the Prophets. We ask that they reach out and guide the souls of the *Eleda* to their reward, knowing that we shall see them again when the day comes for our light to be eclipsed." Meressa looked up. "And we give thanks to our friends from across the stars for their kindness in bringing closure to the families of the lost." The kai and the other priests bowed to the altar and then again to the Cardassians. Unsure of the correct etiquette for the moment, Hadlo and Bennek hesitantly mirrored the motion, sharing a questioning glance.

Bennek could see that the cleric was troubled by the kai's benediction. The uses of language, the gestures and ritual—there were several points between the Bajoran rite and Oralian funeral sacraments that were alarmingly alike. The old man clearly read the intention in Bennek's face, the need to speak it aloud, and he gave the slightest shake of the head. "Not now," whispered Hadlo. "We . . . we must tread carefully."

The energy of the moment bled out of Bennek in an instant, and he felt crestfallen. "But, Master, do you not see that—"

Hadlo held up a hand to silence him. "Remember where we find ourselves, Bennek," he husked. "Amid those of our own kind who see no value in the Way, on alien ground among those who may be misguided. We must take care to ensure that these people are kindred spirits. We must find the right moment."

Ico glanced at Kell as the gul let out a low breath between his teeth. She raised an eyebrow and spoke quietly so only the *Kornaire*'s commander would be able to hear her. "Am I to take it that you do not find this ceremony to be as enlightening as I do?"

Kell grunted softly. "'Enlightening' is not the word I would have used, Professor. 'Primitive,' perhaps. 'Distasteful,' even." He looked at her, amused with himself. "You are the expert on alien cultures, are you not? Tell me, what can we expect to see next? Rousing hymnals? The ritualized slaying of some small and inoffensive animal?"

She resisted the impulse to sneer at Kell's words and simply cocked her head. "I do not believe so. What data our observers have gleaned shows no predilection toward behavior of that kind. Bajoran religion appears to be beneficent, at least within the bounds of the inherently repressive nature of all enforced faiths."

"And did your observers tell you how long these interminable benedictions go on for?" Before them, the Bajorans had lit a series of oil lamps and joined in a solemn, metered chant.

Ico smiled thinly. "I believe that some formal ceremonies can last for several hours." She looked away, watching the Oralians. Hadlo and his junior Bennek were sharing words as well, but too low for Ico's hearing to pick up the speech; it mattered little, however. Her skills included the training to read the physical cues of humanoid body language, and with men like these clerics who were unschooled in the arts of obfuscation and dissembling, it was almost child's play to divine their emotional states. Bennek balanced on the cusp of youthful enthusiasm, dazzled by the sights and sounds of the new environment around him, while Hadlo reeked of desperation and the steady drumming pulse of fear. She'd sensed it in the old man the moment she had first seen his face, his watery brown eyes staring up at her from the screen of a padd. Ico could read the cleric's emotional index as easily as she could the text of a book. Then, as now, she knew he was the correct choice to participate in the *Kornaire*'s mission. All that was required was a steady, vigilant hand to ensure that he led the Oralians down the path that was being laid out for them.

Her attention returned to Kai Meressa and the Bajorans as the ritual for the dead came to a slow, stately conclusion. It fascinated her, the way that the Bajoran faith was so clearly threaded through everything that the aliens said or did. The same shapes and motifs appeared in their clothing and their architecture, the oval symbols recurring again and again. Ico was quietly content that she had been born into an era where Cardassia had grown out of such unsophisticated beliefs; she was the product of a Union where belief in the strength of her people's destiny was enough, without the need to resort to the invention of phantom deities. There had been a time in Cardassia's past when they too had been hidebound by dogma and creed. Ico's placid face hid an inner grimace as she imagined her species in thrall to weak men like Hadlo and his Oralian nonsense. But the Cardassian civilization had matured, finding new strength in its austerity, and the cleric's Way was withering and fading; perhaps, in time, Cardassia would be able to educate the Bajorans so they might find a measure of the same maturity.

The ceremony concluded, the Bajorans broke apart into groups, some remaining in the courtyard, others leaving. Dukat noted that the natives of apparent high rank bore distinctive jeweled rings and chains about their right ear. Every Bajoran he saw had the earring, but some sported simple silver or steel versions, while the men and women who stood with the First Minister wore ones studded with gemstones and precious metals. He followed Kell and Ico, with the others from the *Kornaire* trailing behind him, through a tall set of doors that were carved from a dense black wood inlaid with copper plates beaten into friezes. He looked up and saw renderings of Bajoran warriors armed with cannons, primitive crossbows, and strange kite-like gliders engaging in battle with one another. The copper was worn and smooth to the touch.

Pa'Dar came to his side. The scientist had his ever-present tricorder in his hand. "These carvings are ancient," he noted, peering at the device's screen.

Dukat nodded. "I've seen something similar in the mineral baths at Corvon."

"Not like this," said the other man. "The Corvon mural dates back to the pre–Hebitian era. These . . ." Pa'Dar put out his hand and ran gray fingers over the metal. "Perhaps there's something in the structure confusing the scanner. According to my tricorder, these plates are more than fifteen thousand years old."

Dukat looked around, taking in the high ceilings of the Naghai Keep, the ornate columns ranging up the walls, the floors of polished granite slabs. Banners and tapestries hung in alcoves behind humming stasis field generators; there were towering paintings of landscapes and Bajorans in robes and tunics that seemed little different from the clothes worn by Verin and the others. The soldier felt a sudden and palpable sense of history pressing in on him from all around, almost as if the age of the castle were a scent in the air.

The other minister, the one named Jas, was speaking to Gul Kell as they walked. "Ladies and gentlemen, now that the sober matter of the *Eleda* has been concluded, I would like to extend to our guests from Cardassia Prime an invitation to remain and dine with us. I have had my staff prepare a meal." The minister threw a nod at one of his functionaries, a dark-skinned female with a shorn skull, and she in turn signaled two guardsmen to open another door, revealing a wide hall beyond. "The hospitality of the Naghai Keep and the Jas clan are yours," he smiled.

Dukat crossed over the threshold of the room, and his senses were assaulted by a hundred different odors of cooked foods, of spices and mulled wines, fruits and vegetables in a panoply of colors and shapes. He tasted the scent of something that had to be roasted fish on his tongue and, despite himself, felt his mouth flood with saliva. Weeks of passable *rokat* fillets and that barely palatable *tefla* broth from the *Kornaire*'s food stores were suddenly like a bad dream. All around a wide, ring-shaped table in the center of the hall there were heaped serving trays of Bajoran dishes, alongside metal drums of steaming herbal infusions and heated wines.

It was more food in one place than Dukat had ever seen in his life.

Pa'Dar blinked at his tricorder. "This ... feast is compatible with our biology," he announced, clearly sharing a degree of Dukat's amazement.

"Of course," insisted Kubus, a note of affront in his tone. "I provided the keep's cooks with a complete dietary guide for your species." He chuckled self-consciously. "You may not find it as appealing as *taspar* eggs or fine seafruits, but I promise you, you will be intrigued by our native dishes." He gestured to a plate. "Try the *hasperat*. It's some of Bajor's most popular fare."

They took their seats, but Dukat felt a tightness in his chest that he couldn't readily explain. The scents of the food washed over him; he hadn't realized that he was hungry, but the smells were mouthwatering, and a wave of greed tingled in the tips of his fingers. Part of him wanted to take all he could and gorge on it. He glanced around, watching Kell and Ico, Hadlo and the Oralians, all of them following the lead of the Bajorans and helping themselves to brimming glasses of drink and plates piled with edibles. Dukat wanted to do the same, but something stopped him—and for a moment he was the young boy from Lakat all over again, growing up hungry, the table at his home always spartan. His lips thinned.

It wasn't as if he had been born into poverty—far from it. The Dukat family was relatively well-off in the scheme of things, a middle-tier clan with good holdings and a respectable income. Many lived in far worse conditions.

But life in Lakat, life all across Cardassia Prime, was one of austerity. Shortages were a matter of fact on a world where meager farmlands might produce only a few barrels of grain each season.

And now he was here, on this world of verdant green fields and wide oceans, surrounded by these plump-faced people with their smooth skins and rich clothes, and before him they had laid out enough food to feed an entire Cardassian family for a year. Dukat recalled the poor level of sustenance that his lower-ranked subordinates were forced to live on, and the obscenity of the moment settled on him. The Bajorans ate and talked, and they were wasteful with it, some of them leaving half a course on their plates before moving on to something else, letting their servants take the serving dishes away. He wondered if the leavings would go to feed the staff, or if they would simply be discarded. The idea of such ostentatious, thoughtless wastage set his teeth on edge, and he fought down a surge of resentment. *What right do these aliens have to live so well when my people must fight for every mouthful?*

"Dalin Dukat?" He turned to see Kubus Oak studying him. The Bajoran offered him a glass of purple-hued fluid. "Try this, it's a vintage springwine from the vineyards in the hill provinces. I've found my Cardassian associates enjoy it."

Dukat took the proffered glass stiffly and sampled a little. It was rich and potent. "You have had many dealings with the Union," he noted. He remembered the man's name from one of Kell's briefings; the Obsidian Order had characterized the merchant minister as an opportunist with grand plans for himself and a somewhat mercenary attitude. Dukat knew the type well.

Kubus nodded. "That I have. I've always found your people to be most scrupulous. It's a pleasure to see that relationship grow stronger." He smiled. "You're not eating. Is there nothing here that is to your liking?"

Dukat returned a cold, humorless smile. "I don't wish to

seem ungrateful. It is just that ... you have so very much. It's hard to know where to start."

The minister smiled back at him, turning away as someone else took his attention. "Take what you want, Dalin. There's more than enough."

"Indeed," the Cardassian said quietly. He took another sip of the springwine and let his eyes range around the room, finding Bennek grinning over a plate piled high with some sort of pastry. The cleric was talking to a Bajoran woman, one of the servant girls, and for a brief instant Dukat imagined he saw the glint of a different kind of hunger in the young man's eyes.

Dukat stared into his goblet, seeing the swirling sapphire liquid within as if it were the resentment that burned inside him. These Bajorans knew none of the hardships that his people did, and it angered him. How could Hadlo and Bennek speak of the blessings of beneficent guardian powers that watched over Cardassia, and then come to a place like this and realize how much their people were forced to go without? The scales of the universe were unbalanced if lean and vital Cardassia had to live hungry while Bajor, with its static and inward-looking culture, feasted every day. Dukat held up his glass and looked through it, at the food and the people and the vast walls of the hall beyond; and once again, the flare of raw greed rose in him.

Take what you want. Kubus's words echoed in Dukat's thoughts. "We will," he whispered to himself, raising the glass to his lips.

As the evening drew in and the meal moved to a conclusion, Jas Holza found the moment of definition that had been eluding him all day. As a statesman, he had learned from his father that the key to understanding his enemies and allies was to find the nature of them at the first meeting; that impression, the visceral and immediate truth of it, would never fail to be the correct one. All Jas had to do was listen to himself, and heed it.

As he watched Gul Kell polish off a leg of *porli* fowl, the definition suddenly came to him. *The Cardassians are like grass vipers. Watchful and measured about everything they do, but always ravenous.* He smiled slightly, self-amused. The gray skin made the comparison complete, and Jas recalled the dry, reptilian texture of the gul's flesh when they had shaken hands. *But what do they see when they look at us?* He hoped it wasn't *porli* fowl.

Kell dabbed at his mouth with a napkin. "Ministers," he began, glancing at Jas and Verin. "I hope you will forgive my bluntness on this matter, but I would like to speak to you of the future."

"Oh?" Verin leaned forward. "In what fashion, Gul Kell?" Jas wondered if the aliens registered the faint disdain in the old man's voice.

The Cardassian summoned a server to pour him more wine. "The friendship of the Union has much to reward those who accept it. The Detapa Council believes that a strong society is one in partnership with its neighbors."

"Quite so." Kubus threw the comment in from down the table, catching the edge of the conversation. From the corner of his eye, Jas noticed that the elderly Cardassian cleric was listening in as well.

"And what do you think, Gul?" Verin asked. The old man had seen the slight tic as Kell spoke of his masters; but then, the alien wouldn't be the first soldier to chafe under the commands of his civilian masters.

"I am a humble servant of the Cardassian Union, no more. I follow my orders, gentlemen, and today those orders are to extend the hand of friendship to Bajor."

"You're talking about trade," said Jas, a wary note entering his voice.

"Our planet wants for little from other worlds," said Verin

abruptly. "We need nothing from Cardassia. The Prophets granted us a home that fulfills all our needs."

Kell nodded toward Kubus. "Some feel differently, is that not true? Bajor does engage in commerce with other worlds throughout this sector."

"It would be more accurate to say that our colonies do," corrected the First Minister firmly. "We export very little. And what does come from offworld to Bajor herself does so in only the most limited quantities." He glanced away dismissively.

Jas saw the Cardassian look at the other alien at his side, the one wearing the plain tunic. At first Jas had thought it was another male, but when it spoke he realized abruptly that she was a female of the species. The shapeless, unflattering uniforms the Cardassians wore did nothing to highlight the differences between their sexes. "Are you not curious about what other races may have to offer Bajor?" she pressed. She gestured at the food. "Clearly, your generosity shows *you* have much to offer others."

"You are too kind," Verin replied, but his smile never reached his eyes. "Hospitality is a core tenet of our culture, Professor Ico. The Prophets tell us to treat all visitors with respect . . . no matter what their origins."

"And we thank you for it," Hadlo ventured, saluting with a nod of his head.

Jas put down his goblet and looked directly at Kell. "Gul, I think you are pressing us to ask a question that you would like to answer. You spoke of bluntness, so why not be blunt, and say what you wish to?" He ignored the glare Verin shot him.

There was the briefest glimmer of irritation on Kell's face, a hardening of his jaw, and then it was gone. "Perceptive, Minister Jas, very perceptive." He nodded. "Very well. We have seen your vessels, craft like your scoutship *Eleda* and the frigates that greeted us on our arrival in the B'hava'el system. What if I told you that Cardassia has technology that could double the speed and range of those craft? New advances in deflector shield technology, spiral-wave disruptors far more powerful than the energy cannons you currently employ. Is that not something you would find useful?" Kell indicated Colonel Coldri and Captain Jaro across the room from them. "I imagine your military officers would find such devices of great interest."

"And you would demand much in return!" snapped Verin.

"Bajor's wealth in minerals and foodstuffs is quite apparent," noted Ico.

The First Minister's eyes narrowed. "We have been careful to ensure that our planet has remained in balance for thousands of years. To begin taking more than we need from her would upset that equilibrium."

Jas rubbed his thin beard. "Admittedly, swifter starships would be of use to us. Our settlements on Golana, Valo, and Prophet's Landing would benefit. It would bring them closer to us."

Verin sniffed with contempt. "The people on those worlds chose to leave the safety of the homeworld, Minister. If they have put themselves at a great distance from Bajor, then that is a matter for them. They should not be coddled."

Jas said nothing; Verin's platform among the Council of Ministers had always been an isolationist one, and he had never made a secret of his disdain for Bajor's colonial efforts.

"You are proud of your world, and rightly so," allowed Ico. "Would you not consider the merit of giving your planet greater security?"

"Bajor has made no enemies," Verin retorted. "We are not an expansionist people. We keep to our own borders, unlike other species."

Unbidden, Jas's hands tightened into fists. He thought of his scoutship, of all his vessels out in the void. Better technology might have saved the crew of the *Eleda* from their ignominious deaths in deep space.

Kell looked across the table at the First Minister, ignoring the old man's thinly veiled insult. "And yet, one need only examine a starchart to see that your sector lies between the frontiers of a handful of alien powers." He waved a hand at the air, as if he were taking in the space all around them. "The Breen Confederation. The Tzenkethi Coalition. The Federation. Even the Tholians or the Talarians might find their way here." Kell smiled coldly. "None of them would be as good a friend to Bajor as Cardassia."

Ico nodded. "It is well known that the Federation has designs on expansion into this area of space." She looked to Hadlo for agreement. "I doubt that if they came to Bajor they would do it out of respect for the souls of your dead."

The cleric hesitated. "The United Federation of Planets is a largely secular nation," he said finally, with distaste.

"We are aware of that," Verin bristled. "We have no dealings with them." A grimace formed on his lips. "They . . . do not approve of our societal structure. They consider our *D'jarra*s to be an impediment to our progress."

"Your caste system," said Ico. "How like the humans to be so judgmental. It is clear to me that your culture functions perfectly well in a stratified arrangement. Cardassia would never be so bold as to think we could tell you how to run your world."

Kell's lips drew back into a smile. "We believe in the partnership of equals." He met Jas's gaze. "Is that not the basis of all strong friendships?"

Jas nodded slowly, the image of the *Eleda*'s shattered hull rising to the surface of his thoughts.

Verin took a careful sip of springwine. "All of Bajor respects what you have done for our citizens," he said levelly, "and you have our gratitude. But your overtures will find little purchase here. If that is truly why you have come to our world, then your journey has been wasted."

The rest of the meal continued with awkward small talk and there came a moment when Dukat felt as if he had eaten his fill: not because he had no more room in his stomach, but because after a while the richness of the Bajoran food had soured on his tongue. Glasses of Kubus's spring-wine did nothing to wash away the cloying taste, and as the meal slowly drew to a close he found it progressively more demanding to stay in the same room as Kell and the others, watching them chatter and go around in circular conversation. Picking his moment, he excused himself and stepped out of the hall. On their way in, as they had walked the keep's corridors, Dukat had noticed an arched door opening onto a wide stone balcony, and he strode over to it.

Night had fallen across the planet while the feast had progressed, and the sky was dotted with low, thin clouds. Unfamiliar constellations looked down on Dukat as he wandered to the edge of the battlements. As if it were a reflection of the heavens above, the city spread out below the keep was a mixture of dusky patches of parkland and municipal districts glittering with lanterns. He raised a questioning eyeridge as he spotted faint plumes of smoke issuing up from the streets. His first reaction was to wonder if there was some sort of discord in progress, that those were fires set by malcontents; but he heard no sounds of gunfire, nothing that could be considered violence. On a breath of wind came the faint noises of music and revelers, and his lip twisted. *More feasting and carousing? Is that all these aliens do?*

The wind brought scents with it as well, and Dukat sniffed at the air like a hunting dog. He detected a pleasant, slightly resinous odor.

"Bateret leaves," said a voice. "We burn them. It's a *Peldor* Festival tradition."

Dukat turned to see a Bajoran man standing in an open-topped stone cupola some short distance down the length of the ramparts. *A soldier?* The Cardassian read the man's manner instantly from the way he stood, the wary edge in his voice. The Bajoran turned toward him hesitantly, as if he were uncertain it was permissible for him to speak to Dukat. The dalin saw a simple chain glitter on the man's ear, and he took in the ochre-colored uniform, the holstered gun at his hip. He noted how the Bajoran's hands never went anywhere near the pistol. *Not a soldier then, perhaps. But certainly one used to dealing with unknown threats.* The corners of Dukat's mouth drew up in satisfaction at the thought of being considered in such a way. "You are holding a festival in our honor?"

A brief flash of amusement crossed the Bajoran's face. "Uh, no. I'm afraid not. You just timed your arrival to coincide with one of our annual celebrations." He nodded toward the city. "The Gratitude Festival. We ask the Prophets to help us with our troubles and watch over us in the coming year." He sighed. "It'll be over by tomorrow." The Bajoran paused. He was clearly finding the situation awkward.

Dukat elected to say nothing; until this moment, every alien he had met on this planet had been a politician or a priest. He found himself wondering about the men who served below them, the workers and the warriors like this one. *Like me.*

"Do you have celebrations like this on your world?"

Dukat looked back at the city. "Some. On Union Day, all of Cardassia unites in honor of the formation of our society. We mark the anniversaries of the deaths of our ancestors, the births of our children and . . . and their namings." His throat tightened a little on the last few words, and he frowned at himself.

The Bajoran heard the catch in his voice. "I have children. A boy, Bajin, and a girl, Nell."

For a brief instant, Dukat considered turning around and leaving; instead he found himself answering. "I have a son," he replied. "He has yet to be named."

"A newborn?"

Dukat shook his head. "He is a few months old. I have been on detached duty and unable to return home to join his mother for the ceremony. Both parents must be present for the naming to be formally recognized by the state."

"But you have chosen a name already?" The Bajoran came closer.

Dukat nodded. "Procal, after my father. I fear my wife may have other ideas, however." He felt the weight of the holograph rod in his wrist pocket, and the pictures came to the front of his thoughts once again. His saw his family, out there in Lakat, waiting for the supplies to arrive. And here he was, only a few feet away from a room brimming with food he could not give them. The greasy aftertaste of a Bajoran meat dish he had eaten came up at the back of his throat and his hands gripped the stone lip of the battlements.

"I'm Darrah Mace," said the other man.

"Skrain Dukat."

Darrah accepted this with a nod. "You're military."

"As you are."

"Not exactly." Darrah frowned. "I'm a Militia officer, but not a line soldier. I'm a law enforcer, part of Korto's City Guard." The Bajoran followed Dukat's gaze out over the conurbation. "I imagine the demands of our duties are similar, though. Sometimes, family has to be served second."

Dukat shot a look at the man, and he was ready to censure Darrah for his forwardness. The urge dissolved as quickly as it had come upon him. *Careful, Dukat,* he told himself. *Do not reveal too much to these aliens.* For all he knew, this chance meeting might have been engineered deliberately by Verin and the others to take the measure of the Cardassians. *And if they are anything like us, this man will report every word we have shared to his superior officer the moment I leave.* The furrows on his brow deepened. He was allowing the matter of the naming ceremony, of his concerns for the welfare of Athra and his son, to play on his mind. The resentment was there again, and some of it fell at the feet of Kell. The gul knew Dukat's circumstances, and he had denied the dalin's request for a temporary leave of absence prior to the Bajor mission.

The Bajoran didn't seem to notice the turmoil behind Dukat's eyes. "We all have our responsibilities," he said, and Dukat detected an air of resignation in the other man's manner.

He was still forming a reply when a figure stepped out onto the balcony behind him. "Skrain. There you are." Kotan Pa'Dar approached him. "Minister Jas has provided us with guest quarters for the night in the keep's east tower. Professor Ico felt it would be best if we accept. A refusal might offend the—" He caught sight of Darrah and hesitated. "Our hosts."

"Of course." Dukat gave the Bajoran a nod. "Perhaps we will speak again?"

"Maybe so," offered Darrah.

Pa'Dar spoke quietly as they walked away. "What was that about? You were talking with the alien?"

"It was nothing," said Dukat, with a finality that silenced the scientist.

5

There was something about a library that instilled a sense of reverence in Gar Osen. Just as he would have on entering a temple of the Prophets, or one of the great halls in the monastery, his voice fell into soft, respectful tones. Before he accepted the calling of the Prophets, he had grown up in a house filled with books—his mother was a minor playwright—and Osen had understood from an early age that books were a doorway to other worlds, to the past or to schools of thought that were vastly different from his own. He had never lost the veneration that being in such surroundings brought upon him. It was second only to the satisfaction he felt in the temple, when he spoke with the Prophets.

Even now, late at night with the light of the floater-globes hovering in the galleries at their lowest setting, the chamber was still impressive. The Naghai Keep's library was one of the finest private collections on Bajor, with works that the Jas clan had gathered from across the planet since the era of the First Republic. Gar had seen the deep vaults beneath the library proper where they now walked, where stasis field pods kept documents that were millennia old safe from the ravages of time. Admittedly, the keep's current master, Jas Holza, did not have the same sense of respect for the library as his father had shown, but the minister was savvy enough to know that it was a treasure. Still, there had been times when Kai Meressa and Vedek Cotor had applied gentle pressure to ensure that the minister kept hold of certain works instead of selling them to collectors in other provinces.

At his side, the kai gestured upward to point out the three levels of the collection's stacks. "It's hard to imagine, but this library began in ancient times as a simple compilation of agricultural charts and works of botany." Cotor was nodding in agreement, and behind them the two Cardassian clerics, Hadlo and Bennek, walked slowly, tipping back their heads to take in the scope of the place. "It houses works of all kinds, from fiction through to sciences, religious works, historical documents. An original copy of Shabren's Prophecies resides here, and it is said that in this very room the treaty of the Nine Tribes was first drawn up, ushering in the age of the Third Republic . . ." Meressa drew her hands together. "Forgive me. History is a passion of mine."

"A most impressive collection," offered Hadlo. "You spoke of religious works here? Is that typical of your world, that they would be part of a clan's personal holdings? Doesn't your church keep important books itself?"

Cotor shook his head. "You misunderstand, Hadlo. The Naghai library is commodious, of that there is no doubt, but it is not primarily a store of holy works." The vedek's head bobbed in agreement with his own words. "The monastery at Kendra, some distance to the south, is Bajor's greatest repository of devotional literature."

Meressa smiled, her face lit with amusement. "Ah, I think the monks at Kiessa might take umbrage at that statement. They like to think that they lay claim to that status." She halted at a hexagonal table in the middle of the chamber. Lined in wood and cut from local red stone, the broad desk presented a reading screen and an ornate crystal keyboard. "This device is a stand-alone database of all known writings, protected and preserved. As Minister Jas has often bragged, if you cannot find what you wish to read in its written incarnation, you will likely find it in a virtual one stored here." She patted the table. "But, as Vedek Cotor notes, we believe it is important that we preserve as much of our written culture as we can in its original form."

Bennek nodded. "The Oralian Way shares that sentiment, Your Eminence. If no substance of a faith remains, then it may become like smoke on the wind."

Hadlo frowned briefly at the younger cleric's words before continuing. "Forgive my companion if he speaks with more drama than is necessary. Esteemed Kai, I would very much like to hear more about the Kendra monastery, and of the tenets of your faith." He paused. "During the meal, I heard the young prylar speaking of a *pagh*. You used that word during the ceremony for the lost in the courtyard . . ."

Meressa glanced at Gar. "Osen? Why don't you explain the term to our visitors?"

Gar swallowed hard; he hadn't been expecting to take a direct part in any of the discussions. "Of course, Eminence." He cleared his throat and touched a hand to his ear, where his *D'jarra* signet dangled. "The *pagh* is the name we give to the elemental life force of all living things. It is the ephemeral energy of the soul, the source from which we draw our strength and our courage. Our will to live, if you like."

"Your spirit, then," said Bennek.

"Correct. In our faith, we conceive the *pagh* as a flame, a candle that is set burning by the Prophets in the Celestial Temple at the moment of our birth. At times of great hardship that flame may burn low, it may even be snuffed out if death claims us unexpectedly. But we believe that through our faith in the Prophets, they sustain us, replenishing our *pagh* through their love." He touched his bare left ear. "The light of that energy blooms through our flesh here."

"Fascinating," said the Cardassian. He raised his hands to his face. "In the patterns of the Way, we see the blessings of Oralius in a similar fashion. Her eternal strength flows through us and keeps us strong. We don masks to symbolize our union with her, and the energies that animate us . . . like your *pagh.*"

Hadlo nodded sagely. "And like all things, it can turn to light or to darkness. It is the duty of the Oralian Way to show our people the road into the light." Gar saw a new understanding bloom on the alien's face. "Kai Meressa, it is our belief that Oralius plots a path for every one of us, for a greater fate than we may know. At this moment, I feel as if I am on the verge of a revelation!" The old man's voice rose. "Yes. This journey here to Bajor, our meeting. It is her will."

Cotor smiled. "Then perhaps too it is the will of the Prophets that we are here to greet you, Hadlo."

The elder cleric's eyes glittered. "This simple moment . . . five souls in a chamber steeped in history . . . My friends, dare we think on the import of such a thing?" He stepped forward and touched Meressa on the arm, and she returned the gesture. "We reach out and find kindred spirits among those not of our world. What does this tell us?"

Gar's mouth went dry; it was difficult not to be caught up by the quiet potency of the Cardassian's words. He understood at once how the old man had risen to such high office in his faith—there was a way about Hadlo, a sagacious, metered passion that made one want to listen to his words.

The kai showed the same enthusiasm. "It tells us that barriers of species and distance cannot deny the simple truths of existence."

"Yes! Yes!" Hadlo's face split in a grin. "My friends, we share the same path! We can learn so much from one another. The Way of Oralius, the road of your Prophets . . . What if they are intertwined?"

Gar glanced at Bennek. The younger Cardassian was muted, his face the mirror of Osen's. It was hard to know what to make of the conversation unfolding before them. Both the priests were wary, and yet they were both daring to hope that Hadlo could be correct. To find aliens who shared a belief system that echoed their own—the theological implications were simply staggering.

Meressa nodded. "Hadlo, you must come to the monastery at Kendra. I will see to it, and there you shall put this question to the Prophets themselves."

Shock unfolded on Vedek Cotor's face. "Eminence! You are not suggesting that—"

She cut him off with a look, and Gar realized what she was about to suggest. He too wanted to protest, but words failed him. The prylar hesitated, trying to find a way to frame his objection, and found none.

"If your Way truly does parallel the path of the Prophets, then there is a manner in which we can be sure. At the monastery we hold in honor a most sacred artifact, one of many that the Celestial Temple has seen fit to grant us over the centuries." At Hadlo's quizzical look she indicated an image cut into a stained-glass window at the far end of the chamber. "A Tear of the Prophets. A sacred Orb sent by them to guide us in our lives."

The Cardassians looked up to see the hourglass shape set amid an image that showed the Celestial Temple opening in the heavens and the Tear falling toward Bajor, toward the open hands of a man in the robes of a vedek. Gar felt a peculiar tingle in his chest at the thought of laying eyes on the real thing. The Tears were the physical manifestation of the Prophets, and to be in the presence of one was to touch the aura of gods.

"Eminence," said Cotor, "you know as well as I that any

encounter must be deliberated and ratified by the Vedek Assembly! With all due respect to Hadlo, I think they may be reluctant to allow an alien to enter the presence of the Orb of Truth!"

The kai glanced at him. "And will our visitors be content to remain for months while your fellow vedeks debate the matter over and over?" She shook her head. "No, Cotor. I exercise my right as Kai and I say this will happen." The priestess spread her hands. "Hadlo is correct. Throughout the feast and through the night we have talked and seen the congruence between our faiths. I am not content to have it come to an end there, not when a chance to know the absolute truth is in our power." She touched the old cleric's arm. "I will see to this. Through the Tear, the Prophets will turn their gaze upon you and know you. The truth will be revealed."

Hadlo returned the gesture. "Thank you . . . my sister."

Bennek felt giddy and off balance. After the Bajorans left them in the keep's sumptuous guest lodgings, he found he had to sit upon one of the wide loungers in the atrium between the chambers shared by the Oralians. Hadlo returned from speaking to the other members of their party and came to sit with him.

"Have . . . have you informed Gul Kell of the Kai's invitation?" Bennek asked.

Hadlo shook his head. "I will speak to him tomorrow. I will notify him we will not be returning to the *Kornaire* on the shuttle."

"This 'orb' the Bajorans spoke of . . ."

"Kell is faithless. He is a nonbeliever and he would not understand. I will simply tell him that the Bajorans have asked us to make a pilgrimage to the Kendra monastery, nothing more. That is not a lie."

"It is not the whole truth, either," Bennek insisted.

"Master, I am uncertain about the swiftness with which this is progressing. Yes, I hoped, as we all did, that we might find some common ground with the Bajorans, but I hear you talk as if our faiths are like lost twins, and it . . ."

"It frightens you?" asked the old man softly.

"Yes."

Hadlo nodded. "That is a natural reaction, my friend. Great moments of change always carry with them the fear of the unknown." He gave Bennek's shoulder a pat. "Have faith in Oralius. She watches over us. She has given us this chance for deliverance."

The cleric's words deepened Bennek's confusion. "Deliverance from what?"

The old man's voice fell into a hush. "Bennek, you know that I see you as my successor. You alone have the will and the strength of spirit to take the Way forward despite all the hardships we endure. In the face of the hatred and aversion from our fellow Cardassians, you have remained strong, true to Oralius even as those fools in the Detapa Council and the military have fought to expunge us." He squeezed Bennek's shoulder, taking on a fatherly tone. "I need your support."

"You have it," Bennek replied immediately. "Never feel you need to question that."

Hadlo smiled. "I know. And for that, I will clear the mist from your eyes, my young friend. I will tell you what I have not said to the other clerics who came with us from the homeworld." He looked around the chamber. "These Bajorans . . . They are a gift to us, a blessing from Oralius herself. She has seen that our faith is slowly being eroded from the Cardassian soul, and she knows that we are living on borrowed time."

Bennek nodded ruefully. The purges and the arrests back home were getting worse as the months went by. More and more branches of the Oralian Way were being forcibly closed under the weakest of pretexts created by the Detapa Council or Central Command, laws were being enacted that made it difficult for church members to find employment or sustenance, and nothing the followers of the Way did had any impact. The future of their faith hung by a thread, and that was why they had been so desperate to take part in the Bajor mission, as a last attempt to show the legitimacy of their church as a valid part of Cardassian culture.

"Meressa spoke of truth," continued Hadlo, "so let me do the same. The truth is, Central Command has been looking to the Bajor sector with ambition for some time, but they lack the diplomatic prowess to reach these people. But we, Bennek, we do not. We are the common link between Bajor and Cardassia, because we have our faith."

"What are you saying?"

Hadlo smiled thinly. "You saw Kell and Ico as they attempted to pour honey in the ears of the First Minister and the others, and found only distrust. The Bajorans look at them and see aliens, soldiers! Their first reaction is to suspect them! But we are different!" He tapped his chest, fingers tracing the lines of his robes. "The Bajorans look at us and see kindred spirits. A sister faith. We have a bond that transcends everything else. While Kell's clumsy overtures were rebuffed, the seeds of friendship we planted tonight fell on fertile ground! We will make ourselves requisite to any future alliance between Cardassia and Bajor, because that relationship will have to be built upon a foundation of *faith.*"

Despite the warmth of the chamber, Bennek's skin prickled with a chill. He saw it just as Hadlo described. The Detapa Council and the Central Command needed the Oralians to facilitate this mission, and if that was so, then the Way had suddenly been granted leverage against those who would see it destroyed.

The old cleric saw the light of understanding in his expression. "We cannot preserve the other branches of our faith, but this chance that Oralius has granted us means we may protect our own ministry. We can ensure that the Way will survive. We can preserve it, stop Cardassia from turning into a secular, faithless wasteland!" His eyes flashed. "Do you understand the magnitude of this, Bennek? We may be the very last chance to save our credo from oblivion!"

Bennek was silent for a moment. "What about the Bajorans?" he asked finally. "What part will they play in this?"

Hadlo frowned. "This is about us, not them. What I told the kai was not a lie. I do believe that Oralius and the Prophets may be two facets of the same great truth."

A bleak thought occurred to the young priest. "The men who perished aboard that ship, the *Eleda*. Was that really a misadventure?" He thought of the wreckage in the *Kornaire*'s cargo bay and of the words he had said over the bodies of the dead in the name of Oralius. "Were the dead only a pretext to bring us to Bajor?"

The cleric's face darkened. "Bennek, listen to me and understand." He leaned closer. "We are on the edge of annihilation. If we do not take steps now, the Oralian Way will be eradicated and Cardassia will be doomed to a future of hatred and destruction, a path that will lead only to ashes and blood. We must do whatever is necessary to preserve the Way."

Bennek met the older man's gaze. "Even if the price is our integrity . . . our souls?"

There was no doubt, no hesitation in Hadlo's reply. "Yes. Is that so great a cost to keep the flame burning? What do two men mean when weighed against the future of our entire species?" He nodded to himself. "Oralius asks for a sacrifice, Bennek. We must not turn away from her."

Bennek searched inside himself for a reply, finding nothing but an echoing hollow.

✦ ✦ ✦

Lonnic halted Jas as he crossed the anteroom toward his chambers. "Sir," she began, "you have a visitor. He refused to wait and let himself in."

"Oh?" Jas said, with an arched eyebrow. He strode forward and pushed open the ornate door to his office and found Kubus Oak seated in one of the deep chairs across the room from his desk. The minister was puffing at a smoking pipe between his teeth.

"Holza, good morning." Kubus waved the pipe in the air. "You don't mind, do you? I like to take a draft as an eye-opener—"

"Actually, I do." Jas went to his desk and opened a window, letting in the sunlight and the cool air. He gave Kubus a level stare, working to take back some authority in the confrontation. The other man had cheerfully set the moment against Jas, putting himself in the superior, relaxed position. That did not sit well.

"Ah. Forgive me." Kubus used his thick thumb to douse the pungent *hiuna* leaf. "It's an old habit."

Jas rested against the edge of his desk. "I thought you were going to return to Ashalla with the First Minister."

"It would seem not," Kubus said languidly. "Verin told me to remain in Korto while the Cardassians are still here. As much as he hates to rely on me for anything, he thinks my presence will keep them at ease until they leave. I'm a known quantity to their kind."

"Indeed?" Jas kept his manner neutral, but inwardly he was frowning. It was enough that the alien clerics had decided not to go back to their ship with Kell, and that in turn was complicated by the fact that the gul had ordered his executive and a couple of soldiers to remain "as an escort." Jas had not been prepared for the contingency, and matters of maintaining security were foremost on his mind. Now, would he have to deal with Kubus Oak at the keep as well, the man constantly at his shoulder, second-guessing him? He still wasn't sure where the other minister's loyalties lay. *To himself, and there alone, more than likely.* Jas had yet to get the full measure of the man. *Is he a potential ally, or is he a tool of Verin?* The latter was the least likely, but then again the old man hadn't made it to the office of First Minister without making some odd political alliances along the way.

"Last night was interesting," said Kubus. "I thought it might benefit us both to examine the way it played out."

"It was a diplomatic function, not a springball match," Jas retorted, with rather more force than he intended to. He sighed. He had not slept well, spending the night mulling over every word and gesture he had made to the aliens. Verin's narrow-minded manner had single-handedly derailed any chance at a pact.

"Diplomacy is as much a sport as springball. Only the stakes are higher."

Jas tapped the intercom unit on his desk. "Tomo, get in here. And bring some *deka* tea."

Kubus sniffed. "I thought we could discuss this alone."

"Lonnic's viewpoint is the sharpest I know," Jas countered. "That's what I employ her for."

"As you wish."

Jas wanted Lonnic in the room for support. His sleepless night had left him with worry gnawing at the pit of his stomach, the ghost of self-doubt clinging to him. Had he made a mistake bringing the Cardassians to Korto? Deep down, Jas knew he wasn't the minister his father had been; perhaps this time his reach had exceeded his grasp.

Lonnic entered, followed by a servant who laid out a tray of steaming *deka* tea before leaving them to their conversation. Kubus inclined his head in greeting, and Lonnic returned the gesture. She had her padd in her hand, her fingers poised to string notes into the touch-sensitive surface of the electronic slate.

"I have to confess, I was a little surprised by your reaction at the reception, Holza." Kubus helped himself to a generous cup of the tea. "Your response to the Cardassians was more conservative than I had expected. Gul Kell practically offered us a trade agreement, but you were less than enthusiastic."

"I'm merely being cautious," Jas replied, taking a cup for himself.

"Ah, caution, is that it? And yet you were not so unadventurous before, when you boldly offered to host the alien delegation here. I did enjoy that speech you gave at the Gratitude Festival." Kubus smiled thinly. "Why the change of heart? Are you out of your depth, Holza? Have you decided to join Verin's reactionaries?"

"'The fool plants where he wishes,'" quoted Lonnic, "'the wise man sees where the sun falls first.'"

Kubus snorted. "A country homily, how quaint. So Jas is the wise man, then? I'm pleased to hear it. I would hate to find myself in partnership with someone who lacked the wisdom to pursue opportunity."

Jas raised an eyebrow. "We're partners, Oak? When did that happen?"

"When the Cardassians came, my friend. You and I are in this together." Kubus patted the chair. "Here, on this side of the river we sit with opportunity in our laps, and over there"—he gestured to the east, in the direction of the capital—"in Ashalla, there are old men of limited vision who will waste this chance if we let them. I want to make sure you know that, Holza."

Lonnic sipped at her tea and watched the interplay between the two ministers, gauging the reactions and the thoughts behind her employer's face. In the five years she had been Jas Holza's adjutant, she had come to know the man well—even intimately, for a time, before he had suc-

ceeded his father into the hereditary office of minister for
Korto—and she could read the emotions behind his politician's façade. Undoubtedly there was merit in Kubus's
words, but like Darrah, Lonnic couldn't shake an elemental
dislike of the man. His manner was high-handed and superior; Kubus was rich and well traveled, spending more time
at his holdings on the colonies than on Bajor itself, and he
affected a smugly cosmopolitan attitude as if he were more
worldly than those who did not venture offplanet. But then
again, Jas had several political allies whom Lonnic found
quite distasteful in person. Expedience often meant dealing
with those one considered objectionable.

What made the matter worse was that Kubus was right:
the Cardassians did represent a unique prospect for Bajor.
But then again, so did the overtures from the representatives of the United Federation of Planets, and a dozen
other smaller planetary governments. Just because the Cardassians had come to Bajor, right to their doorstep, was not
a valid reason to welcome them with open arms. Perhaps it
was xenophobic of her to think it, but there was something
about the manner of the gray-faced aliens that made her
feel uncomfortable to be in the same room with them. She
sipped another mouthful of tea and listened.

"Let's look at this from a pragmatic point of view,"
Kubus was saying. "Suppose we open the gates to an alliance between Bajor and the Cardassian Union. The pos-
sibilities for trade alone are huge. Their technology could
help our people advance in leaps and bounds." He waggled his finger at Jas. "I saw the glint in your eyes when
Kell spoke about faster warp drives and better starships.
And think of what else they have that we don't. Medicines,
advanced energy sources, knowledge of the greater galaxy around us. Will Bajor thank us for turning down the
chance to have those things?"

"And such trade, if it took place, would be facilitated

through certain channels?" Jas asked. "The Kubus clan's shipping line, for example?"

The other man nodded. "In association with the Jas clan's concerns, of course. After all, if we are the men who bring this bounty to Bajor, is it not right that we take some reward from it?"

"You mean beyond improving the quality of life for our people?" Lonnic asked.

Kubus shot her a look. "I won't deny that I see this as a way to better my own lot, and that of my clan. And you should do the same, Holza." A note of reproach entered his voice. "After all, you have responsibilities to the district of Korto and your people. I think I would be correct in saying that your current circumstances could stand to be improved, yes?"

"What are you implying?" The mood in the room cooled rapidly.

"I'm not in the business of making implications, Minister," continued Kubus. "I prefer to deal in facts." He put down his cup and leaned forward intently. "Let us be honest, Holza. Your position in the Chamber of Ministers is not what it once was. Verin and his cronies have done what they can to take advantage of your recent misfortunes and diminish the stature of your office."

Lonnic saw a nerve twitch in Jas's jaw. It was an open secret that the First Minister was quietly scornful of Jas's political prowess and saw him as a poor shadow of his father.

Kubus continued. "I know you nurse the hope to one day stand for election to Verin's post, but for now that goal moves further away from you with each passing moment." He paused, taking a breath. "But if you were to take a leading place in assembling an agreement with the Cardassians, the political capital you would gain would strengthen your position. You could rise to the front rank again."

"My only interest is to do what is right for Bajor," Jas replied carefully. "My rank, and Verin's view of it, are secondary to that."

"And how will you do that if you are insolvent and powerless, Holza? Remember, I know about your meeting in Batal. I know about the problems that you face."

For the briefest of instants, Lonnic saw something like shock on the minister's face before he shuttered it away, composing himself. She felt her blood run cold. Jas had yet to explain to her the reason for his sudden and secretive trip across the equator to the city of Batal. For several months now she had been aware that he was keeping something from her. At first she thought it might be an illicit assignation—it wouldn't have been the first time Jas had taken an interest in another man's wife—but the minister's increasingly grim manner after each jaunt gave her cause for concern. Now she read a degree of the truth in Jas's face, and it chilled her.

Kubus watched her and suppressed a smirk. "You haven't even told your adjutant? Perhaps you were trying to protect her from any future consequences?"

"Sir," Lonnic said, "what is he talking about?"

"I'm talking about Golana," said Kubus. "The bold colonial endeavor funded by your clan, far from home and far from stable."

Jas met her gaze. "There have been some serious issues at the colony, Tomo," he explained. "The situation there has . . . deteriorated."

Lonnic's mouth went dry. The Golana settlement was a legacy of Jas's parents, established nearly two decades earlier by the clan's mining pioneers. Even then, it had been a gamble. It was a verdant, Bajor-analogous planet, ideal for an outpost site; but it was distant from the homeworld, well outside the span of closer colonies like Prophet's Landing and Valo II. After the initial rush to colonize, it had been difficult to induce new homesteaders to make the long voyage; but she never dreamed that there were problems out there. "What happened?"

"The storm season last year was particularly harsh. A large percentage of the crops failed. There were deaths. Several of the families resident there broke their contracts and left. The population count is currently too low to maintain criticality."

She nodded, understanding the pattern. Without a crucial number of people to keep the colony running, the Golana settlement would eventually collapse and be abandoned. All the millions of litas invested in the planet by the Jas clan would be wasted.

"I've been sending ships and supplies, trying to shore up the outpost." Jas frowned. "It hasn't gone well."

"That's the reason for the closed-link communications? That's why you went to Batal?"

Jas eyed Kubus. "Yes. I was meeting with one of my scoutship captains. What they had to tell me was not encouraging." The minister folded his arms and looked at the other man. "How did you learn of it?"

Kubus shrugged. "I have my methods. Rest assured that First Minister Verin knows nothing of the matter. Frankly, if something does not occur within sight of Ashalla, he has little interest in it."

"What do you intend to do with this information?" Lonnic demanded.

"Nothing," said the minister. "But I bring it up now to illustrate a point. If we had faster, better starships, Golana would be brought closer and this issue would not even be a concern. But as it stands, you run the risk of wasting your clan's fortune on a colony you cannot hope to support."

"And if I close the settlement down," murmured Jas, "I give Verin another stick to beat me with."

Kubus nodded. "All the more reason to make an alliance

with the Cardassians. A single one of their freighters would solve all your problems."

"Perhaps."

Lonnic heard the turn in Jas's voice and fixed him with a hard stare. "We should not be so quick to trust the aliens," she broke in. "Yes, in the short term we may be able to reap the benefits, but what do we open ourselves up for in the days that follow? Cardassian starships moving freely through our space? New economic pressures placed on our worlds by the Union's demands? Suppose, after a while, they decide they want to take from us instead of trading? Once we open these gates, we won't be able to close them again."

"The Cardassians would never have been allowed to enter our system if there was the slightest chance they were here on a military footing," Kubus retorted. "Li, Jaro, and all the rest of the Militia, they would never permit it!" He grunted, shaking his head. "The fact is, the Cardassians simply don't have the capacity to mount an invasion of Bajor! Why expend soldiers and matériel when they can follow a peaceful path? Cardassia Prime is too concerned with their own internal problems, and their naval forces are tied up in border skirmishes with that Talarian rabble." He leaned forward. "Let's not forget, *they* came to *us*. We have the home advantage here, Holza. If we let the prospect for a pact pass Bajor by, then perhaps your gloomy adjutant here will be proven right, and they will come back with battle cruisers instead of priests!"

Jas was silent for a while, and Lonnic could see him weighing the arguments in his thoughts. "If we did advocate an agreement, Verin would never accept it. Even together, Kubus, you and I and what allies we have would not be enough to sway the Chamber of Ministers. Without another impetus to propel it, the First Minister will block any petition and we will be left looking foolish."

Kubus smiled. "Don't worry about that. We'll have all the support we need."

"What do you mean?" Lonnic asked.

The other minister glanced at her. "The Prophets will provide."

The door hissed open and Kell crossed the threshold into the *Kornaire*'s primary laboratory module, casting around until he spotted the woman Ico at a console in the far corner of the room. He was glad to be back on his ship; the towering ceilings of the Bajoran castle had made him feel uncomfortable, and he had forced himself to resist the urge to look up over and over, as if his senses were warning him of something threatening overhead. Kell preferred the close, controlled spaces of his vessel, the decks and corridors he knew as well as the ridges on his own neck.

He studied the faces of the civilian contingent as he passed them by. Only one or two of the half-dozen scientists dared to look him in the eye. Most of them hadn't even left the lab decks to venture into other parts of the ship. He imagined they were simply marking time, waiting for the mission to be over so they could return to whatever interminable research projects they had been plucked from. He saw one of the younger men, the one called Pa'Dar. Kell had seen him in conversation with Dukat about the vessel. *It would behoove me to place a closer watch on that one,* he mused. Unlike the others, Pa'Dar had willingly taken meals in the mess hall and seemed interested in the running of the ship. Such behavior left Kell suspicious; there was no doubt in his mind that the secretive forces of the Obsidian Order had an operative on board the *Kornaire*—it was standard practice to put a spy on every line starship, so the rumors went—and with these scientists foisted upon him it was likely they had used the group to insert another. *But then again, Pa'Dar is the obvious choice,* he told himself.

Too obvious for the Order; then again, it wouldn't be beyond them to attempt a double-bluff . . .

He shook the thought away. This trying mission was playing on his mind.

"Gul," said Ico. "Thank you for coming. I felt it would be simpler to display my findings here rather than on the bridge."

"I appreciate the need for containment of information," he replied. "Show me."

Ico manipulated the arc of control tabs on the panel before her, and a large screen on the wall opened into a virtual display of the star system, each of the fourteen worlds in the ecliptic appearing with designations and data tags that streamed with information. A curved red line showed the course that the *Kornaire* had taken from the outer edge of the system in toward Bajor. Kell noted how the Bajorans had done their best to ensure that the Cardassian ship had traveled on a circuitous route that kept it as far from the other worlds as possible. If anything, such an action showed how little they knew about the capacity of Cardassian sensor technology. Coupled with long-range scans from other ships and the reports of covert probe drones, the *Kornaire* had a good spread of information about the Bajor system to draw upon.

"Our initial estimates were incorrect," said the woman.

Kell eyed her. "In what way?"

Ico didn't look at him. "If anything, we were far too conservative in our approximations. There's a reason these aliens have never ventured far from home, Gul. They have everything they need close by." She altered the image to bring up a series of models of the planets, which scrolled past one by one, each bringing up ovals of text showing mineralogical determinations. "Stocks of feldomite, dilithium, iron, kelbonite . . ."

"What about Bajor itself?" he insisted.

She nodded and worked the console to show the planet that they now orbited. "We've used our time carefully. To ensure the aliens were not aware of the operation, I had my team adopt a rotating scan frequency modulation combined with a shift matrix in the *Kornaire*'s sensor pallets—"

"How your team did it concerns me less than what you learned." Kell was getting impatient with the woman. Although he found the scientist an interesting diversion from the military officers he normally associated with, Ico had a tendency to display more self-interest than was seemly for a civilian.

"Of course," she replied, letting his interruption roll off her. The image of Bajor unfolded into a topographical map that changed color, areas glowing in different shades to highlight geological strata and mineral deposits. "I have conducted an intensive scan of the planet and the close orbital moons, confirming the intelligence provided by the Obsidian Order. Bajor is indeed a treasure-house, Gul Kell." She pointed out areas on the map. "It is very rich in many key strategic ores and minerals. For example, several parts of the planet are dense with seams of raw uridium." Ico folded her arms. "From what I can determine, it seems that the natives have made only a few cursory attempts to excavate the substance, and in a largely inefficient manner. A more intensive program of strip-mining would generate a much greater yield, perhaps with the construction of an orbital refinery platform to facilitate more effective extraction."

Kell grimaced. "Yes, I'm sure the Bajorans would be *happy* to allow us to level their hillsides in order to fulfill the needs of our shipyards." He snorted.

Ico gave him a neutral look. "It was my understanding that the purpose of this mission is to establish the value Bajor has to the Cardassian Union as a resource, not how we may make the locals happy."

"What was it that you said to me before?" Kell glared at her. "This is only one ship, Professor Ico. What would you have me do, wage war with it and plant the *Galor* pennant on a pile of corpses in the plaza of their capital city?"

"I would never have the temerity to think I could provide military acumen to a decorated officer of the Second Order, Gul," she replied smoothly. "I am a scientist, and it is my function to observe and calculate, and draw conclusions from what I witness. Perhaps, if the Central Command did not insist on provoking the Talarian Republic, there might be more vessels to prosecute the more important missions for the Union."

"Are you suggesting that this . . . this fact-finding jaunt has as much value as defending our borders against raiders?" Kell loomed over her, but the insufferable female remained aloof.

"I know you feel slighted by the orders you were given," she continued. "Be assured I would not say the same to anyone else." Her smile was cool. "I imagine you would prefer to be out at the perimeter, engaged in combat." She cocked her head. "Your daughter is there now, is that not right? Stationed with the punitive fleet at Torman?" Ico gave a theatrical sigh. "But neither of us have what we wish, Gul Kell. I wish to see Cardassia thrive, and to do that she needs resources, but for now the option to annex Bajor is beyond us." Her voice hardened. "What I find disappointing, and what I do not doubt Central Command and the Detapa Council will also be dismayed by, is the paucity of response you generated from the Bajorans."

Kell's temper was rising, but he kept it in check. "I did as I was ordered to. I offered them our technology and they were uninterested." He made a curt gesture with his hand, hoping to make the woman flinch, but she remained impassive. "I dislike this interminable diplomatic rhetoric. Already I am sick of it." He drew himself up. "I told Command when my orders were delivered to me, this mission is pointless. All we can do is gather what intelligence we can and then return to Cardassia." He nodded at the screen. Kell wasn't sure what irritated him the most: that the woman was so perceptive, or that on some level he agreed with her. "Let them send politicians next time," he grated. "This is their arena, not ours."

Ico gave a short, sharp bark of laughter. "My dear gul! We are Cardassians. We are all of us political animals."

He turned his back on her and made to leave.

Kell was halfway across the laboratory when Ico spoke again, her words deceptively light. "It's a pity," she began. "At a time like this, a man who returned to the home-world with a bloodless victory for his people would be hailed as a hero."

He paused, turning. "I have no need for plaudits," he said carefully, "I take my glory in serving Cardassia."

Ico approached, smiling that flat, predatory smile of hers. She saw straight through the lie in his words. *What man wouldn't want to be lauded? But what chance is there for triumph in this backwater, surrounded by pious, stolid aliens?*

"Just so," she allowed. "And would it not serve Cardassia to bring her succor?"

He frowned. "You're talking in circles, and I have little tolerance for such things."

"Have you seen the datastreams from home, Danig?" Her voice became more intimate, as if she were confiding some personal secret. "There have been incidents, violence in the streets."

Kell hesitated. His attention had been solely on the ship and the mission. He had not had a moment to review the information feeds. The gul wondered where Ico had got access to that data herself.

She continued. "The Oralians have been causing unrest. Apparently, after Hadlo joined the mission and left Cardassia, some of his followers chose to believe that he had in fact been executed by the state, that this endeavor was merely the cover for that deed."

Kell sneered. "They flatter themselves. If Hadlo was to be killed, he would have been gunned down in the street, not spirited away in some conspiracy." He met the woman's gaze. "What have they done?"

"Some violent clashes have been reported between religious militants and the armed forces. There are rumors that agents in the employ of the Talarians may be assisting the militants. The Oralians have come in from their enclaves outside the cities and disrupted transport routes, started riots."

"Where?"

"Senmir, Corvon, and Lakat." She hesitated. "Your first officer is from Lakat, isn't that right? Dalin Dukat? I wonder if he is aware of the situation."

The gul ignored the comment. "The Talarians? They'd never dare to make trouble on Cardassia. They know how hard we struck back after they violated our borders. They wouldn't risk our retaliation." He sniffed. "Obsidian Order propaganda, nothing more, designed to isolate those Oralian fools even further."

"As you wish," she replied, without weight. "I only tell you what I have heard."

Kell's eyes narrowed. "You're very well informed, Rhan. Some might think too well informed for a mere scientist."

"I'm not responsible for what others think of me," said the woman, turning back to her work. "As I told you before, my duty is to observe and theorize. We all serve Cardassia in our own ways."

When he was back in his quarters, the gul opened a protected link to his security chief. "Matrik," he snapped, "the surveillance on the contingent from the science ministry, have you found anything of interest?"

The junior officer shook his head warily. "Nothing substantial as yet, sir. One of them appears to be concealing a minor drug addiction, but nothing that may threaten the ship's security. I have been directing extra attention to Kotan Pa'Dar. He's been associating with the dalin quite a bit."

Kell frowned. "Forget Pa'Dar. Dukat's smart enough not to socialize with spies. He's not the one. Watch Ico. Put all your resources on her."

"Sir?" Matrik's face showed confusion. "You believe she's a shadow? Her files were—"

"Just watch her," Kell commanded, and stabbed the disconnect key.

6

As they walked the cloisters of the monastery at Kendra, Gar's attention was drawn to the haunted look in the eyes of the alien cleric. Finally, the older Cardassian caught his gaze and gave him a rueful smile, his expression filled with sadness.

"This place is magnificent, Prylar," Hadlo told him. "You have truly been blessed by your Prophets."

"This is one of many places dedicated to our faith," said Gar. "Each province has a central monastery like this one, and several smaller temples and reclusia. Most of them are built on holy sites that date back to before our recorded history."

"Incredible," breathed Bennek. The other priest was lost in the scope of the building, pausing to study every tiny detail of the decorations and opulent hangings inside each alcove.

A question came quickly to Gar's lips. "Do you have similar places of devotion on Cardassia?"

A shadow passed over Bennek's face, and Gar immediately regretted asking. Hadlo patted the younger man on the arm. "Our faith . . . Once it was celebrated in places such as this one, but now we have no temples of such merit. Time and the will of secular men have taken them from us. These days, the Way spreads from tents and shanty towns, in caverns and basements. It is no longer safe to praise Oralius in stone and mortar as well as in our flesh."

Gar didn't know what to say, and he hesitated, searching for the right words. The kai, her pleasant face fixed in
an expression of deep compassion, came to his support.
"Sometimes we forget how fortunate we are to have such
things," Meressa said to Gar, Cotor, and Arin. Arin was a
ranjen, a theologist and one of the resident priests at the
monastery, and he had joined the group on their walking tour of the grounds. "We should thank our Cardassian
brothers for reminding us of that." She looked to Hadlo.
"I hope you will not think ill of me to say it, but I have
always felt that a place of worship is as sacred as one wishes
it to be. It need not be built of stone and iron. It need not
even be a place with walls and roof . . ." She tapped her
chest. "The heart is the grandest temple of all."

"You are quite correct," said Hadlo, some of the grim-
ness leaving his face. "Would that all my kinsmen had such
clarity of insight." The alien glanced back at Gar. "Please,
Prylar, do continue. I wish to know more."

Meressa gave him a nod of assurance, and Gar licked his
lips. "Certainly. Well, uh, the monastery here at Kendra has
just over a thousand clerics in residence at any one time,
some of them on retreats from other parishes, some taking part in missions of faith, some of them serving as full-
time staff. We have a mix of lower-ranked prylars such as
myself, along with more senior ranjens and vedeks . . ." He
jutted his chin at Arin and Cotor, who both nodded back.
"Many come to take meditative walks along the Sahving
Valley." Gar paused by a window and pointed out into the
clear day; in the middle distance, the mouth of the grassy
vale was visible. "Others come to study our library, as we
discussed in the keep. There's also the Whispering Hall . . ."

Arin made a noise of assent. "Many scholars have said
the hall is the most spiritual place on Bajor. There is a
peace there that few other reclusia can match."

"Indeed," said Cotor. "And of course, there is the Kendra Shrine." He gestured toward the end of the long, wide cloister. An oval doorway stood before them, the doors cut from a dark, dense wood and decorated with lines of thick latinum. The large entrance allowed passage to the shrine proper, and around it there were smaller doors of normal dimensions. Through these, pilgrims of certain piety could enter smaller prayer chambers with only a single stone wall between them and the monastery's most holy of holies, the Orb of Truth.

Gar felt a tingling in the soles of his feet as he walked closer, an electric sensation, a vertiginous rush as if he were approaching the edge of a steep, sheer cliff.

Bennek was pointing at the doors. "I have a question." He made an oval shape in the air before him. "The symbol of the nested ellipses and circle appears again and again in your society, and not just in your religion. I have seen it on insignia, on the uniforms of your Militia. What does it mean?"

"It is the unity of Bajoran existence, my friend," began the kai warmly. She indicated the etchings cut into the shrine door. "The circle at the lowest level represents the world of Bajor, her people, and, in a greater sense, all that is corporeal. The first oval that envelops the circle and extends above it is the universe around us, all that lies beyond Bajor. The last oval, the largest, which surrounds the other two shapes, symbolizes the Prophets. It signifies the place they have in our lives, watching over everything, knowing all, protecting and nurturing us."

"And the line?" Bennek traced the column that rose from the crest of the circle, bisecting the two larger ovals. "What does that mean?"

"It is the pathway that unites all: Bajor and her children, the universe and the Prophets."

The Cardassian's brow wrinkled. "I see that. But why then does the pathway extend beyond the realm of the

Prophets?" He indicated the top of the doors, to where the rising line emerged alone.

Meressa smiled. "That, Bennek, is the gateway to the unknown, the unfinished road. It represents our eternal quest for knowledge and understanding."

"Fascinating," murmured Hadlo. "Your Eminence, what I have seen here today brings me to a single conclusion." He glanced at the Bajoran monk. "Prylar Gar spoke of 'missions of faith,' and after your warm reception I find myself compelled to make a most serious request of you and your church."

The kai's expression was neutral, but Gar felt a thrill of anxiety. "Go on, brother. We will hear what you wish to say."

The Cardassian cleric's fingers knitted together and he gazed at the Bajorans one by one; but as he spoke, the prylar couldn't help but notice that Bennek's face had turned rigid and stony, as if the younger cleric were afraid to utter a word. "I am flattered you would call me brother, Kai Meressa," continued Hadlo. "And in that spirit, I would humbly make entreaty to Bajor. I ask your formal permission for the Oralian Way to establish an enclave on your world."

"An enclave?" Arin echoed. "You wish to build a church here?"

"Not exactly." Hadlo shook his head. "An embassy, of a kind. A theological legation from which my fellow Oralians can come forth to learn from your scholars and seek the connections between our two faiths." He sighed. "There is so little opportunity for such reflection and contemplation on Cardassia Prime. But this world? I have rarely found a place so open to spirituality."

"The Vedek Assembly will have to be consulted," Cotor said quickly, speaking before the kai had a chance to reply. There was open misgiving in his manner. "To grant a place for an alien credo on our soil . . . There is no precedent for such a thing."

Meressa sniffed in mild derision. "The Prophets are not so venial or so weak as to be afraid of another man's view of the universe. They welcome the challenge of new ideas. I would hope the Vedek Assembly would not do the opposite."

"It is a serious request, Eminence," Cotor pressed.

Hadlo hesitated. "Please, I do not mean to be the cause of dissent—"

"You are not," said the kai firmly, "and I will see to it that your appeal goes forward with my backing."

Hadlo bowed. "Thank you, Eminence. I firmly believe the coming together of our faiths heralds great things."

"I know it," Meressa replied, with quiet honesty. "And if you will come with me, Hadlo, I hope to show you why." The group crossed a line of golden tiles set in the marble floor of the cloister, to a series of stone basins on the outer walls of the great shrine. Temple servants were there holding bolts of white linen, and with automatic reverence Gar and Arin backed away. Arin, as a ranjen and a rank higher, took one step back while the prylar took two. Gar's fingers curled into his palms, and he fought to push down the nervous energy coiling in his chest. To be so close to the shrine and yet be unable to go any further—it filled the young priest with conflicting emotions that were hard to separate.

Abruptly, he was aware that the kai was looking directly at him as she washed her hands in the clear waters from the basin. She dried them with the white cloth, but instead of moving to the next phase of the ritual cleansing, she turned and came across to him.

"Eminence?"

"Ask me," she said quietly, pitching her words so that only the two of them could hear what she was saying. "Go on, Osen. Give voice to the question that has been stuck in your throat since last night."

It would have done him no good to feign ignorance;

Meressa was perhaps the most intelligent, most compassionate, certainly one of the most insightful people he had ever met. Any thought of politely deflecting her question faded, and he let out a thin sigh. "Eminence, why are you doing this? You are about to usher an alien into the presence of the Prophets! And you have ignored Vedek Cotor's rightful concerns over such an action!"

She nodded. "I have indeed, my young friend. And shall I tell you why?"

He straightened. "You are kai. You do not have to explain your decisions to a mere prylar if you do not wish to."

"But I do, Osen, and I will." She touched him on the arm, and her hand was cold from the chilly water that fed the basins from the spring beneath the monastery. "You are a little like Cotor. You are clever, but you are also afraid. You have never stood in the presence of a Tear."

"I have not yet had that honor," Gar husked.

"Part of you longs for that moment, and part of you is terrified of the prospect of it, yes?" He nodded woodenly, and she continued. "As was I." The kai smiled. "And, perhaps, you are jealous of Hadlo? You wish it were you?"

Gar felt heat rise in his cheeks. "Yes. I do, Eminence," he admitted. "I know I should rise above such things."

"You are only mortal. And there *will* come a time when Gar Osen will stand before the ark in that chamber. But not today." Her hand dropped away. "I will confide in you, because before I do this I feel as if I must."

"But . . . the ritual . . ."

Meressa silenced him with a gesture. "Rites and prayers are only frames for our faith in the Prophets. Truth is what they ask from us, Osen, truth and love. I have always been one to test the hidebound ways of our church to stop us from becoming parochial. That is why the Vedek Assembly has Cotor here to watch me. I vex them with the choices I make and the things that I do." She studied him. "They ask me why I have an untested prylar from a provincial city on my staff." Meressa glanced at Arin, who stood watching the Cardassians. "They ask me why I overlooked my ranjen's dalliances with illicit substances and rescued him from the ignominy of a colonial posting. And now they will ask me why I hold out friendship to these aliens and offer them the chance to walk our path." The kai leaned close to him. "It is because I sense the future. The Prophets gave me insight, and I feel it coming. I am certain that only through leaps of faith, through trust, can we progress."

All at once Gar's breath caught in his throat as he realized what Meressa was telling him. "Eminence, no! You must say no more! You cannot speak of it!"

But she kept talking, and Gar couldn't turn away. "The *pagh'tem'far.* The sacred vision granted by the Prophets. When I first encountered an Orb, they showed me such sights . . ." Her vision became hazy, and Gar knew she was seeing that moment again in her thoughts. "Such images and sensations that it will take me a lifetime to meditate on the meaning of them all. But I recall one thing with clarity. One moment with such sharpness that it burns inside me still."

"You must not," Gar managed. "The visions gifted by the Tears are for those alone who experience them, not for others. You must not tell me."

She smiled gently. "I think the Prophets will not mind this once. If it convinces you that I am right, then they will not be upset by it." Meressa gazed into his eyes. "I saw a future yet to come. The Celestial Temple revealing itself, and in the heavens above, a giant's iron crown floating among the stars. I glimpsed an age of unity for Bajor, all of it stemming from one moment. The arrival of those not of our world, but also connected to it. An alien who is no alien."

Gar swallowed hard. "And . . . and you believe that these Cardassians could be these offworlders the Prophets showed you?"

"I cannot be certain. That is why they are here. The Orb of Truth will answer that question." She was silent for a moment. "Now do you see?"

The prylar felt rooted to the spot. That the kai herself had trusted him with her personal insight—it was a heady sensation. He nodded, unable to frame an answer, and she left him there pondering her words.

Bennek's fingers were light on Hadlo's shoulder. The Cardassian turned to face his junior and saw the worry there on his face. "What is it?"

"I question this," said the young cleric. "You have no idea what they expect of you, of us. We know so little of their ways . . ."

Hadlo smiled slightly. "What are you afraid of, Bennek? Do you think they will drink my blood or brainwash me? It is a temple, nothing more. They will show me their great and holy relic, and I will give it the reverence it deserves, and then we will move on to matters of greater import."

Bennek spoke in a whisper as Hadlo used the linen to dry his hands. "You meant everything you said to them, all this talk of enclaves?"

"I did," he replied. "We must look to all possible outcomes. We will forge a friendship with these people, but with one eye toward Cardassia. If the Detapa Council attempts to expunge us, a place to find sanctuary with sympathetic souls would be of great use."

Bennek was about to say more, but then the kai approached him. "Hadlo," she said, offering him her hand. "Are you prepared?"

"I suppose I am," he told her. "Is there anything I should say or do once we enter the shrine?"

She smiled warmly at him. "Open your heart and your mind. The Prophets will do the rest."

✦ ✦ ✦

The doors closed behind them with a solid, heavy thump, and Hadlo's fixed smile faltered a little. The realization came upon him in an instant; what if Bennek's concerns were justified? The cleric had a point—the Oralians really didn't know much about the ways of the Bajoran church. What if Meressa asked him to do something strange, something *unholy*?

Hadlo clamped down on that line of thinking, rejecting it as foolish; but the nagging voice in his head would not be silenced.

"This way," said the kai, leading him forward.

Inside, the shrine chamber was circular, with walls that vanished away toward a ceiling covered with intricate murals of alien figures, great oceans of stars, and unfamiliar landscapes. There were freestanding walls twice the height of a man ringing the center of the shrine, spaced at regular intervals. As they moved around them, the Cardassian glimpsed a shallow dais and upon it a wooden box. A honey-colored light seeped from the container, spilling out across the room. He noted that Meressa did not at any moment look in the direction of the box.

She drew to a halt in the shadow of one of the barriers and indicated the dais with a sweep of her robed arm. "I will go no further," said the kai. "This is the *pagh'tem'far*. This moment belongs to you alone, Hadlo. Step to the ark and look within."

He felt his throat become arid. "What ... what will happen?"

Meressa bowed her head. "You will look into the Tear, and the Tear will look into you."

Hesitantly, Hadlo stepped through the gap between two of the walls and into the very heart of the Kendra Shrine. He saw the box more clearly now, what Meressa had termed the "ark." The container was made of old wood, polished smooth by the action of thousands of fingers upon its surface. Complex Bajoran ideograms decorated the edges, illuminated in the soft yellow-green glow from within. Through misted oval lenses in the sides of the ark, Hadlo defined the shape of something infinitely complex, turning and shimmering.

A thread of old memory rose up inside him. *A boy's bare feet padding along the rough stone floors of the Temple of Oralius, decades before it had been torn down and ground to rubble. His new master's hand on his shoulder, guiding him away from a mother whose trade for his life now meant she could afford to feed his brothers and sisters. Young Hadlo, at first not understanding, coming to face the priestess with the mask of the Fate upon her. The sudden knowledge that he was in the presence of something greater than himself. The need to subsume himself within it.*

He felt a stab of panic. The Cardassian was not sure what he had expected to see, but it had not been anything like this. Some sculpture, perhaps, or the mummified bones of an old dead saint. He held up his hands and watched the waves of light cross over his skin. His flesh tingled and the image wavered; for a moment he saw not the gray quality of his own species but the pale tones of a Bajoran.

Hadlo blinked and the illusion vanished. The box compelled him toward it, and he found his fingers moving across the wood. It was pleasant to the touch, as if it had been warmed by the glow of a summer sun. Seams parted and the ark opened to him, almost of its own accord; a helix of glittering, shifting intricacy lay there, casting its light over his face. And inside it . . .

Inside Hadlo saw—

Whiteness hazed his sight, burning the stone reality of the shrine away from him, casting the Cardassian into a footless void of numbing darkness.

I am falling and falling and falling—

There were voices speaking in tongues, chattering in Old Hebitian, crying out his name in Lakarian dialects, laughing and hooting. Hadlo looked down and saw pale flesh upon his hands. He raised them to his face and there were no ridges upon his neck and about his eyes, only a raised serration across the bridge of his nose. A heavy weight of metal links dragged upon his ear.

No, this is not who I am—

He felt rough caresses over his legs and bare feet, a touch like old dry parchment. Hadlo's gaze dropped to see serpents crowding around him, rising up like a tide. Gray vipers moving about his body as if he were not there, more and more of them now, burying him under their obdurate mass.

He cried out and threw them off, stumbling away. His feet plunged ankle-deep into drifts of ash, and the cleric turned, his robes catching in a tormented wind, tearing his pastel hood from his head. Hadlo glanced up and saw the vestiges of an obliterated city ranged around him, beneath angry clouds that spat flames and lightning.

He heard the distant screech of disruptor fire, the crack-and-thump of chemical explosives. The ash was everywhere, thick in layers that coated the stone ruins, turning and wheeling in motes that clogged the air in his lungs. He made out toppled towers and shattered statues robbed of their majesty, cracked domes and piles of dead bricks. Hadlo struggled to make some sense of the murdered vista, searching to find some commonality, some indicator.

Is this Cardassia? Or Bajor? Which is it? Which one? Answer me!

From the wall of howling, windblown ashes came shapes that formed into figures of hooded men and women, the masks of Oralius tarnished and broken over their faces. Hadlo lurched forward and grasped the closest one, snatching the façade away. It disintegrated into powder in his fingers and beneath there was nothing but a bare skull, the grinning mask of the dead. He recoiled, feeling hot streaks of tears down his face.

Is this what will be? *He shouted the words to the smoky air.* Oralius, answer me! Is this what will come to pass if I turn back, or if I press on? I must know!

Glowing warm light fell on him once again, and Hadlo saw

Orbs; not one, but many of them, emerging from the drifts of black ash, burning it away with their radiance. He reached for the closest one, sensing salvation within the turning helix of light; but as his fingers touched the surface, the object faded as hordes of snakes coiled in around it, dragging it away. He swung around, casting about, but each Orb did the same, diminishing and disappearing beneath a mass of serpents. They left him in the darkness, with no light to show him the path.

Hadlo's hand went to his face. He touched the familiar bony ridges around his eyes and then there was nothing but whiteness.

Bennek watched his master take the cup of liquid with a trembling hand. The old cleric seemed to be barely aware of where he was. When the kai had emerged from the shrine with Hadlo at her side, the deathly pallor of his master made the priest gasp. Hadlo's color was returning with each passing moment, but the hollow look in his eyes made Bennek wonder what sights he had seen inside the sealed chamber.

Meressa looked on with quiet concern. "The aftermath of an Orb encounter can be quite trying."

Ranjen Arin produced a small sensor wand from a pocket in his robes and waved it discreetly over the old cleric. "If my readings are correct, he does not appear to be in any physical distress."

"The tea contains extract of *makara* root, a medicinal herb. It will serve as a calmative," said the kai.

Bennek's ridges tensed. "What did you do to him in there?" he demanded, but before he could say more he felt Hadlo's hand on his arm.

"It's all right." The cleric glanced at the woman. "Kai Meressa, forgive my young friend. He is sometimes so impulsive . . ."

The other Bajoran priest, Gar, leaned in. "Are you well, Hadlo?"

The old man nodded. "Yes." His words were quiet and

muted. "I . . . I was unprepared for what I saw. I'm all right now. Just a little . . . bewildered."

Meressa nodded sagely. "The *pagh'tem'far* is an intense experience. What the Prophets choose to show us can come as a shock, but we must be open to it. Only through study, through the careful consideration and interpretation of the vision, can we reach true understanding of it."

Bennek eyed the cleric. "You . . . you *did* see something?" He sat beside the old man. "What was it?"

When Hadlo spoke again it was like a voice from the grave, faint and sepulchral. "A future," he husked. Then suddenly the priest stiffened, as if he had remembered where he was, and in what company. "A future," he repeated, and this time he spoke with the same potency that Bennek knew of old. "I saw a road ahead, my friend." He got to his feet and took Meressa warmly by the hand. "Thank you, Eminence, for this great honor. If there was but the slightest iota of doubt in my mind that our coming together here was right, it has been washed away. I am alight with a new determination, sister, and for that there are no words to express my gratitude."

Meressa's wary smile became relaxed. "I am so very pleased to hear that, brother." Bennek saw the kai and Prylar Gar exchange a loaded glance.

Hadlo nodded. "With your permission, I should like to return to the Naghai Keep." He let out a deep sigh. "I have much to think on."

The kai bowed and turned to speak to Gar. Bennek drew close to the elder. "Hadlo?" he asked, doubt clouding his face.

The old man looked at him, and his eyes were alight with certainty. "Come. We have much to do."

Lonnic stared at the strings of characters on the padd but did not really read them. Her eyes were unfocused, the text turning into a string of meaningless blobs against the digital screen. The glass of amber *copal* before her was barely touched; she had taken one or two sips in the hour she'd been sitting on the taphouse's veranda, but done little else. She'd left the keep and come out into the city proper to put distance between her and her concerns—but the conceit that her worries could be walled up inside the old castle and she could walk away from them was foolish. Every word of the conversation between Jas Holza and Kubus Oak was trapped there behind her eyes, and she was going back to it over and over, worrying the issue like a *hara* cat getting the last licks of meat off a bone.

The whole Golana problem; it hung around her, dragging on her thoughts. On one level she felt betrayed by Jas for cutting her out of the crisis, while on another she understood the choice he had made. Kubus had been correct when he suggested that Jas had done it to protect her. *But I am his chief adjutant,* she fumed. *I should have known.* And then there was the matter of the fate of the *Eleda.*

A shadow fell across her table, blotting out the afternoon sun, and Lonnic looked up to see two men in uniform.

"Hey," said Darrah, and indicated the empty chairs across from her. "Did some foolish man break a date with you? How rude."

She gave him a wry smile. "Constable Darrah, and Watchman Proka. What brings you to this part of Korto?"

Darrah sat. "Oh, you know. Law officer stuff." He threw a glance at the chronometer on his cuff. "Actually, we're on break for a moment, isn't that right, Migdal?" He shot Proka a look.

"We are?" said the watchman. "Oh," he continued, "I mean, we *are.*"

Darrah nodded. "Catch a server, will you? Get us a couple more of those." He tapped Lonnic's *copal* glass, and Proka stepped away to summon a waitress.

Lonnic raised an eyebrow. "Drinking on duty is not permitted,"

Darrah shrugged. "One glass doesn't count as drinking. At least, not where I come from." He settled himself in the chair. "Besides, me and you talking? That counts as a business meeting."

"A taphouse is hardly businesslike."

He raised an eyebrow. "I beg to differ. I've done some of my best police work in taverns like this." He paused, watching her. "You know, I only ever see you here when something's bothering you. Want to talk about it?"

Lonnic was thinking about what to tell him when a group of noisy children ran past, laughing and shouting. A couple of them were wearing crude masks made of gray paper that mimicked the shape and form of a Cardassian face. "Will you look at that?" she said.

"They're just kids," Darrah said easily. "They're fascinated by anything that's unusual."

Lonnic's expression darkened. "And they aren't the only ones." She looked around, taking in the people at the other tables on the veranda. "I've lost count of the number of times I've heard the word 'Cardassian' float over from someone else's conversation since I got here."

"Better than 'spoonhead,'" said Darrah quietly. "What did you expect, Tomo? Offworlders are always a crowd-pleaser. We get so few of them, and even then they tend to stick to the spaceport quarters in Ashalla or Dahkur."

Proka returned with two glasses of *copal* and sat, taking a slow sip of the Bajoran cider.

"Sometimes I think that's better for all of us," Lonnic replied, tapping her own glass. "You haven't seen things at the keep. All the attendant *D'jarras*, when they think they're out of earshot, I hear them talking about the Cardassians." She grimaced. "The women are *fascinated* by them all right."

"Oh," Proka said with a blink. "It's like that, is it? Huh."

"Well, I have heard that talk as well," noted Darrah, reaching for his drink. "You know how people wonder." He tapped his shoulders. "All those ropey muscles on their neck, folks start thinking that maybe they have them in other places as—"

Lonnic thumped her glass on the tabletop. "Stop right there. It's bad enough I'm hearing it from giggling servant girls, now I have to get it from you?"

Darrah's wan smile faded. "C'mon, Tomo, don't take this so seriously. I'm sure the aliens are probably thinking the same things about us."

"I don't trust them," she said flatly. "I don't trust the Cardassians, and I don't trust Kubus Oak or the First Minister or anyone involved in this." She took a gulp from the *copal*. "There. I said it."

"Verin's a sour old coot," opined Proka.

"Well, Kubus. Yeah, I don't like him either, but . . ." The constable watched her expression. "You didn't seem this angry about it when we talked in the precinct."

"That was official business," she retorted, and had another sip of the cider. "Now I'm on a break." Lonnic glanced around to be certain that no one was listening in on their conversation. She was on the verge of telling him about Golana, but she reeled back. Instead, she revealed something else. "You know the *Eleda?*"

"The scoutship," said Proka. "The one the spoonheads brought back." Darrah shot his subordinate a terse look at the casual epithet, but the watchman pretended he hadn't noticed.

Lonnic nodded. "Just how was that vessel wrecked? I knew the captain by reputation, and he was good at what he did. I find it hard to imagine he nose-dived into an asteroid."

"Is that what the sensor logs say happened?"

She sighed. "The Militia isn't saying much. They've only

released the most basic of information about the fatalities. It's all very sketchy, at best."

Darrah's eyes narrowed. "What are you getting at? You think this wasn't death by misadventure?"

"The *Eleda* crew perished under dubious conditions, that's a given," she insisted. "I've pulled in favors with my contacts at the Space Guard division, and from what I've learned they haven't been able to make an accurate post-mortem on the wreckage."

"The aliens rigged it?" Proka hesitated with his glass at his lips.

"That's a bit of a leap," added Darrah. "Just because you're wary of the offworlders, that doesn't make them murderers."

She eyed him over the lip of her drink. "You're the law-man, Mace. Aren't you supposed to be the one who is suspicious of everybody and everything?"

"I am," replied the constable. "I'm a trained, professional skeptic, so you ought to leave this sort of thing to me." He gave a crooked smile. "Honestly, you've been with Jas too long. You see conspiracies everywhere."

Lonnic sipped the *copal*. "I work in politics, Mace. There *are* conspiracies everywhere."

"Huh," added Proka. "Makes me glad I'm just a watchman. I'll stick to kicking in doors and cuffing felons. Simpler."

"I spoke to one of them, you know," Darrah volunteered. "His name was Dukat, one of the officers, I think." The meeting with the alien had been preying on his mind since that evening, and something about it made Darrah want to get it out in the open. He felt as if he were doing something wrong keeping it to himself.

"When did that happen?" asked Proka.

"In the keep, on the ramparts. I was taking a walk around the perimeter, checking the security arrangements. The Cardassian was there. I think he came out to get some air."

Lonnic was listening carefully. "What did he say to you?"

"He asked me about the Gratitude Festival. I don't think he really understood what it was for."

"What did you make of him, then?" Proka asked. "They seem like a stiff-backed lot from what I can figure out."

Darrah shrugged, recalling Dukat's words, the look of sad distance on the alien's face. *I have a son. He has yet to be named.* "He seemed . . . like anybody else. We talked about our kids for a bit, then another one, one of the scientists, came and got him." He chewed his lip, reviewing his impressions of the Cardassian. "They seem like us. There's good and bad in everyone, right? Aliens included? Anyone who cares about his family can't be a million light-years different."

Lonnic grunted. "For all you know, they might eat their young."

"Yeah," added Proka, warming to the subject, "or maybe the females are like *palukoo* spiders and they chew off the heads of the men once they're done mating."

"Speaking of that, how are things with Karys?"

Darrah glared at the dark-skinned woman. "Fine. She's fine."

"She seemed to enjoy herself at the festival."

"We all had a good time." He frowned. "I . . . I don't get to take her out as much as I would like."

Proka kept talking, missing the undercurrent of tension in his superior's words. "You know, we used to have a betting pool running at the precinct about how long your marriage would last. What with her being *Ih'valla* and you being *Ke'lora,* I mean." He took a draught of cider.

"Really?" Darrah replied, ice forming on the word. The watchman didn't appear to notice; it baffled Darrah how a man who brought such attention to detail as a police officer was so oblivious to his unintentional rudeness in social situations.

"Yeah," Proka went on, "I mean, we all know it's been rocky for you."

"You all know?" Darrah repeated, shooting a glare at Lonnic, who maintained a passive expression.

Proka nodded to himself. "Women of that caliber are very high-maintenance," he said sagely. "They expect a man to improve his lot in life. Otherwise, they can walk right out the door—"

"Thank you, *Watchman.*" Darrah ground out the words, putting acid emphasis on Proka's rank. "Perhaps you ought to consider a career as a counselor instead of a law officer?" He reached over and took Proka's glass from his hand. "Break's over. Take a walk."

And finally, realization of what he'd been saying caught up with the man, and Proka smiled weakly. "Uh. Yes, boss." He got up and left.

Grimacing, Darrah glared into the depths of his own drink. "How can that man still be walking around with his foot stuck in his mouth?"

"You know," said Lonnic, after a long moment, "he does have a point."

"Oh, not you as well?" Darrah growled. "Does everyone have an opinion on my marriage?"

"I'm just saying . . ." she began, gathering her things together to leave. "People from the *Ih'valla* caste are always flighty. It might help if you took a little time off from the precinct. Remind Karys why it was she married you."

"I will," he told her, without looking up. "Once this situation is put to bed, I will. Once the Cardassians have gone home."

Dukat stood and watched as the *Kornaire*'s space-to-surface cutter returned to the exact spot inside the Naghai Keep where it had arrived, dropping to the ground in a gust of exhaust. He considered it for a moment, smiling thinly at the Cardassian precision of the gesture. The inner cordon of the castle was bare now, the temporary pavilion that had been erected for their arrival now gone. He understood from Pa'Dar that there would be no official farewell ceremony beyond a couple of handshakes from some of the local ministers and the granting of some Bajoran gifts.

Dukat's smile faded. Not for the first time, he found himself questioning the entire purpose of the mission. He would never have ventured to voice those thoughts within earshot of other members of the *Kornaire* crew, even though he knew most of them—up to and including Gul Kell—felt much the same way. *We should have come here with a flotilla of warships and then offered them our friendship. One hand outstretched, the other with a gun in it.* There were plenty of "client systems" inside the Cardassian Union who had been induced to make agreements with Central Command in just such a fashion—Celtris, Rondac, and Ingav, among others—and Bajor would have made a fine addition to them.

But Cardassia cannot afford to waste valuable combat vessels on a diplomatic mission when they are needed at the frontier. Our warships are thin on the ground. How many times had he heard that? Too many officers, too few ships. That explanation had been passed to him by Kell, by other senior officers, when he pressed for a command of his own, for a long overdue promotion. *I hear the words but I do not believe them.* There were ships out there all right, but they were being granted to men and women whose elevation through the ranks owed more to politics and nepotism than to their individual merit. Kell's own daughter lacked the experience and skill of Dukat, and yet she was in command of a fighter squadron in the disputed regions. Kell himself owed his position to a parent in the Legate congress.

After the feast, Dukat's thoughts about Bajor had crystallized. He was convinced now that the planet could—it *should*—come under Cardassian aegis. All it would take would be a few vessels and the willingness to understand these aliens. After only a few days, he felt a new awareness forming in him. The Bajorans were wayward, insular children, with dogmatic habits and a limited perspective on the greater universe around them. What they required was clear: the guiding hand of a stern parent to turn them toward a more productive life. *All the luxuries they squander, heedless of how other worlds suffer. If Cardassia had such riches, my people . . . my* family *would be safe and secure. These aliens need our supervision.*

But he was in no position to make that happen. Perhaps, if he were in command of the *Kornaire,* Dukat could change the course of this operation; but with a man as stolid and unimaginative as Kell at the helm, the mission would end before it could truly begin.

His hand went to his wrist pocket, to the holograph rod. *At least it means I will be home soon. Back to Athra and my son.* If he could do nothing on Bajor to help his world, perhaps back on his world he could do something to help his wife and child.

The shuttle's hatch hissed open and released one of the noncommissioned gils assigned to the craft's duty crew; but from behind the junior rating came Kotan Pa'Dar, his face darkened with effort. The scientist's eyes locked on Dukat and he came running to him, puffing. "Skrain! I'm glad I found you!"

Dukat frowned at the other man's near-frantic manner. "Kotan, what are you doing?" The scientist had transported to the ship hours ago. "You're supposed to be up there."

"I had to speak to you!" Pa'Dar said between panting gasps. "I didn't want . . . to go through channels. I knew Kell would . . . would never let me contact you for a personal reason, so I had the glinn take me on the cutter."

Dukat waved a hand at the scientist as if he were dismissing a nagging insect. "Explain yourself. What personal reasons?"

Pa'Dar looked him in the eyes, and the officer saw pity in the other man's gaze. "I knew it," Pa'Dar said quietly. "I knew Kell would keep it from you. He infuriates me."

"Watch what you say!" Dukat barked. Despite the fact that he agreed with Pa'Dar, it was wrong to allow a civilian to openly denigrate a member of the military. "I ordered you to explain yourself!"

Pa'Dar swallowed hard and made an effort to calm himself. He drew Dukat to one side, into the lee of the parked shuttle. "There's word from Cardassia Prime. I heard Professor Ico speaking with Kell. There has been rioting, the Oralians have come into conflict with the military." He grabbed Dukat's arm. "There's fighting on the roads outside Lakat, Skrain! The city has been cut off!"

"Athra." The name fell from his lips. With a sudden burst of motion, Dukat pushed away from the scientist and strode into the shuttle.

The glinn at the flight controls looked up with a start as Dukat dropped into the command chair next to hers. "Dalin? Is there a problem?"

"I want communications," he snapped. "Give me a direct feed via the *Kornaire*'s subspace array, immediately!"

The glinn blanched at his tone. "Sir, that will require an authorization code."

He bent forward and punched a set of numbers into a control console. "There! Get it done. I want a real-time link to Cardassia Prime, now!"

The pilot hesitated as the console emitted a negative chime. "Dalin, that code . . . It is not cleared for direct comm protocols. Only Gul Kell can authorize that."

Dukat teetered on the verge of shouting at the glinn; but he knew she was right, and if Kell knew about the reports from home and he hadn't bothered to bring them to Dukat's attention, he wasn't likely to simply let his first officer place a priority message. Dukat's face burned with fury, at the Oralians, at Kell, at himself for acting in such an emotional manner.

"I can help you." Dukat's head snapped around to see Bennek standing next to Pa'Dar in the cutter's entry bay.

Anger propelled Dukat out of the cockpit and to the young cleric, their faces only a hand's span apart. "You'll help me?" he rumbled. "After your people put the lives of my wife and child in danger, you will help me?" Dukat's words became a snarl.

"I know nothing about that," Bennek replied. "I have a communications code that was provided to the Oralian Way by the Detapa Council. It will only open a channel via the civilian network, but you are welcome to use it." He nodded at the control console. "Will you permit me?"

His fists contracting into tight hammers, Dukat could only nod stiffly. He watched the priest fold back his hood and bend over the panel, fingers sweeping over the keypad. The glinn examined the display and her eyes widened. "Dalin, the connection is being made. I have a tie-in with the *Kornaire*'s hyperchannel array."

Bennek looked back at him. "Who do you wish to speak to?"

There was a pressure in his chest as Dukat formed the words of his reply. "Contact the Ministry of Justice. The office of military legality. I will speak to Procal Dukat . . . my father."

7

"**S**krain?"

The old man's voice was thick with sleep, and Dukat realized abruptly that the time difference between Korto and the capital on Cardassia meant it had to be before dawn. He deflected a stab of irritation, for an instant taking a step back and examining his actions. Dukat was allowing himself to behave emotionally when the best course would be to remain detached and clearheaded. His fingers drew together and he fought to moderate his anxiety. "Father," he began, "I'm sorry I woke you." He threw a look over his shoulder and saw that the hatch behind him was shut. The pilot, Pa'Dar, and Bennek had left without speaking, respecting his privacy.

On the tiny cockpit monitor, Archon Procal Dukat settled himself on the chair before the desk in his office where the comm screen sat. Thickset and firm of face, he still maintained the look of a street fighter about him even as the passing years robbed him of his robustness. Skrain, wiry and athletic in build, took after his mother more than the man on the other end of the line, but only in his physical aspect. Inwardly, Procal and his son shared much more in terms of their manner and personality. It was one of the reasons why they disagreed so often, why they had disagreed the last time they had spoken; but both of them understood that this was a matter of greater import than their differences. Unspoken, the two men automatically put their quarrels aside.

The elder Dukat adjusted the robe about his shoulders and threw a glance toward the shadowed bedroom door across the room. He kept his voice low but intense. *"You received the message, then?"*

Skrain's brow furrowed in confusion. "From you? No."

His father chuckled without humor. *"Of course not. Why should I have expected any different? Central Command told me you were on a mission of utmost sensitivity. Communications of a military nature only."*

Skrain shook his head. "It doesn't matter. We're speaking now." He leaned closer to the small screen. "Tell me what is going on. My wife . . ."

Procal frowned, matching his son's expression. *"Skrain, this channel is likely being monitored."*

"Athra and my son," Skrain continued, keeping his voice level. "Tell me."

The old man's eyes met his. *"As soon as I heard about the Oralians and the rioting, I did what I could to reach the Medical Campus at Lakat . . ."*

"What?" The word burst from Skrain's lips. "Is she hurt?"

His father held up a hand to halt him. *"The week you left, Athra and my grandson took ill. It's an infection from tainted water. Many people have been affected."* He sighed. *"I made sure they were placed where they would get good care."*

"Thank you." Dukat replied numbly. His face tingled with a rush of blood. At once he felt a churn of emotions: anger and worry, shock and humiliation. All he wanted in that instant was to be home, at Athra's side.

"Skrain," the archon continued, *"listen to me. The Detapa Council has issued a statement about concerns over insurgent attacks. The Oralians are in an uproar here. The military have sent*

in peacekeeper divisions to calm the unrest outside Lakat and the other cities in the southern territories. Nothing is getting in or out, including supplies."

"How will they get the medicine they need?" Skrain snapped. "I have to—"

"Skrain." His father said his name with such quiet force that it stopped Dukat in his tracks. *"What can you do? Unless you're planning on stealing Kell's starship and flying it home, what can you do?"* The old man shook his head. *"This is what it means to serve Cardassia, son. This is a harsh lesson, but you cannot shrink from it."* His voice shifted, taking on the authoritarian tone Dukat remembered from his childhood. *"Do your duty. I'll do what I can to help Athra and the boy."* He reached for the disconnect key.

"Procal," said Dukat. "His name is Procal."

The old man halted and nodded to him, then cut the link.

For long moments, Dukat sat there in the acceleration chair and looked at his hands, the gray fingers tightening into fists, releasing, tightening again. He felt helpless and he despised the reaction, a hard loathing coiling inside his chest, pressing against his ribs. He wanted to shout, to break something, but the turmoil had no point of escape. He glared out of the canopy of the cutter at the walls of the Bajoran castle beyond, and a sudden flare of hate shot through him—for Kell, for the Oralians, for the aliens, for this damnable mission.

Burning in his directionless fury, he almost shattered the control panel when the ship-to-ship communicator chimed, announcing an incoming signal. "What is it?" he snarled at the intrusion.

Kell's indolent voice answered him. *"Another officer might consider that tone to be insubordinate, Dalin. However, I'm willing to overlook it, given your personal considerations at the moment."*

Dukat's teeth set on edge, recalling his father's earlier comment. *Of course Kell had been listening to us. I would have expected nothing less.*

The gul continued. *"I've been in contact with Fleet Jagul Hekit. He concurs with my appraisal of the situation here. The Bajorans are intransigent and there are matters of greater import closer to home that require our attention. We're to complete our secondary intelligence-gathering scans of Bajor and disengage."*

Dukat hid a sneer. The *Kornaire* had been in-system for barely a solar week, and already Kell had colluded with his old mentor Hekit to have the mission cut short. The gul's open loathing of anything that smacked of "diplomacy" colored his every decision. Dukat immediately fathomed Kell's train of thought; forced into taking the mission to Bajor, he had done only the least required of him to consider it completed so that he might move on to something that would gather more credit for the avaricious officer. Kell craved high rank and made no secret of the fact that he wanted to be prefect of his own planet. In his mind, the gul had doubtless decided the Bajor delegation was a worthless assignment even before they had left Cardassia Prime.

Kell must have seen something of his thoughts on his face. *"Come, Dukat, I'd expect you to be pleased. My orders are to go to high warp once we break Bajor orbit and return to base. I thought you'd relish the chance to get home."*

"Yes," Dukat replied, even as he knew that something did not ring true. "And there is more, sir?"

Kell nodded. *"Indeed there is. The jagul informed me that an investigation has begun into the incidents with the Oralians on Cardassia. Apparently, Central Command now suspects that these disturbances were prearranged by senior figures in the church. Suspects are being gathered to be put to the question. Tribunals are already being convened."*

"Hadlo?" Dukat hesitated. Masterminding urban disorder

and open conflict? Such behavior seemed out of character for the staid old cleric, but then there was a part of him that didn't care, a part of him that wanted someone to blame.

"*Correct,*" said Kell. "*Isolate and detain him. I want him back on board the* Kornaire *immediately. See to it personally, Dalin.*"

"Sir," he replied, but Kell had already cut the signal.

Pa'Dar glared at Bennek, his arms folded over his chest. "How can you deny that you know nothing of the actions of your cohorts?"

The priest frowned, trying to find a way to explain the situation to the scientist without patronizing him. "You have to understand, I can no more know the thoughts of my fellows than you could tell me the workings of someone in the Ministry for Public Health! We are one faith, yes, but beneath the gaze of Oralius there are many branches of the church." He could see Pa'Dar was not listening to him. "One faith, many voices. Do you not follow me?"

The other man sneered, and his voice carried down the length of the cutter's central bay. "What I *follow* is reason and rationality, not some masked shadow-theater that encourages dissension and unrest!"

Bennek glanced around nervously. He was regretting his offer to Dukat; while the dalin was sealed in the cockpit beyond them, the cleric was alone with the glinn, Pa'Dar, and a couple of men from the enlisted ranks. The two gils in particular hovered at the edge of his vision, intimidating him with their hard glares and the set of their jaws. Bennek's fingers clutched at the baggy cuffs of his pastel-colored robes and bunched them. "If my brothers have done these things, then there must be a good reason for it!" He blurted out the words with more bravado than he felt, too late realizing that the others might take them for defiance and strike him.

The glinn eyed the priest. "My grandmother went to your temples," she told him. "She died from blood poisoning, even though she gave the clerics every last lek she had so that they would recite for her. She thought they would save her."

Bennek blinked, his jaw working. "I'm ... I'm sure they did their best to make sure her last days were peaceful ones."

"Money better spent on medical care," Pa'Dar grated. "That's the problem with you people. You're all backward-looking." He pressed a thick finger into Bennek's chest. "Prayers and mythology won't make Cardassia strong again."

The young priest tried to frame an answer that wouldn't raise the ire of the others, but before he could speak, the cockpit hatch hissed open and there was Dalin Dukat on the threshold, his eyes hooded and flinty. His gaze locked on Bennek and he took two quick steps toward him. Reflexively, the youth backed away and bumped into a curved support stanchion. The cleric nearly stumbled, the larger of the two gils looming over him, blocking his retreat.

"Where is he?" demanded Dukat. Bennek's throat went dry as the officer's hand fell to his belt, dithering over the holstered pistol at his hip. "Hadlo?"

Like a striking snake, the enlisted man's hand shot out and grabbed a fistful of Bennek's robes, pushing him to the wall of the compartment.

Bennek glanced at Pa'Dar, hoping that the civilian might come to his aid, but the scientist said nothing, watching. "Please," he began, "I am so sorry for the conduct of my brethren on Cardassia, but you must understand we knew nothing of it!"

"I will not ask you again," Dukat growled. "Where is Hadlo?"

The cleric wanted to be strong; he was willing himself to say nothing, but the terror washed through his veins in a cold flood and he stuttered out the answer. "Th-the keep. In the rooms the Bajorans granted us."

Dukat gave the gil an almost imperceptible nod, and the trooper jerked his wrist, pushing Bennek away so that he stumbled to the deck in a heap. The dalin went to the airlock and stabbed the control pad. "Keep him here," he told the pilot. "See that he doesn't speak to anyone."

Bennek looked up to find that nobody was offering to help him to his feet. "Dukat!" he called. "We're not to blame!"

Without looking back at him, the officer hesitated on the airlock ramp. "I don't blame you, Bennek," he said, with an icy calm that was more frightening than his earlier moments of fury. "You think you are a good man. Perhaps you are right. It's misguided beliefs that allow good men like you to do terrible things. That's where the blame lies."

Dukat took care to moderate his stride and his outward mien so that the aliens he passed in the corridor would not realize that something was amiss. He found his way quickly to the east tower and paced into the area where the Oralians were staying. The other clerics, the minor functionaries who rarely seemed to speak in Dukat's presence, came to their feet at he stalked past them toward the door of Hadlo's room.

One of them reached out to touch his arm, the other bringing a hand to his lips in a gesture calling for quiet; in return Dukat shot the priest a steely glare and tore his pistol from its holster, ripping the peace bond ribbon around it with a tight snap. With a single sharp blow from the heel of his hand, Dukat forced open the electromechanical lock on the door and entered, slamming it shut behind him. He kept the disruptor at his side, his finger an inch from the trigger plate.

Hadlo was kneeling in the center of the room. The old man had moved all the furniture to the walls, the table and the wooden chairs pushed out of the way so that he had a spread of open floor to work on. There were sheets of paper everywhere, arranged in a ragged halo around the cleric, and Dukat recognized some of them as scrolls like the one that Bennek had used in his recitation for the dead. Hadlo was scratching at them with a stylus, writing in the margins and adding spidery lines of text in every blank space he could find. He shot a watery look at Dukat and paused. "I have to complete this," he said vaguely. "Come back later."

"Get up," Dukat snarled, angry at the priest's defiance. "If you wish to do this with some dignity, then stand up!"

The old man looked at him again, and it seemed to Dukat as if Hadlo were seeing him for the first time. Hadlo did as he had been told to, padding forward on bare feet, hands outstretched. "Do you know this?" He waved at the papers. "Have you seen the vipers, my brother? Ashes and the future." The cleric shook his head as if he were trying to clear it. "It's difficult to marshal all the images. There's a code, I think. A code. Yes."

Dukat raised the pistol. "I'm placing you under detention by the order of Cardassian Central Command. Attempt to resist me and you will be shot."

He expected the cleric to fold and panic just as Bennek had, but instead a cool smile emerged on the old man's lips. "Who ordered this? Gul Kell?" He nodded before Dukat could answer. "Yes. Very well. Take me to him."

Dukat tapped the communicator bracelet on his wrist. *"Kornaire,* this is Dukat. Lock on and transfer two to shipboard, immediately."

Hadlo kept on smiling, even as the transporter beam enveloped him and swept him away.

✦   ✦   ✦

As Gul Kell reached the security compartment, his lip curled in cold amusement to find Rhan Ico standing at the heavy hatchway before Dukat. The dalin's expression was all chained anger and repression, while the woman wore the same default mien of watchful neutrality. Everywhere he turned on this mission, Ico was there. It was getting to be comical, in its own sinister way.

"Report," he ordered.

"The cleric did not resist arrest," Dukat explained, in a way that made it clear he was disappointed. "I have secured him in holding quadrant two. He has made repeated demands to speak with you."

Kell raised a thick eyeridge. "Well. Perhaps I should indulge him, then." He took a step toward the hatch, and as he expected, Ico interposed herself.

"Gul, I would like to attend you. It's of interest to me to hear his comments regarding the unrest on the home-world."

"Is it?" Kell replied. All three of them knew full well the scientist had absolutely no authority to be granted such access; her posting, after all, was only that of a civilian adviser outside the starship's chain of command.

"With respect," began Dukat, "Professor Ico's remit does not extend to prisoners in custody."

"Quite so," said Kell, tapping the keypad to open the hatch. "But I'm choosing to extend it for the moment."

"Sir," said the dalin, "Central Command will—"

"Central Command is not *here*," Kell growled. "I am." He beckoned Ico to follow him. "Return to the bridge, Dukat. I want privacy."

"As you command." The other man's reply was terse.

Once the hatch closed again, Ico gave him an arch look. "Thank you for accommodating me, Gul." She paused. "If I might say so, your junior officer appears quite unhappy with the situation at hand." Ico had a knack for making

everything she said appear to be no more than an innocu-
ous observation; she always spoke without weight.

Kell didn't look at her. "Dukat's a fine officer, but he
lacks an understanding of the nature of command. Some
hounds need to be kept on a tight chain."

"Some hounds bite," she added.

They came to a halt at an oval space opening onto a
narrow chamber. A humming force field hazed the view
into the cell, traces of yellow sparks flickering at the edges
of the glowing emitter bars surrounding it. Hadlo stood in
the center of the holding compartment, watching them.

"There's no need for this," he said, pointing at the field.
"I'm not a threat."

Kell rubbed his chin. "I'll let a tribunal decide that,
cleric. Your fellow zealots have made quite a mess in your
absence. I'm sure the people will be interested to know
what hand you had in that." He glanced at Ico. "How many
deaths so far, Professor?"

"Fifty-three," said the woman. "Some of them children
and the infirm."

Kell shook his head, concealing the relish he felt at
having the priest incarcerated. "Terrible business. I'm sure
you'll be made to answer in full for it."

Hadlo came forward in an abrupt rush. "No, listen to
me. Your attention is in the wrong place! This is not about
Cardassia, it is about Bajor! About both!" His face flushed
dark gray. "If you could open your eyes, if you could listen!
I've seen it!"

"Seen what?" A sneer crossed the gul's face. "Has your
silly little sect given you some holy revelation to impart to
us?"

"In the temple at Kendra, in the shrine there, I saw such
things as a man like you could never comprehend!" thundered Hadlo, suddenly animated. "The Bajoran kai showed
me, and the Orb . . . the Orb was the vision!"

"Orb?" The word stuck in Kell's mind, and he dwelt on it for a moment. He recalled a fraction of data from his pre-mission briefing, the vague intelligence reports from the Obsidian Order about the aliens and their culture. Doubtless the reports were deliberately unclear where the Order chose to keep the more sensitive data to itself—such a practice was not uncommon—but there had been mention of some sort of relics of religious significance to the Bajorans. He glanced at Ico and saw with some interest that the woman's previously offhand attention toward the cleric had gained a new intensity.

"I saw our worlds, the ashen wilderness and the snakes. Death and destruction laid forth, the blinding smoke . . ." He trailed off, gasping. "As real to me as you!"

Kell snorted. "Oh, how pathetic. This is the best defense you can offer? Your perfidy is revealed and all you can do is play the madman? Visions? What idiocy."

"I saw tomorrow!" The cleric let out the words in a screech. "The future emerging from the Orb of Truth, skeins of possibility unraveling! And the shape of them vanishing, taken away and stolen by serpents . . ."

Ico's eyes narrowed, and she took a step closer to the force field. "Stolen," she repeated. "You saw the Orbs being taken away?"

He nodded curtly. "One by one."

The gul grimaced. "Rhan, please do not tell me that you of all people find some shred of cogency in this babble?" He shot Hadlo a hard look. "It's clear to me. He is either arrested by some sort of dementia brought on by his primitive beliefs, or he is concocting a web of nebulous statements in an attempt to appear more knowledgeable than he is!"

"Perhaps," Ico said.

Kell laughed. "Aren't you a woman of science? A student of the rational? Do you actually put any credence in talk about Orbs that show the future? This is the desperation of a condemned man, nothing more." He sniffed. "I have seen all I need to see."

"Science is the pursuit of knowledge," she said quietly, speaking with steady intensity. "I want to know more about these Orbs." There was something in her words that told Kell she knew far more about them already than either he or the cleric did.

"Yes. Yes!" Hadlo came so close to the glimmering barrier that the emitters rose in pitch with the proximity of his body. "And that will only come through me, through the Oralian Way!"

"If that was an attempt to convert us, it was a weak one," Kell retorted.

The old man's face twisted in a snarl, and suddenly the gul was seeing the pious, imperial manner he remembered from their earlier confrontations. "I would never dirty my faith with you, Kell! I speak of larger issues, of survival and what must be done to ensure it!"

"Go on," said Ico.

He stabbed a crooked finger at them. "You want to open the path to the Bajorans, but they will not listen to you. They see only aliens, the shadow of expansionist warmongers and soulless clinicians! Without weapons, you will never gain a foothold on Bajor! You know it and I know it! They reject you, they distrust you!" He laughed bitterly. "If it were not for us, if the children of Oralius were not with you now, they would have turned you away at the edge of their space!"

Kell's jaw stiffened. "Be thankful you had a use, you old fool. But now, like any tool that has failed to perform, you'll be cast aside. You and your whole sect."

"Not if Cardassia wants Bajor!" roared Hadlo. "I can give it to you! Kai Meressa will listen to me, she trusts me. The Bajoran church holds great sway over their people . . .

If the kai welcomes Cardassia, then Bajor will follow in her footsteps and not even the First Minister will stand against her. I can bring that to pass. Already she has granted my petition to create a theological enclave on her planet. I have taken the first step!"

"You would make your faith the bridge between our two worlds? This is your bargain?" asked Ico.

"That's what you want, isn't it? A channel to their riches and resources?"

The gul folded his arms over his chest. His mind was racing. Here he was, hoping for nothing more than a chance to gloat over the cleric's reversal of fortunes, and instead the old man had offered him a chance to gain the glory Ico had taunted him with earlier—a bloodless victory. The lure of the moment made his mouth flood with saliva. "And suppose you did this, priest," he began, "what would you want in kind?"

Hadlo rocked back, the flush of emotion on his face fading. "Assurances. You will use your authority with Central Command to call off the persecution of my kinsmen. The Oralian Way will be allowed to go on as before."

Kell spread his hands. "I am only a gul of the Second Order. I think you overestimate my influence."

Hadlo glared at him through the transparent barrier. "Spare me your false modesty, Kell. We all know you are well connected. You could do this if you wished to."

Kell shrugged. The cleric was right. "Perhaps so. But it will be difficult to withdraw after your fellow Oralians have done so much damage."

The old man's eyes narrowed. "There is little doubt in my mind that the majority of the unrest was stirred up not by followers of the Way but by men who impersonated them at the government's behest." His voice was low and loaded with cold fury. "But still. I understand there must be closure for the common folk. I submit instead, then, that

the Central Command might learn that the Oralians who
did these things were not of my branch of the Way, but of
another. Perhaps the followers of the Desert Path sect or
the Church of the Love of the Fates."

Ico nodded. "Those are the smaller, less pliant factions
of your religion, if I recall correctly. I imagine you would
not be saddened to see them reduced in number?" She
smiled coldly. "My dear Hadlo, I must apologize to you.
I had thought you to be soft and idealistic, lacking in the
ruthless instinct of the Cardassian spirit. I see now I was
incorrect. You can be without pity if you want to."

"This 'enclave' of which you spoke," said Kell, "it will
be a retreat, then? An embassy of sorts on Bajor?" Hadlo
nodded. "It would serve the Cardassian Union well if the
pilgrims you sent there were to include certain *additions*
among their number."

"If you wish," Hadlo replied.

The gul glanced at Ico, and then at the cleric once
again. "To ensure your sect remains free of persecution,
what you speak of would need to be implemented in quick
order. If I contact Central Command and tell them that I
am ordering the *Kornaire* to remain in Bajor orbit, they will
need assurances."

"Let me out of this cage and I will make it happen. You
have my word. I will do this for the future of my world
and my faith, I swear it on the Recitations."

"Gul," said Ico silkily, "if I might prevail upon you to
communicate with my colleagues at the ministry, I think
I will be able to bring some weight to bear on the matter." She smiled demurely. "I have some substantial contacts
across the spectrum of our government."

"Those that exist toward the darker end of that spectrum, I don't doubt." Kell grimaced. "Very well." He tapped
a control, and the energy field stuttered and faded. The gul
studied the cleric. "Cardassia expects much of her sons and

daughters. If they are lacking, then her mercy will be fleeting and her anger quite terrible." He tapped the comcuff on his wrist. "Bridge, status."

"Bridge here, this is Dukat," came the reply. *"Drive control reports systems at the ready, sir. Homeward course is laid in. We are ready to break orbit once the last of the ground party has been secured."*

Kell's lip curled. "My previous orders are rescinded. Stand down from flight stations and remain in orbital mode. Prepare a Priority Black hyperchannel link to Cardassia Prime and connect it to my quarters."

"Sir?" Confusion was evident in the other man's voice. *"We are not leaving?"*

"No, Dukat. There's been a change in the mission."

The applause faded away, and Jas nodded into it, maintaining the same careful expression of studied intellect that he had grown up seeing on his father's face. Camera drones drifted over the assembled dignitaries like untethered balloons, moving this way and that so the view of the podium could be transmitted to screens around Bajor. Unlike the relative privacy of the *Eleda* memorial, this was a big affair, outside the keep walls in the gardens where the city and the plains beyond were clearly visible as a backdrop. The setting was a good bit of theater, and Jas made a mental note to compliment Lonnic on her deft placement of the stands. His gaze ranged over the faces around him and he forced himself not to dwell on the gray expressions of the Cardassians. Even after weeks of seeing the aliens in the corridors of the castle and elsewhere, he was still finding it difficult to adjust to them; but he was a politician and he was experienced at concealing things.

He launched into the concluding part of his speech. "And so, it gives me great pleasure to announce that our new friends from Cardassia will join us here in Korto District on a permanent basis, so that we might learn from one another and build a stronger understanding between our two peoples." Jas gestured toward the plains; from this distance a good eye would be able to pick out the square of land marked for construction, purchased by the aliens through Kubus Oak's corporate holdings. "This enclave will be a symbol of friendship and cooperation, and an opportunity for Bajor to look beyond her own horizons, to the galaxy beyond." There was more applause, and the minister bowed slightly before stepping away from the podium. Regal in her full formal robes, Kai Meressa stepped up to take his place, with the Oralian cleric Hadlo at her side. As they stepped past one another, Jas could not fail to notice that the fatigued, wary cast to the old man's features—so evident when the aliens had first arrived more than a month ago—was gone, replaced by a new, boundless confidence. The kai reflected the same energy and passion; Jas had no doubts that anyone here did not understand that the enclave had only come to be because of her single-minded drive to make it happen.

Verin had opposed the proposal to welcome the Cardassian priests from the moment Meressa had announced it on the floor of the forum in Ashalla. Jas recalled the stony cast to the First Minister's face as the kai had given a heartfelt entreaty to the Chamber of Ministers; while she talked of "hands across the stars" and twinned faiths, Jas stole a glance at Kubus and found the other minister smiling to himself. Kubus had been correct when he had told Jas that the Prophets would provide the impetus for a Bajoran-Cardassian treaty, and that was exactly what had happened. For his part, Verin all but called the kai naïve and did his best to exercise his influence to reject the proposal. *But Bajor is a world of the faithful,* thought Jas, *and the word of the kai carries greater weight than a politician's ever could. She spoke with the will of the people and the clergy behind her.*

He wondered if Verin Kolek understood where his isolationist outlook had taken him; with a little over a year remaining in his term of office as First Minister, his defiance of Meressa and his continued intransigence toward the offworlders had done nothing but weaken his position in the eyes of the people and the other ministers. Verin's political allies were leaving his side one by one, shifting to follow the same path as Jas and Kubus; foremost among them was Lale Usbor, a moderate from Tamulna. He was everything Verin was not—warm and open, thoughtful and considerate. Kubus was already talking about Lale in terms of the elections, grooming the man for high office. The current First Minister would not return to that posting for another term, that was as clear as the sky. It was telling that Lale was here at the ceremony and Verin was not; the First Minister had cited some poor reason not be in Korto for the announcement, but it was a snub, pure and simple. Jas imagined Verin fuming in his office in Ashalla, unable to comprehend why the people were ignoring his conservative counsel; for all the man's political acumen, at heart Verin was a staid, inflexible traditionalist. It was remarkable how the arrival of the Cardassians had rotted the roots of the old man's power. Bajor was fascinated by the aliens and wanted to know them, while the First Minister just wanted them gone.

Hadlo and Meressa were speaking of the great import of this moment, of the historic coming together of two cultures and two faiths, of their hopes that the Korto Enclave would be the first of many. Jas nodded in all the right places, just as he knew he should, but inwardly he was elsewhere. The churn of anxiety had returned, the questions rolling over one another in his thoughts. *Is this the right path? Am I making a mistake?* He caught Kubus looking at him, and the Minister for Qui'al gave him a shallow nod. The other man had wasted not a moment in applying his political and business capital to the development of the Oralian enclave, and Jas was going along with him. For better or for worse, Korto was now at the center of things on Bajor. Where that would lead his city was something that Jas Holza could not predict, and the thought chilled and excited him in equal measure.

The reception inside the Naghai Keep was, if anything, more opulent than the gathering laid on for the Cardassians on their first arrival. Dukat ate and drank nothing, feasting instead on his own frosty anger. Not for the first time, he wondered if Gul Kell was deliberately placing him in circumstances that would test the dalin's patience. The dalin had grown increasingly withdrawn and sullen since his commander's abrupt alteration of orders. One moment Dukat had been there on the bridge, ready to give the word that would take the *Kornaire* back home—he had Athra's face in his mind's eye, and the reality would be only a day or two away at high warp—and the next Kell had told him to stand down.

How many times had he run the holograph rod through the player since then? How many messages had he sent to his father, to the medical clinic in Lakat, without answer? Every day they remained here was like razors over Dukat's flesh, the wounds worsened by the silence from the home-world. *Only communications of a military nature.* He hated that phrase. And Kell, constantly pushing him and gently mocking him, denying him even a moment to step back from his duties and look to his family. For a Cardassian, it was torture, and Kell knew it.

Is he pushing me to see how much it will take to have me break? There was cold malice in his commander's behavior. Kell knew as well as Dukat did that now that the Bajor mission was hailed as a success on the homeworld, Dukat would be rewarded for his part in it. The promotion he deserved would finally come to him; and so in one last attempt to spite his first officer, Kell wanted to make Dukat lose his control. He glared at the gul across the chamber. *Nothing would make him happier than to sign off my last performance report under his command with a negative rating. I will not give him the satisfaction.*

His comcuff chimed, and Dukat raised his wrist to his mouth. "Responding."

"Skrain?" Although it went against military regulations, although it would have given Kell exactly the excuse to chastise Dukat if he had been aware of it, in sympathy to his plight, Pa'Dar had agreed to do what he could to assist the dalin in keeping lines of communication open to Cardassia. However, for the most part the man's contacts at the Ministry of Science had been able to give him little more information than the censored government newsfeeds that played in the *Kornaire's* common room.

But now the tenor of Pa'Dar's voice made Dukat go tense. He heard something there that made his bones chill. "Kotan. What is it?"

There was a pause as the civilian tried to find a way to frame his next sentence. *"Skrain . . . one of the adjutants from the medical division was conducting a survey this week, of the fallout from the situation in Lakat. They showed my colleagues records from the clinic . . ."*

The room around him seemed to become hazy and indistinct. Dukat heard the rumble of his blood in his ears, the chatter of the voices merging into incoherence. His boots felt rooted to the spot.

"I'd left some messages to contact me if anything matched . . . if there were any names . . ." He sighed. *"Your father ensured that the data would find its way to me."*

"Tell me," Dukat said in a leaden whisper.

"Your wife was released from medical care four days ago. She has made a full recovery."

"My son?" he demanded.

When Pa'Dar spoke again, it was as if the marble floor of the keep was yawning open to swallow him whole. *"The data indicates . . . an unnamed male child of the Dukat clan perished from complications due to a lack of medical supplies. I'm so sorry, Skrain."*

Dukat blinked and for an instant the haze faded. He saw Hadlo leaving the chamber through the door to the east tower. Then he was moving forward, propelled by a building surge of heat in his chest, a furious anger that shattered the cold cage he had built to contain it. His hands tightened into claws as the raw need for revenge swept away everything else in his mind.

Darrah Mace turned the corner on the lower level of the east tower, grateful for the opportunity to do something as straightforward as a foot patrol. The pomp and circumstance of the reception and the announcement made him uncomfortable. Too many people, too big an area to cover adequately, too much chance that some moron would turn up and make trouble. There had been some posturing on the planetary comnet by a few of the usual suspects, from the crackpots to the more serious activists like the Alliance for Global Unity, all of them decrying the arrival of the aliens; but then there were just as many lunatic postings by people who welcomed the Cardassians, and some in ways that were less than seemly. With Colonel Coldri's help, Darrah had put on extra security to ensure the offworlders were well protected from both the people who wanted them gone and the ones who wanted to bask in their glory.

Those thoughts fell from his mind when he almost collided with one of the black-armored aliens as he rounded a bend in the corridor. He jerked back with an automatic apology on his lips; then he recognized the face. "Dalin Dukat?"

The Cardassian blinked. He seemed distracted. "Constable Darrah."

Something rang an alarm bell in Darrah's mind. The seasoned lawman's sense for people was giving him a warning, but it was difficult for him to map it to the alien's body language. He didn't know the Cardassians well enough to be sure, but there was anger in Dukat's eyes. He looked as if he were moving with purpose, and the intention behind it was not a benign one.

"I'm looking for the cleric. Hadlo."

Darrah nodded. "He passed me a moment ago. Going up to the guest chambers, I think." He moved slightly so that Dukat couldn't simply walk past him. Darrah frowned and took a chance. "You're walking like you have a quarrel with the man."

Dukat's eyes flashed, and Darrah saw a wary mask drop into place over his expression. "I need to speak to him."

In that moment, Darrah knew his instincts were correct. "Well," he said, "don't let me stop you, then." He didn't move, and Dukat stepped out to pass around him. "Strange, though," Darrah continued. "Pardon me if I'm wrong, but you don't strike me as the kind of man who'd spend much time at temple."

Dukat took a few more steps and hesitated. "I'm not. I have unfinished business with the cleric."

"Right." Darrah watched him carefully. *"Unfinished business.* I see that kind of thing a lot in my line of work." He chuckled dryly. "I guess you could say it's kind of a flaw in the Bajoran character, if you get my meaning. We're a passionate people, you know? Sometimes we get so angry about things we lose focus on everything else. Especially when it's a matter of unfinished business." The constable shook his head. "We hold those kinds of grudges forever."

For a moment, he thought the Cardassian was going to say something to him. Instead, the alien turned away and walked up the stone steps to the upper tiers. Darrah blew out a breath, his hand over the phaser in his holster. *If they kill each other, does that count as a diplomatic incident?*

The door slammed open and Hadlo looked up from the flask of water on the table before him. He put down the half-full glass and presented the intruder with a smile.

"Dalin Dukat. Here you are again. You're making a habit of this." In the next second the insouciant expression on the cleric's lined face was gone as Dukat's hand clamped around his neck. He was forced to the window of the chamber, air tightening in his lungs. "What are you doing?" he wheezed. "Release me!"

"My son is dead because of you," The other man bit out the words with icy, quiet fury. "You think you can play with people's lives like pieces on a game board? What gives you the right?"

In spite of himself, Hadlo's face creased in amusement and he began to laugh gruffly through the dalin's viselike grip. "Can it be that an officer in the homeworld's military is too unsophisticated to grasp the very nature of his own species? Are you that raw and untempered, Dukat, that you do not understand?" His laughter intensified, and the other man grimaced, shoving him away.

"I should kill you," Dukat growled. "Crush the life from you and then do the same to those other spineless zealots who hang on the hem of your robes!"

Hadlo straightened himself, brushing dust from the front of his clothing. "But you won't," he replied, taking a sip of water. "The Oralian Way is the bridge to Bajor now. *I* am that bridge, Dukat. If you have any loyalty to Cardassia, you will understand that. I will live, because it benefits Cardassia to have me live." He eyed the officer. "And as much as you are your child's father, you are Cardassia's loyal son first, yes? As am I." Hadlo put down the glass and walked to stand before Dukat. He tipped his head back to expose his neck. His hands were at his sides; the cleric presented the most open target for the dalin's furious ire. "Make your choice, Dukat. What devotion sings loudest? Vengeance for a child that did not live or greater glory for your world and your species?"

The priest felt a stab of fear as he saw something harden in Dukat's eyes, and he wondered if he had gone too far; but then the soldier's tightened fists fell open and he turned away.

Hadlo sighed. "I regret the passing of your child. I promise I will dedicate a prayer to Oralius in his memory."

Dukat turned back to throw him a look, his hooded eyes glittering. "We will talk of this again, priest. And on that day, your faith will not protect you."

Evening was drawing in as Gar Osen wandered the ornamental gardens, turning the events of the day over in his mind. At the side of the reflecting pool, he saw a familiar figure, the sky-blue robes closed around Bennek as the Cardassian leaned over the shimmering surface, peering into the depths.

The alien cleric looked up as he approached. "Brother Gar. Hello."

Gar smiled tightly. He wasn't entirely comfortable with the Oralian's way of addressing the Bajoran clergy. "Bennek. I had thought you would be preparing for tomorrow." He nodded at the distant construction. "You are joining Hadlo on his inspection of the enclave site, I believe?"

"I am." The Cardassian seemed weary. Gar understood; it had been a busy few weeks. Part of him was still reeling. Barely a month ago, the offworlders had seemed little more than a distant idea, something that other people spoke of second- or thirdhand. Now they were here, on Bajor, and it seemed they would not be leaving anytime soon. "It's so peaceful here," Bennek said wistfully. "I cannot think of a place where I have ever felt such spirituality." He looked back at the pool. "Cardassia has nothing to match this, Gar. As much as I love my homeworld, it has become a hostile place for our beliefs. I relish the chance to engage the Way in a place where I can honestly think upon it . . . instead of listening with fear for the sound of our persecutors' footfalls."

"I am glad we can help you . . ." Gar said warily. "The kai believes we can learn much from one another."

Bennek nodded. "I have spoken to my brethren on Cardassia Prime. Pilgrim ships are being prepared. They will come to seek knowledge . . ." His voice dropped. "And perhaps, a small measure of sanctuary."

How many? The question leapt to the front of Gar's mind, but before he would voice it the alien came forward with one of his own.

"What would you do, Prylar, if your faith were in danger? If the Prophets were being threatened?"

Gar blinked at the sudden intensity of the query, and he answered without thinking, from the heart. "My faith is greater than I am. I would do whatever I had to do to protect it."

Bennek looked up, and Gar could see his eyes were fixed on the distant site of the enclave. "Yes," he whispered, "as shall I."

FIVE YEARS AGO

◆ ◆ ◆

2323 (Terran Calendar)

8

"**My** client categorically denies all charges." The words were firm and clear, and they carried across the courtroom to Darrah Mace as he slipped quietly through the door.

The speaker was a thin, austere woman; she was of that indeterminate approaching-middle-age that Mace found so hard to pin down. Bajoran females got older in different ways than their men, and even after his years in the police service Darrah was never comfortable when he was called upon to guess a woman's age. He usually ended up offending someone.

It was warm inside the windowless room; they were a level below the entrance atrium of the Korto City Watch Precinct, sandwiched between the duty offices and the holding cells below. In theory, the building kept all the city's law and order operations under one roof; in practice, it was inadequate to the task. The poor ventilation was just one of the reasons Darrah didn't venture down here that much. Since rising up the ranks to inspector status, there wasn't often call for it. He needed a good reason to be here; and today his good reason sat in the dock, looking equally angry and mournful.

The public defender continued, and as she did so Darrah placed her face. *Els Renora*. She was an acid, waspish sort, but she did her job well. "I would point out to the court that scans of Captain Syjin's ship revealed no traces of the materials he was accused of transporting. At best, what we have is circumstantial evidence of an alleged crime backed up by hearsay." She drew herself up. "I move for a dismissal."

A squat Cardassian got to his feet from the prosecution's bench and wandered past the magistrate, gesturing at the air. "All those scans prove is that the accused is very good at cleaning up his vessel." The alien lawyer sniffed. "The fact remains. Quantities of *maraji* crystals were found in the domiciles of pilgrims at the Korto Enclave. When questioned, they positively identified this man as the trader who provided them."

"I'm a freighter captain, not a drug dealer!" Syjin snapped, his voice high and tight. "I never touch that kind of cargo!" He bared his teeth. "And I know the law! That stuff isn't illegal on Bajor anyway, not that I would carry it, because I wouldn't!"

The prosecutor gave him a sideways look. "No. But it *is* illegal in the Cardassian Union, and according to the terms of the alliance between our two worlds, the enclaves are classed as Cardassian territory, where our legal codes apply."

Els shot Syjin a glare. "Be quiet," she told him, "you're not helping."

"I counter the defense's request with a demand that Syjin feel the full weight of that law and be turned over to Cardassian authorities for legal processing." The prosecutor paused, letting that sink in. "I ask the magistrate this: Are you really willing to damage the goodwill that has built up between Cardassia and Bajor over the last five years for the sake of an untrustworthy—"

Syjin started to complain, but Els silenced him with a curt gesture.

"—and petty delinquent with a record of many criminal infractions? Release him to Cardassian justice, and the truth will be determined swiftly and immediately."

The woman faced her opponent. "I think we've all heard about the *swiftness* of Cardassian justice," she said coldly. "But Captain Syjin is a Bajoran, and this is a matter for Bajorans to resolve."

The magistrate, a heavyset woman with dark skin and a mane of gray hair, regarded Syjin severely. "Your point it well-taken, Ms. Els, but the conservator is correct. The captain has a record of many minor infractions, up to and including the transportation of proscribed materials."

"We're talking about simple food items here, Magistrate," said Els. "My client's past infractions, the most recent of which occurred more than four years ago, were minor deeds that incurred fines, not the transit of highly addictive narcotics, and he has answered for those."

"Nevertheless," continued the magistrate, "unless there are mitigating circumstances—"

Darrah was on his feet and striding forward. "I'll vouch for him."

Syjin's face flushed with relief, and his defender's eyebrow arched. "Inspector Darrah Mace of the Korto City Watch," noted Els. "A highly respected law officer."

"And a personal friend of the captain," said the Cardassian. "Hardly a neutral voice."

Darrah ignored the alien and looked directly at the magistrate. "I've known this man since we were children. He's had his issues with the law—the Prophets know, I've been the one to arrest him once or twice—but Syjin's not that kind of smuggler. The sort of crime you're describing—it's beyond his character to perpetrate."

"Then how do you propose we deal with this situation, Inspector?" asked the magistrate.

"At the very least, he should be incarcerated and his vessel dismantled," snapped the conservator.

Darrah continued. "I recommend a full investigation. Captain Syjin may retain his master's license for the interim, but he should be prohibited from leaving the system until a conclusion is reached. The Watch will have his vessel held in impound."

"*What?*" Syjin bleated, but in the next second he realized that Darrah was saving him from life in a Cardassian penal facility, and he fell silent.

The magistrate mulled his words for a long moment. "Very well," she nodded. "Inspector Darrah, I'm releasing Captain Syjin into the custody of the City Watch. If your investigation comes up empty, he will be free to return to his business. If not, then we will reconvene and discuss sentencing." She stood up. "This hearing is concluded."

In the corridor Els approached him, with Syjin following behind. The pilot's face was flushed with emotion. "Thanks for the assist, Inspector," said the woman. "He's lucky he has friends like you to look out for him."

"You think the Cardassians will keep pressing this?"

She shook her head. "They wanted a quick and clean conviction, someone to blame the misdeeds of their own people on. You denied them that, so I imagine this whole thing will quietly go away . . . just like the Oralians they *caught* with those crystals." She said the word in a way that told Darrah she had little faith in the veracity of the Cardassian prosecution.

"Damn spoonheads . . ." Syjin bit out the words. "Why did they pick on me? All I did was bring in some cases of *yamok* sauce!" He ground his teeth. "*Kosst,* if they take my ship I'll have nothing!"

"Calm down," said Darrah. "You're grounded for a while, that's all."

Syjin met his gaze, and he saw fury in his friend's eyes. "I'd never touch that filth, Mace. You believe me, don't you?"

"Of course I do, you idiot. Do you think I would have

spoken up for you if I thought you were trafficking in drugs? I'd have sent you down myself!"

The shock and adrenaline of the moment made the pilot's voice shaky. "I was a breath away from it. My own people would have given me up to the aliens, just to keep them happy! Is that how it is? Are the Cardassians making the law on Bajor now?"

Darrah and Els exchanged glances. Both of them had seen similar incidents recently, with the government backing down in favor of Cardassian interests when push came to shove. These days, it seemed more and more that the Union had a hand in things on Bajor. Darrah felt a stab of guilt; his own promotion and raises in pay had come in part from his work as security coordinator for the Korto Enclave. He placed a hand on his friend's shoulder. "Look, just be grateful. Go see Gar in the temple and thank the Prophets your luck is still holding."

"I'll do what I can to expedite the investigation," added Els.

"Good—" Darrah's words were cut off by the chime of his communicator. He tapped the badge. "This is Darrah, go ahead."

"Boss, it's me." Proka Migdal's voice grumbled from the air. *"You wanted me to remind you about the pickup."*

Darrah frowned. "So I did. Thank you, Constable. Darrah out." He glanced at Els and Syjin. "I've got to get to Ashalla, I'm handling Minister Jas's protection detail today."

Syjin took his hand and squeezed it. "Thanks, Mace. I'll make this up to you, I swear it."

Darrah gave his friend a nod. "You can count on that."

The flyer was on the primary pad out behind the precinct building, and Proka had ensured that it was prepped and ready to go. Two officers from the constable's division were already aboard, running last-second security checks. Unlike

Darrah's ochre tunic, they wore lighter shades, and each man had a dermal induction communicator adhered to a spot on their mastoid bone; the device allowed the bodyguards to keep both hands free while still in contact with the police comm net. Darrah slipped into the pilot's chair and cleared his flight plan, taking the aircraft up in a swift vertical climb.

The flyer was quick off the mark, far more speedy than the older model aeros he had piloted after first joining Korto's Watch. He glanced at the thruster controls and saw the circular operator pads that were distinctive of Cardassian-made technology. Ion thrusters, impulse drives, and warp engines were among the most popular imports from the Union. An indicator flashed on his panel, and Darrah eased the throttle bar forward, guiding the police flyer around in a half loop to turn it eastward, toward the Perikian Mountains and the capital city beyond.

Korto flashed past underneath, the sharp silver towers and the low golden domes catching the midday rays of B'hava'el. Darrah drifted to the edge of the flight corridor, humming over the open parks and the square emerald patches of the municipal lakes. The outer districts thinned and they passed the city limits; then a few moments later the flyer was nearing the Cardassian enclave. Immediately, a traffic warning signal blinked on Darrah's panel, informing him to divert around the airspace over the area. Of course, as a law officer Darrah could have legally entered the zone without needing any of the clearances required of a civilian flyer, but without a good cause he would find himself up on charges for doing so.

Pivoting the aircraft so that he could watch the enclave roll by, Darrah studied the sprawl of the oval patch of thermoconcrete with its hard-edged structures. It had none of the poetry of Bajoran architecture; all the Cardassian buildings were squat and functional, hugging the ground, glittering dully in the daylight. What open areas there were within the outer fences were covered with wide smartplastic pavilions and bubbletents. In his dealings with the Cardassians and the Oralians—he found himself thinking of them that way, as two separate entities—Darrah had often been inside the enclave, but he had always felt he didn't know the full extent of it. The space had grown in five years from the original square of land a few hundred *tessipates* in size, but the aliens seemed careful not to encroach toward Korto. The farmers whose plainsland fields they had purchased were happy to sell up, gaining a lifetime's worth of money in one transaction, doubtless moving to the coast, where the weather was always fine and they didn't have to grub in the dirt for a living.

The Korto Enclave was the first and it was the largest Cardassian holding on the planet; but it wasn't the only one. The aliens had brought a new kind of prosperity with them, and several city-states were only too pleased to follow the model of Korto in order to have a taste of it. Qui'al, Kubus Oak's district, had a sizable outpost; so did Tamulna, Hathon, Gallitep, and Karnoth, with the latest zone currently being laid down in Tozhat. Oralian pilgrim ships and Cardassian freighters were a common sight over Bajor, the reptilian shapes of the vessels moving in and out of the docking bays at the Cemba commerce station in high orbit. At the corner of his eye, Darrah saw a shape moving in the sky, dropping toward the port in Korto: a Cardassian cargo lighter. The aliens had been pressing the council of ministers for a while about Bajor's customs regulations, citing the need to bring their ships straight down to the enclaves instead of passing through local port security. Darrah remained firm on that issue, as did a lot of the ministers in the capital; but he knew that nothing would prevent the aliens from using matter transporters to simply beam materials to the surface if they wished to. *And what might they want to deliver that they don't want us to see?*

He shook off the grim thought and angled the nose of the flyer toward the eastern horizon.

Lonnic Tomo's gaze drifted up to the observation galleries above the forum's floor, and she was surprised to see there was hardly anyone up there. Certainly, she'd expected there to be correspondents from the media services, but instead there were only a few official faces, security personnel and the like. On her level, in the center of the triangular space that was the focus of the Chamber of Ministers, Kubus Oak was gesturing and talking in that hard-edged, gruff voice of his. Security had been tightened once again, and Lonnic wondered if he was disappointed his performance would not be broadcast planetwide. To say that Kubus enjoyed the glare of publicity was an understatement; he basked in it, and he knew how to use it to his advantage, unlike her employer, who sat quietly before her between Kalem Apren, the minister for Hedrikspool, and the young Militia officer Jaro Essa. Jas Holza kept his own counsel more and more these days. At times Lonnic felt they were just drifting, going where the winds of Bajor's politicking took them.

"Five years," Kubus said, the glimmer of a smile on his lips. "Hardly the smallest blink of time when measured against the great legacy of our civilization's history. And yet, in that small span, so much has happened to change the way that Bajor sees her place in the universe." He spread his hands. "I'm not afraid to say that we were in danger of becoming insular. Inward-looking and stagnant. But the Union trade alliance we forged and the clergy's historic enclave partnership brought new understanding to our planet."

Kubus walked toward the apex of the triangle, to the short bench where the First Minister and his adjutants sat.

Lit from behind by a single thin window that let in Bajor's daylight, Lale Usbor was the picture of studious, careful thought. He was nodding in all the right places, giving exactly the right impression at exactly the right time. *How such an unremarkable man ever made it to that high office I'll never know.* But that was a lie; Lonnic *did* know. Lale became First Minister after Verin Kolek's landslide defeat, and that had been on the back of the pro-expansionist, pro-openness, pro-Cardassian factions guided by Kubus, Jas, and the ministers swayed by the bright-eyed words of Kai Meressa.

Lonnic's eyes fell on the woman, seated across the forum with several other figures from the Vedek Assembly. Five years, and the time had not been kind to the kai. The vital and passionate priest that Lonnic remembered from the Korto Enclave's dedication ceremony was a shadow of her former self, pale and drawn, in robes that seemed to swamp her. Once in a while, she would speak and there would be flashes of the old Meressa, but for the most part the kai allowed her adjutant Ranjen Arin to speak for the church. Lonnic looked away. Yerrin syndrome was an uncommon illness and it didn't kill you all at once. Meressa had promised to continue to fulfill her role as kai for as long as she was able, and for that at least Lonnic was thankful. She couldn't imagine someone like Arin taking her place. He was too easily swayed by the currents of popular opinion.

"Can anyone deny that our stronger relationship with our Cardassian neighbors has *not* been beneficial?" Kubus was asking. "The aftermath of the hurricanes that struck Musilla Province last year would have claimed many more lives, if not for the advanced medical technology our first responders now possess. We have new sensing systems. Cardassian-designed warp cores give our starships greater reach."

A man with a shock of dark hair and a thick brow made

a derisive noise in the back of his throat; it wasn't loud, but in the clear air of the chamber it was enough for everyone in the room to hear it. Kubus paused and turned to face the other politician. "Minister Keeve Falor seems to have something to say," he said, with an arch sniff.

Keeve. Lonnic had heard the man speak several times and had been impressed by his directness and refusal to compromise. She might have been able to admit that she admired the minister a little, if not for the fact that he had become a persistent thorn in the side of the pro-alliance factions. Keeve embodied the character of many ordinary Bajorans, the son of a merchant who had married into a higher *D'jarra* and used his connections to get him elected to public office. He was a staunch nationalist, adamant that Bajor should be free to choose its own future unfettered by alien influences. Kubus liked to paint his opponent as a reactionary in the mold of former First Minister Verin, as a borderline xenophobe, but in reality Keeve was nothing so unsophisticated.

"You say Bajor has benefited, Minister Kubus," Keeve replied, "but perhaps it would be more honest to say that the city of Qui'al, the Kubus clan, and their allies have benefited the most. Those technologies of which you speak, yes, they did help our people at Musilla, but where were they during the mine collapse at Undalar? What good did swifter ships do for the colonists who were forced to abandon the Golana settlement?" Lonnic saw Jas stiffen at the last statement, but her employer said nothing. Keeve continued. "Perhaps these circumstances were not given greater priority because they were not interests of yours."

"Minister Keeve," said Lale. "That is quite an inflammatory statement. I would be careful to cast such aspersions in this august forum. The issues behind the Undalar accident and the withdrawal from Golana are well documented, and they had nothing to do with Minister Kubus."

"That, sir," Keeve said tightly, "is a matter of perspective."

For an instant, Lonnic's attention was drawn away by someone moving in the gallery. She saw Darrah Mace enter and take a seat next to another man in a Militia uniform.

"Commander Jekko," Darrah said quietly, giving the other officer's hand a firm shake. "Are you well?"

"Inspector," came the reply. "The Prophets are keeping me safe." The other man had an oval face with a white stubble of beard and sparse hair. He didn't take his eyes off the forum below. "How's Karys and the cubs?"

"They're good. Not so much cubs anymore, though. Bajin's growing into a fine example of a moody teenager, and Nell spends my money almost as fast as my wife does."

"Ah, fatherhood," said Jekko dryly.

Darrah scanned the room and found Lonnic and Jas. "I miss anything?"

Jekko shook his head. "Kubus Oak preening some. Nothing you haven't seen before." He paused. "You still got Proka Migdal on your team?" Darrah nodded. "Huh. You tell him, he gets tired of rubbing shoulders with Cardassians, I've got a post for him on my detail. You're wasting him over there in Korto."

Darrah sniffed. "Yeah, I'll be sure to pass that on. Or not." He nodded at Keeve Falor, who was in the midst of a terse response to something Kubus had said. "Why do you want to entice my men over to you, anyhow? You getting bored with the close protection stuff? The way Keeve rubs people the wrong way, I'll bet there's no shortage of folks you have to keep him safe from."

"He's a firebrand, that much is certain," said Jekko. "But these days I'm doing more of the adjutant stuff, less of the bodyguard." His fingers drummed on his right knee; the other man had taken a Nausicaan knife there during a stop-and-search when the two of them were only a few years out of the Militia academy. The injury had never really healed correctly. "And a good gun hand is always hard to find."

Darrah leaned closer. "Maybe *you* should come work for *me*. Benefits of rank and all, I'm sure I could call in some favors to get you an assignment—"

Jekko snorted. "I don't think so. Too many spoonheads in Korto for my liking. Don't trust them. Never have."

Darrah's lip twisted. "What, and you think *I* do? This is me you're talking about, Darrah Mace. I'd arrest the Emissary himself if he looked shifty."

Jekko gave him a sideways look. "You're a good lawman, Mace, you always have been. You got good instincts, better than me, even. It's just the other stuff you're a bit slack with."

Keeve was on his feet now, his voice pitched at a level that matched Kubus's resonant tones. "Minister, perhaps you could consider for one moment addressing the negative implications of the alliance. Instead of glossing over them?"

Kubus frowned. "I'm sure you would be more than happy to do that for me."

"The so-called bounty from Cardassia does not arrive on our shores out of the goodness of their alien hearts," Keeve replied. "Minerals and precious metals from our star system are migrating across the border to the Cardassian Union at an increasing rate. Kelbonite and mizainite ore from our moons, uridium from Bajor herself, and I have been made aware that the Detapa Council has been petitioning for some time to have those quotas increased."

"It's only fair that we pay for what we are given," Kubus retorted. "We supply the Cardassians, and they supply us."

"And how long do we let that continue?" Keeve looked around, and Lonnic saw nods from his supporters. "Are we going to let these offworlders drain us dry? What happens when the ores they want become harder to locate? Will we let them turn tracts of our land into mine works?" He glared at Kubus. "Such things have already happened in Qui'al District, as I understand."

"What my clan does with our holdings is not a matter I wish to discuss," said the other minister.

Abruptly, the priest at Kai Meressa's side rose. "If the chamber pleases, I would like to interject. The discussion here dwells too much on the material." Ranjen Arin puffed out his chest. "You are ignoring the great spiritual interchange that has come from our friendship with the offworlders. The insights of the Oralian pilgrims have brought new light to our understanding of the Prophets and our faith."

Keeve shot Arin a measuring stare. "Forgive me, Ranjen, but I am only an ordinary man and not blessed with such great knowledge of the Prophets as you are. All I see are these so-called pilgrims bringing *their* faith and who knows what other things to our planet." He placed his hands on the table before him. "If they are so open, sir, then why do they keep to those enclaves? How can they learn from us and we from them if they are isolated?"

"The path to the Celestial Temple." There was a moment of silence before everyone on the floor of the chamber realized the words were spoken by the kai. "It can only be opened by those with open hearts, open minds. The Prophets know this, and we must know it too."

Keeve's expression hardened, and Lonnic wondered if he would be willing to speak against someone so venerated and respected as Kai Meressa. "Some of us do not see that path as clearly as you do," he replied finally, returning to his seat.

First Minister Lale cleared his throat, breaking the tension of the awkward moment. "We have drifted from the issue. I have called this meeting in order to allow debate on a new matter relating to the Bajoran-Cardassian agreement." He nodded to Kubus. "Minister? If you will continue?"

"Thank you," said the politician smoothly. "Jagul Danig Kell of the Cardassian Union has brought forward an offer from his superiors to further cement the close association between our two species. We have all heard of the incidents in recent months relating to piracy and loss of our shipping. We are all aware that the aggressive and secretive Tzenkethi Coalition are expanding their sphere of influence into the Bajor Sector." He looked at Jaro Essa. "And for all the hard work and selfless sacrifice of our brave men and women in the Militia Space Guard, we have only so many ships to go around. Not enough to protect every civilian vessel."

Jaro's stony face never showed a flicker of expression, but Lonnic could see the stiffening of tendons in the officer's neck; Kubus was, regrettably, quite correct.

"To that end, the Second Order of the Cardassian Central Command has offered to place a squadron of its cruisers on station in Bajoran space." A ripple of debate followed the statement, but Kubus kept speaking. "The ever-present threat of the Tzenkethi alone shows the merit in such a generous gesture."

"A squadron?" said Kalem Apren. "How many vessels is that, exactly?"

"Standard Cardassian deployment would be six to eight starships, plus support vessels," Jaro said flatly.

Lonnic glanced at Jas. The minister remained silent, adding nothing to the debate, only watching.

"Eight or more alien warships?" Keeve retorted. "In sight of Bajor, on a permanent footing? Is that what you are proposing?" He shook his head. "There are more than enough Cardassian vessels in our space as it is, acting as 'escorts' to their freighters." The minister gestured to Jaro, and his tone turned acid. "I would suggest that instead of accepting this *gracious* offer, we instead divert matériel and energy from trade issues toward accelerating construction of defense vessels of our own!"

Jaro nodded slowly. "I agree. A strong Bajor is an armed Bajor."

Keeve mirrored Jaro's motion. "Would it not be better for Bajoran interests to be protected by Bajoran starships?"

"What you suggest is already in motion, Minister Keeve," said Lale mildly, seemingly unperturbed by the other man's building irritation. "But it will take time to complete and deploy new wings of assault ships and corvettes."

"The Cardassian offer could serve as an interim measure," Kubus broke in. "It would be a great benefit."

"For us?" Keeve retorted. "Or for them?"

The ministers dispersed across the chamber's atrium, and Lonnic walked with Jas, scanning the faces of the other men. Predictably, there had been no conclusion to the matter of the Cardassian offer; the issue would be debated again and again until one faction or another gained enough momentum to resolve it. She saw Darrah in conversation with the officer from the gallery, the two of them standing in the shadow of one of the tall statues that held up the roof of the domed chamber. Each figure represented a lawmaker or leader from the various Republics. She found herself wondering what opinions they might have had of the circumstances currently unfolding on their homeworld.

Darrah nodded a farewell to the other officer—a commander, she noticed—and crossed to them. Past the inspector's shoulder, Lonnic saw Minister Keeve talking to the other man. "Mace," she said quietly, "you know him?"

"Jekko?" He nodded. "We served together. We came up through the academy as squadmates."

She was going to say more, but Jas pushed past her and

approached Keeve. Lonnic saw something in her employer's eyes that she couldn't read.

"Falor," began the minister.

The other man hesitated. "Holza." His voice was cool and unwelcoming.

Jas struggled to find the right words. "I want you to understand my position in this—"

Keeve held up a hand to silence him. "I respect your clan and what you've done for your district, Holza, and because of that I'm willing to stand in the same room as you. But if you're coming to me now in hopes that I'll go back on what I said in there, you're sadly mistaken."

"It isn't that," Jas replied, frowning.

Keeve continued. "I know there are some ministers who will put on a show in the forum and then speak differently when they're behind closed doors. I'm not one of them." He leaned in. "Kubus and Lale are weakening Bajor, and if you're not opposing them, you're aiding them." The minister turned to walk away.

"We can have this alliance and still keep our independence," insisted Jas.

Keeve spoke again without looking back. "I'm certain you believe that."

Darrah felt compelled to break the moment of awkward silence and gestured with his hand. "Minister? Your flyer's this way, if you'd follow me."

Jas nodded distractedly, "Yes, Darrah. Of course."

Darrah couldn't help but notice Kubus Oak's level stare as they walked back across the atrium. The inspector kept a watchful eye, scanning the room for anything that might be a threat, just as his orders stated. From behind, he caught the fringes of a hushed conversation between his friend and the minister.

"There's a part of me that cannot disagree with Falor,"

Jas was saying. "I feel responsible, Tomo. I helped open the gates to the Cardassians."

"You did what you thought was right," Lonnic returned.

"Did I?" Darrah heard the morose note in the man's voice. "Today I wonder."

The inspector looked again, his gaze once more finding Kubus. He was smiling and talking quietly with Ranjen Arin; of the kai there was no sign. There was a voice in the back of Darrah's thoughts, the old, automatic deference his *D'jarra* imposed upon him, something telling him to concentrate on matters that were in his purview and not these issues that soared far above his rank. Except, he couldn't let it go. Perhaps Jas was right, perhaps it was his responsibility; but then a look at Kubus Oak told Darrah that this situation would have come to be even without the support of Jas Holza. A man like Kubus was not one to have his agenda brushed aside. He frowned as they walked onto the flyer pads. "Sir? Back to the keep?"

Jas shook his head. "No. I need some time to think. The coastal villa, Inspector. Take me to my retreat."

9

After several days in the cargo compartments of the *Lhemor*, there were still instances when Bennek felt overwhelmed by the stale odor of chemical sealants and old rust. The freighter creaked and groaned like a man with diseased lungs; last night, after vespers, with gallows humor Pasir had opined that the corrosion was all that held the decrepit starship together. This was the fourth journey the *Lhemor* had made from Cardassia Prime to Bajor, and Bennek was quietly amazed that it had survived even one.

"Oralius protects," he said aloud, and he hoped she would continue to do so. He worked his way down the narrow companionway from the storage spaces to what passed for the crew decks. The cleric hardly ever saw the freighter's small complement of staff. Civilians all, they spent most of their time at their duty stations and ventured into the rear compartments only if there was a problem. They had been paid reasonable wages for their service aboard the vessel, but the Way's limited reach in Cardassian society meant that the people the church could employ tended to be either members of the congregation or those who did not care where their leks came from. Bennek was convinced that the *Lhemor*'s captain remained in a state of permanent inebriation; certainly, he had never encountered the man without him stinking of *kanar*.

While the cargo compartments had been converted into rough dormitories for the faithful, there were a couple of other spaces used by the priests. Bennek let the door to one of these areas judder open in front of him and entered. It was a bare room with a simple computer console and a screen. A blinking glyph showed him that a subspace signal was being decoded, although Bennek held out little hope that the third-generation encryption software built into the communication suite would provide a challenge to the scrutiny of any Obsidian Order monitors. The cleric sat and glanced out of the room's only viewport, an oval window set in the grimy hull. Outside, stars turned to rainbow streaks of warp light swept past; and there just off the flank of the *Lhemor,* maintaining the same perfect separation and implied threat as it had throughout the flight, was the frigate *Kashai.* The warship was a continual reminder of the Central Command's presence, provided as an "escort" for the pilgrim transport but as much an overseer as it was a protector. No Oralian ship was allowed to venture into space without such a companion, and not for the first time Bennek wondered what work those ships did as they shadowed the pilgrimages.

All too often he had seen things that he was unable to explain away. Groups of men and women from churches of the Way he had never visited, who disappeared from the pilgrim groups the moment they reached Bajor. Cargo modules sealed tight, with no identification, that were there when they left Cardassia and gone when they returned. Bennek had spoken of these things several times to Hadlo, but on each occasion the senior cleric had replied with nebulous admonishments and poor justifications.

With a solemn bell tone, the screen illuminated and the old man's face peered out at him. A haze of interference made Hadlo's expression seem blurry, but there was more to it than that. The cleric was more sallow than normal, and the shadows collecting around his brow' ridges were deeper. Only his eyes seemed alive; they were animated and fierce. *"Bennek,"* he said abruptly, *"you seem disturbed. Have you been called away from something?"*

Bennek shook his head. "No, Master. The pilgrims are well, they are taking part in a reading from the Hebitian Records. Pasir is leading the group in my absence."

"Who? Pasir?" Hadlo blinked. *"Don't recall the name."*

Bennek frowned. Hadlo had personally assigned the younger priest to his group only a few months earlier, after the government had closed Pasir's temple outside Tellel on some minor technicality. The man had proven to be a deft minister, and his knowledge of the Recitations was excellent.

The old man waved a hand at the screen. *"You need to be watchful, Bennek. There have been more incidents since you left Cardassia Prime. Things are worsening."*

"What do you mean? More arrests?" The grim truth was, despite the assurances that Danig Kell had made to Hadlo five years ago, the Detapa Council and the Central Command had done little to scale back their persecution of the Oralian Way. At best, things were as bad now as they had been then; at worst, entire congregations in the outlying provinces were disappearing. More than ever, theirs was an embattled faith.

Hadlo's voice dropped to a breathy whisper. *"We can trust no man, my friend. Only Oralius can show us the way, and her face is forever hidden from us! Clouded, do you see? I alone am blessed in that I can see this for the truth it is. The serpents, Bennek! Beware of the serpents in the ruins, the ashen wilds . . ."*

Bennek's heart sank. He had put off leaving the old cleric alone for months and months, refusing Hadlo's orders to go to Bajor and take a direct hand in the running of the enclaves. His fear for his mentor's grasp on reality was very real, but it had been a long time since Hadlo had spoken of his experience at the Kendra Shrine, and Bennek had hoped he would not hear of it again. The messianic qualities of Hadlo's "visions" frightened him, and he was afraid that reason might desert his friend and teacher. Bennek had boarded the *Lhemor* because Hadlo had promised to join him on the next starship. As the old man whispered on, he realized that assurance had been forgotten as well.

"The touch of the Prophet's Tear showed much to me. I see it unfolding. There is talk of rising up against the oppressors." He ground out the words. *"A holy war."*

Bennek's blood ran cold. "That would be a mistake," he said, forcing himself to remain outwardly calm. "To do so would give our enemies the reason they crave to destroy us. If one Oralian raises his hand in anger, they would cut us down like animals . . ." His throat tightened and his gaze strayed to the window, to the threatening shape of the warship pacing them. "We must endure, Hadlo. We must exercise caution!"

The old man rubbed at his face. *"Listen. With each passing day it becomes clearer to me that our birthworld is the place of ashes. It is not safe for us here anymore. Bajor . . ."* He looked away. *"Bajor may be the only sanctuary for our faith."*

"Hadlo, I—" The screen went dark, and Bennek was startled into silence. For a moment he nursed a pang of fear, worried that something might have happened at the other end of the line, but then slowly he understood that the cleric had simply severed the link, having said what he wanted to say.

"Bennek?" He jumped at the sudden voice and turned in his chair to see Pasir at the half-open hatch. The young priest's narrow face had the same perpetual cast of eager interest it had shown on the day they had first met. "Pardon me. The door was open . . . I concluded the Recitation and I came looking for you."

"It's all right," Bennek replied, licking dry lips. "You

just startled me, that is all." He hadn't heard the cleric's approach, even though the metal decks of the *Lhemor* seemed to squeak everywhere one laid a foot.

He looked at the console. "You were speaking with Hadlo?" When Bennek nodded, he continued. "A very great man. He has done so much for the Way. He has given so much of himself to it." His expression shifted toward concern. "Is there news from Cardassia Prime? Is something wrong?"

Bennek sank deeper into the threadbare seat and sighed. "Pasir, my brother, we all face great trials. You yourself are a victim of the government's continued attempts to 'encourage' us to leave the social order."

The other man nodded. "Indeed. That is partly why I wanted so much to come to Bajor. The chance of a spiritual refuge holds great promise for me, for all of us."

"Perhaps," Bennek replied, "but we must resist isolation, on our homeworld and in the enclaves. I am afraid that our kindred do not see the whole mural, only the smallest part of the painting . . ."

"What do you mean?"

"The Detapa Council divides the branches of our faith and misinforms us, keeps us from coming together so that we might oppose them. At home we are blinded to the threats that surround us, and on Bajor those of our people in the enclaves think themselves safe." He shook his head. "I know they are not."

"But haven't the Bajoran clergy accepted our friendship? Don't their people know that we are travelers on twin paths?"

"I'm not speaking of Bajor or the Bajorans." Bennek's voice took on a gloomy tone. "I wonder, how many of our pilgrims are agents of the Obsidian Order? How much of our mission is for them and not for Oralius?"

Pasir laughed. "Spies? You know the hearts and minds

of every one of our people aboard this ship! Look at me, Bennek! Could I be a spy? Could any of us give up the Way for something so tawdry?" He placed a friendly hand on the other man's shoulder. "Our unity makes us strong. Without it, we have nothing."

Bennek saw the light of enthusiasm in the young man's eyes and it lifted his spirits. "You're right. Thank you for the clarity of your insight, Pasir. I imagine we will both need that when we reach Bajor."

He got a smile in return. "I must confess, I am greatly looking forward to meeting our Bajoran counterparts. I've read much about their Prophets and their Celestial Temple. It will be fascinating to meet with one of their priests." Pasir paused. "You spoke to me of the prylar Gar Osen. I should like to meet him."

"He is a ranjen now," Bennek corrected. "He has been granted a higher honorific, in connection to his work as a theologist and friend to the Way." He gave a nod. "He's a lot like you. He has a passion for his faith that shines on all that he does."

Pasir's smile deepened. "Then, with Oralius's grace, once this venerable old craft reaches Bajor, I hope to make his acquaintance."

Bennek shot a look at the ceiling as the deck above gave a mournful creak. "With Oralius's grace," he repeated.

Dukat peered into the discreet console on the arm of his chair, studying the image there. The display on the hooded console was arranged in such a manner that only the ship's commanding officer could see it; it allowed Dukat to slave any station on the *Kashai*'s bridge to his immediate oversight, and if required, he could belay any order a crew member executed with the stroke of a keypad. At the moment he was looking through the frigate's targeting matrix, the screen showing the status of the disruptor grids, a lazy aiming halo drifting up and down the hull of the freighter moving in the warship's shadow. *A single disruptor salvo could end them; they would be cast to the void and none would know the* Lhemor's *fate.* Dukat's finger drummed on the edge of the console. He needed only to move it slightly to blow the ship apart and rid Cardassia of a few more Oralians. He let his mind wander, imagining the ramifications of such a deed. Would he be punished? Hardly. Perhaps there would be some cursory investigation, but nothing of consequence. If anything, he would be guilty of acting on his own initiative instead of waiting to be ordered to destroy the zealots. *That might be bad enough,* he mused. *Central Command does not like men who think too much for themselves.*

From the corner of his eye he saw the door slide open, and he turned in his seat to see Kotan Pa'Dar cross warily toward him, stepping around the control podiums of the frigate's compact two-tier command deck. The civilian didn't enjoy being in the presence of so many military men. He walked with the air of a weak child in a room full of idle thugs. "Dal Dukat," said the scientist. "I did as you requested." He waved a padd. "The analysis is most interesting."

Dukat took the padd and saw Pa'Dar glance at the dal's monitor. The civilian's eyebrows rose as he realized what it displayed. He shot the commander a look of sudden alarm.

"Call it a thought experiment, Kotan," he said languidly. "How many bolts would it take to blast that scow from space?"

His amusement deepened as the other man hesitated, unsure if Dukat was asking him a question or just making an idle threat. "I would think that would be a rash course of action," Pa'Dar said finally. "We are not the Klingons. What you posit is more in line with their crudity of behavior, Dal."

"Quite so." Dukat had made it clear that Pa'Dar wasn't to call him by his first name in front of his crew, and he was pleased the civilian kept to his orders. "It is only a drill for my weapons officer, nothing more." He grinned slightly, enjoying Pa'Dar's discomfort. "I wouldn't want for there to be a malfunction in the disruptors . . . a misfire, perhaps." Dismissing the matter, he went back to the padd and paged through it. Dukat found himself thinking of Kell, his former commander. Now promoted to the rank of jagul and enjoying a posting at the Union embassy on Bajor, he recalled the man's irritation at their mission into this sector five years earlier. Although his dislike for Kell hadn't waned, Dukat did in a way understand him a little better. Commanding his own starship, albeit a small craft, gave Dukat fresh insight. The tyranny of boredom that came from uneventful missions such as this one would try any officer's patience, and that, he imagined, was why Danig Kell had taken such care in making life hard for Skrain Dukat. Small cruelties passed the time.

Dukat snapped off his monitor, irritated by the thought that he might share some characteristics with the man.

"Your phantom," offered Pa'Dar, indicating the padd. "I ran a full diagnostic on the *Kashai*'s sensors and I concluded that it was not, as your officers suspected, a reflection from the freighter's poorly shielded reactor core."

Dukat's eyes narrowed. The intermittent sensor contact had been plaguing them since they entered the Bajor Sector, appearing at the fringes of the frigate's detection range, hazing in and out at odd intervals. With Pa'Dar's contingent of experts from the science ministry on board as passengers, the commander had decided to make use of them and turn the civilians to the problem. He made a mental note to reprimand his scan officer for failing to come to the same conclusion. "It's a ship."

Pa'Dar nodded. "Given what can be determined by its

course, motion, and energy patterns, I would hazard a guess that the vessel is Tzenkethi in origin."

"That would fit a profile," Dukat allowed. "They're known to be active in this region. It's most likely a scout, pacing us to see if we might make good prey for a raid." His fingers tightened on the padd. A Tzenkethi scoutship was an agile opponent, but the *Kashai* was well armed and swift at sublight speeds. In an engagement, Dukat had no doubt that his vessel would emerge the winner. Skirmishes between Cardassian and Tzenkethi ships had become a regular feature of travel through the Bajor Sector; the aggressive aliens seemed to have little concern about picking fights well outside their own borders.

"Based on my projections of their ion trail's decay rate, I suspect that the ship is diverging from our course." Pa'Dar split his hands apart to illustrate his conclusion. "If they continue on that heading, they will enter the Ajir system."

"Ajir?" Dukat repeated, turning back to his monitor. He called up a report on the star system. "Single star, several unremarkable balls of ice and rock, a large cometary debris zone. No inhabitants." He considered it for a moment. "A waypoint, perhaps."

"I concur," said Pa'Dar. "The Tzenkethi are known to prefer the refuge of star systems to the void of deep space. It's an accepted trait of their race."

Dukat tapped the screen with his finger. "We could alter course, go to high warp, and make it to Ajir before them. If they were following us, they were scanning us, and that is tantamount to an act of espionage against the Cardassian Union." The prospect of a combat engagement tingled in his fingertips.

"To do so would require you to abandon the *Lhemor* and leave it undefended," Pa'Dar replied. "It could even be a ploy to make you do just that." He frowned. "If I am correct, I believe the Detapa Council's orders are that the Oralians are to be escorted all the way to Bajor."

Dukat raised an eyeridge. "And how would you know the intents of the Detapa Council, Kotan? I wasn't aware they kept the Ministry of Science informed of such things."

Pa'Dar's frown deepened. "You know full well my family's connections within the council. Some things became known to me."

"Indeed?" Dukat did know; Pa'Dar's clan was applying pressure to the man to give up his dalliance with the sciences and take up a political career. That he continued to resist showed character on his part, something Dukat saw little of in most civilians. He sighed. "But you are quite correct. And far be it from me to go against the will of Cardassia's most esteemed council." He got to his feet and glanced down at the helm officer. "Glinn, you will maintain our present course and speed. Enter this data into the ship's log and alert me if the alien makes any sort of approach." He handed the woman Kotan's padd and beckoned Pa'Dar to follow him. "I will be in my duty room."

When the door closed behind them, Dukat gestured to a chair in front of the chamber's low table. Pa'Dar sat and glanced around; the dal's office was lined with screens showing data feeds from different parts of the ship, but many of the panels were blank. Pa'Dar knew from experience that the *Kashai*'s main computer had detected his entrance into the room and automatically concealed any information that a civilian of his security authorization was not cleared for. He paid it no mind; it was just another part of the way of obfuscation, concealment, and secrecy that was the Cardassian manner.

"Are you hungry?" asked the dal. "I decided that in order to acclimate myself, I would try a meal of Bajoran dishes." He crossed to the replicator slot, examining the labels on a series of isolinear rods. *"Veklava. Hasperat.* These names mean little to me."

"Skrain." Pa'Dar shifted uncomfortably. "Just now, on the bridge. You were making sport of me, yes? You did not actually intend to fire on the Oralians?"

"Would you be perturbed if I did?" Dukat glanced at him. "You've made it clear in the past that you have little regard for the followers of the Way."

"True," Pa'Dar admitted, "but in the end they are still Cardassians."

"Barely."

Pa'Dar continued. "Sometimes I wonder if they could be convinced to lay down their allegiance to their dogma and become part of society again."

Dukat gave a dry laugh. "You have changed since we were last together, Kotan. If anything, you've become softer."

"I just feel that now is the moment for Cardassia to look inward and put her own house in order. It's been a year since the Talarian conflict was brought to a conclusion, but Cardassia Prime still feels as if it is on a war footing."

"Cardassia is *always* on a war footing," Dukat grunted. "And the Talarian conflict was not *concluded,* Kotan. It came to a stalemate. The two things are not the same. Just because we have withdrawn from Republic space and no longer engage them in open battle, it does not mean we can turn away from them. They still represent a viable threat. Along with the Breen and the Tzenkethi, they hold walls around Cardassia on three fronts."

"And because of that, we expand toward Bajor?" Pa'Dar replied. "We should be consolidating, not expanding. Our people need to apply restraint to the factions in the council, marshal our citizens, and deal with the Oralian matter."

"And how would you accomplish the latter?" Dukat asked, raising an eyebrow.

"Most who follow the Way do it out of habit. If the Cardassian Union gave them the same leadership in their lives, they would reject the church. I would give them that and offer them a choice. Disavow their religion and reintegrate or leave the homeworld."

"To Bajor, perhaps?" Dukat selected a few data rods and put the rest aside. "Pack off the troublemakers and the zealots?" He nodded to a small screen showing an exterior view of the *Lhemor.* He smiled thinly. "Kotan Pa'Dar, I do believe that the colors of your clan are showing through that scientist façade you wear. Anyone listening to the words you just said would think you were a politician and not a man of learning."

"I speak plainly." Pa'Dar bristled at the officer's tone. "I know that is a rarity among the circles you move in."

Dukat chuckled again, and Pa'Dar knew he was mocking him. "So tell me, then. You have the solution to Cardassia's social ills. What about her other needs, eh?" He gestured around at the *Kashai*'s dun-colored walls. "Our naval forces were depleted in the process of teaching the Talarians some discipline. We cannot rebuild faster because we don't possess the minerals we need. Bajor does, but they will not trade it to us. We get only a trickle, too little too slowly. How would you address that?"

Pa'Dar felt the color rising in his ridges, the flesh darkening. The open challenge in Dukat's words was clear. If he backed down he would lose whatever respect the dal had for him. His jaw hardened. *Very well. I will say what I wish to, and hunger take Skrain Dukat if he takes offense over it.* "The answer is plain to see. The Bajorans feel intimidated by us. What we see as normal behavior they see as aggressive and demanding. To make them open up to us we must be more like them. Cardassia needs to foster a peaceable route toward collaboration. If we force them, they will dig in their heels and become intractable. Warships and soldiers like you won't do the job."

To his surprise, Dukat's expression changed and he nodded in agreement. "I think you are correct, Kotan. If there are mistakes being made on Bajor, it is that our kind expect the aliens to adhere to our patterns." He shook his head. "They won't. And if Cardassia had the time, I would say that your route would be the one to take." He activated the replicator, turning his back on the scientist. "But we will not. Cardassia does not have the luxury. The Talarians will nip at our borders once again, it is their nature. We have seen ample evidence today of Tzenkethi audacity, and then there is the constant pressure of the Federation's influence. If we bide our time, we allow all those enemies to gain strength over us." He nodded again. "Let me tell you what must be done. Bajor must be made to understand how lucky they are to have the Cardassian Union as a friend. They should give us what we need and do so willingly. They don't appreciate that they should be grateful for our patronage, and that must be pointed out to them in the strongest of manners. Anyone who cannot see that, Bajoran or Cardassian, becomes an impediment to our greater good."

"That . . . that has all the color of a threat, Dukat." Tension settled in Pa'Dar's muscles. In a cold, immediate rush of insight, he saw something different, something callous and hard in the other man's manner. It was as if a vast chasm had suddenly opened up between them; but then again, perhaps it had always been there, and only in this moment had Pa'Dar recognized it.

The commander drew a number of steaming plates from the replicator's maw and placed them on the table. The scents from spiced meats and pastries brought back memories of the feast in the Naghai Keep, but suddenly Pa'Dar felt his appetite fading. "Threats are only intentions never made manifest," said Dukat, taking a seat and a large chunk of meat. "Why waste time on them? Bajor must be taught, and teaching requires the application of lessons." He glanced up and saw that Pa'Dar had not touched the food. "You're not eating. Is there nothing to your liking?"

The scientist got to his feet. "I will take my leave of you, Dal Dukat. I'm afraid I find everything here . . . distasteful."

As the door closed behind him, Pa'Dar caught a ripple of laughter at his back.

10

Darrah Mace thumbed the entry control on the lock pad to silent and entered the house quietly. From the outside, most of the windows were dark, and he didn't want to wake the children if they were sleeping. Sliding the door shut behind him, he stopped sharply, narrowly avoiding walking straight into the chest-high statue in the hallway. The sculpture had only been in the house a few days, and he still hadn't got used to its being there. Another gift from Karys's mother, the artwork was apparently quite valuable, but to Darrah it looked like the torso of a nude, corpulent woman crossed with a bunch of broken sticks. He thought it was unattractive and obstructive, and to his wife's displeasure Bajin had expressed the same opinion. Only Nell, ever the conciliator, had said something nice about Grandmother's efforts, and even then she had damned it with faint praise. Darrah imagined that they would follow the same pattern they did with every such gift from his in-laws; it would stay in the house for a couple of months before he shifted it to the basement to be out of the way with all the others.

He threaded his way through the wide bungalow, following the faint smell of food coming from the kitchen. The shutters across the window were open slightly, and through them Darrah could see the glow of the city below the hills. The view was one of the best things about the place, and on a clear day he could stand there and pick out the habitat district where their old apartment block still stood. He slid open the kitchen door on its rails and found his wife at the table, picking at a carton of food with one hand, reading a booklet with the other.

Karys closed the book and inclined her head. "Kids are asleep."

"I gathered." Shrugging his tunic onto an empty seat, he sat down opposite her, and she immediately got up, putting distance between them. Mace sighed and helped himself to a glass of *kava* juice. It was too warm, but he was too thirsty to care. "Is there anything to eat?" He cast an eye over the containers on the table, the debris of a take-out meal from one of the vendors down in the commercial quarter.

"There was a couple of hours ago," she retorted. "At supper. You remember supper, Mace? I think you had it with us when Nell was still crawling."

The jibe barely registered. He flipped open the lids of the boxes and his lip curled. Cooked fish smells assailed his nostrils, smoky and potent. "What is this?"

"*Rokat* fillets and seafruits in *yamok* sauce."

"That's *Cardassian* food. Since when did we live on alien grub in this house?" He shot her a glance. "I want something Bajoran."

"You're dealing with the Cardassians all the time now. I thought you'd be used to their foods. And besides, since when did you have a choice in deciding who eats what?" Karys came back toward him, bristling, and Mace knew she was gathering the momentum for an argument. "If you were around more often, you might have a say in it."

Mace shoved the boxes away and took a gulp from his juice. "I pay for this house. I pay for space for your mother's damned monstrosities in the hallway. The least you can do is have something I can eat in the place when I come home!"

"*When* you come home!" She seized on the words.

"You promised me things would be different when we moved here, Mace!" Karys put her hands flat on the table. "The assignment with the enclaves, you said it would make us better off and you said you'd be home more often. But you're not. Nothing is different!"

"Nothing?" he shot back. "You have the home you wanted, I got you out of the stackers, gave you a life more to the taste of an *Ih'valla*. What more do you want?"

"I want my husband in the house!" Her voice started to rise, and she checked herself. "For more than a few hours a week, at least!" She shook her head. "I see Rifin Belda at services and I feel like I'm turning into her!"

Mace frowned. Belda was the wife of the late captain of the *Eleda,* and she had struggled hard to continue on with her life, left alone with two children after her spouse had been lost. "Belda's husband is dead."

"And she sees his memorial more than I see you."

Mace's temper flared. "That's not true, and you know it." He blew out a breath. *"Kosst,* Karys. What do you want from me? I'm trying to give you the best life I can, keep you safe. Don't you understand, if I don't work this hard, all this goes away?" He gestured at the house. "How many times do we have to rake over this old ground?"

"So I should be grateful and silent, is that it?" She snorted. "Do you know, my sister sent me a comm from the colony today. We talked for a long time."

Mace rolled his eyes. "Oh, I'm sure that went well. She can't stand me."

"She offered to get me passage out there, Bajin and Nell too. Suddenly I'm wondering if I should accept!"

He got to his feet and drained the rest of the drink. "You're going to go to Valo II? To a rural border colony? I don't think so."

"What makes you so sure?" demanded Karys.

"Because you'd go insane. After a couple of weeks of

looking at fields and trees you'd be desperate to come home." His voice shifted into the harsh tone he used in prisoner interrogations. "You hate being away from the center of attention, Karys, and that's what Korto is these days. You like being cosmopolitan." He flicked at the food containers. "You like being daring and worldly, the wife of a City Watch inspector who deals with exotic offworlders every day." Her face darkened, and he knew he'd struck a nerve. "But you can't have it both ways." Mace felt buried tensions churning inside him, the legacy of dozens of half-finished arguments and directionless animosities forcing themselves to the surface. Part of him wanted to stay and unleash them, and for a long moment he balanced on the edge of giving them voice; but then he turned and snagged his jacket from the back of the chair.

"Where are you going?" she snapped.

He deliberately ignored the pleading tone in her words.

"To get something to eat."

Darrah hopped a near-empty tram at the foot of the road and took it to the night market at the base of the hill. Hunger always made him terse and short-tempered. He found the first street vendor he came across and handed her a couple of lita coins, getting some savory *porli* strips in a rough *mapa* bread roll. He wolfed it down and then got another, along with a cup of ice water. Licking grease from his fingertips, Mace caught sight of himself in the polished chrome of the vendor's food wagon. His face was set hard in a grimace, jaw locked and eyes narrow. The echo of his anger with Karys was still resonating in his bones. *Walk it off,* he told himself.

He wandered into the alleys of the market, between the narrow walls of the stalls selling clothing and trinkets, hot and cold foodstuffs, entertainment software or old books. When they saw him coming, some of the sellers rather indiscreetly used cloths to cover parts of their stalls to hide their wares. He didn't doubt that some of the vendors were trading pirated isolinear disks; there was a strong trade in illegally copied holo-programs from the United Federation of Planets that the City Watch was continually trying to stamp out, which kept rising again no matter how hard they worked to eradicate it. Others kept their stock discreetly hidden, like the men who traded in programs of a more questionable kind. Although it didn't fall directly in his jurisdiction anymore, Darrah was aware that sales of that kind of material had spiked in Korto and other cities where there were enclaves. It appeared that some Cardassians had an interest in Bajorans that went beyond the cultural; and the trade wasn't just one way, either. The idea that Bajorans wanted such intimate information about the reptilian aliens made his gut twist. He made a mental note of faces and resolved to pass the information on to Myda at the precinct in the morning.

Darrah looked up at the ornate chronometer that towered over the night market. It was a little after twenty-three-bells. In the past, the stallholders would have been tearing down their pitches by now, rolling up their stock, and dismantling the stalls before calling it a night, but if anything the bazaar was running at a good clip. There were customers in every alley, and Darrah noted that the majority of them were Cardassian. *They like the warm nights,* he recalled, thinking of something that Lonnic had told him. The vendors were staying open later in order to service their new patrons. *They come into the city at dusk during the summer months.*

The offworlders fell into two groups. There were knots of Oralians, who were never in anything less than a group of three or four, hooded figures shrouded by pastel robes of dusky pink and sky blue. The pilgrims dallied mostly around the stalls selling used paper books or tourist trinkets depicting items of local interest like the *bantaca* spire and the keep. Small resin models of the Kendra Monastery and laser-cut crystals in the shape of an Orb ark were the most popular purchases, or so it seemed.

The other Cardassians were the soldiers in their beetle-black armor, men from the escort warships in orbit or the so-called "support staff" out at the enclave. Darrah never saw any signs of weapons on them, but he imagined that the carapace plates of dark metal could easily conceal small blades or beam guns. These aliens walked either in a tight group, with the same watchful motions as a recon unit in enemy territory, or else they were alone, loping from stall to stall, talking in low tones to the dealers.

In accordance with council ordinances, colored ribbons on the stall frames denoted the permissions and contents of a given booth, but most of the stands also had banners dangling alongside them with Cardassian text written in a sketchy, poor hand. Darrah couldn't read them, but he knew the food vendors had banners explaining that their cooking was compatible with Cardassian digestive tracts, or that offworlders and "friends of Oralius" were welcome. He frowned at the signs and walked on, crossing under the clock tower, finishing his water and discarding the cup.

It wasn't just the aliens themselves that showed their influence on things in the city. At the toy stands there were little kits one could purchase that would make a model of a *Selek*-class starship from paper and glue. He saw commemorative *Peldor* Festival plates from the year the *Eleda* crew had been returned, disks of white porcelain with montage images of the funeral at the Naghai Keep. There were clothes on sale, knockoffs of the fashionable items worn by the higher *D'jarra*s that resembled the cut of Cardassian tunics and Oralian robes; and there were more subtle things, like the way the traditional icons of hearth and home were being supplanted by symbols of space and new horizons.

Once it had been a rarity for Darrah to cross paths with an alien, and now that he did it every day, it seemed so natural. He glanced up as a flyer hummed past overhead. He knew immediately that the vehicle had a Cardassian engine—the tone of the drive was dull and tight, unlike the grumbling throb from less powerful Bajoran-made craft.

"Ho, Mace!" The voice cut through his musings, and he turned to see Gar Osen beckoning him from the steps of the marketside temple.

"Ranjen," he said, coming over. "What are you doing here?"

Gar indicated the small temple. "Just a small bit of church business about tomorrow's new arrivals. It went on a little longer than I thought it would."

Darrah nodded. There was another boatload of Oralians arriving at Cemba Station the next day, and both he and the priest had to be there.

Gar gave a wan smile. "You know how it is, *Inspector*. The higher up the wheel you turn, the more things you have to deal with." The flyer was settling on the road nearby. "I was just leaving. Do you need to go somewhere? I could have my driver give you a lift . . ." He trailed off, and Darrah knew that his old friend was reading him. "What's bothering you, Mace?"

"I haven't even opened my mouth yet. What makes you think there's something bothering me?"

Osen frowned. "I'm your friend and I'm your priest. If I can't tell when something is wrong with you, I'd be failing on both those counts." He gave the man in the flyer a shake of the head and gestured back into the temple. "Come on. Unburden yourself."

Darrah resisted. "I have no burdens, Ranjen."

"No? Well, how about two men just talking, then? I'll ask the Prophets to turn a deaf ear to anything sacrilegious you might say."

✦   ✦   ✦

A day later, and they were in orbit. Gar paused to smooth down the front of his robes and glanced down the length of the commerce platform's reception area. It was a wide space, dominated by a large horizontal window that looked out into the void. He always found the station to have a slightly shabby, down-at-heel atmosphere to it, and if the option had been his he would have preferred to meet the Oralians on Bajor rather than up here. It wasn't as if the place was decrepit or anything like that; it was just a bit too industrial. It lacked grace, and it was hardly the best first impression to give new arrivals. But there had been raised voices in the Chamber of Ministers about allowing Cardassians, Oralian or not, unfettered passage. It was largely down to the agitation of Keeve Falor that they were here on Cemba instead of holding a reception at the Naghai Keep. The priest sighed. Here, on the outer decks of Cemba Station's main structure, the hemispherical shape of the orbital platform's main hull joined a spiderweb of thin gantries, extending out to tend to arriving and departing starships. Sunlight reflected from the Derna and Jeraddo moons illuminated the vessels in dock; the priest didn't know the makes and models of the ships, but he did know the difference between Bajoran designs and Cardassian ones, and there were none of the latter in evidence. He had heard Darrah say that the Union military liked to keep their ships untethered, and indeed he could discern the shapes of a couple of craft farther out in higher orbits. Yellow-amber hulls glittered, reminding him of the mantas that swarmed in the Dakeeni shallows.

The inspector crossed his line of sight, in conversation with two of his watchmen, talking urgently and glancing at his chronometer. Security was another reason why the reception was taking place on Cemba Station. In Ashalla, Hathon, and Jalanda, there had been demonstrations calling for greater restrictions on the movement of the aliens, and some had concluded with hostility. Darrah Mace and his men were here to make sure that didn't happen today. Darrah was all business now, and he was a different man from the person who had sat with Gar in the marketside temple the night before, angry and sad, trying to find a way to make his marriage work. There wasn't even the slightest hint of concern on the man's face; Darrah was in his element here, in perfect charge of things. Gar understood why Darrah gave so much of himself to his work: *At least there he can feel like he has control over his life.* He remembered the worry, the real fear, in his friend's eyes when he spoke of Karys's comment about going offworld. Osen had soothed him by pointing out that Mace's wife had a history of idle threats, but then again she was touching on something that Gar had been seeing more often of late. There was a small but concerted movement by some Bajorans across the planet to leave it. Ships making the voyage to Prophet's Landing and Valo were taking more emigrants along with their cargo. There were plenty of people whose issues with the government's choices over the alliance had spurred them to leave. He sighed, thinking of the kai's words outside the Kendra Shrine. *This path that Bajor is on, it should be toward unity, not division.* He wished she were here now.

The party from the clergy were talking quietly among themselves, and Vedek Arin was nodding at questions from the cluster of novices that had joined him from Kendra. Arin caught Gar's eye and gave him a perfunctory smile. The ranjen had hoped that Kai Meressa would have joined them for this small outing, but Arin had closed that matter the moment he arrived. *The kai was indisposed.* That was the small lie they were using to save face. According to Arin, Meressa's illness was making it progressively harder for her to leave her chambers at the retreat in Calash. The temperate weather and clear air there had helped her somewhat, but more and more Arin was assuming the role of her day-to-day proxy. Gar resolved to take a skimmer out to the retreat the first opportunity he got.

"There," said Tima, a young novice with blond hair and bright green eyes. She pointed out at the void. "There's the ship."

Gar saw the *Lhemor* as it came around the curve of the window, the long, corrugated shape of the freighter turning to settle against the docking arm. There was a resonant thud of metal against metal as it locked on to Cemba Station, and he saw glowing red lights turn white around the airlock tunnel. The priest saw a second vessel drift past, eschewing the open docks. It had the same manta-wing profile as the other Cardassian military ships, and it moved up and away to a steady distance from the commerce platform. Gar couldn't escape the implication that the *Lhemor*'s escort was watching it like a desert hawk.

After a few minutes, with a whine of hydraulics the hatch at the end of the airlock tunnel dropped into the deck and revealed the Oralians. Gar scanned their faces, seeing a mixture of wary enthusiasm and, in some, slight disappointment. Vedek Arin came forward, and Gar moved with him as the figure at the head of the pilgrim party rolled back his hood, revealing the cleric Bennek. Gar was struck by how much the Cardassian's face had darkened with deep lines that gathered at the corners of his eyes. A smile crossed the alien's expression and he bowed.

"Vedek Arin, Ranjen Gar. In the name of the Oralian Way, I greet you and extend once more the thanks of our congregation for allowing us to visit your world." His smile faltered a little. "The kai is not present?"

Arin shook his head. "She is indisposed, cleric, but she sends her most profuse apologies and warmest greetings."

"The Fates protect her, then."

Gar nodded. "Welcome back to Bajor, Bennek. I hope our honored friend Hadlo is well?"

There was a momentary flicker of emotion in the Oralian's eyes, and Gar wondered what it could signify. "Hadlo remains on Cardassia Prime, engaged in matters of the Way," he explained, "but he hopes to visit you again in the near future."

"Just so," noted Arin. "You know Gar, of course. Let me introduce you to some of our newer novitiates who will be joining us today." The vedek ran through the learners, and Gar caught an unmistakable flush of emotion in Tima's expression when Bennek shook her by the hand. The girl was clearly spellbound by the aliens.

Nearby, Darrah cleared his throat and indicated the corridor beyond the reception area. "Gentlemen? A shuttle has been fueled and is ready to take you down to the planet. If you'll follow Constable Proka, he'll show you the way."

"Of course," allowed Arin. As the vedek launched into a conversation with the Cardassian cleric, Gar watched the rest of the Oralian party disembark. There were more of them than he had expected, and he wondered if the shuttle might have to make two trips to the surface and back to take them all.

One of the males detached himself from the group and came across, a broad grin threatening to break out on his face. "Pardon me, but are you the ranjen Gar Osen of Korto?"

"I am." Gar was surprised to be recognized by an alien. "And you are?"

The Cardassian's grin unfolded and he shook Osen's hand, palm to forearm in the old fashion. "Pasir Letin, Ranjen! I'm excited to meet you. I hope we will be able to discuss some matters of theology." He was walking quite swiftly, and the Bajoran had to quicken his pace to stay in step with him. "I was most fascinated by your monograph on Trakor's Prophecies."

Gar blinked in surprise, momentarily wrong-footed by the other man's enthusiastic manner. "You read that? How did you—"

Pasir kept speaking. "There's been a strong exchange of information among our faiths in recent years. I was particularly struck by some of the similarities between Trakor's divination on the matter of the Pah-wraiths and Oralius's words of rebuke in the Hebitian Records."

The group was approaching the hangar bays, and as he walked, Gar formulated a reply. He was going to ask the Oralian a question, but the opportunity was snatched away as the deck of Cemba Station lurched beneath his feet, pivoting forward, the gravity controls struggling to compensate. There was a brilliant white flash of light from behind them, and the priest felt a wash of searing heat across his back and the bare skin of his neck.

The next sound he heard was the explosion, the screaming roar of broken air and burning backdraft.

The tingle of the transporter died away, and Dukat took his first breath of Bajoran air in five years. He stepped off the reception dais set in the corner of the Union embassy's atrium and crossed the chamber, his boots clicking on the dun-colored stone floor. Passing under a huge Galor Banner, he glanced toward the entrance doors below and saw the honeyed glow of sunlight through the windows set in them. Inside there was nothing but the soft chime of computers at the monitor stations, but out beyond the windows there were figures moving and shifting. Dukat imagined that if the building were not soundproofed, he would have heard shouts and disorder. He scowled. It was one more black mark against Jagul Danig Kell, and he filed it away.

Dukat noticed troopers with stunner rifles loitering near the doors, and with them a group of nondescript civilians in the uniforms of medical specialists. They appeared to be waiting for something. For a moment, the dal considered approaching one of the soldiers and demanding an explanation from him, but then he dismissed the thought. There were other, more pressing issues to deal with, and he wanted to get them out of the way as soon as possible. *The quicker I speak with Kell, the quicker I can be done and return to my ship.*

He presented himself at the security arch and eyed the technician behind the monitor. There was no need for an exchange of greetings; the operator knew who he was, her console reading the ident plate fused into his armor the moment he had materialized on the dais. She gestured to a wide-spectrum scanner matrix set in the floor like a tall, thin tombstone. "If you please, Dal Dukat."

He did as he was bid, letting a pulse of blue light flick across his eyes. In moments, the noninvasive bio-scan and retinal profile threw up a confirmation, and a light glowed on the arch. "You may proceed, sir," the woman said, and looked away, moving on to her next work item.

Dukat passed through the arch, and a discreet door opened in the wall across from him. The turbolift inside rocked gently as it took him into the embassy's inner spaces. The building followed standard Central Command design protocols; it was a bunker within a bunker, a hardened blockhouse constructed from reinforced thermoconcrete on a sonodanite frame, concealed inside a rectangular building made from the densest local stone available. Dukat had been in several facilities of identical form and function, from Arawath to Orias, and each was the same. The uniformity was comforting, in its own way.

The doors opened and Dukat was waved through to the jagul's office by a muscular glinn; and there he found Kell watching an oval holoframe, the transparent display hazing the air over his desk. Dukat saw grainy images, probably from the security monitors out on the embassy walls. A horde of Bajorans, a handful of them in Militia uniforms standing with their backs to the gates, the rest churning back and forth, shouting and brandishing pennants. The officer seemed to be only half interested in the screen, his attention wandering between that and a series of padds showing some kind of schematic.

He indicated the image. "Have I come at a bad time, Jagul Kell?"

"Dukat." Kell drew out the name, ignoring the question. "Here you are. Welcome to Bajor."

Dukat made a show of looking around: The jagul's office was heavily decorated with thick hardwood paneling from Cuellar, and there were artworks that showed scenes of Cardassia Prime, a shelf of antique books. It was the polar opposite of the austerity of Dukat's own duty room aboard the *Kashai*. "I feel as if I have not left the homeworld," he replied.

Kell smirked. "High rank means men are granted allowances." He shifted in his seat and pointedly did not offer Dukat the opportunity to take the empty chair across from his desk. Dukat studied the man. The stocky, uncompromising officer who had once commanded the *Kornaire* was still there, but Kell had grown more portly in the intervening years. An increase in girth was to be expected as a man became an elder, of course, but the jagul was still some time away from earning that level of distinction. The tailoring of his duty armor did its best to conceal it, but there was only so far it could go. Dukat kept a sneer from his lips, holding his contempt and faint disgust for the man in check. *Is this what you have been doing in your glorious posting, Kell? Growing fat on rich alien food, guzzling their drink?*

As if in reply, the jagul took up a glass of springwine and sipped it. "Cardassia endures," he intoned. "Even beyond her borders, Cardassia endures. Tell me, how many more of the Oralian rabble have you brought here?"

"One ship, the *Lhemor.*" Dukat answered the question even though he knew Kell had all the details of the freighter and Bennek's pilgrims. "Other vessels are known to be preparing for voyages. The Oralians in the cities have been encouraged to vacate the population centers. They are being increasingly corralled in the outer territories, in shanty towns."

"Enclaves . . ." Kell mused. "Rather like here on Bajor."

"Central Command estimates that a full third of all declared followers of the Oralian Way are offworld at this time."

"Following the pilgrim path to learn from the Prophets," mocked the jagul. "Well. That would seem to indicate we have them where we want them. Diminishing and ineffectual. The Union will be all the better for it."

"'And the betterment of the Cardassian Union is the goal of all the nation's sons,'" Dukat replied, the axiom coming easily to him. "If I may ask, sir, how have you fulfilled that edict?"

Kell's eye twitched at Dukat's open challenge, but he opened his hands to take in the office. "Look around, Dal. While you loitered with the Talarians, I have worked to cement Cardassia's foothold on this world." He frowned. "Perhaps not with the swiftness that Central Command wishes, but then the road to control must be taken with care."

Dukat made a noncommittal noise and glanced at a small sculpture made of jevonite. "I wonder. Do the Bajorans living here in Dahkur have any inkling of what lies inside the blunt planes of this building?" He raised the object to his eyes, studying it. "They would be most displeased to find you have inserted a covert military base into one of their major cities." He nodded to the walls. "I saw the secure hatches along the corridor." Most of the interior spaces of a facility like this one were prefabricated rooms that locked together like a child's construction blocks, modular components beamed directly into place from ships in orbit. "I'm curious. How did you prevent the Bajorans from detecting the transporter signatures? Scattering fields, perhaps?"

As he expected, the jagul couldn't resist the opportunity to brag. "The trade with our homeworld has provided the Bajorans with some new sensor technology, which they use quite widely," he noted. "Of course, it is possible that those who built those sensors know them well enough to exploit any . . . blind spots."

"Ah," Dukat nodded. "But it's my understanding the Militia also operate sensor arrays using components of non-Cardassian origin."

Kell mirrored his nod. "They do. Hardware that the Xepolites sold them." He sipped at the springwine. "Interesting to consider: Who might it be that sold the Xepolites *their* technology?" The jagul smiled slightly. "You see, Dukat, there's nothing to cause any dismay among our gracious hosts."

"And this?" Dukat pointed at the holoframe. "That's not *dismay,* as you call it?"

Kell gave an arch sniff. "Embassy matters are classified at the highest level, Dal. I'm sure you understand."

"You need not worry about my clearances, Jagul. I'm here at the behest of the Central Command, and my orders are to evaluate the circumstances on Bajor." Dukat detected the twitch of annoyance in Kell's brow, but the other officer hid it quickly.

"It seems I was mistaken," Kell returned. "I was under the impression that you had been sent to Bajor, not on a mission of such great temerity as *judging my command"*—his voice rose slightly—"but because you had fallen out of favor with the Legates."

It was Dukat's turn to hide a flash of anger. The riposte was too measured to have been a chance comment. *How is he aware of my circumstances?* Dukat wondered. *Some agency funneled that information to him. Someone with a long reach.* "If you wish to ensure you don't find yourself in a similar condition, you might wish to curtail scenes like that," he snapped, nodding again at the rowdy demonstrators. He could make out Bajoran ideograms on the banners, and on some, in crude Cardassian, exhortations for them to quit the planet.

"On the contrary, Dukat, I'm allowing these protests to go on. In fact, I'm nurturing them."

"Explain."

Kell waved his hand in the air. "Nonlethal subsonics in the embassy's defense grid. Tuned correctly, over a limited area they can create a sense of agitation in the Bajoran hypothalamus . . ." He shrugged. "Forgive me, I understand the theory but the science of it is beyond me." Kell sniffed again. "When these so-called peaceful protests turn ugly, it serves us. The Bajorans become divided over the issue and Cardassia is shown to be compassionate when I send my medical staff in to help the injured in the aftermath."

Dukat remembered the specialists in the atrium. *Waiting for something.*

"Look at this," said Kell, offering him one of the padds as he snapped off the holoframe. "If Central Command is questioning my motivation, show them this as an example of my plans to better exploit Bajor for Cardassia's gain."

The padd's memory contained schematics for another prefabricated facility, but this was a surface base for military starships. He saw a communications intelligence center, shuttlebays, space for a trooper garrison. Dukat paged to the end. "A Cardassian naval outpost on Bajor's outer moon? They would never let you build such a facility!" He tossed the padd back to the other man. "Is that the best you have to show?"

Kell's jaw stiffened. "You haven't changed, Dukat. Not

one iota. You're still the same man you were when you were my officer, spare and arrogant." He grunted humorlessly. "I had thought you might have matured somewhat. I see I was wrong."

Dukat seethed inwardly, but refused to rise to the bait. "I would submit to you, sir, that perhaps your perceptions may have been influenced by your time among these aliens."

"Really?" Kell drawled.

Dukat fixed him with a hard eye. "It is our mission here to see that Bajorans become more like Cardassians . . ." He let his gaze drop to Kell's gut. "Not that Cardassians become more like Bajorans."

"You forget yourself, Dal," said the other man, putting a hard emphasis on Dukat's rank. "I've always considered your behavior to be insubordinate—"

The door to the office hissed open and the glinn Dukat had encountered outside rushed into the room. "Jagul! There's been an incident!"

Kell glared at him, angry at the interruption. "The demonstrators? As long as they don't attempt to breach the compound, let the Militia deal with them."

The glinn shook his head. "No, sir, it's something else."

The comcuff around Dukat's wrist vibrated with an alert signal, and he raised it to his lips, moving away from Kell's desk. "Report."

"In orbit," the glinn was saying, "the Bajoran commerce station . . ."

"Dal," Dukat recognized the voice of Dalin Tunol, his executive officer. She was clipped and businesslike. *"We have registered an uncontrolled energy discharge in the vicinity of the Cemba orbital platform."*

"An explosion?"

"Confirming . . ." There was a pause. *"Dal, the freighter* Lhemor *appears to have suffered a core breach. The vessel was completely destroyed, and the detonation has caused major integ-*

rity loss on the platform. Reading power failures across the station. It's coming apart."

Dukat shot Kell a look, but the expression on the jagul's face made it clear the other man was as surprised by the turn of events as Dukat was. He spoke again. "Tunol, coordinate with all Union ships in orbit. Lock on and transport out any casualties, immediately. Give priority to Cardassian life signs."

"We're attempting to comply, sir, but the radiation bloom from the blast is fouling our sensors."

"Do what you can. Dukat out."

Kell shot to his feet, knocking over the wineglass and spilling the contents over his desk. "Did you have anything to do with this?" he demanded.

Dukat's eyes narrowed. "A question I was about to put to you."

11

Placing his feet so he could stand evenly on the canted decking, Darrah Mace leaned forward and put his hand on the blast door. Patches of frost were already starting to form on the surface of the duranium plating, and the chill radiated out of the ice-cold metal. He threw a look at Proka Migdal, who was worrying at a messy cut above his eyebrow. "Vented?" asked the constable.

"Vented," repeated Darrah. On the other side of the hatch there was nothing but the airless vacuum of space, and it was steadily leaching the heat from the sealed-off corridor.

Proka indicated an air vent over their heads. "Not a trickle coming through there, which means we're without life support. No telling how long what we got is going to last us. Couple of hours, maybe."

Darrah turned away, walking back along the carbon-scorched plates, picking his footing. "At least we still have gravity."

"For the moment," said the other man. "That could drop out anytime, too."

"That's it," Darrah said dryly, "you just keep thinking positively."

"You got a plan, boss?"

He eyed his subordinate. "What? Making it up as you go isn't a plan?"

"Not as such, no." Proka sighed. "I tried communications and the station intercom again, but there's nothing there. Sounds like a rainstorm coming over the channels."

Darrah nodded. "That tells us what the blast was, then. Radiological, not chemical."

The constable paled. "You . . . you think we caught a dose?"

"Likely. Don't fret. You're too ugly to have children anyway." Rounding the corner of the twisted corridor, they returned to the ragged group of survivors. The Oralians and the priests clustered together, many of them praying. There were a few men and women from the station crew they had found trapped in compartments off the companionway; but far more of the rooms had been sealed tight by emergency maglocks or else they yielded nothing but corpses.

He paused, crouching where Gar was lying on the deck. A Cardassian was at his side, probing at his torso. "You know something about medicine?" The ranjen's skin was pale and his breathing was thready.

The Oralian priest looked up. "Only a little. I'm not sure how much I can apply to one of your people." He gave a weak, fragile grin. "I . . . I was just talking to him when it happened . . . Then the blast, and I didn't think, I just pushed him down . . ."

"What's your name?"

"Pasir . . ."

Darrah placed a hand on the alien's shoulder. "Pasir, listen to me. You saved the life of a good friend of mine. That means I owe you one, so as payback I'm going to get you and everyone else out of this mess, okay?" Pasir nodded. "You just look after my friend here and let me do the rest."

He stood and crossed to Proka. Bennek, the senior cleric, was talking in a low, intense voice to one of the Bajoran novices, a blond girl whose face was wet with tears. The Oralian priest threw Darrah a nod; he was deferring to the inspector.

"Boss," began Proka, "You think there's other people still alive, on the other decks?"

"If there are, there's not much we can do for them." Darrah heard the leaden tone in his own voice. "With all the blast hatches sealed and the lifts offline, we're trapped on this tier. First things first, we concentrate on getting *these* people to safety." He paused, massaging his arm. The explosion had thrown him straight into a stanchion and popped his shoulder out of place. With Proka's help, he'd reset it, but the agony lingered on. He pointed and winced. "Shuttle's on this level. We get to it, we can get away. It's not like we're in the deeps here, after all. We're in Bajor orbit. I'm willing to bet the sky all around is swarming with rescue ships. We just have to get to them."

"You make it sound easy,"

"I always do." Darrah gave him a smile. "I'm going to move ahead, scout down the length of the corridor to the shuttle dock. You stay here, keep the civilians from panicking."

"Got it."

He was stepping away when he saw the unfocused glaze in the other man's eyes. "Mig? What is it?"

Proka glanced up. "How did this happen? One second we're walking and talking, the next . . ." He trailed off. "I was at the front, I just heard the noise. Dennit was at the back, and she . . . I mean, the hatch came down and sealed off the compartment behind us."

Darrah nodded slowly. "Yeah. Dennit and a half-dozen of the Oralians. It would have been quick, Mig. We can thank the Prophets for that."

"She was going to come along to the *prayko* game tonight," said the constable. "I always thought she was a bit stuck-up, but—" He stopped and swallowed hard. *"Right.* Keep the civilians calm. Got it, sir."

Darrah left him and picked his way between the survivors. His nose wrinkled at the mingled smells of blood, burnt skin, and the ozone from sparking short circuits. The corridor, normally square-shaped, was deformed and bent. He imagined it was like walking down the inside of a piece of bent pipe. He navigated around junctions and areas where support frames had collapsed. He was grateful he hadn't lost his phaser in the confusion; setting the weapon to a tight-beam, high-energy setting, he cut through a girder that blocked his way. With care, he stepped around the still-glowing metal edge and found the decking angled away from him, turning into a steep slope. The detonation—*and what in fire's name had it been?*—had apparently hit Cemba Station with such force that the platform had twisted under the impact. The realization made Darrah's throat go dry. The survivors in the corridor were probably alive only by some random chance, a freak interaction of the platform's structural integrity fields forming a temporary bubble in the middle of the spaceframe. He thought about the rooms they had been unable to get into, the way the hatches were distorted and jammed in place. Anything organic inside there that was hit by the concussion wave would be unrecognizable now, just a paste of meat and bone. The lawman's stomach turned over at the thought, and along with the roil of adrenaline shock still coursing through his system, Darrah felt hot acid bile coming up his throat.

He sank back on the decking and panted, forcing himself to calm down. "Focus, Mace," he said aloud. "Don't puke. That would be embarrassing for everyone."

After a moment, he came up into a crouch and went forward in a ducking walk, bending to get under a half-open blast door that had locked in place. His skin tingled with an electric discharge in the air, and Darrah caught the sound of a resonant humming. Beyond the blast door was the boarding tunnel to the shuttle. He laid eyes on it and spat out a string of particularly choice gutter epithets.

A short distance from where he stood, using improvised handholds to keep himself up on the tilted floor, the corridor was blocked by a wavering green force field that prevented him from advancing any farther. He glanced around and saw the glowing emitter heads set in the ceiling and the walls. He knew that blasts from his pistol would destroy them and kill the field immediately; but what had made him curse with such venom was what lay on the other side of the energy barrier.

He could see the boarding tunnel clearly, and in fact he could see the shuttle too, still attached to the severed length of the corridor. It was drifting less than a linnipate from the station's hull, with nothing but airless space and a cloud of metallic debris between them, severed cleanly. In any other circumstance, Darrah could have covered the distance in a few moments, but with no environmental suit, no way to stop the rest of the corridor outgassing what atmosphere remained the moment the barrier went down, the damned thing might as well have been on the other side of the galaxy for all the good it would do. He swore again, and then turned back to retrace his steps.

Gar blinked, and it hurt like blades scraping the inside of his skull. There was a hand on his chest and a hazy shape hovering over him. "Careful, careful, brother. Try not to get up too quickly. You may have a concussion."

The ranjen nodded, and that made his head hurt even more. He felt as if a heavy weight had been attached to the back of his neck, and each time he moved it pulled on him. "Ah," he managed. "I . . . I'm all right. Comparatively speaking."

The dimness around him resolved into a smoky corridor full of injured and fearful faces, and the shapes that spoke became a pair of Cardassians. "Ranjen Gar, thank the Way," said Bennek. "I feared you might not wake again."

"Don't move too fast," said Pasir. "You took a nasty blow to the head, and there are burns down your back."

"I feel them," Gar admitted, wincing at new pain. "That's the Prophets telling me I'm not dead." He got into a sitting position and looked around. "Where . . . where is everyone else? The vedek?"

Arin appeared out of the shadows, lit by a flickering illuminator strip. "I am here, Osen. By the Temple's Grace, we have lost none of our number." He sighed. "I wish I could say the same for our Cardassian cousins."

Gar looked at Bennek and the alien gave a solemn nod. He listened as the cleric explained what had taken place— the detonation, the shock wave, the loss of life. "But how could this happen?" he asked when the priest had finished. "Was it some kind of accident on board your vessel?"

"The *Lhemor* was elderly," noted Pasir. "And in that statement, I am being generous."

"Perhaps," said Bennek, "but would not any critical failure have been more likely to happen while we were at warp, when the ship was under the greatest stresses?"

"That doesn't necessarily follow." The law officer Proka added his voice. "Ships coming in to dock are more accident-prone than ones at sail."

"That's if it was an accident at all," returned Bennek.

"You can stow that kind of chatter right now." Gar heard footsteps, and Darrah Mace came into sight, his face grim and smeared with soot. "What matters is getting everyone here to safety. Air's running thin and our time's going with it."

"Inspector, perhaps it would be best if we remain here," suggested Arin. "The Militia know we are aboard Cemba. They won't abandon us."

Darrah shot the vedek a look. "That's true, but with

all due respect, it's been my estimation that those who sit and wait for a rescue are usually the ones who don't live to see it."

His words sent a ripple of concern through the survivors. Gar shifted, ignoring his pain. "Mace, what about the shuttle?"

"Not an option," he replied, in a manner that brooked no argument. "We need to come together, find a different way off this wreck."

Gar had Pasir help him to his feet. "What else is on this level? Does anyone here know?" he called out, choking back a guttural cough.

"I do," said a voice. The ranjen limped to a man in a technician's oversuit. The girl Tima was bandaging his arm with strips torn from her robes. "Working this tier. Consumables maintenance." The man's cheek was bloody where he had taken a lick of flame from the explosion, and his earlobe and *D'jarra* earring were a mess of flash-burned metal and livid, liquid scarring.

"What's your name?"

"Lirro," he slurred.

"Lirro, tell us what's on this deck," said Darrah, coming to Gar's side.

The man ran through a series of descriptions, shock making his voice dead and mechanical. After a moment, Gar stopped him. "Wait. You said cargo bays."

Lirro nodded. "Small ones. For temporary storage."

Gar glanced at Darrah. "Mace, a cargo bay means a cargo transporter. If there's still power to that compartment, we could beam off!"

"*If* there's still power," said Proka.

The inspector hesitated. "The thought occurred to me. But there's another problem. Cargo transporters are optimized for inert materials. They're fine for noncomplex structures, but the pattern buffers don't have the density to handle organic life-forms. You put a person through one of those and you're likely to lose a good percentage of the original molecular configuration."

Proka nodded. "You'll come out the other end a drooling moron . . . *if* you're lucky."

Bennek raised a hand. "All true, unless you have an operator who can compensate for the signal degradation."

Gar glanced at the Cardassian. "You know how to do that?"

The cleric nodded. "You were not born a priest, my friend, and neither was I. Before Oralius called me to walk the Way, I was a public transporter clerk in Lakarian City."

A crooked smile appeared on Darrah's face. "Okay. *Now* we have a plan."

There was a heart-stopping moment when the smoky interior of the cargo bay melted away from him and Darrah felt the transporter beam take hold. The last thing he saw was Bennek fiddling with the knot of wires dangling from the control console, then sprinting around to join him on the hexagonal pad. *What is he doing?* The panicked thought was barely formed before his mind, like the rest of his body, came apart in the matter stream and discorporated.

Then he was in a white space that was full of sound. He felt something cold tug at the skin on his neck, and he blinked furiously. Strong hands took his arms and guided him forward. He swallowed and took a cautious breath.

His eyes refocused on the face of a severe-looking bald man in a Militia uniform. The man waved a tricorder at the inspector and nodded. "You're fine. The electrolytic booster shot I just gave you will kick in quickly, but for the time being don't do anything strenuous."

"Right." He glanced around the transporter room and found Bennek. "Where's everyone else?"

"Medical bay," said the bald man. "You're on board the assault ship *Clarion*."

"My ship." The words came from another man who approached them with a purposeful gait. "Colonel Li Tarka, Space Guard."

"Inspector Darrah Mace, City Watch. Thank you, sir."

Li had the stone-cut manner of a career soldier, a face that was all hard angles and a crest of regulation-length oil-black hair. "You the one who got them out?"

Darrah shook his head and indicated the Cardassian priest. "That was Bennek here."

The other man made a small noise of surprise. "Quick thinking, Mr. Bennek, establishing a transport bridge with our ship's systems. We never would have been able to get you people off the station otherwise."

Bennek smiled weakly. "All matter transporters work on the same principles, Colonel. I knew that once the bridge was established, the *Clarion*'s integrators at this end would compensate for any signal loss."

"There's a lot of people who owe you their lives," Li replied, and Darrah could sense that the other man found it difficult to attribute such behavior to an alien.

"Aside from us, how many others made it to safety?" asked Darrah.

The bald man frowned. "A few escape pods were ejected from the platform and one of the bulk lighters on the far side of the docking array. There were some beam-outs, and we're tracking them down at the moment, but some were probably lost in transit. The numbers are grim, Inspector. Cemba Station alone had a crew of two hundred and ten people, and there were five ships of varying tonnages at dock there."

Bennek paled. "Oralius, watch over and preserve them," he whispered.

"I've already spoken to your man Proka," Li continued

in a brusque manner, and belatedly it registered with Darrah that the colonel was here to interrogate him, not to greet him. "Why don't you tell me what you think happened, Darrah?"

"A reactor malfunction aboard the *Lhemor*, maybe a cascade failure from a plasma breach?" He sighed. "I don't know. I'm not an engineer, Colonel, I'm a police officer."

Li's flinty expression never altered. "Then I'm surprised your first assumption is that it was an accident."

Bennek gasped. "Someone did that deliberately?"

The colonel directed the bald man to a wallscreen. "Kored, show them," he ordered.

The display lit up with waveforms of sensor data. Darrah recognized the basic shapes from the thousands of pieces of forensic data he came across in his caseload.

"I don't understand," said the cleric. "What are we looking at?"

Darrah pointed. "Scanner readouts. The Watch take the same kind of readings at crime scenes, looking for biological signatures, energy discharges, latent clues."

"This is the raw feed," Li explained, "and we're not done sifting the patterns yet. The *Clarion* was close by when the explosion took place. We were conducting operational drills, one of which happened to be a sensor test."

Operational drills. That was likely a euphemism for running in combat mode close to the Cardassian ships. The Space Guard made no secret of their dislike of the alien vessels being near Bajor, and Darrah had heard that some commanders had taken to testing the resolve of the Union crews by running weapons-hot battle drills right under their noses. For a moment he entertained the wild notion that the colonel might be responsible for what had happened—what if some nervous Bajoran gunner had set his sights on the *Lhemor* and accidentally fired on it?—but then he dismissed the idea. The Cardassians were watching, and the sky would have been a war zone by now if that had happened.

"See here." Li indicated a particular set of waveforms that crested from the mass of signals in the microsecond after the detonation. "Do you know what those are?"

"It's artificial," Darrah replied, his mind automatically kicking into investigative mode. "You can tell by the dispersal pattern. I'd say definitely not the result of a malfunction." His lips thinned. "Someone put a bomb on that freighter."

"The discharge originated just below the warp core," said Kored.

"Any line on a trigger signal?" He leaned closer, running the display back and forward. Behind him, he could hear Bennek murmuring more prayers under his breath.

"Negative. It's possible it's there, but we haven't been able to pick it out yet."

Darrah nodded to himself. "A timer, then, or a proximity switch." He halted the waveform display again and glanced at Li. "Colonel, are you seeing this as well? The peaks here and here?" He indicated two distinct energy spikes. "Those are molecular markers."

"Ultritium and triceron. Both extremely lethal explosive compounds," said the officer.

"That's an exotic mix," Darrah said immediately, his mind racing. "Undetectable by transporters and most civilian sensor suites. A military-grade munition, probably."

"I concur, Inspector. You know your job."

Darrah nodded. "Activists from the Circle have been making noise in Kendra Province recently. We've been on the lookout for bombings. I was briefed by General Coldri on some worst-case scenarios . . ."

"The device, it's not Cardassian." Li eyed the priest. "At

this point, the weapon profile only fits three possible origins. Gorn, Nausicaan—"

"Or Tzenkethi," said Darrah.

"Order! *Order!*" The First Minister struggled to be heard over the chaos in the chamber as everyone in the room tried to talk at once. Lonnic looked this way and that, catching snatches of shouted words and angry retorts. At her side, Jas Holza's face was an immobile mask. He was growing more withdrawn with every day.

Finally Lale slammed his fist on the table in front of him and the sound echoed like a thunderclap. The wave of voices from the ministers ebbed for a moment, and the man drew himself up. "At last. Are we children? This is an emergency session, and a matter for serious debate, not for squabbling and posturing."

Lonnic raised an eyebrow. It was the first time she had ever seen anything like annoyance from the First Minister, and from the reactions of the other politicians, it was the first time they had seen it too.

Lale Usbor sat, and by degrees his usual manner reasserted itself. "Now," he said, with bland graveness, "we have all read the report prepared by General Coldri's people." He nodded to where the Militia representative sat, flanked by Jaro Essa and Li Tarka. The three senior officers were like statues, their gray uniforms accenting the image. "It makes a damning case."

She heard a faint sigh and flicked a glance to Darrah, who sat nearby, his hands locked together around a padd. Much of the man's vitality had disappeared in the hours following the Cemba incident; he seemed like a ghost of his former self, the easy smile and straightforward manner dimmed in the aftermath of the bombing. Lonnic imagined that she would have been no different, had it been she who barely escaped the station instead of him. Of all the people on the ships and the platform, Darrah's group of survivors had been the largest. Kubus Oak had already made noises about awarding him some kind of citation, but Lonnic had gently deflected the suggestion. She knew Darrah well enough to know what was going through his mind right now: *If only I could have done more.*

Kubus was nodding in agreement with Lale. Seated to the far end of the long ministerial table, the politician had been joined by three of the aliens. Kell and Dukat looked quietly dangerous in their dark battle gear, while the other one, the scientist called Pa'Dar, seemed uncomfortable to be there. She found it odd that there were no representatives of the Oralian Way. The last Lonnic had heard, the cleric Bennek had played a major role in the rescue. *Why, then, is he absent?*

"Minister Kubus, if you would?" Lale nodded to the other man, who got to his feet.

"Thank you, First Minister." Kubus squared his shoulders. "At the chamber's behest and with the assistance of my honored colleague Minister Jas of Korto District, I took the liberty of making an independent verification of the sensor data provided by General Coldri and the Space Guard. It is my duty to inform you that their conclusions match those of my staff. It appears, within a probability of more than seventy-five percent, that the terrible act eighteen hours ago, which obliterated the freighter *Lhemor* and caused the loss of countless lives and property, was indeed the result of a timed explosive device concealed aboard the vessel. Holza?"

Lonnic's employer stood up, and he read from a padd in his hand. His delivery was passionless and static. "We have determined that the device was of non-Bajoran origin. While other avenues of investigation are open, it appears most likely that the device was fabricated by the Tzenkethi."

Kell cleared his throat. "If I may speak," said the Cardassian. "That conclusion mirrors those drawn by my men." He nodded at the scientist.

Pa'Dar blinked and took his cue. "It is our deduction that the bomb was placed on board the *Lhemor* shortly after it tethered at the Cemba commerce platform. All records pertaining to the ship's departure from Cardassia Prime revealed no discrepancies, no signs of any illegal entry or other suspicious circumstances."

The jagul grimaced. "The Tzenkethi are well known for their brutal, callous tactics. In my opinion as a soldier of the Union's fleet, it is well within their character to perpetrate such an act."

Another rumble of discontent rang around the room, and Lale tapped loudly on the table before him to forestall another outbreak of shouting. "Ministers, we are all aware of the Tzenkethi issue. For some time they have been a thorn in the side of shipping and colonial efforts on the outskirts of our sector."

"They are territorial," Keeve Falor spoke up suddenly, his words clipped. "Yes, the Tzenkethi are a dangerous foe, but they're raiders and pirates." He glared at Kell. "They don't plant bombs."

The Cardassian commander returned Keeve's glare. "With all due respect, Minister, have you engaged them in battle? I have. I know firsthand what they are capable of."

"So you have drawn Bajor into your skirmishes with the Coalition, then?" Keeve seized on his words. "Is this a new benefit to our much-lauded trade alliance? Must we now pay in Bajoran lives as well as in our minerals and ores?"

"There were many Cardassians lost in the incident as well as our own people," said Kubus. "It is insensitive of you to ignore that, Falor."

"Don't you mean many *Oralians*, Oak?" Keeve snapped back.

Kell raised a hand. "I understand Minister Keeve's anger

and his need to lash out. I feel the same. But Cardassia is not your enemy. This is the work of jealous minds, ladies and gentlemen. The Tzenkethi Coalition has preyed upon the borders of the Cardassian Union for many years, envious of our holdings and the many client worlds that we have as our partners."

"Is it not true that Tzenkethi agents have attempted in the past to sow dissent on your home planet?" Lonnic's lip curled. Kubus's question seemed rehearsed, part of a schooled performance.

The jagul nodded. "Correct, Minister Kubus. And now I fear they may have come to your world to do the same, doubtless driven by a desire to disrupt the Bajoran-Cardassian trade alliance."

"Intensive inquiries are under way as we speak," said Coldri. "Investigators from all branches of the Guard and the Watch are coordinating efforts to isolate the perpetrators of this act." Lonnic sensed Darrah stiffen at the general's mention of the City Watch. Coldri's severe expression remained impassive as he continued. "Mark me, this atrocity will not go unanswered."

Kell brought his hands together in front of him. "On behalf of the Central Command and the Detapa Council, I am willing to offer any assistance that I can."

"He could start by releasing the *Lhemor* wreckage for forensic analysis," said Darrah, speaking in low tones that did not carry.

Before Lonnic could answer him, Jas turned to the inspector. "The Cardassians are very strict about their funeral rites. It is a matter of great importance to them that the remains of their dead are not viewed by anyone other than family members."

"Convenient," Darrah murmured. "We only need to see the debris, not the corpses."

"We have to respect their wishes." Jas said the words,

but he didn't seem convinced of them. Darrah folded his arms and sat back, saying nothing. Lonnic knew he'd come to Ashalla expecting to add something to the debate, but instead he was being given no chance to contribute. *He's here so Jas and Kubus can be seen with him, the hero of the Cemba incident . . .*

"Your gesture is appreciated, Jagul Kell," Lale was saying. "Perhaps you could have Mr. Pa'Dar pass his finding on to Major Jaro?"

The Cardassian nodded. "Consider it done. But if I may, First Minister, there is more we can offer." He tapped the copper sigil on his chest plate and gave a theatrical sigh. "Minister Keeve's words make me look again at the events of these past days, and I realize that there is more Cardassia could have done to ensure that our associates on Bajor did not find themselves in harm's way." Lonnic noticed an air of tension between Kell and the officer at his side, Dukat. "With that in mind, I will make this offer. The Second Order of the Cardassian Union freely offers a support contingent of picket ships for deployment in association with Bajor's Space Guard, to bolster the security of your system and ensure that a horror of this magnitude will not occur again."

Keeve Falor and his supporters were on their feet immediately. "A support contingent? What exactly does that term mean, Kell?" he spat. "Bajor does not need military aid! Bajor can defend itself!"

"Can it?" Across the room, Kubus Oak shot Coldri and his men a hard look, his words thick with acid sarcasm. "Recent events would seem to indicate otherwise!"

And once again, the chamber erupted into a storm of shouts and reprisals.

It was dusk by the time Darrah was back in Korto. The flyer's skids had barely settled on the precinct's landing pad and he was already out of the pilot's chair and then out of the hatch in swift steps. Proka was waiting for him, shielding his eyes from the settling dust cloud kicked up by the thrusters. The constable must have seen the thunderous expression his superior was wearing, because he blinked. For Proka Migdal, that was quite a reaction.

"Didn't expect you back so soon, boss. Did it not go well?"

"Waste of my damned time," Darrah shot back, advancing across the apron toward the precinct building. "I don't know what the *kosst* they do in that place all day aside from snipe at each other and make life hard for the rest of us."

"Huh," Proka nodded. "Politicians, eh?"

Darrah shot him a look. "I saw a crowd outside the building as I came in to touch down. What's all that about?"

"Fallout from that business in Dahkur. It's a vigil, or some such. People angry about the Militia using violence to break up the demonstration. They're holding them in every province."

Darrah didn't reply. In all the activity after the *Lhemor* bombing, it had almost slipped his mind that there had been unrest of a different kind outside the Cardassian Embassy across the continent. There had been injuries, civilians fighting constables. *What is happening to us?* The question echoed through his head. It seemed like every time Darrah looked up, he saw more signs that his planet was losing its way.

"Remember when all we had to deal with were honest criminals and the odd smuggler here and there?" Proka had picked up on his mood; he was intuitive that way, which was one of the reasons Darrah used him as his second in command. He made a tutting noise under his breath as they entered the building.

Inside, the precinct was an exercise in controlled chaos.

The entrance atrium was full of people pushing and shoving. One group was singing a hymn and holding *duranjas*, the ceremonial lamps lit to honor the newly dead, but the majority of them were calling out for the attention of the duty officers. Some were asking after friends and family who'd been on Cemba, others were just ordinary people frightened by the things they had seen on the newsfeeds.

He saw a familiar face among them, a man threading his way toward the exit and making little headway. "Syjin."

The pilot turned and pressed through the crowd to them. "Mace, Migdal. Hey."

"What are you doing here?"

Syjin managed a weak facsimile of his usual broad smile. "The, uh, port authority called me in." He showed them a datadisk in his hand. "My ship's been released from impound because of what happened in orbit. Apparently, they rushed through the paperwork and cleared me for flight status."

"Because of the bombing?" Proka asked.

Syjin nodded. "The Space Guard has called in all available civilian ships on planet, and that includes mine. All qualified captains have been seconded to the emergency management bureau to assist with the cleanup operations. There's a lot of wreckage drifting around up there, and the military needs all the help they can get making it safe." He licked his lips. "I should thank you again. If you hadn't vouched for me, I wouldn't have a ship at all, wouldn't be able to help."

Darrah took it in. He knew that Coldri's forces were stretched thin, but he hadn't realized the situation was severe enough to force them to deputize civilian crews. "I thought the station's core was still intact."

"Mostly," Syjin replied. "The explosion knocked it out of position and it's settled into a decaying orbit. From what I heard from the other crews, it looks like it'll have to be towed out by tugs and scrapped." He blinked and looked away. "I knew a lot of good people on Cemba."

Darrah nodded, his angry mood dissipating in the face of his friend's simple grief. Bajor's shuttle crews and freight pilots were a small community and a tight-knit bunch. He had no doubt that tonight a lot of absent friends would be toasted in starport bars across the planet.

For a moment, an uncharacteristic flare of hate crossed the pilot's face. "You catch those Tzenkethi bastards who did this, Mace."

"We don't know for sure it was them," he said carefully.

Syjin eyed him. "It's all across the 'feeds. They said they were trying to assassinate the kai."

Proka's brow furrowed. "She wasn't even up there."

"That blowhard from Qui'al was on the broadcast. Kubus. He practically blamed the Guard for not stopping it."

"You saw it?" Darrah asked.

Syjin shook his head. "No, Karys told me. She saw—"

"Karys?" Darrah was brought up short by the mention of his wife. "You talked to her?"

The pilot pointed in the direction of the offices. "Sure. She was here, with another constable, the dark-haired girl. She was pretty upset, looked like she had been crying."

Darrah broke away and pushed his way back into the precinct.

He found her on the upper level, in an interview room. Light from the fading day filtered in through the window blinds. Constable Myda was with her, working a tricorder. Karys was pale, her face streaked with tear tracks. She clutched a tissue between her fingers. There was an untouched cup of *deka* tea on the table in front of her. Both women looked up as Mace slid open the door.

"Karys?" The tone of his voice was enough to communicate what he was afraid of.

She shook her head. "Bajin and Nell are fine, they're at services."

A strange mixture of fear and elation shot through him. He was so pleased that his children were safe, and yet the look on his wife's face was enough to tell him that something was very wrong. He caught a glimpse of himself in the mirrored window of the observation room next door. He saw the same cold terror there that he had witnessed every time he had been forced to give someone bad news. *Your son has been killed. Your wife is missing. We're doing all we can. I'm sorry.*

He blinked, snapping himself out of the moment. "What happened?"

Karys stifled a sniff. "Mace, wait. Just let me do this." She nodded to Myda. "I'm ready."

"All right," said the constable, giving her commander a quick glance. Myda aimed the tricorder at the table and thumbed a control, and abruptly Darrah realized what was going on.

The small holographic playback emitter inside the device cast a fan of orange-hued light across the table, and the shape of a dead man's torso and head appeared, rendered in a ghostly laser glow. Karys made a choking sound deep in her throat and nodded once. Myda tapped the control again and the image disappeared.

"The likeness data was sent from the emergency bureau facility in Ilvia, sir," she told him quietly. "I'm sorry, Inspector. Your office should have been informed automatically."

"I was in Ashalla," he replied. "I wouldn't have gotten the message." Mercifully, the face of the dead man had been free of any serious injury. He'd handled many of these identifications himself in his days as a street officer, and he knew the signs, the visible mismatching where the medical computers had made a virtual reconstruction of a countenance instead of the real thing. At least Karys had been spared that.

"It's him," said his wife. "That's my cousin, Jarel."

"Identity confirmed by next of kin," Myda said into the tricorder. The device gave an answering beep.

"What was he doing on Cemba?" asked Mace. "I never knew he was there . . ."

"He was . . . he was supervising the transport of some materials. Mistwood from Rigel, for a piece he was working on." She sniffed again. "That's Jarel. He obsesses over the details."

Mace hadn't known the man well; he remembered him vaguely from family gatherings, a gangly fellow with a braying laugh. Mace had always been an outsider at those things.

"You should have contacted me," he told Karys. "I would have done this for you."

"You were in Ashalla," she repeated, a razor under her words.

He felt each one hit him, guilt striking like ice in his gut. Mace shot Myda a look. "Can you give us some privacy, Constable?"

Myda nodded. "I'm done, sir. There were no personal effects. Your wife's free to leave."

When the door closed he went to her and held her, but Karys was rigid. "Talk to me," he said finally.

"This is too much," she told him. "After the explosion and then I thought you were gone, but you were safe and . . ." Karys choked off a sob. "And now Jarel. It's made me realize something, Mace. Something I've been hiding from, denying to myself."

"Tell me."

She pushed away from him. "I'm *afraid*, Mace! I'm afraid all the time now, for myself, for the children, for my family, for you . . . I see those aliens everywhere I go, and if not them then people who are angry about them being here, or angry with the government and the Watch . . . I don't know this place anymore!" Fresh tears crossed her cheeks. "I think we should go."

"Go? You mean, leave Korto?"

"I mean leave *Bajor!*" she shot back.

He was incredulous. "Karys, how can you say that? This is our world. This is our home."

She went to the exterior window and snapped open the blinds. Mace saw the people outside the precinct, tired and angry faces lit by lamps. "But for how much longer?" Karys's question hung in the air, and Mace found he had no answer for her.

12

The light winds across the plains ruffled the white domes of the enclave's pavilions, the smartplastic pergolas snapping and clicking against their duranium supports. The Bajorans would have considered the day to be hot, with a close and unfocused heat radiating down from a sky shrouded in thin cloud, but by Cardassian standards it was cool and temperate. Pasir crossed through the open alleys between the prefabricated buildings, his head down, with the hood of his robes up and his hands lost inside the folds of the sleeves.

The majority of the thermoconcrete blockhouses were outwardly identical, with only various two-digit reference numbers laser-burned into the lintels to differentiate one from another. Any locals who passed through this part of the enclave would be struck by the bland similarity and walk on. They would have had to stay for several hours to notice that certain groups of Cardassians never ventured inside certain buildings. It had been made clear to the Oralians with discreet but steady menace that any blockhouse with a code number above three was off-limits to them; and there were lots of three buildings and four buildings, even a larger five and a six under construction beneath another of the massive sunshades. And then there were the devices attached to the dome-tents that looked like thermal regulators but were actually something quite

different. The surfaces of the pavilions were clever con-
structions, a sandwich of energy-conductive layers that, if
correctly programmed, could give the impression of heat
sources and metallic objects moving beneath it—or make
the same appear invisible. Even the most naïve of the Oralians knew that the Bajoran Space Guard had surveillance
satellites observing every enclave on the planet.

Pasir smiled a greeting at a couple of pilgrims passing in
the other direction, and he came to the open space in the
dead center of the enclave compound. There was a small
fountain there, and it drew the attention of every Cardassian
who passed it; the sight of water being used for something so
frivolous as a decoration was fascinating to them. A natural
spring was a closely guarded resource on a world like Cardassia Prime, where even the energy cost to replicate something as simple as potable water was rationed by the government inspectorate. Here, on Bajor, water was disposable.

Of course, the construction of the fountain was not
something that had happened by chance; the Union had
the practice of architectural psychology down to a fine art.
Just as the capital cities of Cardassia had looming watch-
towers and intimidating statuary to reinforce the state's
symbolic power over the individual, so the fountain had
been built here to reinforce certain emotions in the minds
of those who lived in the enclave. Pasir sat on the lip of it
and cupped a hand in the clear water, taking a sip.

"Excuse me." It was a woman's voice. "How long is it
until sunset?"

The priest glanced up and found a somber-faced female
backlit by the afternoon sky. "Oh, please forgive me. I'm
afraid I left my chronometer in the refectory."

"Ah," she nodded. "It is difficult to reckon the hours
here, don't you find?"

"Quite." He returned her nod. His next words were in
the same light tone of voice. "You have something for me."

Rhan Ico shook her head, matching the flat, conversational speech level. "Not at the moment. But we're going to move soon. I'm in the last stages of preparing the process for your insertion. It's not your first experience of this?"

Pasir's narrow face remained fixed in a pleasant smile. "I'm sure you've read enough about me to know the depth of my experience. I'm quite ready."

She nodded. "I understand it can be painful." When he didn't answer, she spoke again. "Congratulations are in order, by the way. Your work aboard the *Lhemor* . . . The effect has been exactly as we hoped. Better, even."

He looked away, watching for any observers. The gesture seemed casual. "I admit that I was forced to improvise in the aftermath. Fortunately, I was not placed in a position where I had to compromise my legend." Pasir smiled briefly. "I underestimated the resourcefulness of Bennek and the Bajoran law enforcer." He spread his hands. *"Oralius protects,* as they say."

Ico gave him a level stare. "Or so they hope." She sighed. "I've grown weary of hearing their dogma every day, but Kell has ensured that I remain posted here instead of at the embassy in Dahkur."

"He suspects?"

"Of course. He's not a fool. But he knows little." She gestured around. "This is his small way of attempting to spite me."

"Ah." Pasir's head bobbed. "A petty man, then. But you have made good use of your posting on Bajor. The intelligence you've accumulated is quite compelling." He paused, thinking. "But Dukat . . . He appears to be a serious concern."

"Leave Dukat to me," said Ico. "He's young and ambitious, and a staunch patriot. Despite his loathing for us, I think I can use that to make him work to our agenda."

The priest took another sip of water. "Tread carefully, Rhan. He is the random factor here."

"I know."

"Should I be aware of anything else?"

She frowned slightly. "One of my subordinates—from my legend, you understand?—a man named Pa'Dar. He's exhibiting some rather independent behavior, sniffing around in areas outside his responsibility."

Pasir made an affirmative noise. "Removal, then?"

Ico shook her head. "No, that would be too problematic at this stage. Pa'Dar's family is well connected with the Detapa Council. His death would raise too many questions. Just be aware."

"I always am," said the priest. He paused and glanced down at his hands. "Regarding the . . . insertion. I'm concerned there may not be enough time for a full—"

She shook her head. "We are working on an accelerated timetable in that area, yes. But everything is in hand. As I told you, the moment is being prepared for. In the interim, we'll begin some of the less visible corrections."

"As you wish." The hollow sound of a gong rang through the clearing, and Pasir got to his feet.

"What is that?" asked the woman.

"The call to vespers," he explained. "I'm assisting Bennek in the recitation tonight, and I must prepare. He wants to make some sort of speech at the funeral service tomorrow."

Ico's lip curled. "Thank you for reminding me. I must find a convincing reason not to attend. I do find theological rituals so offensive."

"Ah, pity them, Rhan." Pasir's tone was lightly mocking. "The Oralians have so little left now. They're almost extinct."

"Yes," she agreed. "When the time comes, we will have to work harder to expunge the Bajoran faith. It will not be so easy with the aliens."

Pasir walked away. "One step at a time," he said, without looking back.

✦ ✦ ✦

The voices of the assembled hundreds in the grounds of the Naghai Keep pealed off the walls of the ancient castle, swelling the verses of old High Bajoran as the death chant neared its conclusion. As tradition had it, the families of each of the *D'jarra*s would speak a few lines, then pause as others picked up where they left off, but there were many who felt so strongly that they spoke the entirety of the chant, tears on their faces and throats cracking with emotion. There had been some suggestions that morning of policing the approach roads to the keep, to try to hold the numbers at the remembrance ceremony down to a minimum. Darrah Mace looked over the sloping ornamental gardens, at the throng gathered there, and realized that he had made the right choice ordering Proka to put away the barricades. Korto was united in grief, just like every city on Bajor. The ritual would give the people the closure they needed to bring the Cemba incident into sharp relief. Those who had lost someone they cared for would know that the Prophets were watching over them, and those who were afraid would have, at least for today, the unity of their neighbors around them.

Karys was holding hands with the children, their heads bowed. She'd hardly spoken to him since their conversation in the precinct, spending time on the comm trying to gather together the remnants of Jarel's diffuse life. Her cousin had no partner, no parents or siblings of his own left to mourn him, and Karys's mother, ever insensitive, was not sorry to see him gone. It fell to Mace's wife to arrange his burial, but she had refused point-blank any offer of assistance. Bajin caught his eye and nodded solemnly; his son had stepped in to help Karys without any request on her part, and the boy's quiet support made his father proud. Nell remained morose. She was still finding it hard to process, that some alien beings from light-years distant would come to Bajor to kill her uncle. Mace hated the fact that he had no explanation to offer her.

The lawman felt a heavy sense of dread pressing down upon him. In a blink of memory, he thought back to the *Eleda* ceremony and the deaths that had brought that to pass. Changes had been wrought that day, and now the same was happening here again. The road to the future was being marked out in the blood of Bajoran men and women. The horrific image made him shudder, and with a sudden, terrible certainty, Darrah Mace knew that what was happening today would not be an end to it. He saw himself standing in the same place, his face lined with stress, and blood there on the streets, the funeral chant repeated over and over into infinity. A million deaths, and a million more, more and more and more—

The ringing of the Bell of Souls shattered his moment of dark insight, and Darrah blinked, feeling cold sweat on his neck. He forced away the images in his mind and swallowed hard. Some distance away, on the podium set up among the ornamental gardens, Kai Meressa was being helped down from the dais by Gar and Tima. She had stood for the entirety of the chant, despite her fragility. Darrah watched her descend the steps. The kai seemed unreal, like a thin papery sketch of the woman he had first seen in the flesh five years ago. It was hard to reconcile the sight of her with the vital, passionate preacher of the past. That she held on steadfastly to life was a testament to her strength of will, and even the most dissenting of voices in the Vedek Assembly did not dare to speak openly of inviting Meressa to give up her rank and retire. Truth be told, there was not a man or woman among her subordinates who had so captured the hearts of the Bajoran people as Meressa had; when she finally left them, he had no doubt it would throw the church into disarray. Darrah forced himself to look away, the specter of death pressing in on his thoughts all over again.

Vedek Arin said some words. The platitudes seemed to work on the mourners, but to Darrah they fell on stony ground. He heard the echo of Meressa's voice in them, and wondered how much of the kai's prose the bland little priest had sifted through to gather material for his own speech; but it was with surprise that he looked again at the podium and saw the Oralian cleric Bennek step up and draw back his hood.

The alien's face was streaked with dark tears, and the simple power of the emotional display silenced all the Bajorans ranged around him. Cardassians were gray and dour, they were cold and passionless—that was the commonplace, trite perception of their race. The raw grief that flooded from Bennek was real and potent; it was shocking, in its own way.

He spoke, his voice crossing the gardens. "I am moved beyond my capacity to describe," began the cleric, his gaze seeking out faces in the crowd at random. "You, our brothers and sisters of Bajor, have taken the hand of friendship from my people, and this horror has been your reward. I am filled with such depthless sorrow as I have never known. Like many of you, people who were important to me were taken, swept away in fire, and it is for them that I join you in prayer today. The souls of all those lost on Cemba Station, aboard the *Lhemor* and the other vessels, they were stolen from us by vengeful hearts and heartless, callous killers . . ." Bennek choked back a sob, and despite himself Darrah felt a prickling in his eyes as his heart tightened in empathy; but the cleric's next words stopped the breath in his throat. "I see a path unfolding before our worlds. As Oralius blesses me and your Prophets do the same, I see it. It is a road watered by bloodshed and fear, forced upon us by those who seed darkness upon the light." He raised his hands. "All of us, Bajoran and Cardassian . . . we stand upon the threshold of this path, and we must choose wisely or else we doom ourselves to the darkest of futures. We must not embrace hate and fear, even in the face of such terrible consequences. Avarice and greed will poison us. We must look to tomorrow with our eyes open and clarity in our hearts, we must listen to the powers that watch over us. I will strive to be better than I am, and I know you will do the same in the name of the Prophets." Bennek brought his hands together. "Only in accord can we turn away from the dark road. Only in unity can Bajor and Cardassia find the way." And with that, Bennek's shoulders slumped, as if all the energy in the man had been spent in the flood of his outburst. "I . . . I weep with you," he husked, and stepped away from the podium. Darrah saw Tima at the foot of the platform; like many of the people in the crowd, she had been profoundly moved by the cleric's sincerity.

There were no problems as the crowd dispersed. Darrah watched with one eye, afraid that someone, some bereaved person angry at the world for their loss, would lash out; there was none. Instead, a somber stream of mourners threaded out of the gardens in clusters, supporting each other through their grief.

As they joined the departing groups, he spotted a gathering of figures and heard the snap of a raised voice. Karys shot him a sideways look, a warning, but he chose to ignore it and drifted closer. Mace saw the drifting shape of a camera drone and a news crew, and abruptly he knew who they were crowding around.

"But can we stand here and do nothing?" said Kubus Oak to the correspondent, his jaw set. "Are we to be a reactive people? Will our only reply to this atrocity be to weep and bury our dead?" Some of the people gathered around the minister made angry noises and shook their heads. "We cannot let this go unanswered! It was our fail-ure that allowed these good people to perish. When the

Prophets talk of judgment for the honest and the willing, we must hear that and ask ourselves, how would we be judged if we did nothing to bring justice to the ones who ended these innocent lives?"

Darrah grimaced. "The man has no shame," he said quietly. "This is a funerary ceremony, not a podium in the Chamber of Ministers."

"He's a politician," Karys replied. "It's what they do."

Mace was disgusted at Kubus's opportunism, turning the day to his own ends, using the service as a platform for his agenda. Grim-faced, he led his family past.

"There must be a reprisal," Kubus was saying, "and with the people's support I have convinced the First Minister and the government for exactly that—" He caught sight of Darrah and changed tack. "It is because of men like Inspector Darrah Mace that many more lives were saved . . ."

The camera pod turned in midair and trained a lens on Mace and his family. The controlled anger on his face flashed across newsfeeds planetwide, and for one long second he wavered on the cusp of decrying the politician for his callous grandstanding; but then he turned away. "I'm taking my family home," he said simply, and left Kubus and his circus behind. He heard the politician take his brush-off and say something about "grief" and "stress." Nell's hand touched his, and he glanced down at his daughter.

"I don't like that man," she told her father. "I don't think you should talk to him."

"You're right," he replied. "Come on. Let's get out of this place."

The transmission was authentic, and the fact that it had been sent without her authority made Lonnic Tomo furious. She gripped the padd in her hand and strode swiftly down the corridors of the keep; the hard manner she displayed made certain that none of the other staffers dared to stand in her path or waylay her. Lonnic tore open the door to Jas Holza's chamber, an accusation on her lips; but instead she saw something that made her fury jump tenfold. Kubus Oak was sitting on the ornamental couch by the window, helping himself to a generous glass of spring-wine.

He sniffed. "Doesn't your adjutant knock before she enters a room, Holza?"

Lonnic glared at her employer, who seemed thin and tired, pressed into the depths of the chair behind his desk. The surface of Jas's workspace, what had once been such a model of efficiency and care, was now a mess of padds, printout flimsies, and other detritus. It mirrored the man's manner these days, untidy and directionless.

"Tomo," said the minister, "I'm in conference. Can this wait until later?"

"No, sir, it cannot," she replied, gathering back her momentum. She ignored Kubus and stepped forward, placing the padd down on the cluttered desk with a snap. "This communiqué was in the comm traffic stack. A signal to the commanders of two of the clan's scoutships."

Jas didn't look at the padd. "I know what it says, Tomo. I wrote it."

"Did you?" she asked, shooting a look at Kubus, the question slipping out before she could halt herself. For a brief moment, Lonnic saw a flash of the old Jas Holza, irritated by her inference; but then it was gone as quickly as it had appeared. With a nearly physical effort, she clamped down on her emotions and took a breath. "Sir, why didn't you consult me on this? In my opinion, this is a serious misstep—"

Kubus made a bored noise. "Is it necessary for a minister of the Chamber to ask the opinion of his adjutant on every single matter? Do you pass your eye over every communiqué, over every little bit of text?"

Lonnic kept her gaze on Jas but answered Kubus. "This is hardly a minor matter, sir. It bears further scrutiny!"

Jas looked away. "It's done, Tomo. It's what was necessary."

Necessary. The word echoed in her thoughts. The contents of the communiqué were a terse set of orders for the best-equipped scout vessels in service to the Jas clan's prospector fleet, giving them the coordinates for a rendezvous a few light-years distant from Bajor. The two ships were to meet with two more vessels, a pair of heavy assault ships from the Space Guard under the command of Li Tarka. Their mission was to scour all the star systems within a globular search perimeter for any signs of Tzenkethi raiders, utilizing the powerful Cardassian-made sensor gear mounted on the prospector ships. Jas had ordered his own civilian crews to join a reprisal fleet.

Kubus sipped the wine. "We cannot let the Cemba incident go unanswered. It was our failure that allowed these good people—"

Lonnic rounded on him, interrupting. "Yes, Minister, I've already heard that speech once today. I saw the newsfeed."

"Then you understand the seriousness of the situation."

"What I understand—" She stopped; she was on the verge of shouting. With a breath, Lonnic moderated herself and started again. "What I understand is that your rhetoric, Minister, has pressed the council into making a rash and ill-considered decision!"

Kubus arched an eyebrow. "Is that right? The First Minister seems to think otherwise, as does General Coldri."

"Coldri's a pragmatist. He's only going along with this because you've left him with no choice," she retorted. "If he disagrees, he will look weak in the eyes of the public." Lonnic stiffened. "You're expecting civilians to go out looking for a fight, against an enemy that we're not even sure was responsible!" She glared at Jas. "And you're letting him do it."

Kubus put down the glass. "Of course the Tzenkethi are responsible! Oh, I don't doubt the Coalition will deny it to the hilt, but we know their kind, and so do the Cardassians! They're animals . . . Force, swiftly applied, is all they understand." He sat back. "We will show the flag, let them know Bajor is not a soft target for their picking. Colonel Li is a fine soldier. He won't shrink from this."

Lonnic shook her head. "I cannot believe what I am hearing. What happened to due process, to a court of law? Are we just leaping to revenge? Is that how we make government on Bajor in this day and age?" Her hands contracted into fists. "This isn't the Era of Republics anymore, Minister Kubus! We're not city-states warring against each other with swords and bows, swearing pacts or vendettas over the smallest slights! We've grown beyond that!"

The other man shook his head and glanced at Jas. "Holza, how can you manage with such a naïve woman on your staff?" Kubus looked back at Lonnic. "You're a fool if you think that Bajor has lost the taste for retribution. We may be sophisticated and civilized, but so were we ten millennia ago, and we knew then as I know now, blood can only be paid in blood!"

"I don't agree," she bit out. Lonnic could feel the moment slipping away from her. She felt as if the floor beneath her feet were turning thick and muddy, swallowing her up. She had no purchase here, nothing to grab on to. *It's done.* Jas's words resonated in her mind.

"I'm sorry, Tomo," said Jas flatly, "but I am in agreement with Oak. My order stands. It . . . it is for the best."

Lonnic's hands came together and for a moment she lost focus. He was right; there was nothing she could do now to stop Kubus working Jas as his proxy. She cursed silently. *This is my fault,* Lonnic told herself. *I saw this com-*

ing and I didn't do enough to stop it. Now it's out of my control.
She glanced at her employer and saw Jas for what he had
truly become: a puppet, the pawn of a man with a stronger
will and a longer view. Tomo had hoped for so long that
Jas would one day show the character that she knew he
had deep inside, that he would step out of the long shadow
cast by his late father. But instead, he had slipped back the
other way, retreating under the coattails of the charismatic
and strong-willed Kubus, taking the easy path.

I can't do anything here. The words formed in her
thoughts, and against the dejection she felt a sudden flare
of hope. "I can't do anything here," she said. "That's clear to
me now. But I can serve a purpose out there."

Jas's eyes narrowed. "What do you mean?"

"The fleet," she replied. "Those scoutships represent an
important part of the Jas clan's holdings. Someone should
be with Colonel Li's flotilla to oversee our interests." *And
perhaps,* she thought, *I can prevent a shooting war.*

"No," said Jas. "It's too risky. Send someone else."

"It would communicate an important message," Kubus
offered. "Lonnic Tomo, a ranking member of the Korto
District governmental body. It would show the seriousness of our intent." The minister was clearly content with
the idea of having Lonnic and her dissenting voice out of
the way.

Jas shook his head. "No," he repeated, and there was an
element of dread in his voice. "You'll be going directly in
harm's way, and I won't have that. What if something happened to you? I don't . . . I don't want you to be hurt." The
minister trailed off, embarrassed by his own reaction.

She picked up the padd and drew herself up to her full
height, for the moment ignoring the fact that Kubus was
in the room with them. "I'm doing this, Holza," Tomo told
him. "I need to do some good." She turned and glanced at
Kubus before walking out of the room. "I can't do it here."

✦ ✦ ✦

Bennek looked up at the knock on his door. The evening had become a blur; he was still caught in the emotional backwash of the funeral ceremony, and even the ride back to the enclave outside the city had swept past him in a haze of sadness. He held pages from his copy of the Hebitian Records in his hands, his fingers tracing the care-worn edges of the aged *brangwa*-hide scrolls, but his eyes were unfocused, not really reading the words in the tight old script of his ancestors. He knew the texts so well that he had no need to look at them—he could speak them by heart—but to hold the pages gave him some degree of peace, of connection to his faith.

The cleric wanted that so desperately now, but it did not come. He felt adrift, unable to voice his feelings to the others; and Pasir seemed to always be elsewhere, off to the embassy in Dahkur or back in orbit on errands.

The knock came again. It was hesitant. With a bone-deep sigh, Bennek climbed out of his wicker chair, crossed the warm confines of his room in the blockhouse, and opened the door.

Outside there was a Bajoran woman, cast slightly in shadow by the setting rays of B'hava'el. He saw immediately from her posture that she was cheerless; there was a kind of gentle vulnerability that radiated from her in waves. "Bennek?" She spoke his name with reverence.

The voice sparked recognition in him. "Tima?"

"Can I come in?" she asked. "I came out from Korto . . . I wanted to see you."

"Of course." He opened the door wider and allowed the woman inside. "Can I get you something?" Bennek gestured to a chair and she sat.

"Water?"

He nodded and poured them both glasses from the seal-jug on his desk. The cleric was hesitant. Bennek was unprepared for the girl's unannounced arrival. She ran a hand through her blond hair and blinked. He could see her better now, and he noticed the shimmer in her striking green eyes. She'd been crying, and he felt a stab of guilt, as if he had been the cause of it.

"Are you well?" he asked. There was the slightest tracery of a scar just below her hairline on her temple, where she had been injured on board the Cemba platform.

Tima nodded. "The doctors told me there will be no lasting damage." She gave a shallow sigh. "I never really thanked you for what you did on the station," she began.

She had been terrified; Bennek had offered her words of comfort. He shook his head. "I did only what Oralius asks of all of us, to care for our fellow beings."

She looked at the floor. "I was so scared, and I ... I didn't want to say anything in front of Vedek Arin. ... I couldn't . . ."

She confided in me because I am an alien, he thought. *Because she knew I would not judge her for being afraid.*

"You are a good man," she continued. "I wanted to tell you that."

Her words made him hesitate. "I ... Thank you, Tima." Bennek watched the Bajoran girl, drawn to her face. She was so delicate, the straw-colored hair about her head falling in golden lines, the blush on her flawless cheeks like a piece of living artwork. He recalled his first impressions of the Bajoran females he had seen years ago in the Naghai Keep. *Like the desert nymphs of mythology.*

"What you said today, in the gardens." She swallowed. "Bennek, your words moved me in a way that I've never felt before. You were so honest, so truthful." Her hand fell upon his, and it was warm. "But you're so lonely."

"I ..." He tried to find a response, but her statement disarmed him with its simple directness.

"I can see it in you." Tima nodded. "Even across the gulf

of our species, I can see it. You're vulnerable and alone. You are surrounded by companions, but there's not one of them you can confide in. I feel so sorry for you. I want to help."

How can she know me so well? It was a shock for the cleric to realize the woman could intuit his thoughts and feelings. *And she's right. Hadlo is far from here, and his mind is ranging still further. Pasir and the others, they are so earnest but so distant from me. But this one . . . She is here with me now. In all ways.*

"I want to learn from you," Tima said carefully. "Tell me of Oralius and the Way, tell me how she touches the path of the Prophets."

He nodded. "I will, if that is what you wish." He reached for the scrolls, but Tima stopped him.

"But not now. Will you let me give you something first?"

"Yes." His throat turned to sand.

Tima's hands came to his cheeks and his to hers. She was warm, warm all over, her body like the orange sunlight of his homeworld. Bennek's eyes closed, and he tasted çool water on her lips.

13

The sky above the port was unusually clear. Launch platforms that normally echoed with liftoffs and landings were quiet, with almost every ship in service in operation off-planet. The only activity was from the ground crews, working at fuel stations or maintenance carts, waiting for the return of the civilian ships that the emergency bureau had pressed into disaster management duties. They had to work at keeping turnaround times to a minimum, so that low-duration ships could spend as little time as possible on the ground and the maximum in orbit clearing the debris. The shock wave from the explosion of the *Lhemor* had ripped parts of Cemba Station and the other ships at dock into a cloud of hull fragments and wreckage; for the past few nights everyone on Bajor's northern continent had been treated to skies streaked with shooting stars as the smaller sections burned up in the atmosphere. But there were larger, more lethal pieces up there, some leaking toxic material, some dense enough that they would strike down a city if they fell on a populated area. The crews in orbit were working around the clock to neutralize the threats. Darrah looked up into the blue sky, wondering where Syjin was at that moment, what the itinerant pilot was doing to keep his planet safe.

Darrah had managed to catch a few words with the captain of a cargo lighter down from the lunar colony on

Derna. Darrah wasn't there to ask after the progress of the cleanup; he wanted to know about the *Lhemor*.

Since the funeral ceremony, sleep had become harder to find. While Karys dozed fitfully beside him, Mace stared at the ceiling, trying to distill the churn of thoughts in his mind into some kind of order. Kubus's rhetoric and the circumstances of the explosion lay on him like a lead weight. Every moment his thoughts drifted from what was at hand, and he found himself thinking back through the desperate hours on Cemba. He struggled to recall every moment of his time up there on the docking platform. Had he seen something that hadn't registered at the time? Someone suspicious? Something that rang a wrong note? Like all the other survivors, he had given a detailed statement to the Space Guard, but he couldn't shake a sense that what he'd told them was somehow incomplete.

Try as he might, there was nothing that came to mind, and that disturbed Darrah Mace most of all. The Cardassians said that the charge that claimed the *Lhemor* had been placed on board the freighter after it left their star system, and since the ship had been at high warp all that time, the only time a bomb could have been planted was upon arrival in Bajor orbit. But Darrah was sure of one thing. He'd watched the hatches to the freighter open, seen the docking tube extending. No one had entered, and only the Oralians had left. He had come to be sure of that at least. His attempts to follow through on his suspicions were getting him nowhere, however. The Cardassians had been the first on the scene, and ships under the control of Jagul Kell had swiftly tractored away anything that remained of the *Lhemor*'s structure, claiming it under diplomatic auspices. Now the inspector was here, hoping to find some clue from the men and women who were working up there amid what amounted to the planet's largest crime scene—perhaps some report of an unusual sensor reading, or a piece of the *Lhemor* the Cardassians had missed. But so far, nothing.

Darrah's hands knitted together. Suspicion prickled the flesh on the back of his neck as if it were a physical presence. It came down to a simple equation in back of the lawman's thoughts. *Something isn't right here, and I need to know why.*

The mutter of conversation from one of the hangars drew his attention, and Darrah's eyes narrowed at the sight of a Cardassian speaking with one of the ground technicians. Darrah had spoken to the tech earlier; the woman was on the crew of a heavy impulse tug that usually worked the plasma trawlers from the Denorios Belt. Her words became clearer as he approached.

"I can't help you," the woman said sharply. "I don't make the rules, I'm just duty chief on the ground. You want passage, you need to speak to the pilots and captains, and they're all up there." She jerked a thumb at the sky. "So unless you want to wait for the next ship down for tanking, you might as well go back to your enclave." The Cardassian man—Darrah saw now that the alien was one of their civilian types, without the robes of an Oralian or the duty armor of a military officer—made to say something, but the tech cut him off. "Besides, you got enough of your own damn ships in orbit, don't you? Why can't you hitch a ride with one of them?" She walked away, ending any chance at further conversation.

The Cardassian turned, frustration on his face, but the expression swiftly changed to alarm as he caught sight of the law énforcer. His eyes darted left-right, as if he were looking for an escape route.

"Are you lost?" offered Darrah. He nodded in the direction of the flyer pads out toward the far end of the port compound. "These are the yards for the interstellar and orbital ships. Atmospheric flyers are over there."

"I . . . I don't require a flyer," came the hesitant reply.

Darrah studied the alien and a name came to him. "Pa'Dar. You're the scientist. I saw you with Kell in Ashalla."

He got a nod in return. "That is correct. And you are Inspector Darrah, yes?"

"What are you doing here, Mr. Pa'Dar?"

The alien shifted uncomfortably. "I should be going, I think . . ."

"I'm asking because I have your best interests in mind." Darrah slipped easily into his default manner for addressing suspects. "There are a lot of upset people in the city. People who blame Cardassians for what happened in orbit."

"It wasn't our fault," Pa'Dar replied, but Darrah saw that the response was something automatic for him. He didn't believe it. After this long working alongside the aliens, he knew them well enough to read the cues of their body language as well as any Bajorans. It was one of the skills that made him a good police officer.

"Why don't you tell me why you want to go offworld." Darrah closed the distance between them, making their conversation more intimate, less open. "And why you want to do it without your superiors knowing."

Pa'Dar schooled his expression, realizing too late that he'd given away something of himself. "The Union's ships are otherwise engaged, and I merely wanted to see the site for myself."

A lie. Darrah knew it immediately. He decided to take a chance. Based on what he knew of the Cardassians, their culture was stratified into those in service to the military, the government, and the civilian populace. Each was looked down upon by the group above theirs, and Darrah had no doubt that as a scientist, Pa'Dar was used to being beleaguered by Kell's men. "Your Central Command hasn't been very open with its findings, despite what you said in Ashalla."

There was a flash of understanding in Pa'Dar's eyes, and

Darrah smiled inwardly. *He doesn't trust the answers he's been given, just like me.*

"There's no error in making a secondary evaluation," came the reply. "It's my job to take a closer look at things," he concluded.

"Mine too," added Darrah.

Pa'Dar stepped away. "I think I should follow the suggestion I was given and return to the enclave. I do not believe I will be able to do more here." He inclined his head, his disappointment clearly evident. "Until we meet again, Inspector Darrah."

"Mr. Pa'Dar. Perhaps when that happens, we might find something more to talk about."

"Such as?"

"Call it common interests." For a moment, Darrah considered holding him, but what reason could he have given? He watched the alien thread his way toward the flyers.

Behind him, the chatter of the ground crew picked up and Darrah turned to see them break into motion. It was a sure sign that a ship was coming down, and within moments he saw a dot leading a white contrail out of the sky. It was an oval shuttlecraft with stubby winglets, the kind of short-range impulse ship that plied the spacelanes inside the B'hava'el system. Darrah watched the craft land, noting the symbol on the hull; the ship was one of a few auxiliaries in the service of the clergy, and as such it was exempt from the authority of the emergency bureau. When the embarkation ramp hit the apron, the third man out of the hatch was Gar Osen, gathering his robes in a fist to keep them from flapping in the wind generated by the idling thrusters.

Gar saw Darrah and waved to him. "Come to meet me?" The priest meant the words in jest, but the lawman detected a definite edge of weariness.

Darrah shook his head. "Just passing through." He glanced over Gar's shoulder. "Is the Kai with you?"

Gar's expression saddened. "No. No, Vedek Arin had the pilot take us down over the sea first, so we could take Her Eminence back to the retreat at Calash."

"Where have you been?"

"Derna," said the ranjen, indicating the sky. Bajor's fourth moon was just visible, peeking slightly over the horizon. "A dedication ceremony, nothing more, but the kai insisted on joining us. I wish she had not."

Darrah nodded. "She's no better, then?"

"Meressa says the Prophets are testing her," Gar said in a fatigued voice, "that they are testing all of us. She refuses to be sidelined, as much as Arin would wish it."

The lawman said nothing. He had known a friend of his father's who had died from Yerrin syndrome. The old man had not gone easily, lingering for years with the pain as his own blood slowly turned to poison in his veins.

Gar sighed. "Let's talk of other things. Have you spoken to Tomo recently? She didn't come to services this week, and she's seemed more distant than usual."

Darrah blinked. "You haven't heard?"

"Heard what? I've been on Derna for the last three days. It's a bit rural up there."

"Of course . . ." He took a breath. "Osen, she's gone. She joined the task force going out to look for signs of the Tzenkethi."

"What?" Gar blinked in surprise. "What could she hope to do there?"

"I'm not sure," Darrah admitted, "but when we last spoke she was agitated by something. She told me that she could make a difference if she went with them."

The priest frowned. "Well. I'll say a prayer in her name, then." He sighed. "It makes me sad to say it, but Vedek Arin was one of those who supported Kubus's petition for the fleet's mission. I find some very unpleasant commonalities in the interests of those two men."

Darrah patted his friend on the shoulder and leaned in. "There are more who agree with Kubus than those who don't, especially here in Korto." He kept his voice low so that it wouldn't carry far. "All the events of recent days, the Cemba incident and the deaths. I can't shake the feeling that something more is going on. Something hidden from us."

Gar's eyes widened. "I will admit . . . I too have had some concerns of late. But is there any evidence? You're a lawman, Mace. You know what's needed."

He nodded again. "You're not saying anything that hasn't occurred to me already, believe me." Darrah's chrono pinged suddenly and he shot a glance at it; the alarm was warning him that he had a staff meeting back at the precinct. "I have to go. Look, we'll talk some more about this later. In the meantime, just . . . keep your eyes and ears open, eh?"

Gar nodded once. "A priest always listens. It's one of the things we do best."

Gar watched his friend go before following the rest of the group toward the flyer bays. He drew into himself, thinking on Darrah's words. Mace was always a suspicious soul, that had been true for his entire life, and in his line of work, it fulfilled a function that did the community good. For Gar, it did not come so easily. He had joined the priesthood because he believed in the fundamental good in people, but what good could there be in those who had caused such a horror as the bombing of the *Lhemor*? The Oralians were a decent, honest group of souls who came with genuine reverence and honor for the Bajoran faith. Since that night in the library of the Naghai Keep, he had learned much of their Way and of the parallels it shared with the worship of the Celestial Temple. It made him feel sick inside to contemplate that serpents with hate in their hearts might lurk among them.

"Brother Gar!" He turned at the sound of his name and halted in surprise. In his pastel robes, the Cardassian cleric Pasir was crossing the landing pad toward him.

He bobbed his head in greeting. The Oralian priest's usual open smile was absent. Pasir seemed muted, and he kept glancing around as if he were afraid of being seen by someone.

"Gar," he said, coming close. "I am so pleased I found you. I've been looking for you for days, but I heard you were offplanet."

"I was on Derna."

Pasir nodded. "Yes, I know. I had nowhere else to turn. I did not want to chance speaking to anyone else."

The Cardassian was afraid. Gar scanned the alleys between the hangars for any sign that Darrah could still be around, but he saw none. One of the prylars from the shuttle threw him a look from the hatch of the skimmer that was to take them back to Kendra. Gar glanced back at Pasir and saw the pleading on his face. "Go on ahead without me," he called out. "I'll get a flyer and follow you." The prylar nodded and shut the hatch behind him. The skimmer took off, leaving Gar and Pasir alone.

"Thank you, Ranjen, thank you." Pasir gripped Gar's arm. "You have no idea how important this is."

Gar studied the alien, thinking of his parting words to Mace. The Cardassian wanted him to listen, and he found he wanted to know what the Oralian had to tell him.

"There's something I have to show to you," said Pasir. "Something terrible, something that threatens both our faiths." His voice dropped to a conspiratorial whisper. "I am being coerced, brother. Men with huge and frightening plans hold sway over me, and I cannot let it go on any longer. I must confess." The alien's eyes were filled with desperation. "Will you help me?"

"Pasir," Gar began. "If you are afraid for your life, I can

see you safe. Inspector Darrah Mace of the City Watch is a close personal friend, and I—"

"No! No one else!" hissed the cleric. "You're the only one I can trust, Osen. The only one I know that is untouched by the stain of the Obsidian Order. Spies and liars, all of them. They caused the *Lhemor* to be destroyed. They are the root of the danger." His fingers tightened on Gar's arm. "Please, just come with me."

At last Gar gave a slow nod. "All right. Lead the way, and I will listen."

The door to Kell's private office closed behind Dukat with a faint thud of magnetic bolts, and at the edge of his hearing he picked up the whine of a broad-spectrum jamming array. Even here, in the heart of the Union embassy, the jagul was taking no chances that his security would be compromised.

Dukat felt ambivalent with an empty holster at his side; the guard at the turbolift had taken the dal's weapon and placed it in safekeeping. Although he still had a push-dagger secreted in the sleeve of his uniform, something about having the capacity to disintegrate Danig Kell where he stood always made Dukat feel more comfortable in the man's presence.

Kell made a steeple of his fingers across the top of his desk. "Don't stand there like a trainee before the commandant, Dukat," he snapped. "Get over here."

Dukat didn't move. Instead, he gave the woman seated before Kell a level stare. "Your summons indicated that this was a meeting of senior officers only. There's a civilian in the room."

Rhan Ico arched an eyebrow. "Really, Dalin Dukat, there's no need for such formality. The jagul and I have been engaging in a very entertaining discussion."

Ico's words confirmed what he suspected: Kell's "meeting" had started much earlier—it was only now that Dukat was being allowed to join them. His lips thinned in a sneer. He was reaching the end of his patience with Kell and the situation on Bajor. He had come to Dahkur seeking a resolution, and in that moment he decided that he would have it. Returning to Cardassia with nothing to show would only serve to reinforce his already ill-starred status with Central Command.

Kell's face was heavy with anger, and for the first time Dukat guessed that it wasn't directed at him. As he crossed the room, Dukat saw that the power of the confrontation taking place here did not lay with the jagul; it lay in the hands of the woman. *What must she have said to him before I entered?* Dukat had a reasonable idea what it might have been.

"I've received several intercepts from officers on ships stationed in Bajor orbit," Kell was terse. "It seems that the *Kashai* has been conducting sensor sweeps of the orbital debris zone around the Cemba Station without consent from this embassy. This was done on your orders, Dukat."

"I don't deny it," the dal replied. "I offered the service of my ship and crew to the squadron commander involved in recovery of the *Lhemor* wreckage. He refused, despite the fact that the *Kashai* has a full complement of technical staff currently standing idle." He paused. "I decided to act on my own authority."

Ico made a small noise of amusement, but Kell found his words anything but entertaining. "And that, Dal, is why you have so few friends at Command. You show too much temerity. A Cardassian officer follows orders."

"A Cardassian officer serves his Union," Dukat retorted. "How does waiting dead in space do that?" He folded his arms. "It was your intention to marginalize me from the moment I arrived, and now, even in the face of this . . . this *incident*, you continue to do so."

"The tragic circumstances that led to the loss of the *Lhemor* and the deaths on Cemba Station are under investigation," Ico added. "They are not your concern, Dal."

Dukat threw back his head with a bitter bark of laughter. "What do you take me for, woman? Do I look like a simpleton to you? Please don't insult my intelligence again. Save your lies for the Bajorans." He bared his teeth. "I think everyone in this room understands what took place on the *Lhemor.*"

"You have a theory?" Ico said blandly. "Oh, please do enlighten us."

Dukat's hand balled into a fist, and he resisted the urge to backhand the insouciant smile off the woman's face. "How many agents of the Obsidian Order have you inserted into Bajor since the first contact delegation, I wonder? Five, ten? Twenty? A hundred?" Dukat stabbed a finger at Kell. "More than he knows of, I would imagine."

Ico's insipid smile never faltered, not for one moment. "I'm afraid I don't follow you, Dal. I have no knowledge of espionage. I'm only a scientist, a cultural ethnologist and observer."

"Of course you are," Dukat retorted. "A very well-informed, very well-connected scientist. And yet there seems to be precious little of your work in the public record, Professor Ico. When did you last publish? There was nothing current in Cardassia's libraries that I could find before I left for Bajor."

Her smile widened. "You wanted to learn more about me? Oh, I'm flattered."

The woman wasn't going to give him anything that easily, he could see it in her manner. He looked at Kell, seeking a softer target. "She told you what happened, didn't she? That's why she's here."

The jagul eyed him. "Contrary to what you might believe, Dukat, there are decisions made above your rank that you are not and will never be privy to."

Dukat glared at Ico. "The Obsidian Order destroyed the *Lhemor*. It wasn't the Tzenkethi. Even with the holes in the Bajoran security perimeter, the Tzenkethi would never have been allowed to do something like this. *We* would have stopped them first."

Ico inclined her head and mused, as if Dukat were positing some mildly diverting conundrum for her to untangle. "An interesting supposition. Let's consider that possibility, then, shall we? Purely as a hypothetical thought experiment, you understand?" She straightened in her chair. "Imagine that the Obsidian Order did indeed initiate the destruction of the freighter *Lhemor* and the resultant loss of life, both Oralian and Bajoran—"

"There were Union soldiers on that station as well," Dukat grated.

The woman continued. "What motive might the Order have for such a deed?"

"Chaos and mayhem are your stock-in-trade," he spat. "You thrive on it. Keep others off balance while you plot and scheme."

Ico chuckled. "I would imagine that chaos is far'from the goal of the Obsidian Order. Such organizations seek stability, Dukat. Harmony for all Cardassia." She shook her head. "No, I submit to you that, given the scenario you imagined, the net result of the *Lhemor*'s destruction will bring a staged change in Bajoran extraplanetary policy that will bring them closer to the Cardassian aegis—"

"You spineless fools." He snarled the words, heavy with venom, and with such vehemence that for the first time Ico's featureless mask of indifference slipped.

"Watch your tone!" Kell snorted. "I'll have you cashiered."

Dukat ignored the threat. *"That* is the endgame for your great plan? You've been here for five years and that is the best you can do?" He snorted derisively. "You don't know anything about these people! Both of you, you sit cosseted inside your compound and your enclave, playing off against one another, living well while Cardassia continues to starve!" He was shouting now, anger roiling in the air like smoke, and he glared at the woman. "Obsidian is opaque, but you are transparent. Do you think that your desires are hidden from the rest of us?" He leaned forward. "I know what you want. I know all about the legends of the Orbs."

When Ico spoke again, her voice was icy and he knew he had struck a nerve. "A metered progression is the best approach to any cultural intervention when direct military force is not an option."

Dukat sneered. "I understand why I was sent here now. You've become comfortable and hidebound, like the Bajorans. What's needed here is boldness." He shot Kell a hard look. *"Temerity,* Jagul."

Kell came to his feet. "You insubordinate whelp! How dare you stand before me and judge my orders! You will respect my rank and do as I command you!"

"No." Ico stopped Kell dead with a single word. She wasn't looking at them anymore. Instead, the woman's eyes were unfocused, seeing inward. "He's correct."

"What?" Kell's bluster faltered.

"He's right. It has been five years, and still Bajor remains in a state of grace, outside the rule of Cardassia. We have been remiss. Too much effort spent on infrastructure and not enough on operational concerns . . ." She turned to face Dukat, and it was as if he were looking at a different person. The studied mien of Rhan Ico faded like mist and in its place there was a dissimilar woman. She looked at Dukat in the way that he would sight down the barrel of a weapon toward a target, nodding to herself. "Let me cut to the heart of your frustration, Dukat," she told him. "What angers you about the *Lhemor* is not that the ship was obliterated, that Bajorans and Oralians, even loyal Cardassian soldiers, died in honorable service to the needs of their nation ..." Ico shook her head gently. "No, the root of your fury is that the military was kept in the dark. *You* were kept in the dark."

Dukat's jaw set hard, his skin stiffening with annoyance. If there had been any doubt still remaining in his mind that Ico was in the Obsidian Order's service, it fled now in the face of her cool insight.

The edges of a cruel smile tugged at the corners of her lips. "But the time for that is over. Perhaps we can use your passion to a better end." She studied him, looking him up and down. "What do you have to offer your Union, Dukat? Are you just an ordinary officer with pretensions above his station ... or could you rise above your rank to become something more?"

"I will do what Cardassia requires of me." He bit out the words. "Even if that means I must serve alongside you."

Ico looked at Kell. "The dal has brought me some fresh perspective, Jagul. It's time to move things along. We must work harder to isolate the Oralians and reinforce Cardassia's influence over this planet."

"And how do you propose we accomplish that?" Kell demanded.

"I can tell you how," Dukat replied. "I understand these aliens. I've seen how they think, how they feel, and what they want." Unbidden, memories surfaced in his thoughts. *On the battlements of the Naghai Keep on the eve of the great feast. Dukat and the lawman, Darrah, talking as two men, nothing more; then again, in the corridors of the castle, as hate filled him and the need to take Hadlo's life burned in his skin.* The Bajoran's words came back to in him a flash of insight. *We're a passionate people. We get so angry about things we lose focus on everything else.* "The Bajorans hold grudges forever," he told them. "They nurture them like their children. All we need to do

to blindside these people is to bring them to rage. You only
made them afraid. We need to make them furious."

"I refer you to my earlier statement." Kell was sour.

Dukat leaned forward and picked up a padd from the
jagul's desk. On it was a report of two Bajoran warships that
had recently departed the star system. The raw anger he had
felt when he entered the room waned, replaced by a colder,
more controlled resentment. They were forming a pact here,
he realized. Without open words or accords, Dukat, Ico, and
Kell were opening the way to the fall of an entire civilization. *For the good of Cardassia. For Athra and my family.*

"I know exactly how to do it," he told them.

Lonnic entered the *Clarion's* triangular bridge at the apex,
the hatch doors retracting into the deck at her approach.
On the upper tier of the command deck men and women
in gray uniforms sat working consoles, and on the lower
level in the engineering pits she saw enlisted crew busy at
banks of power controls. Colonel Li's station was offset to
the starboard side, ringed with elliptical panels that relayed
all the data the ship's commander required from the heavy
assault ship's systems.

The *Clarion* was unlike the scouts of the Jas clan's fleet
or the civilian liners Lonnic was familiar with. The military
ship was all steel walls and sparse construction; the compartment they had provided her with was barely the width of
her closet back home on Bajor, with a netting hammock-
bed instead of the sleeping pallet she was used to.

Li beckoned her across the bridge, speaking to one of
the other crew members. "Does it match the profile we
have in our database?"

The officer nodded. "Confirmed, Colonel. It's not a target we've designated before, but the energy silhouette and
warp trail decay curve are right on the line."

"Good. Start a sensor file on this one, designate it as

required, and then have the navigator plot me a speed course for intercept."

"Acknowledged." The officer stepped away, and Li turned his attention to the adjutant.

"Ms. Lonnic. I wanted to let you know. The crew of one of your scoutships, the *Kylen,* has reported in. They've confirmed a report we received of a possible Tzenkethi contact a few light-years from our current position. Those sensors of theirs are quite impressive."

She nodded. "We're going to approach it, then?"

"Just as soon as I have my ship in order. I want to get this done quickly and cleanly, then get home to my wife and son." His words were clipped. Lonnic could see he didn't want to tarry out here in the depths of the sector any longer than he needed to. Like the rest of the *Clarion* crew, he wanted decisive action rather than a long, drawn-out operation.

Something concerned her. "Colonel, you said you received a report? From one of the other vessels?"

He shook his head. "A subspace signal from Bajor, relayed from the crew of a freighter."

"Who sent the signal?"

He glanced at a console. "It was a ministerial mandate, from the office of Kubus Oak. The freighter is one of his."

"Kubus?" Lonnic felt herself tense. "With all due respect, Colonel, can you be sure the data is, ah—"

"Trustworthy?" Li broke in. "That's why I had the *Kylen* make a close approach to the location. They confirmed it. A single Tzenkethi marauder at anchor in the Ajir system."

Lonnic's mistrust was acid in her throat. "All the same, perhaps we should proceed with caution."

"My intentions exactly," he snapped back, prickling at her manner. "And when we're done with caution, if I detect one atom of explosives on board that ship, we'll space them." The colonel shot her another look. "There were friends of mine aboard a Guard cutter tethered to

Cemba Station, Ms. Lonnic. Not a one of them got out alive. I intend to offer the Tzenkethi the very same."

She fell silent. *Did Kubus know that Li has a personal stake in this reprisal?* The answer was obvious. *Of course he does. Doubtless Li Tarka was selected over Jaro Essa to lead the mission for just that reason.*

The bridge officer called out to his commander. "Ajir course plotted and laid in, Colonel. Action stations at standby."

Li settled back into his chair. "Sound alert condition and make for maximum warp cruise. We have some unfinished business to conclude."

Lonnic glanced up at the tripartite viewscreen just as the *Clarion* leapt beyond light speed, streaking the darkness with bands of white.

Gar glanced out of the flyer's sloped window, watching the lowlands flash past in a blur of greenery. In the distance he could see the hazy peaks of the Kendran Range; below the mountains were the floodplains of the River Yolja, but it was impossible to see them through a thick bank of ashen-colored clouds sweeping eastward toward them. In the distance the priest could make out tiny bright glitters where lightning was flashing to the ground. The storm would be upon the lowlands by nightfall, and the summer tempests were always harsh, despite the work of the weather modification satellites.

The sight of the storm deepened Gar's sense of discomfort, and he turned back to face Pasir in the pilot's chair. "How much farther?"

"Not far now," the Cardassian said briskly.

Gar sighed. "Pasir, please, you cannot simply expect me to remain silent while we fly about the planet. You speak of secrets, of something you call the Obsidian Order, and then take this ship without filing a flight plan . . ."

"I did file a flight plan," Pasir corrected. "Just not the one we're actually using." The flyer hit a thermal, and the alien deftly navigated through it.

"I wasn't aware you were such an accomplished pilot."

Pasir shrugged. "I'd imagine there's much about me you're unaware of." He said the words with cold dismissal.

Gar's resolve hardened. "I think we should turn around," he said firmly. "Go back to Korto, find Darrah. Whatever your problem is, he will be able to help."

"That's not going to happen."

Gar moved forward, reaching for the communications panel. "I'll contact him—"

The Cardassian's hand shot out of his robes with a compact pistol in his grip, and he cracked Gar's fingers with it, smashing them against the plastic. The Bajoran howled in shock and pain, clutching his broken knuckles to him.

"What do you want?" Gar demanded.

"Silence," Pasir said, in a voice that was knife-sharp.

He's going to kill me. The thought pressed into Gar's mind, sudden and hard. *If I don't get away from him, I will die.*

The Cardassian glanced at him. "Don't do anything else," he began.

Gar threw himself out of his chair and into the alien, crying out again as he tried to grip Pasir's gun hand with his ruined fingers. An impact slammed him forward, and he felt the aircraft's throttle bar shift beneath him. There was a surge of engine noise, and the flyer's blunt nose slipped off the line of the stormy horizon and down toward the ground.

14

The Tzenkethi ship drifted in the shallows of the gas giant's outermost atmospheric layer, tracing faint eddies of hydrocarbon-rich mist around it. When in flight mode, the elongated fuselage resembled a smooth, seamless teardrop; the hulls of marauders of this class were inspired by ocean predators from the abyssal deeps of Ab-Tzenketh, but at this moment the clean lines of the vessel were marred by the vent hatches that lay open along its flanks. Absorption grids trawled the planet's clouds for consumable chemicals and raw matter for the fuel stores, while mile-long antennae no more than the thickness of a hair trailed out behind. The patterns of radiation flux shifting between the gas giant and the numerous moons that crowded its orbit stroked the aerials, and the vessel drew the energy in to bolster its stores.

The ship's mission was almost at an end. The sortie had been a disappointing one, with little in the way of prey craft to pursue and nothing but dead space and distant sightings in between. In another half-rotation, once the matter banks were fat and sated, they would furl the antennae and close the grids before making a high-speed warp sprint back into Coalition space. Home base would be under their keel soon after.

Inside the ionosphere, the play of the planet's radiation belts ensured that the Tzenkethi marauder's sensors were fouled by great drifting clouds of electronic fog; only a small pilot pod in a higher orbit, attached by a diamond-filament tether, floated high enough to be clear of the effects. It was the single crew member aboard the pod who detected the arrival of four starships as they emerged from the sunward side of the gas giant, their shields raised and their weapons running hot.

"Compensating for atmospheric interference . . ." The *Clarion*'s deck officer worked his console. "Set. I read a metallic mass in the upper atmosphere, four thousand kellipates distant, quadrant blue."

"Weapons," said Colonel Li. "I want synchronous fire. Program for salvo barrage, phasers and missile tubes one through four."

Lonnic's fingers gripped the cushioned back of the colonel's command chair. Standing behind him appeared to be the only place on the assault ship's bridge where she wasn't in someone's way. She saw the formation of the reprisal fleet on one of Li's consoles. The two scoutships in Minister Jas's employ were keeping abeam of the bigger military ships. Their forward-mounted phase-cannon turrets lacked the power of the weapons on the battle vessels, but in concert they could still be deadly.

"Merculite warheads loaded in all tubes," reported the deck officer. "The marauder is reacting. They're reeling in their observation pod. I'm reading an aspect change."

"Might be contemplating a dive into the troposphere," Li said, half to himself. "Can't have that." He looked up. "Sensors! Go to full power, active sweep. Rattle their decks a little."

"Colonel," said Lonnic, "are you going to fire on them without any formal declaration?"

He didn't bother to look at her. "I don't recall the people on Cemba being given any warning, do you?"

"No . . . but if the crew of that ship are not responsible, would you want it said that Bajorans showed the same callous disregard for life that the bombers did?"

Li grunted. "Ms. Lonnic, I don't give a damn what is thought about me. Our space was invaded and an atrocity was committed. If I had my way, it would be classified for what it is. An act of war."

"Colonel!" Her voice rose. She saw whatever shreds of authority her position as a ministerial adjutant gave her eroding by the second in the face of Li's grim intent. "We have nothing but circumstantial evidence that the Tzenkethi were even involved!"

"Sensor sweep complete," said the deck officer. "I can confirm the presence of volatile stocks aboard the alien vessel, sir. Refined triceron, military grade."

Li looked up at her. "There's your smoking gun. Do you want me to wait for a signed confession?"

"Many warships carry triceron explosives," she insisted. "Colonel, at least offer them a chance to surrender. Otherwise, we'll never know the truth about what happened." Lonnic saw the hesitation in his manner and she pushed on. "There could be more devices on Bajor, a network of terror cells, other marauders . . . There might be valuable intelligence."

At last the commander nodded. "I'll admit, the thought had occurred to me." He gestured to the deck officer. "Suspend firing countdown. Get me communications. Tell the Tzenkethi, stand to and prepare to be boarded."

"Transmitting," came the reply.

Lonnic felt cold sweat prickling the back of her neck as she watched the tactical plot on the portside viewscreen. The alien ship did not reply; instead it turned, rising up through the exosphere of the gas giant, gathering itself in.

"Aspect change!" shouted the deck officer. "Marauder entering attack configuration!"

"It seems we have an answer," Li told her. "Weapons, track and fire—"

On the screen a plume of brilliant white plasma lanced up from the rising shape of the alien ship and flashed past the wing of the *Clarion*.

A warning shot? The question echoed through her thoughts, even as the realization struck Lonnic that the blast had been anything but that. On the tactical plot, the glyph symbolizing the *Kylen* blinked twice and vanished. Lonnic's heart leapt into her throat. There were eight men on that ship, and she knew every one of them.

The scoutship's fate was sealed when her captain, inexperienced in confrontations with hostiles, moved too far out of the *Clarion's* formation. The territory of the Tzenkethi—which the aliens classed as their ship and a generous measure of space around it—was being invaded and their automatic reaction was to take up a belligerent posture. The voices of the invaders they heard over their translator matrix heaped insult upon insult, daring to demand access to the marauder itself. The Tzenkethi crew's reaction was instant and lethal.

With a near full-energy bank behind it, the plasma projector released a murderous warshot that tore through the *Kylen's* shields. Gaseous matter with the temperature of a solar core bored through duranium hull plating and opened the small scoutship to the void. The *Kylen* disintegrated, speared on a rod of sunfire.

The second scout, the *Pajul,* peeled off and showed the alien her impulse grids, gaining distance as the Tzenkethi pivoted and charged for a second strike. The alien moved swiftly, turning to avoid a barrage of missile fire from the assault vessels as they detonated in a chain of proximity-fused explosions. The blast wall tore open the pilot pod trailing on its tether, killing the occupant, and slammed a kinetic shock through the marauder's hull.

Another plasma spear probed out after the *Pajul*, missing its mark.

Lonnic clung to a stanchion as the *Clarion*'s gravity compensators struggled to keep up with the ship's swift maneuvers. She pressed herself against the cold metal, willing herself to diminish. *What am I doing here?* She cried silently. *I can't stop this! I thought I could, but there's nothing I can do!* A childhood fear surged through her as the assault ship rocked under impacts from the Tzenkethi weapons. Lonnic remembered the ghost stories of her grandfather, of the tales of the dead lost in space who became angry *borhyas* that drew on the souls of those about to perish. She felt fear crowding in on her, her blood turning to ice water. In that moment she understood that all the power her esteemed rank could muster on Bajor was utterly worthless to her here; and in her mind's eye she saw Kubus Oak's self-indulgent smile, as if he were watching her life tick away and taking amusement from it.

A panel across the bridge flashed with electric discharge and a body fell away from it, skin crisped black-red and wreathed in sweet-smelling smoke. Lonnic fought back a retch from deep in her stomach.

"The *Pajul*'s taken a glancing hit," said a voice. She couldn't be sure who had spoken. "Venting plasma. They've dumped their warp core, but they still have mobility."

"We can't help them," Li retorted. "Bring us about, order all ships to put power to weapons. Sweep in and rake the target!"

"Yes, sir!"

The pit of Lonnic's gut dropped out as the *Clarion* turned sharply again.

The inner walls of the Tzenkethi ship's hull were studded with powerful field nodes that reinforced structural integrity and internal gravity envelopes. It was this design aspect that lent a deadly agility to the marauder, allowing the starship to perform actions that craft several times smaller would struggle with. The marauder pivoted, shedding the energy of velocity in a wash of radiation, snapping about to face the two Bajoran assault ships bearing down upon it. Phaser fire ripped across its shields, turning the transparent ovoid barrier orange where each shot landed. Backwash from emitter overloads ran down the length of the marauder even as the ship powered forward. At the last moment, the Bajoran ships broke away in climbing turns—but too slow to avoid the scintillating nimbus of the main plasma cannon. The *Glyhrond, Clarion*'s sister ship, lost meters of ventral hull plating as the blast blew out her deflectors and scorched an ugly wound along her belly.

Still in a turning fight, *Clarion* came on as the Tzenkethi warship crossed over the pole of a rocky moon in close orbit around the gas giant. The marauder angled after the *Pajul,* snapping after the wounded craft for an easy kill.

"Firing again," snapped the deck officer, ignoring a cut that streamed blood into his eyes. "Colonel, we're about to lose shielding fore and aft."

"Then put all power to the guns," came the command. "He's fixated on that scout. We'll give him something else to think about."

Lonnic heard the words but didn't really take them in. She was terrified, seeing the battle only as fragments, as pieces of the whole. She thought about the men on the *Pajul,* and in her panic she couldn't recall the names of any of them. *This is wrong. It's wrong it's wrong it's wrong—*

"The scout's lost motion control!" She heard the shout clearly. "*Kosst,* they're going to hit it!"

In a last-ditch attempt to extend out of the engagement and put some distance between his ship and the Tzenkethi guns, the captain of the prospector scoutship *Pajul* channeled everything he could spare into his failing impulse motors; but with the death of his engineering officer only seconds earlier, there was no one to tell him that the power relays were about to collapse. Something critical fractured inside the *Pajul*, and it spun out of control toward the marauder instead of away from it.

The Tzenkethi ship wrenched over in a punishing kick-turn, but it was too late. The scout impacted the port quarter of the marauder and skipped off the hull, shredding itself. A power surge threaded through the alien ship, and the sallow glow of the vessel's intercoolers flickered toward shutdown.

"*Pajul* destroyed . . . Target's shields are down!"

"What?" Lonnic opened her eyes, expecting the next thing she heard to be the rush of vacuum as the *Clarion* was obliterated.

Li was out of his chair, leaning over a sparking console. "What's the status of the *Glyhrond?*" he barked.

"Damaged, but stable. They're operable, but they're out of the fight."

Lonnic forced her way forward, stepping over fallen stanchions and waving away clots of acrid smoke. "Colonel, what happened?"

He stabbed a finger at the screen. "The Prophets have decided to hand down some justice, Ms. Lonnic. The *Pajul*'s sacrifice has tipped the balance." He blew out a breath and glared at the alien ship. "Damn them, but they're tough bastards." He nodded to the deck officer. "Missiles?"

"Tubes two and three jammed. One and four loaded and ready to fire."

She blinked. "You . . . you're going to execute them?"

"They opened fire first, woman. You saw it."

"They're territorial!" she snapped, her voice breaking.

"Of course they attacked us!" Lonnic blinked. "Why . . . What am I saying?" She shook her head, the stink of burning plastic and blood filling her nostrils. "Why am I defending them . . . If you're right . . ."

Li's face darkened. *"If,"* he repeated. "If I am right." He glared at his deck officer. "Communications. Tell the Tzen-kethi to surrender. They won't be harmed. They'll be taken back to Bajor under arrest for the attack on the freighter *Lhemor.*"

But the crewman wasn't listening. He called out across the smoke-blackened bridge. "New contacts, bearing two-one-seven mark seven!"

Lonnic's heart hammered in her chest. "More Tzenkethi?"

"No." Li bent over his console. "Cardassian. A pair of light cruisers. They're closing . . ." Fear bloomed inside her at the uncertainty on the colonel's face.

"Confirmed," said another crewman. "Identity confirmed, Cardassian Union warships *Daikon* and *Kashai.*" The operator hesitated. "Sir, those two were among the ships orbiting the homeworld when we left."

"They followed us?" Lonnic shook her head. "I don't understand."

The deck officer came forward. "Colonel, I think they were here all along. Their impulse trail leads back to one of the outer moons of this planet. They must have been concealed in its magnetosphere, hidden from us and the Tzenkethi."

Li's expression turned stony. "What is this?" he spat. "Hail them, right now! I want some answers!"

The crewman shook his head. "No reply, Colonel. They're reading us, but they're not responding."

"Then get me Bajor!" he shouted. "Subspace comms, this very second!"

"Impossible, sir," said the officer. "The *Daikon's* broadcasting a scattering field. They're jamming all transmissions."

Lonnic moved to the damaged, flickering view of the two amber-colored ships on the main screen. "Why are they here?" she said aloud. "The Chamber of Ministers ordered the fleet as a Bajoran response . . . Have they come to claim the Tzenkethi for themselves?" She thought of Kubus Oak once more. *How was he involved in this?*

"Sir!" The deck officer called out again. "Reading energy patterns from the Cardassian ships. Transporter signatures."

Lonnic whirled as Li punched up the reading on a console. The colonel's smoke-dirtied face creased in a frown. "They're beaming something over to the marauder . . . Metallic masses. Some kind of container units."

Lonnic craned her neck to see the display. On one of the smaller inset screens there was a graphic of the alien ship overlaid with patterns of moving dots. As she watched, the dots began to blink out one by one. "What is that?"

The blood drained from the deck officer's face. "Life signs. Tzenkethi life signs. Something's killing them."

Without deflector shields to protect the marauder, there was nothing to prevent the dispersal modules materializing on every deck of the Tzenkethi starship. The octagonal drums were faceted with oval nozzles that snapped open automatically. Under pressure, a fine mist of vapor issued into the thick air of the vessel, the dilution spreading out in a wave. Autonomous hazard protocols in the marauder's atmospheric systems, programmed to detect and isolate compartments in the event of just such an occurrence, worked sporadically thanks to the battle damage the ship had suffered in the skirmish with the Bajorans. For the most part, the countermeasures were unable to stop the advance of the contagion through the decks of the ship. In its wake, the biogenic toxin left nothing but death.

◆ ◆ ◆

In the engine compartment of the *Glyhrond*, the ship's captain turned from the stuttering control interface of the vessel's warp core as a high-pitched whine sliced through the air. He turned and saw the glitter of a matter stream forming and a wash of relief coursed through him. *Rescue is coming,* he thought. Li was sending over men to help them get his ship back on an even keel. "Thank the Prophets—"

The words died in his throat as the object in the transporter beam solidified and took on definition. A drum, just under the height of a man, decorated with what looked like Cardassian military sigils. He reached out to touch it as the whine died away, just as latches on the upper surface retracted to present him with a series of oval vents.

Less than a heartbeat later the captain was on the deck, his lungs leaking from his mouth and nostrils in a stream of black slurry. All across his ship, his crew began dying in the same swift and pitiless manner.

"Get the shields back up *now!*" bellowed Li. There was genuine terror in the colonel's voice.

"Bioweapons . . ." husked the crewman. "They're beaming them in all over the ship!"

Lonnic was shoved away as the deck officer grabbed at the console next to her. He stabbed at the controls, getting nothing but negative responses. "Deflector shields are inoperative!"

She stumbled away, half-falling, half-running toward the far side of the bridge; but there was nowhere for her to go, no escape route open to her. "Why are they doing this?" she cried out. Lonnic's stomach churned as she fought down the urge to vomit on the decking. On the sensor plots the dead hulls of the Tzenkethi marauder and the *Glyhrond* were like specters, and she imagined them as charnel houses filled with the poisoned dead. The adjutant grabbed at the communications panel and pressed the transmitter key. "Stop this! I am Lonnic Tomo of the Korto District . . . Cease your attack, please!"

Behind her, Li was shouting at his men to seal the bridge's environmental systems, even as an alert tone sounded over the intercom. Lonnic dropped into the chair in front of the console, ignoring the body of the unconscious operator lying next to her on the floor. She looked down at her hands and, with a physical effort, forced them to stop trembling. The woman marshaled all the resolve she could gather and steeled herself, drawing in the studied comportment that was her usual manner in the corridors of power. Lonnic took a deep breath, and a strange smell touched her senses, sweet and cloying like rotting flowers.

She spoke into the communicator pickup, an icy calm descending on her. "This is Lonnic Tomo aboard the Bajoran Space Guard warship *Clarion*. We are under attack by Cardassian vessels. They have already . . . killed the crew of the *Glyhrond* and a Tzenkethi marauder, and—" She felt wetness in her throat and coughed, bringing her hand to her mouth. Spots of dark blood dotted her palm. "I—"

The rotting stink was overpowering her, and she tried to speak but nothing came. Lonnic's eyes stung and cramps spiked through her, knotting her muscles. From nowhere, an uncontrollable shuddering wracked the woman's body and a wash of agony came with it. The pain knifed through her and she fell from the seat to the deck. Her vision blurred and darkened as the biogenic toxin burned into the optic jelly of her eyes. The last thing she saw was Colonel Li dropping to his knees, his face a ruin as he wept streams of crimson.

Prophets, please, Lonnic begged, *I don't want to die out here!*

Her prayer was not answered.

✦ ✦ ✦

The troop of black-armored figures stepped into the command compartment of the marauder, picking their way over the heap of alien corpses at the hatch. There were gouges in the metal where the Tzenkethi had clawed at the door as they tried to escape.

Dal Dukat studied them. *As if they would have found somewhere to flee to,* he mused. A Cardassian would have met his fate with stoic defiance, not the panic that these creatures had obviously displayed. He glanced at one of his squad. "Ensure you gather all the corpses and have them placed out of the way. We need to retain their biomass."

"Yes, sir," said the glinn. She paused, cocking her head and placing one hand to the temple of her environmental suit's helmet. "The rest of the sweep teams are reporting in. Engine core and environmental controls are secure. Secondary tiers have been vented to space."

Dukat walked forward into the streamlined oval space of the room. "Any stragglers?"

The glinn nodded, her suit making the gesture into a broad motion. "Some. A few made it to a decontamination pod before the dispersal reached them. They've been terminated."

Dukat nodded back and studied the ramps that curved up from the lower level of the command deck and inverted to meet the roof of the chamber. The upper surface of the deck was almost a mirror of the lower one, with consoles and oddly shaped chairs distributed in a circular formation. He could feel the faint shift in gravity as he moved closer; to make more efficient use of space aboard their craft, the Tzenkethi used tailored gravitational fields so that walls and ceilings could become work areas. Dukat made a face. He preferred to have all his staff spread out across a single plane; but this operation called for flexibility, so he would tolerate the situation for the duration.

The glinn was examining the sensor readings from the tricorder built into her suit. "Toxin percentile is now within acceptable limits. The pathogen has burned itself out."

Dukat glanced up and saw an identical hesitation in the faces of his boarding party. All of them accepted the glinn's determination, but none of them wanted to be the first to test it. Dukat smiled coldly and reached up, detaching his visor with a single swift twist of his hands. He folded the helmet back over his shoulders and made a show of taking a lungful of air. All of them had injected heavy doses of a neutralizing agent before they transported aboard the marauder, but it would have done little to save them if a pocket of the deadly germs still lingered.

The dal tasted the metallic tang of blood in the air. The ship stank of death; it would be another discomfiture to endure until they had completed the mission. One by one, his officers mirrored his actions as Dukat gave the command consoles a cursory examination. The displays showed streams of Tzenkethi script tumbling like waterfalls, lacking the obvious order of a Cardassian radial display. "Get a translation matrix uploaded into these systems," he ordered. "I want this ship under power and ready to move as soon as possible."

"Sir, the engineering team report that the drives are largely intact. Shields will take longer to repair."

"Have them take whatever they need from the *Kashai* and the *Daikon* to get the job done, men and hardware," he replied, "but quickly. We have less than a day before the Bajorans are declared overdue." Dukat turned away and tapped his comcuff. "Tunol, respond."

The *Kashai*'s executive officer answered instantly. *"Here, Dal. What are your orders?"*

"You have command now, Tunol. Once we're done here, I want you to set a course for Bajor, warp three. Make your route a lengthy one, do you understand? The timing of your return to Bajor is critical."

"*Confirmed, sir,*" she replied. "*I've taken the liberty of pre-programming target strike points into the weapons systems. The* Daikon *will handle your exfiltration after the attack.*"

He gave an approving nod. Tunol was an intelligent woman and she showed a methodical insight. Dukat had been quietly pleased with her utter lack of qualms when he outlined the scope of the operation to her. "Good. I'll supervise the transfer of command from here."

"*Dal,*" she added. "*The Bajoran derelicts . . . Without power, they've been seized by the gravitational pull of one of the gas giant's moons. Shall I take them under tow?*"

"No." He glanced at the glinn. "You. Weapons?"

"The plasma cannon will be operable in short order, sir."

"See to it." He turned back to the communicator. "Tunol? Have the cruisers take some distance from those Bajoran scows. We'll obliterate them before they impact the moon."

"*Confirmed, sir. Kashai out.*"

Dukat found the station for the marauder's commander and sat on the broad, cushioned disk. A cluster of circular screens and abstractly proportioned panels hung around him, suspended on the ends of metal armatures that rose from the floor or dangled from the ceiling. He toyed with them, turning and adjusting so he could sit in relative comfort and examine them. One screen showed a view beyond the blunt prow of the marauder, through the vapor of discharged breathing gases and wreckage fragments that were the remains of the skirmish between the Tzenkethi and the Bajorans. One of the assault ships was drifting past on a slow tumble, the nose turning, presenting itself to the dal.

Dukat considered the crews aboard those ships. Unlike the Tzenkethi, who were declared enemies of the Cardassian Union, the Bajorans were, under the letter of the

Detapa Council's law, an allied people—and yet he had ordered the murder of more than a hundred of them without a moment's hesitation. And now, as a plan of his design gathered momentum, Skrain Dukat's hand lay on the weapon that would cause the deaths of countless more Bajorans.

As his men worked quietly around him, he looked inward, searching for the moral balance that guided so much of his actions.

The morality of a Cardassian can only be understood by a Cardassian. The morality of a soldier of the Union is that which serves the Union best. His father had first said those words to him, repeating one of the great axioms of service. There had been moments in his life when Dukat had entertained doubts—and only a simpleton would be so foolish as to believe that no man could be without questions, soldier or not—but this was not one of them. Dukat considered the place where he found himself: isolated from Central Command because of the independent streak he had exhibited during the Talarian conflict . . . *No matter that it had won him many battles!* Reviled by Kell for daring to defy the jagul, for shining a light on the corpulent fool's lack of progress with the Bajorans, and in an uneasy partnership with Ico and the Obsidian Order. More than anything, it was the latter that sat most poorly with him. The Obsidian Order represented everything that was cancerous about Cardassia; they were an institutionalized form of decay that preyed on the military and the people even as they pretended to serve the same ends as Central Command.

His gloved hands tightened into fists. *The Order serves only the Order.* That too was wisdom that his father had given him, and firsthand Skrain had learned the truth of it. It galled him to think that he was in partnership with them on this, but he was a pragmatist and he saw that no other choice was open to him. *Ico and her kind may be a cancer on Cardassia, but there are other more pressing malignancies that must be excised first.* The pitiable Oralians, with their sad weakness and their primitive beliefs. The recalcitrant Bajorans, refusing to come to heel like ill-trained riding hounds.

Warfare is always a matter of priorities. Another axiom from his training came to mind. *The priority today is not my loathing of Ico's nest of vipers, but to secure a future for Cardassia. For my people and my family.*

"Sir," said the glinn, interrupting his musings. "Plasma cannon is now operable."

He gave the order without hesitation. "Destroy the Bajorans."

The snarling chirp of Darrah's communicator dragged him from the abyss of a deep and dreamless sleep. He rolled from the bed, ignoring Karys's angry muttering, and padded barefoot across the floor to the chair where he had thrown off his uniform. He glanced out through the slats across the window, one hand reaching up to massage the back of his neck. Tension sat across his shoulders in a thick yoke of stiffened muscle. Light rain was drumming on the glass, and he blinked as a distant flash of lightning glittered in the distance. His fingers closed around the communicator brooch as the faint grumble of thunder reached the house.

"This had better be good," he growled, raising the device to his lips.

He heard Myda's ever-weary intonation. *"Wait one moment, Inspector. I'm patching in a signal from the keep."*

"What?" His annoyance flared in unison with another lightning bolt. "Off duty means off duty—"

The very real fear he heard in the next voice made him stop dead. *"Inspector Darrah? This is Tima, I'm a novitiate serving with Ranjen Gar . . ."*

And suddenly Darrah was very much awake. "Is he all right? What's wrong?"

The girl was on the verge of tears. *"He's gone! He was supposed to be back here hours ago, with Vedek Arin's party from Derna . . ."*

Darrah nodded. "Yeah, I saw him at the port. They didn't arrive?" He shifted the slats and peered out at the encroaching storm front.

"The others did. Ranjen Gar stayed behind. They said he was with an Oralian, a cleric called Pasir . . . They took a flyer to Hathon . . ."

"Then he's probably there. Try the Hathon city central comnet—"

"We did!" she insisted. *"And Traffic Control as well. The flyer never went to Hathon, Inspector! No one knows where it is!"*

"Osen . . ." Darrah's throat tightened as he whispered his friend's name. Abruptly, he found Gar's last words to him echoing through his thoughts. *I will admit I too have had some concerns of late.* Darrah clamped down hard on the instinct to jump to a conclusion, but it was hard to hold back the notion that the priest could have been dragged into something dangerous.

"What's wrong with Gar?" Karys called from the bed.

He waved her into silence. "Myda, are you still on the line?"

"Yes, boss," said the law officer.

"What have you got from Traffic Control?"

He heard a heavy sigh. *"Running a search right now, sir, but so far it seems that the flight plan filed by the Cardassian was a dud. I got a report from one of the precinct air units that a flyer matching the same description was seen heading west toward the Kendra mountains."*

Darrah instinctively looked in that direction, and straight into the teeth of the thunderstorm. "No crash beacons, no alert signals?"

"*Not a one, sir. It's like they vanished.*"

"Not on my watch," he growled, flinging off his night-shirt. "Tima?"

"*Y-yes?*"

"We'll find Gar, don't worry."

"*Thank you, Inspector.*" He heard the click as Tima dropped off the network.

"Myda!" Darrah snapped. "Put together a search pattern and a rescue team, have them assemble at the port. Drag whoever you need to out of bed, and get a fast flyer routed to my house right now."

"*Boss,*" came the wary reply, "*the storm's a real monster. Weather control has been trying to pull the teeth on this one, but it's going to hit scale four before daybreak.*"

"Just do what I said," Darrah retorted. "If Gar's lost out there, it's not the Prophets who are going to rescue him, it's us." He tapped the communicator, ending the conversation, then grabbed at his clothes as another bass rumble of thunder swept across the city.

Karys stood, a sheet wrapped around her. "Mace, what are you doing?"

"My job," he replied, pulling on his uniform.

The rain intensified, clattering against the window. "Look at it out there," she retorted. "You know how lethal the tempests can get this time of year." His wife touched his shoulder. "I know the man is your friend, but you're a ranking officer of the Watch. You could let someone else handle this."

He nodded. "You're right, Karys, I could." Mace snatched up his gear belt. "But I won't." Above the sound of the rainfall, he heard the whine of antigravs. Myda had done as he'd ordered.

Her hand closed around his wrist. "You're risking your life for him."

"He'd do the same thing for me." But as he looked into

her eyes, Darrah knew that there was more to it than that, more than just the duty of his friendship with Osen. *This isn't any random misadventure taking place here. Something else is going on, something connected to Cemba.*

The police flyer was settling into a low hover over the roadway outside the house. Grabbing his overcoat and his phaser holster, Darrah ran out into the rain without another word.

15

The rain across the roof of the enclave blockhouse was a constant rattle now, a sound like handfuls of gravel being thrown against the thermoconcrete construction. Outside, the pavilions snapped and cracked as they flexed on their supports, the cables holding them in place humming with vibration. Bajor's sky was dark and heavy with menace, the night gloom mirroring Bennek's soured mood. Aside from the sporadic flashes of lightning, the only illumination cast over the cleric's room was the sullen glow of the communications screen.

The connection was thick with static; it was coming to Bajor on a side channel outside the normal frequencies open to Cardassian civilians. There was an illegal circuit concealed in the back of the communicator that, if it were discovered, would have meant instant arrest for the cleric. The fact that Hadlo was using it now to contact him filled Bennek with dread.

A flicker of lightning cast quick bars of white light through the room behind him, and on the screen Hadlo's pale face reacted. *"Bennek! By the Fates, are they already there? Are they firing? I can't hear any shots—"*

"It's just a storm," said the priest.

Hadlo nodded rapidly. *"Oh, indeed, my friend, the storm is breaking upon us. This is the moment of our greatest testing, Ben-*

nek! The hammer falling . . . The clouds of ashes and the serpents rising . . . Do you see it as clearly?"

"What do you want?" Bennek almost shouted at his old mentor, afraid and angry all at once. Over and over he was forced to endure the priest's directionless, unfathomable ramblings, and each time he spoke with the elderly man it seemed worse. Hadlo had never been the same since that day at the Kendra Shrine, and as much as Bennek was loath to give voice to it, he was deathly afraid that the priest had lost all sense of reason.

His sharp words seemed to make some impact on Hadlo, and the old man stiffened, regaining his poise for a brief moment. *"This is the time. This is the moment I warned you of when we spoke in the library of the Naghai Keep. The purge has begun. All our churches are burning, Bennek. Burning."*

"Purge?" The word almost choked him.

Hadlo nodded, the image jerking and fracturing. *"Kell's promises to us have been finally broken, open to the world. The military are rounding up everyone who follows the Way. Shattering the masks and setting the scrolls to the torch."*

"No!" Bennek gasped. He glanced at the leather bag on a nearby shelf that contained his copy of the Recitations and his recital mask, suddenly needing to reassure himself they were still there.

"Listen to me, boy!" said the cleric, his eyes wide. *"I have gathered as many of the faithful as I can, and we are fleeing the homeworld."*

"You . . . you're on a starship?"

"Yes." Interference turned his words into a buzzing rattle. *"I cannot say much more. They are searching for us, and they may track this signal. It is scrambled, but I do not know how long that will remain secure. Listen!"* His face came forward, filling the screen, and his voice dropped to a whisper. *"We make for the space beyond Quinor, where the plasma storms will keep us hidden."*

"The Badlands," said Bennek. He had heard the Bajo-rans use the name for the area; it was a dangerous place to seek sanctuary, rife with furious plasmatic clouds. Many ships had been lost there, so the stories went, some swept away leaving nothing behind, not even wreckage.

Hadlo was nodding. *"In time we will be reunited, but for the moment you must stay in sanctuary on Bajor. Oralius will keep you safe there."*

"No," Bennek replied. "Master, it is *not* safe here! We are isolated and unprotected, and the enclaves are no longer places of shelter for us. We must come together and—"

"No!" Hadlo shouted, the feedback from his sudden outburst crackling over the static-filled transmission. *"I forbid it! In Oralius's name, you shall not leave that place! Sanctuary, Bennek, sanctuary! You will ensure the Way remains, I have foreseen it in my vision . . . That is your path, boy! You will do it! You will do it!"* Without warning the image vanished, becoming a seething wash of gray static.

Benneck snapped off the console and crossed the room, every footfall leaden and heavy. "I can't do this," he said to the air. "I . . . I am not strong enough to do this!" He savagely grabbed the leather bag and ripped the recital mask from it, gripping it in his fingers. "What do you want from me?" he demanded of the wooden face. "Have you forsaken us? Have you?" The cleric let the mask clatter across the table and he sat heavily. His eyes fell across a bottle of *kanar* that was discreetly hidden in the lee of a support brace, and he reached for it. The bottle was a quarter empty; it had already served him as a panacea in moments when his weakness had overcome him. The cleric twisted off the cap and filled a glass, draining it and letting the mellow fire of the liqueur race through him, steadying his nerves.

There was a knock at his door, and Bennek's hand cracked the glass with a jerk of fright. "They've come," he whispered to the discarded mask. "Come with guns to kill us all." He swallowed another measure as the knocking became more strident. "It's open," he said loudly. "Enter and do as you will."

But the figure that came in from the storm was not a soldier with a phaser rifle. "Bennek," said Tima, shrugging off a rain-soaked cloak. "I didn't know who else to turn to . . ."

In spite of his own concerns, the emotion in the woman's voice made him push everything else to one side. "What's wrong?"

"It's Ranjen Gar. He's lost . . . He was in a flyer with Pasir and they never arrived at their destination." She blinked back tears. "Oh, Bennek, I think something terrible could have happened to them."

"Pasir? No, I can't lose him as well . . ." It was too much for him. Suddenly, as if a wave of despair had dragged him under, the Oralian cradled his head in his hands. "Tima . . . Tima, everything is disintegrating around us. I've been forsaken . . ."

She came to him, putting her arm around his shoulders. "Bennek, no." The Bajoran woman took a shuddering breath. "You must tell me what troubles you."

"But your friend—"

Tima held him, and he found himself wanting only to do the same to her. "His friends are helping him. Let me . . . Let me help you."

With a trembling voice, every fear and every hope poured out of Bennek as the storm battered the walls around them.

The rain lashed across the blackened disks of the flyer pads in hard, windblown waves that made the Watch officers curse and pull their jackets and caps down tight. Darrah glared at the cloud-wreathed sky, daring it to do its worst. *And it will,* he thought to himself. *This is only the leading edge of the storm cell. There's more to come.*

He faced his men. "You've all got the pattern, you all know your assigned sectors. Coordinate through Constable Proka and Myda back at the precinct. The instant you find anything, you radio it in. Clear?" There was a chorus of assent, and he threw a sharp gesture at the parked flyers. "Then get going. But no heroics. I don't want to lose anyone else out there."

As the crews ran to their craft, Proka tugged on Darrah's arm. "Boss? Got a problem. We're a man short. You need a copilot and we haven't got one."

Darrah grimaced, making for his flyer. "I don't give a damn about regulations," he shot back. "I'll search my pattern on my own."

"Can't let you, boss," Proka insisted. "It's filthy sky up there. You take a lightning strike or something—" He snorted. "No heroics, that's what you just said."

"I'm going," growled the inspector, "and that's an end to it."

Proka nodded. "Thought you'd see it that way. So I got you a civvie volunteer instead."

Darrah threw open the gull-wing hatch of the flyer and his gaze fell on the Cardassian sitting in the copilot's chair.

"Inspector," said Pa'Dar. "I was stranded at the port when the weather grounded my shuttle to Dahkur. I overheard the constable, and—"

Darrah looked at Proka. "That's a very creative solution, Mig."

The Watch officer stared back at him. "Needs must. He's a scientist, isn't he? He'll know how to handle the scanners."

Darrah waved the other man off and climbed inside the flyer, dropping smartly into the pilot's couch.

Pa'Dar cleared his throat. "I realize it might be unusual for you to work directly with a Cardassian," he began.

"Why are you doing this?" Darrah cut him off. "The

missing Cardassian, Pasir. He's an Oralian and you're not. I get the impression that most of your people wouldn't miss one of them lost in a storm." Applying power to the thrusters, Darrah guided the flyer shakily into the turbulent sky.

After a long moment, the alien replied. "There are times when things are not as they seem, Inspector. I would think that as an officer of the law, you would be aware of that."

"I suppose so," Darrah admitted. "You know what? Right now, I really don't care. I just want to find my friend, so work those sensors and help me do that." He steered the flyer on a westerly course, and the ungainly police craft shot into the storm.

It was hard to reckon the passage of time in the flyer's enclosed cockpit. Pa'Dar's flight became a single round of chaotic rises and falls as the Bajoran forced the complaining ship through churning air. Outside he could see nothing but the sluice of hard rain streaking the canopy, and every few minutes there was a brilliant glare of blue-white as lightning surged. Pa'Dar glimpsed what could have been towering anvils of cloud or possibly mountain canyons; the image burned a purple blur into his retinas.

Hours. If felt like they had been up there for hours, and his eyes were becoming tired from staring at the relentless sweep of the blank bio-scanner screen. When he glanced over at Darrah, he saw the man's fixed expression of concentration, watching him fight the flyer's controls every second of the flight. The inspector gripped the steering yoke with a dogged resolve that was almost Cardassian in nature. *The man is driven,* Pa'Dar told himself; and on the heels of that came the question that had been plaguing him since the moment he had volunteered. *What drives me?*

At first it had been difficult to frame an answer. Kotan

Pa'Dar was a rational thinker, a scientist with a reductionist mind-set. He was used to problems where the parameters were clearly deduced, where he could apply his knowledge and come to an empirical conclusion; but what was happening around him on Bajor did not lend itself to the same process.

There are connections. He was certain of it. Part of Pa'Dar knew that to be Cardassian was to live in a world where there were always machinations beneath the surface, but he was so close to this, so enmeshed in it that his inquisitive mind could not easily let it go. Rhan Ico's shadowy behavior. The bombing of the *Lhemor.* The wall of silence thrown up around the aftermath of the incident at Cemba Station. Skrain Dukat's manner, the chasm that had opened up in their friendship. All these elements preyed on Pa'Dar's mind, wheeling and turning like the pieces in a child's logic puzzle, never quite fitting into place.

And now this: two priests, one Cardassian, one Bajoran, lost in the tempest. *Another fragment to be woven into the whole?* He wondered what the puzzle would look like when—*if*—it was complete. Was it even something that he wanted to know? Was it better for him to step away and remain ignorant of it all?

A stutter of contact on the sensor panel illuminated for a brief moment, then vanished. Pa'Dar peered at the display, frowning. "Inspector?" he ventured. "There's a lake . . ." He pointed. "In that direction."

"Yeah." Fatigue underlined the pilot's voice. "It's on the edge of the search pattern."

"Can you circle over it?"

Darrah did as he asked, turning the flyer. "You have something?"

The contact returned. "I do," he replied, the lines on his face deepening. "Metal fragments. A single life sign. But the signal is confused. I can't get a clear reading."

"Which one of them is it?" demanded the Bajoran. "Gar or Pasir?"

"I don't know."

Darrah programmed a quick and dirty macro into the police flyer's autopilot and jumped from his chair as the aircraft fell into a wallowing hover over the storm-tossed surface of the water. Darrah knew where they were; the lake was a deep one, a natural formation that fed the Yolja River. He'd gone fishing there in his youth, and he still remembered the stories about it. If Gar's craft had gone down here, it was beyond recovery. The sheer size of the inland sea and the kelbonite in the local rock would mean that tracking the flyer would be next to impossible. It was probably dumb luck that the Cardassian had managed to pick up a reading.

The hatch opened and a fist of wind punched Darrah back into the compartment. He pushed back, securing a rescue vest and descent tether around him. On the hull of the flyer a spotlight snapped on, turning to aim where the sensors told it the life sign was. Mace glimpsed a shape, the arch of a back covered in robes, facedown in the lake.

"Inspector?" said Pa'Dar.

Without a transporter on board, they were going to have to do this the hard way. "Get a medkit ready!" Darrah didn't bother to explain himself. He took a breath of damp air and dropped feetfirst from the open hatch, the tether singing out behind him.

He struck the lake, and a heavy darkness enveloped him. The shock of the icy water threatened to press the air from his lungs, but he resisted, pushing hard back toward the surface and the halo of white light.

Heavy wrappings of cloth swaddled the floating body, water soaking them, making it difficult to handle. Darrah spat out a mouthful of fluid and looped his tether over the drifting shape, pulling hard to bind them together. His hand found the control unit on the rescue vest and he slapped it hard. With a jerk, the duranium-carbide cable pulled taut and the two men were dragged out of the lake, reeled in to the waiting hatch.

Pa'Dar was there, gray hands grabbing at Darrah's shoulders, pulling him inside. In turn, Darrah held firmly on to his charge, dragging the waterlogged form onto the deck of the police flyer. "Medkit!" he shouted.

He tore at the robes, yanking them back to get at the man inside the folds of the priest's vestments. A face was revealed, heavy with scratches and contusions.

"Osen!" Darrah grabbed the Bajoran's head. "Can you hear me?"

Pa'Dar handed him a stimulant hypospray, and Darrah shot the contents into cleric's neck. Gar coughed hard and spat out a stream of blood-laced liquid.

"Where's Pasir?" Darrah shouted over the rumble of the wind through the open hatch. "Where's the Cardassian?"

Gar coughed again and shook his head. "Nuh." He tried to speak. "Dead. *Dead!*" His eyes widened with shock as a flash of lightning illuminated the interior of the flyer and he saw Pa'Dar looming over him. "No! No! Get away!"

"Osen!" Darrah grabbed him. "It's okay. He's here to help."

Gar pushed himself back to the bulkhead. "No," he said weakly.

Darrah turned to the Cardassian. "Any trace of other life signs?"

Pa'Dar shook his head grimly. "Not at all. If Pasir was down there, then he perished."

Darrah sighed. "All right. Mark this location and then get us up above the storm. You can do that?"

He got a nod in return. "Of course."

The Cardassian went to the front of the compartment,

leaving the two Bajorans alone. Sealing the hatch, Darrah paused to snatch a tricorder from the medkit case and swept the sensor over his friend.

Gar was breathing heavily. "Darrah ... Darrah Mace." His voice was thick with pain and effort, husky and rough. "It's you."

"It's me," he replied. "No broken bones. No organ damage. I think. I'm not an expert with these things."

Gar pushed the tricorder away, leaning closer. "I'm fine. But ..." He shot a terrified look at the Cardassian. "Don't let him near me."

"He helped to rescue you, Gar."

"They tried to murder me!" spat the priest. "Pasir! He was insane! He said that it was an abomination ..."

"What do you mean?"

"The ... alliance between Cardassia and Bajor. Between our two faiths. He swore that Oralius was not going to be polluted by corrupt Bajoran dogma."

"He was some sort of fundamentalist?"

"He was a murderer! He pulled a weapon on me." Gar's hands reached out, and his fingers clutched at Darrah's sleeve. "May the Prophets forgive me ... There was a struggle and the flyer went down in the lake. I had to ... I had to ..."

A chill washed through Darrah's bones as he read the truth in the other man's eyes. "You killed him."

"I had to!" husked the priest. "I had no choice!"

"All right," Darrah said, after a moment. "We'll get you back to the hospital in Korto."

"No." Gar's grip tightened. "There are Cardassians in the city. I can't be safe there! Kendra!" He straightened. "Please, Mace. Take me to the monastery at Kendra."

Darrah's disquiet chilled him more than the lingering cold from the lake; in all the years they had known one another, he had never seen such an expression of naked terror on his friend's face. "All right. When you're healed, we'll talk more about this. Until then, you mention nothing about what happened. Pasir died in the crash. That's what we'll say."

Gar seemed to shrink in on himself, his fingers moving up to probe at the flesh of his face. "Yes. Thank you. You're a good friend."

Darrah stepped up to the control console. "Change of plan," he told the Cardassian. "We're going to Kendra."

"What am I doing here?" Jas Holza grumbled to himself under his breath as he filed into the Chamber of Ministers, the last man to enter from the atrium outside. The question had too many facets for his liking; it cut too deep, with neither the literal nor the figurative answers to give him any sort of peace. He sat in his assigned place, hollow inside. In the highly polished surface of the steel table before him, he caught a glimpse of his own reflection. He looked like his father; the sudden realization caught him off guard. Yes, in the warped mirror of the shiny surface, he saw the ghost of his parent in the haggard and beaten man that he was, aged before his time. With effort he pulled his eyes up to where the First Minister stood. Like many of the men in the room, Jas was slightly unkempt, having been called from his opulent temporary lodgings in Ashalla back to the chamber in the middle of the night. Only a few—Lale Usbor most obvious among them—looked as if the impromptu meeting was nothing but a minor inconvenience. Jas's gaze fell on Kubus Oak; all that Jas and Korto had done for that man, and the minister for Qui'al had yet to even acknowledge his presence. Instead Kubus was in quiet conversation with one of his aides. The only man who did meet Jas's gaze was Keeve Falor. The agitator was stern and quiet. He reminded Jas of a pit-fighter waiting for his next bout. *And I? I wreath myself in pity, like an animal walking to the slaughterhouse.*

"Colleagues," began Lale. "My apologies for recalling you at such short notice, but an issue of great import has been brought to my attention, and it must be addressed immediately."

General Coldri, who even on the best of days could only be described as a man of bleak and forbidding aspect, gave the officer at his side a curt nod. Coldri's expression filled Jas with dread.

"Major Jaro Essa," said Lale. "Will you please repeat the information you presented to me before this assembly?"

"Sir." Jaro had a padd in his hand, but he didn't refer to it. "Ministers. As of twenty-two–bells, Ashalla local time, the reprisal force under the command of Colonel Li Tarka was logged as overdue for their scheduled communications check-in. Their last known coordinates were close to Ajir, an uninhabited system in the Coreward Marches. Based on data supplied by the crew of a vessel in the employ of Minister Kubus, they were investigating a possible sighting of a Tzenkethi warship, with intent to censure and detain it in connection with the Cemba incident."

The chamber was silent now, every minister listening intently to Jaro's flat, emotionless report—every one except Jas Holza, who studied Kubus Oak. *Kubus doesn't have any freighters within a hundred light-years of Ajir.* Jas was sure of it; as part of his increasingly unfair association with the man, the minister was privy to some of the Kubus clan's ship movements. *I'm certain of it. But if that is so, then where did he get that data from?*

He thought about the scoutships from his own fleet, the *Kylen* and the *Pajul;* and Lonnic, dear Tomo, who had remained at his side even when other members of his staff had seen his self-destructive course and left the Korto administration. The tone of Jaro's explanation caught up with him. *What is he telling us?*

The major continued. "A short time ago, the detection stations on Andros picked up this signal on a subspace emergency band. Degradation of the transmission indicates that it was under intensive jamming. Only the application of a large amount of energy to burn through the blockade allowed us to receive it. The sending of the message was clearly an act of desperation." Jaro raised the padd and tapped a key.

Immediately the air filled with the buzzing hiss of a communications channel. The next words he heard made Jas Holza's blood run cold. *"This is Lonnic Tomo . . . of the Korto District . . ."* Some heads turned to face him. He saw Keeve's eyes narrow. The static-laced message stuttered, then went on. *" . . . Aboard the Bajorian Space Guard warship* Clarion, *we are under attack by . . . Tzenkethi marauder. They have already . . . killed the crew of the* Glyhrond *. . . Cease your attack, please!"*

The raw panic in Tomo's last words hit Holza like a hammer, and he rocked back in his chair, the color draining from his face. "Prophets," he whispered. "She's dead." He gripped the table in front of him, his head swimming. He felt dizzy and sick.

"It would seem that Colonel Li engaged the Tzenkethi without success," Jaro concluded, the pronouncement a death knell for the men in the reprisal fleet.

A wave of raised voices echoed around the chamber, some in fury, others decrying the destruction. "You've brought this to pass, Kubus!" snapped Keeve. "What sort of botched data did you give the Space Guard?"

Kubus blinked, for a moment showing signs of shock over Jaro's revelation; but in the next moment he was composed again. "I provided only what was asked of me by Colonel Li! What he chose to do with the information was his choice!"

Keeve rounded on Lale. "I was against this so-called task force from the start! A poorly planned operation motivated only by the immediate need for vengeance? Is it any wonder that more Bajoran lives have been lost because of it?" He smacked his fist into his palm. "What is needed is rational thought and measured response, something this administration seems poorly equipped to deliver!"

The argument went on over Jas's head. He stared at his hands, recalling a time when Lonnic had held them. Many years ago now, when they had been young and both untested; and now she was gone, ripped away in the dark, and he would never see her again. Her directness, her honest counsel, all gone. The only voice that had ever dared to stand up to him, to show him the errors of his ways—and then still to stand by him. "Tomo," he husked. "Oh, Prophets. Please keep her safe."

"I am forced to agree with Minister Keeve," grated Kubus, drawing Jas's attention toward the man. "In principle if not in language. He is correct when he stated that the task force sent to censure the Tzenkethi invaders was not adequate to the task." He shot a poisonous glare at General Coldri, which the chief of staff ignored.

"You're trying to blame this on the shortcomings of the Space Guard?" said another minister, one of Keeve's supporters.

Major Jaro folded his arms. "The Militia are an arm of the government," he growled, "and we can only operate to their orders. Would you have us do otherwise? Perhaps martial law would suit you better, Minister?"

"Blame for this must be apportioned . . ." began Kubus, suddenly trailing off as he saw a runner enter with a message tab for the First Minister.

"Blame," Jas said in a low voice. "There should be blame." His hands tightened into fists, his nails digging into his palms. *And I must share in it. What have I become?* He wanted to leap to his feet and shout the words. *An annex for Kubus Oak's dreams of empire? His willing vassal? And all along*

Lonnic was warning me, trying to guide me away, and I ignored her. I knew it was true and I ignored her because I was weak! Jas saw the broken pieces of his life falling down around him. All of it had been in service of Kubus Oak's agenda, not his. The collapse of the Golana settlement and the ongoing loss of the clan's lands and influence. Oak had clothed it in lies made to sweeten the moment, and he had gone along. *Why? Why did I do this? Am I so spineless?*

Jas stiffened and made to rise to his feet, the words pushing at his lips; but there was a new arrival in the chamber, and he turned with Kubus and Keeve and all the others to see Jagul Kell enter the room, a cloak folded over his arm.

The Cardassian bowed to the First Minister. "Sir. I have grave news. Thank you for allowing me to address the Chamber."

Jas wavered, the energy of his turmoil suddenly dissipated by the alien's arrival.

"I have been informed of the loss of your ships and their brave crews." Kell looked solemn. "I only wish that the Cardassian Union could have done something to prevent that terrible sacrifice."

"We fight our own battles," said Coldri with hard emphasis.

"What I am about to tell you may force you to reconsider that, General. Pride, after all, must have its limits." The jagul sighed. "One of my ships has been conducting deep-range scans of stars in the sector as part of a scientific program run by Professor Ico. They detected a vessel, Ministers. A starship of Tzenkethi design, caught by chance in their scan ratios."

Keeve voiced the question on everyone's mind. "It's coming here?"

Kell nodded. "It is. Based on the projected speed and course of the marauder, it will reach the Bajor system in less than five hours."

Coldri was instantly on his feet and speaking into a handheld communicator unit. Jas caught the words "scramble" and "raiders."

"I have contacted Central Command and requested the assistance of any Cardassian cruisers in the area, but they will not get here in time."

"You must have ships here," said Kubus. "Warships."

The jagul shook his head. "Only transports and light escorts, Minister. Nothing that is a match for a Tzenkethi marauder."

Lale nodded grimly. "We will place the planet on full alert, gather what ships we can to form a blockade. If the Tzenkethi come to strike us once more, then we will meet their aggression with all the force we can muster." He surveyed the room. "I would suggest, ladies and gentlemen, that if you have the means, you should seek shelter for your families and make your districts aware of the threat that now faces us."

The chamber emptied faster than Jas had ever seen happen before, but he remained in his chair, once or twice buffeted by the figures that passed him, the ministers eager to remove themselves from a building that would most likely be a major target for any orbital attack.

When he looked up he saw Kubus Oak standing across from him, watching him with a measuring gaze. "Holza," said the other man. "This is a time to be strong, my friend, you understand?"

Jas got to his feet. "A moment ago you were as frightened as the rest of us. Now you seem calm."

Kubus sniffed. "If the Tzenkethi are coming, they'll find nothing to shoot at in Qui'al. And what ships of mine are in-system will be gone within the hour. I'll have little to lose."

"And you'll be on one of those ships?" Jas snapped. "To stand in safety and return only when the dust has settled?"

"I can't have myself put in harm's way." He smiled, as if the idea were comical to him. "Think, Holza, think. This, no matter how tragic, is an opportunity. The intelligent man turns that to his advantage."

"You disgust me," said Jas.

Kubus's face turned stony. "Save some of that judgment for yourself, Minister. Don't let the woman's death give you some sudden growth of conscience."

Jas could find no words and glared at the other man in impotent rage.

"Yes," Kubus sneered. "You may hate me now, but you won't step from the path at my side. You can't. You lack the insight to do it." He came closer and tapped Jas on the shoulder. To any observer, it would have looked like a friendly gesture of support. "You have only a short time before news of the Tzenkethi incursion breaks around the planet. Instead of staring at me, I'd suggest you use the time to get your family to somewhere remote, somewhere safe." He grinned. "After all, in the chaos that follows an attack on our planet, who could say what might happen to them?"

Kubus walked away, leaving Jas alone. With shaking hands, Jas drew a communicator from his pocket and activated a link that would connect him with Korto city.

Orange fingers of sunlight were creeping over the horizon as Darrah turned the police flyer onto a final approach, lining up to touch down on the port's landing pads. He felt bone tired and thick-throated, a chill inside him even though he had dried himself down and changed into the nondescript flight suit in the aircraft's deck locker. He concentrated on the work of flying, but he was troubled. Gar had refused to be drawn on his ordeal and disappeared into the Kendra Monastery the moment they had touched down; and on the flight back to Korto, the Cardassian

Pa'Dar had been equally uncommunicative. Rather than return to the port with him, the scientist had asked Darrah to drop him off at the enclave outside the city. Darrah had no reason not to agree, but the alien did not seem interested in thanks for his help.

The storm was gone now, passed out toward the ocean and diminishing, and beneath the flyer the streets of Korto were still wet, shimmering like dark stone. Darrah blinked hard, his eyes rough with fatigue. He thought of Karys and the bed he had abandoned to rescue Osen. It seemed like a world away, as if he'd been gone for days. "I just want to get back," he said aloud. He'd put the flyer down and then requested someone else to pilot him back to his house. After the night he'd had, it was the least he deserved.

It wasn't until he climbed out of the flyer, the engines winding down in a falling whine, that Darrah realized something was wrong. The port's alert lamps were flashing and there were men running back and forth. Over the noise of the flyer, if he strained to hear it, Darrah could pick out the sirens of police ground units.

He was halfway down the gantry to the port control building when Proka caught up with him. He had a steaming mug of thick brown fluid in his hand. *Raktajino,* spiced with slivers of *kava.* Darrah had little taste for the Klingon beverage, except when he needed a hard caffeine hit to keep him on his feet.

"You're going to want this," said Proka. The look he gave Darrah was not promising.

"Something very bad is happening," said Darrah. It wasn't a question. Proka's face was answer enough.

"Worse than you know." He handed the inspector a hand communicator.

Darrah raised it to his ear. "This is Darrah," he said warily.

"Inspector." Jas Holza's voice was tight with tension.

"Don't talk, just listen. Get to the Naghai Keep and collect my wife and my sons. Take them immediately to my villa. You are to stop for nothing, you are to talk to no one, do you understand?"

"Sir," he said, and the word was laced with the exhaustion that threatened to overwhelm him, "I don't know if I can—"

"Just do it!" roared the minister. "I don't argue with *Ke'lora,* do you understand me? Do what you're told, *do your job!* I don't want to hear a word from you unless it is to tell me they are safe, is that clear?"

Darrah felt a cold burn of anger at the slight. Jas had never invoked the inferiority of Darrah's *D'jarra* before, and now that he had done it the lawman felt irritated and disappointed; but none of that showed in his next words. "Yes, sir. I'm on my way." He snapped the communicator off and glared at Proka as they climbed back into the flyer. "Safe? What the *kosst* is he so worked up about? Safe from what?"

Darrah listened with growing alarm as Proka explained the priority message that had come over the general Militia channel just minutes before Darrah had landed at Korto. An attack was coming, and the planet was going to a maximum state of alert; but by then they were already airborne and it was too late for him to get a call through to Karys and the children.

16

The marauder came in toward Bajor's orbit from high above the plane of the ecliptic, dropping down in a fast, near-light-speed approach across the rim of the Denorios Belt. The ship's commander was canny, using the natural dispersal effect of the plasma phenomenon to mask his approach. The flotilla of Space Guard assault vessels and impulse raiders had little time to respond, but they were well-trained men and women, and it was their home that was at stake. They did not shirk from the engagement. All hails were, as expected, ignored by the Tzenkethi ship.

The first shots were fired with Bajor at their backs, the small two-man raiders leading the interception. The few pilots who survived the engagement would later remark in debriefings how the warship, easily two or three times the mass of a heavy assault vessel, made punishing turns that would have shredded the hull of a Bajoran craft. They outnumbered the marauder, but still they were outmatched.

The darkness became a web of phaser fire and missile trails as General Coldri's crews threw up a wall of destructive energy, fighting to cordon the invader and force it back into open space.

The Tzenkethi ship took hit after hit, but they were glancing blows that the streamlined hull shrugged off, deflector shields glittering and denying anything but the

most cursory damage. The marauder's main armament
threw lances of searing white light against the Bajorans;
impulse raiders caught in the nimbus were blown apart or
sent tumbling, their control systems and crew flash-burned
to ashes. The alien ship turned and avoided every attempt
by the Guard to converge fire upon it, answering with
shots from secondary disruptor cannon arrays. Assault ships
were hit with pinpoint attacks that blew out power grids
or targeted their warp cores, leaving them dead in space or
drifting out of control toward the Denorios Belt. The gun-
ners aboard the Tzenkethi ship seemed to know exactly,
precisely where to hit them, rendering the Cardassian-
made drives fitted aboard the Bajoran ships inoperative.

At last, weathering some minor damage but still combat capable, the marauder slowed to pass through the dis-
ruption it had caused in the Bajoran intercept force, as if
the ship's commander were evaluating his work. No killing shots came, no executioner's blows; the disabled ships
were left behind and the marauder moved on, turning over
Bajor's terminator toward the sunward side of the planet.
Unopposed, it dropped into a low orbit, turning vertical
to present its prow and the plasma cannon emitter to the
unprotected surface of the world.

"Status?" said Dukat, shifting on the alien command dais.

The glinn at the oddly proportioned helm control
turned to face him. "We are ready to move to phase two of
the operation at your discretion, Dal."

Dukat nodded, a faint sneer on his lips as he examined a screen showing the fallout from the engagement.
The marauder was an impressive ship, of that there was
no doubt, agile and lethal. It was a pity that he could not
return with it to Cardassia Prime as a prize, and he made
a mental note to ensure that as much data on the craft was
gathered as possible before the operation came to an end.

The marauder had made short work of the Bajorans, and that had been in the hands of a crew of aliens inexperienced with the vessel. Dukat wondered what it would be like to oppose a Tzenkethi ship at the pinnacle of its capacity. In comparison, these Bajorans were poor sport; they fought in space as if they were still in sailboats on the surface of their oceans. They lacked the hard-won battle experience of the Cardassian navy. He shook his head. "If that was the best they had to offer, we should have invaded this planet five years ago."

"With respect, sir, the Bajorans weren't using Cardassian-surplus warp drives five years ago," offered the woman. "Today, our tactical advantage was much greater."

Dukat made a derisive sound. "You give them too much credit." He glanced at her. "What are they doing?"

"Regrouping, it appears," she replied, reading what she could from the encrypted Space Guard communications networks. "As you planned, the ships that were neutralized are clouding the channels with emergency beacons. There are other defense groups returning to the planet at high warp from the outer edges of the system, but they will not arrive in time to interrupt phase two."

Dukat stood up, looking at the arc of the planet represented on a dozen of the small console screens. "We proceed, then." He drew a padd from a sealed pocket and activated it with a tap of his finger. The device presented him with a string of surface coordinates and firing protocols. There was nothing else, no indication of what was being targeted or why it had been chosen for destruction. He relayed the numbers to the glinn, and when the job was done he deactivated the padd. Immediately, the device went hot in his hands and emitted a puff of acrid black smoke. The internal working fused into a mass of useless matter, and he grimaced at the object before he tossed it to the deck. *The Obsidian Order do so enjoy their little flourishes of drama.*

"Targets locked in. Plasma reservoir is stable. We are ready to fire."

And now, all of them were to play their part in a different kind of theater. Dukat hesitated, looking inward. He searched within himself for the fragments of doubt that had surged to the surface of his thoughts at Ajir. *I have come this far.* The lives he had taken in the prosecution of this mission up to this point had been soldiers. Once he gave his word of command, it would be civilians that would be put to the sword.

Dukat studied Bajor, and his hand came up to a screen to trace the line of the planet's curvature. He looked, and found no uncertainty. It was regrettable, but there were sacrifices to be made, and they would not be the lives of his people, his family. *Never again. I will do what I must.*

He gave the order to fire.

The first bolt fell from the sky in a brilliant streak, atomizing the thin clouds over Korto, a rod of incandescent energy that drew thunder behind as it ripped air molecules apart.

The polarized windows of the police flyer weren't enough to stop the bright flare from hitting Darrah and Proka like a physical blow, and both men reflexively clutched at their faces, shielding their eyes. Darrah saw the hazy image of his bones through the flesh of his fingers, heard the screech and howl of the flyer's controls as an electromagnetic backwash lanced through them.

"Fires take me, what was that?" Proka spat, blinking furiously.

Darrah ignored him, fighting through streaming eyes to hold the aircraft in the sky.

The concussion hit them next, buffeting the craft in a burning updraft. Proka stabbed a finger at the city; they were no more than twenty kellipates distant from the

Korto limits. A huge patch of the settlement down toward the docks was burning. Clouds of vapor roiled overhead.

"Steam from the river," said Darrah. "They hit the low districts." He thought of the stacker blocks where he had once lived, somewhere inside that inferno.

"We've got to get on the ground," snapped Proka. "We can't risk getting caught in—" He balked and pointed at the sky. "Another one!"

Darrah was ready this time, and covered his face with the meat of his forearm. The hurricane scream of the energy bolts struck again, and this time there were more of them, hammering at the air. The flyer fought against him, desperately trying to throw itself into the ground, but Darrah resisted, riding the shock waves even as the wind shear ripped at the hull, shredding the stabilator winglets.

When he looked up again, the entire city was shrouded in smoke, a spreading black cloud pooling in the shallow valley beneath the hill districts. Only the peak and the Naghai Keep were clearly visible, rising above the spreading darkness. The entire attack had lasted less than a minute.

Darrah slammed the throttle forward to full power and threw the ship toward Korto, aiming the nose toward the hills.

"Where are you going?" Proka asked.

"Job's done," he snapped back. "We got Jas's family out, now I'm going to get mine!"

The constable didn't reply. He was craning his neck to see up into the ash-smeared sky. A new storm of killing fire lanced overhead, the angle from the attacker in orbit too shallow to strike the city again.

"They're targeting something to the east," said Proka. "Not the enclave . . ."

Darrah's voice caught in his throat. "The Kendra Shrine."

✦   ✦   ✦

The cloisters of the monastery were filled with prayers and panic in equal measure. Built high into the hillside, the ancient campus commanded an excellent view of the provinces to the west. It was with silent terror that the novices, prylars, and ranjens assembled for dawn mass on the square were witness to the streaks of sunfire falling from the sky to strike the distant blur of Korto's conurbation. The sounds of the detonations were only now reaching them, the shock wave rumbles rattling the ornamental stained-glass windows in the halls.

Then the first blast fell on Kendra, hitting the compound of service sheds and habitats for the visiting penitents at the base of the hill. The concussion turned the ancient glass to molten bullets, the plume of hellish flame behind it erasing the cluster of stone buildings in a heartbeat. The next shot came and tore the tallest towers from the high levels of the monastery. A construction that had stood on the surface of Bajor for thousands of years, that had weathered wars and famines and storms beyond counting, now cracked and crumbled under its own weight, stone breaking with a mournful cry that carried down the valley. No more strikes followed; there were other targets scattered across Bajor's dayside to be prosecuted. No more were needed at Kendra. The damage was done, fires and collapse spreading with roaring, snarling fury.

The sound made Vedek Arin freeze where he stood, halfway down the length of the grand corridor toward the shrine. The polished floor beneath his feet shook as if wracked by an earthquake. His calling as a servant of the Prophets warred with his instinct for self-preservation. The Orb ... Dare he leave it to whatever fate was to come, trusting in his gods to preserve it so that he might flee—or should he enter the shrine and carry out the ark holding the Tear, risking his life to venture inside and perhaps be buried alive? A way behind him, a huge chandelier made of brass and crystal tore free of the ceiling and struck the ground with a colossal crash. Arin's terror leapt a hundredfold and he gaped in panic, rooted to the spot by his fear. He took a hesitant step toward the shrine; he registered that the doors were hanging open. The priest staggered forward, and his foot touched a rent in the floor where a stone tile should have been. He pitched forward, crying out, and he struck the stonework hard. The impact dizzied him, pain blurring his sight. "Prophets . . ." he called out. "Aid me . . ."

Strong hands dragged him to his feet, and the vedek blinked. There was blood in his eyes from a streaming cut on his forehead that sang with pain. Cascades of dust and falling tiles were impacting all around him. "The cloister . . ."

"It's coming down, Vedek!" He recognized the voice, saw the man who was holding him up.

"Osen?" He staggered. "What . . . Were you inside the shrine?"

"I came after you!" insisted the ranjen. "We have to get out!"

"But the Tear of the Prophets is still in there!" cried Arin. "We can't leave the Orb of Truth!"

Gar was dragging him away. "The Prophets will protect it," he shouted over the grind of stone on stone, "and we must protect ourselves!"

Great chunks of the walls and the pillars supporting them were impacting all around them now, and finally Arin surrendered to his fear, letting the young priest drag him away, out of the building.

Outside, the vedek stumbled and fell to his knees, turning in time to see the monastery groan like a dying man and collapse in on itself in a final tide of noise and gray-brown dust. The clouds of powdered stone and ash washed up and engulfed the monks, coating them in the cloying powder, painting them the color of ghosts. Arin looked up into the sky and saw white fire falling toward the horizon, in the direction of Janir and Ashalla.

In Dahkur, dawn had still to break across the city, but the streets were choked with people and vehicles desperate to flee the conurbation. Streetscreens were showing live broadcasts from the destruction wrought in Korto, and the citizenry was panicked.

In the halls of the embassy of the Cardassian Union there was a skeleton crew on duty on the upper levels, soldiers guarding the doors to keep the place secure, but no staff members at the checkpoints or on the office tiers. All of them were a dozen levels below, in the emergency bunker along with the command staff and Jagul Kell himself. All of them but Rhan Ico.

The embassy was replete with protected chambers, a monument to the Cardassian obsession with paranoia and security, but the room that Ico stood in was the most secure of them all, constructed to tolerances and designs that were so secret no living being had a hand in fabricating them. It existed on no plans for the building; there was no door, so access was only via a hidden transporter; it had nothing to connect it to the outside world. The machine-manufactured room was a module that, like the rest of the building, had been made whole on Cardassia and shipped to Bajor to be beamed into place. The walls were laced with complex circuits that could defeat a million kinds of listening devices and sensors. Ico had even heard rumors that the panels contained a bio-neural matrix based on cultured Vulcan brain tissue, which could fog penetration by telepaths. She was confident that no one on the planet could know what was going on in here.

The folded-space transporter unit before her completed its phase-shift cycle with a hiss of displaced molecules and commenced the reintegration process. Inside the sealed receptor capsule a shape began to take form, and she pressed her hand to the transparent wall of the pod. A cool smile unfolded on Ico's lips. It was a genuine emotion on her part, a rare thing for the woman. Certainly, it was not something she would have exhibited in the presence of anyone else. But here, in the room, she was utterly alone, and so she could drop her pretense for a short time. It was, in its way, refreshing.

The transporter completed its work, and the capsule opened to her. Ico reached in and ran a hand over the careworn wooden case that lay inside. Intricate scrollwork in an ancient Bajoran ideogram script framed the planes of the box, looping around convex oval lenses set in the sides of the container. The carved wood was warm to the touch. For long moments Ico's fingers dithered over the small iron latch on the front of the container. The glow of the object inside the ark cast a honeyed illumination that scintillated, compelling her to open it.

"And this is what drove Hadlo to his folly," she said to the air. Ico smirked and pushed aside any thoughts forming in her mind that she might actually give in to the same curiosity. Instead, she gathered up the box and placed it inside a padded cargo container, pausing only to seal it with a beam tool and tag it with an encrypted transporter locater. "The first of many," Ico said to herself.

A faint rumble made her look up at the ceiling. The bombardment of Dahkur had started. She returned to her work, secure in the knowledge that she was in no danger.

The Cardassian warships dropped out of warp inside the orbit of Jeraddo, shedding velocity in flares of rainbow radiation. The maneuver, like every other event in the sequence, was a precisely timed, perfectly choreographed display to present the right image to the Bajoran ships still drifting damaged inside visual range. Their firing grids pulsing, the *Kashai* and the *Daikon* fell toward the Tzen-kethi marauder like swooping raptors. Disruptor bursts arced through the vacuum around the teardrop starship, flashing off the force shields.

"Phase three initiated," said the glinn, gripping the helm console as the marauder shook under the impacts.

The thought had crossed Dukat's mind that if Ico or Kell or any one of a dozen other enemies he had made wished to end his existence, this was an opportune moment for him to do so. All that was needed was someone able to exercise the right amount of influence over Dalin Tunol, to have her turn her aim away from showy near-hits to a direct shot at the Tzenkethi command tier; but Dukat was not concerned. He had picked Tunol for her loyalty and her intelligence. The woman had placed her banner by Dukat's because she knew the kind of man he was. Driven and ruthless, and in the Union such an officer would make his mark or die trying. He had known Tunol was of the same stripe from the moment she was assigned to his vessel.

The ship rocked again, and a plasma conduit ruptured across the bridge, spitting sparks and white gas. "Are the charges set?" demanded the dal.

The glinn nodded. "Countdown is under way, sir. Awaiting your final orders."

"Disengage from ground attack mode and return fire. Simulate damage to the targeting sensors. I don't want any serious hits on either craft." He got to his feet and tapped his comcuff. "This is the dal. Operations team, secure stations and gather at the designated transport points. You have one metric, *mark.*"

"Next run, incoming," The glinn was pale; the prospect of taking fire clearly didn't agree with her.

"Drop the shields after the first volley." Dukat watched

the time dwindle on his chrono. "Make it look like a cascade failure."

A blue light on his bracelet blinked once, twice. *Tunol's signal.* The tingle of a matter transporter prickled his skin as clouds of orange energy snatched away the Cardassian crew, making the ship lifeless for the second time.

The *Kashai* rolled away from the marauder, spitting energy bolts as it veered off. The Tzenkethi ship, suddenly ponderous and wallowing with none of the agility it had exhibited before, spun a lazy turn as if it were making a half-hearted attempt to place its main gun on the light cruiser.

It was the *Daikon* that dealt the blow that signaled the end of the marauder's performance. Concentrating every iota of energy in the ship's spiral-wave disruptors, the Cardassian vessel ripped into the Tzenkethi fuselage, tearing away great divots of hull metal. Something critical failed inside the marauder; in the space of a microsecond orange spheres of explosive detonation appeared in the spaceframe at the bow, the stern, in the warp core, in the central tiers. The *Daikon* veered away as the Tzenkethi ship became a tiny, fleeting sun, an expanding ball of flame consuming the marauder and the secrets that it had so briefly concealed.

Tunol climbed out of the *Kashai's* command chair and surrendered it to Dukat, but the dal waved her away. He had come straight to the bridge without pausing to throw off his environmental suit, and he had no wish to take his place unless he was in a proper duty uniform; but he wanted to see the Tzenkethi ship die, and there it was on the main viewer, consuming itself in fire.

"Mission accomplished," said Tunol, with the hint of a grin.

"A performance worthy of the grand theater itself," Dukat replied. "You played your part well."

Tunol nodded. "The transporter signatures were masked beneath the discharges from the *Daikon*'s weapons. Any sensors directed toward the engagement from the planet's surface or the surviving ships will see nothing to contradict the evidence of their own eyes." Tunol's grin returned. "A dangerous invader, brought down by Bajor's bold comrades in the Cardassian Union."

"Misdirection," mused the commander. "What the eye sees and the ear hears, the mind believes." He could see that Tunol wanted to ask him *why,* she wanted to know more. Dukat knew she was intelligent enough to piece together the reasoning behind the mission by herself, but now was not the time to bring her deeper into the circle he had forged with Ico and Kell. He grimaced. *No. That alliance was made in order to bring this to pass, and now it is done. I have no more need of it.*

Dukat left the bridge for his duty room, turning his back on the screen, the flaming wreck, and beyond it, a scarred and terrified Bajor bleeding from ugly wounds across its landscape. The hatch closed behind him, granting him privacy to discard the environmental suit.

The deception was complete. Dukat detached his thick gloves and stared down at the gray skin of his bare hands. *I have steeped myself in the blood of thousands of Bajorans,* he told himself. *How many of their deaths now lie at my feet, how many in the prosecution of this duty have I taken?*

He took a breath. "Necessity has a price," he said to the empty room, "and one day, they will thank me." Dukat found his chair and sat down, nodding at the rightness of his words. "What I have done today was as much for Bajor as it was for Cardassia."

Darrah brought the flyer in over the city low and fast, banking and turning to avoid heavy clouds of black smoke and the thermals from burning buildings. Many of the elevated highways and tramlines were broken or toppled off their piers, and the streets were choked with rubble and the shifting masses of people. He saw automated fire tenders dodging back and forth, spraying retardants over the worst infernos, but there was so much destruction, it seemed almost pointless for them to try.

The pattern of the firestorm was strange; some parts of the city had been left untouched by the bombardment, city blocks and tenements standing without injury next to blackened canyons scored through the residential district. Sunlight, where it made it through the cowl of smoke, glittered and flashed off broken glass lying in drifts through the streets. The ornamental park near the orphanage was a smoldering patch of black ruin, the aviary domes cracked open like mouths of broken teeth; the devotional tower in the dressmaker's district had broken along its length; there was a heap of metal spines and dull flakes of drywall where the night market was supposed to be. Every scene of devastation bled into another.

Darrah felt cold, chilled to his very core. The sights that lay before him were unreal; he had to struggle to process what he had seen. The city—*his city*—and the streets he had grown up in, that only a day ago he had walked upon, were passing beneath him shattered and thick with ash.

The falling plasma blasts, dropping from the heavens like the spears of a vengeful god; it was as if it were happening at a great distance from him, like a dream. *I will wake and this will all be a phantom. I am in bed with Karys and none of this has taken place. Prophets, please, make that the truth and this horror the lie.*

In the copilot's seat Proka was hunched forward with a hand communicator pressed to his ear, breathing hard and cursing under his breath. The constable was working the dial on the channel selector, skipping across the emergency frequencies. "They hit targets in Lonar as well. Even got some shots as far east as Dahkur." He was grim with the import of his words. Darrah could just about hear the tinny wail of a distant voice crying over the link into Proka's ear. The lawman shifted the frequency dial back to the local channels.

Darrah tried not to listen. He tried to stay in the here and now, but he couldn't stop himself from wanting to know the full extent of the attack. Both men had seen the blaze in the sky, the day-sun that had guttered and died far above them. The invaders were gone, but the shock wave they had created would continue to echo around Bajor for hours, days, *years.*

Proka repeated what he was hearing. "Kendra ... The monastery is gone, totally obliterated. Most of the residents got out, but many are missing and presumed dead. The shrine was buried . . ." He blanched. "They're saying . . . They're saying that the Orb of Truth was destroyed."

Gar Osen's face flashed through Darrah's thoughts. "I shouldn't have taken him back there."

"He might have made it out," Proka offered, but he didn't sound convinced.

"I shouldn't have left him." Darrah went hot with anger. *"I shouldn't have left any of them!"* He wrenched the controls around, sweeping though a bank of wood smoke, and threw the flyer toward the residential districts along the hillside road. His house stood out among the others, among the buildings with their broken windows and wind-ravaged roofs. The lawman's heart leapt; the buildings showed only the signs of shock damage and none of the awful effects of the firestorms and plasma strikes.

Darrah put the flyer down on the ash-coated road and threw off his safety restraints.

"Boss, what are you doing?" said Proka.

"Get out of here," Darrah snapped at him, and he vaulted out of the hatch toward the ruined fascia of his home.

◆ ◆ ◆

The oval front door was halfway down the entrance hall, where it had been blown off its hinges. There were fans of glass radiating out from every window facing toward the ruined city. He saw streaks of blood, still fresh on the wall, and Darrah's throat tightened, silencing him. He had come across sights of violence and destruction over and over throughout his career, in crime scenes all across Korto, but the calm and professional detachment that he fell into there was lost to him. This was *his* home, it was the sight of an atrocity that had bled in from the city, a crime on a scale so large it was beyond him to deal with it.

He couldn't bring himself to call out the names of his wife and children; he was too afraid to do it, for fear that his only reply would be silence. *The blood! The blood on the wall, whose is it?* Karys's, Bajin's, or Nell's? Was one of them up ahead in a room, or sprawled out in the yard, knifed by a piece of flying debris?

"Hello!" He shouted it out, finding the strength to push the word out of his trembling lips. "Who's there?"

He entered the kitchen just as Nell called back to him. In the shambles of the room they were all there, frozen in a tableau. Every detail of the moment etched into Darrah's mind like acid burning steel, fixing the image: Nell, an adhesive bandage covering her cheek, red dots spotting across the shoulder of her white cotton dress, the streaking of dirty tears down her perfect little face; Bajin, shocked into silence at the far door, two bags stuffed with clothes in his arms, his expression ragged with fear; and then Karys.

His wife exploded toward him, and she hit Mace hard across the cheek, the slap stinging him with the force of the impact. He recoiled, not so much from the attack as from the look of pure fury on her face. Karys swore at him and threw another swipe, but he caught her wrist. She spat and tore away from his grip, shoving him back with the heel of her free hand. *"Bastard!"* The word was caustic.

"Karys, you're all right, I—"

"Shut up!" she bellowed. "Don't speak to me! Don't say anything, you don't have the right to say anything to us!" Karys gathered up Nell, as the girl started to cry. "You left us here alone!"

Mace swallowed a gasp of breath. "I had to . . . The minister's family, we had to get them to safety . . ." The words sounded weak in his ears. "No, it's just . . . I didn't know this was going to happen." He cast around at the destruction. "I never would have—"

His wife cut him off with a savage glare. "You left us here, Darrah Mace." Ice gripped his heart. "You put your job before your family, like you did before, *like you always do!*"

"I didn't know this was coming!" he shouted back at her. "You have to believe me!"

She was retreating away from him, taking Nell and moving to Bajin and the bags. Mace read the intentions in her expression before she said another word, and he shook his head. Karys nodded tearfully, denying him. "Yes, Mace, oh yes. We can't stay here anymore. We're leaving."

He took a desperate step toward her. "Where can you go?" he cried. "The city is in chaos, there are thousands of frightened people out on the streets! You think it will be any better in Ashalla with your mother?"

"I'm not going to Ashalla," she snapped back at him. "I told you before, I can't live here. Ships will be leaving." Karys was guiding the children to the door, and Mace felt his heart tearing open as Nell and Bajin followed their mother, casting sad and piteous looks toward him.

"I'll come with you," he said desperately.

"No," she shot back. "You've let us down too many times. I'm leaving, Mace. I'm going to the Valo colony."

Everything Mace had been terrified of losing he had found safe, only to have it snatched from him. "Karys, *please!*" The pleading became a shout that made the children flinch.

On the threshold of the broken doorway, his wife threw a harsh glare at the wounded city beyond. "You care more about Korto than us, you always have. Now you can keep it."

They left him there, mute among the ruins.

17

When the central tower of the Naghai Keep had been constructed, the level below the battlements was known simply as the upper hall. An open space, studded with pillars supporting the roof and the ramparts above, in the days of the Republics it had been where the lord of the castle held his court, the high arched windows that ringed the room allowing him to look out over the region and see the breadth of his realm. In the centuries since that time, the upper hall had been used for many other things, but today it had turned back to some echo of its original purpose. In a mirror of the layout in Ashalla's Chamber of Ministers, a triad of tables were set out across the room, and Lale Usbor sat in the spot where Jas Holza's great-great-great-grandfather had once held domain. Several of the chairs were empty, in memorial to the men and women who had perished in the attacks.

The windows had been replaced only days earlier, and in some places the old polished wood of the floors was still scored where shock wave damage had ripped the aged surface. There was nowhere outside the keep where one could look and not see the devastation wrought in the aftermath of the Tzenkethi incursion. Behind Lale was the main mass of Korto, the proud spires and glittering domes broken and wounded. Here and there floater platforms from Cardassian military engineering squads dithered over sites of importance: the power station, the water purification plant, the central hospice. It had been raining earlier in the day, and the smell of dead fires was heavy in the air. The rainfall sluiced down in streaks of gray, tainted by the ashes that had been thrown into the sky. It would be months before the atmosphere worked the effluent from the attack out of its system; for now, each time it rained, it was a fresh reminder of the assault on their world.

Jas studied the city and felt within for some kind of emotional reaction to the wrecked vista; he could bring back only a cold fury, a detachment to the sight he saw before him. In the weeks since the attack, the deadness had grown worse. In moments of privacy, he had been able to conjure some flashes of emotion when Lonnic Tomo's face was there in his thoughts, but for the most part Jas was consumed by a dark, numbing anger. He saw the same feeling reflected in the faces of other ministers, those of them who weren't too afraid to step outside of their homes, or who flocked like whipped children to the sides of Kell and the Cardassians when they arrived with repair crews and emergency relief supplies, pathetic in their gratitude. They were a microcosm of Bajor as a whole. The people were torn between two polar sentiments: a fierce mixture of furious anger and dull shock at the murderous lethality of the attacks; and, in lesser numbers, a gratefulness toward the Cardassians who had put themselves in harm's way in order to destroy the Tzenkethi invaders. Resentment was on every street, the hard need for retribution burning in the eyes of every man and woman.

With the Chamber in Ashalla sealed closed while engineers worked to make the old building safe, the First Minister had chosen the Naghai Keep for the site of this assembly so that everyone could look out and see the harsh realities of the matters they were here to debate. Jas took his seat, pausing for just a moment to rest a hand on the empty chair to his right. He had yet to name a replacement for Lonnic as his adjutant.

"The Tzenkethi Coalition has formally stated that they did not order the bombing of the *Lhemor* or the attack on Bajor," said Jagul Kell, arching his hands over the table. A wave of derision followed his statement. Jas watched the Cardassian carefully. Offworlders had been granted access to the assemblies many times in the past, but today was the first time that an alien had been given formal permission by the chamber to take part in the debate. Kell sat at the benches as if he were a minister, and Lale was giving the man the same degree of respect and consideration he would give any Bajoran official. It was unprecedented, and yet no one had been able to stir up a majority to prevent Lale's introduction of the alien. Kell let the reactions of the ministers fade before continuing. "The statement is, as I warned you, exactly what we expected. Furthermore, they state that any such attacks, if they were indeed committed by Tzenkethi citizens, were the exploits of renegades and therefore beyond their control."

"They lie to our faces?" spat a minister from Hedrikspool. "Do they take us for fools?"

"Finally," Kell concluded, "the Coalition's governing body wished it to be known that they will consider any attempt by Cardassian or Bajoran citizens to take reprisals against Tzenkethi property or nationals as an act of war, and they will retaliate in kind."

The minister banged the table with a balled fist. *"War?* They started this! These creatures attack us and then make threats? We should blast them from space!"

"Minister," said Lale, cutting off the other man. "We all feel as strongly as you do. Everyone on Bajor has lost a friend or a family member in the cowardly attacks four weeks ago. We all want to see a price paid for that violation, but I called this session of ministers to Korto for a reason." He pointed out of the window. "This city was the first to be struck. It is a symbol of the great hurt done to Bajor. Look at it." There was a moment of silence as all the ministers did as Lale asked them. "Even with the help from our Cardassian friends, this city and the other settlements that were struck, at Janir and elsewhere—all of them need our every effort to rebuild. So I ask you, do we direct our energies to seeking revenge or to ensuring that we have clean water and shelter for those who were fortunate enough to survive the attacks? Do we bury our dead and sing the chants for them or do we let their spirits falter while we take up arms?" The last question was directed to the priests gathered at one end of the triangle. Vedek Arin nodded sagely at Lale's words.

"And what if another attack comes?" Kubus Oak's words carried down the length of the hall. "How will we defend against it?"

Lale laid his hands flat on the table. "Bajor must heal before she can unsheathe her sword," he replied firmly. "I will not set this world down a path to conflict with an enemy we do not even know, without first staunching the wounds we have suffered!"

Kubus nodded. "There is merit in your words, First Minister. A battle joined in the heat of passion offers the chance for mistakes. If the Tzenkethi that attacked us were indeed renegades, we would make a new enemy of the Coalition."

"Precisely," said Lale. "And that is something we cannot afford. No, even though the desire for reprisal burns in all of us, we cannot . . . we *must* not act rashly." He glanced toward General Coldri. The officer was still wearing a healing patch across his face, the result of an injury suffered during the Tzenkethi attack. "Our last attempts to do so may have led us to this place. We must tread carefully."

Kell cleared his throat. "The Cardassian Union will gladly assist the people of Bajor."

For the first time, Keeve Falor spoke up. He had been watching the unfolding conversations with a fixed grimace. "How will you do that, Jagul Kell? I would very much like to know."

The Cardassian inclined his head in a nod, ignoring the open challenge in the other man's words. "My people died in the bombing and during the attacks, Minister Keeve, and that makes this a matter for the Union as much as one for Bajor. Your planet is vulnerable," he said, "and as Minister Kubus stated, while you go about the important task of rebuilding, who will defend you?" Kell gestured toward Coldri and Jaro Essa, who glowered back at him. "The majority of your Space Guard flotilla is spread thinly across your colonial holdings, and many of the ships based near Bajor are in dry dock or incapable of meeting another attack."

"If another attack comes, we will fight to the last man," grated Coldri. Jas heard the tension in the general's voice. Coldri felt the responsibility for the aftermath of the attack, and he burned with the ignominy of his failure to prevent it.

"To the last man," repeated Kubus, "and what then? Bajor will be open to more assaults, worse than before." He shook his head. "No. Pride has kept us from this for too long, and now we are paying the price for it."

Lale nodded. "Minister Kubus is correct. That is why today I propose an advancement into our partnership with our friends from Cardassia. I will accept Jagul Kell's offer of military support to bolster the security of the Bajor system."

"A squadron of *Galor*-class warships and attendant support," Kell said smoothly. "Enough to react to any threat across the B'hava'el system in a matter of moments."

Jas blinked. *More Cardassians? Can that be right?* He glanced around, and to his shock, he saw that almost all of his fellow ministers were nodding in agreement with Lale's words. It was only Keeve Falor who looked on grim-faced and defiant.

"Kubus," said Lale, "you have offered some of your holdings on the moon Derna as a site for the squadron to deploy a command outpost?"

The minister nodded. "I have—" but he was cut off as Jaro Essa stood up abruptly.

"A military base?" The major's normally stoic expression cracked. "First Minister, are you actually proposing that we grant an alien government the right to establish a military facility not just within the boundaries of our star system, but on a satellite of the homeworld itself?" He shook his head. "Do you expect the Militia to accept this diminishment of our authority without protest?"

Lale's voice hardened. "What I *expect*, Major Jaro, is that the Militia will do exactly what the Chamber of Ministers orders them to do. This is a democracy, not a military dictatorship, and we will do what is right for Bajor. The pride of the Militia is a consideration that comes a very distant second."

"This is a mistake!" Jaro snapped, glaring at Kell.

"It is," growled Keeve, unable to remain silent any longer. "I am in agreement with the major. How can we conscience this?" he demanded. "Lale, you are giving an alien navy a foothold at our very door! Have you learned nothing these past weeks?"

"The Cardassians saved our planet from destruction," Kubus retorted. "Without their intervention, the Tzenkethi ship would have laid waste to every settlement, not just a handful! This mutual defense pact will strengthen our world! The Tzenkethi won't dare attack us again if they know we have the Union on our side. And when we are ready to seek reprisals—"

"No!" Keeve slammed his fist down on the table in

front of him, and the sound was so loud it made Jas jerk
back in surprise. "I reject this idiocy, in the name of my
clan and my place in this ministry! I will not place my
name to this proposal, I deny it."

"On a matter of this import there must be consensus,"
Lale warned. "If you reject this, Falor, you will have no
voice in the assembly."

Keeve shoved away the chair behind him and strode into
the middle of the hall. Jas saw his adjutant and the keep's
watchmen react with concern; the minister's rage was so
towering it seemed very possible he might strike Lale. "What
assembly?" he roared, casting around. "Do you mean this
pathetic rabble of frightened, cowed children? Month after
month I have sat here and watched the erosion of Bajor's
government under the slow greed and self-interest of men
like you!" He stabbed a finger at Lale, at Kubus, and the
First Minister's most vocal supporters. "What have you done
but sell our world piecemeal to these aliens?" He rounded
on Kell, but the Cardassian was impassive. "Their so-called
enclaves in every city, their soldiers and priests infesting our
streets, trampling over our culture, our *women?* It is Cardassians that are leading the rape of our lands with mining and
overfarming to feed their planets, it is the Cardassians that
brought the Tzenkethi to our world, and what do you do?"
He turned back to Lale. "Will you give them Bajor?" He
shook his head, his rage ebbing like the tide. "I . . . I will not
remain here to see my homeworld become nothing more
than another annexed colony of the Cardassian Union. Do
any of you have the courage to stand with me?"

Keeve's gaze fell on Jas, and he felt his heart shrink
in his chest. His jaw worked, but no words emerged. He
broke out in a cold sweat, cursing himself for his weakness
once again. His eyes fell to the table, and his hands spread
upon it. *Ashes and blood,* he told himself, *so much and yet so
little has stained me.*

"I thought as much," Keeve said, after a moment. He looked away and addressed the room with a bleak ferocity. "You will, all of you, live to regret the choices you make here today." The politician turned his back on the hall and strode out of the door, never looking back.

There was a long silence before Lale spoke again, his usual tone of neutrality once again in place. "If there are no more comments from the floor, then I move we call for a consensus on the matter of the extended military pact with the Cardassian Union."

Keeve Falor glanced to his side as Jekko caught up with him, concern plain on the face of his adjutant. "Sir . . ." began the man, rubbing at his thin beard.

"Where is my family?" Keeve cut in.

"On the ship, sir. The baggage as well. The freighter's captain told me he's ready to break orbit the moment you come aboard. He'll have you at Valo II in a couple of days."

"Good." Keeve nodded, striding out of the keep and across the courtyard. "I'll take the shuttle straight there from the port."

"Sir," Jekko began again, "what you just did—"

Keeve halted and looked the other man in the eye. The snarling fury the politician had demonstrated in the hall was gone now, and in its place was a cold, controlled manner. "You think I was wrong to walk away? You think I made a mistake?"

Jekko shook his head. "I haven't been in your service for a good decade and more because you're the kind of man who makes mistakes, sir. Frankly, I don't think Keeve Falor has ever made an ill-considered choice in his entire life."

Keeve smiled slightly. "I'm flattered, Jekko."

"But this . . . You were the only one who had the steel in you to stand up to Lale and Kubus and those spoon-heads. Now you just walk away, and you let them have what they want? Where's the sense in that?" He leaned closer. "I trust you, sir, but you have to explain it to me. How does running make this right?"

Keeve's eyes narrowed. "I've never run from anything," he said firmly. "But only a fool fights a battle he can't win." He jerked his chin at the keep. "You've seen how it is in there. Lale has the scared ones scared and the greedy ones bought. Even the men who might stand up for something are so beaten down they can't straighten their backs anymore." He shook his head. "No. If I stay here, I'm a threat. If the Cardassians can make this happen, they won't give pause to removing me or my family or my whole damn clan."

"The Cardassians?" repeated Jekko. "But it was the Tzenkethi who attacked—"

"Perhaps," said Keeve, "but the result was in the Union's favor. As much as I hate to leave my homeworld in the care of cowards, I need distance. Valo II is far enough away to be safe. Out there, I might be able to do something to stem the tide of this insanity. On Bajor, I'm just a target."

Jekko nodded slowly; he could see the logic of his master's words. "The fight's not over yet," he said firmly. "Whatever Lale decides in there, the Vedek Assembly still has a considerable influence. The clergy could overturn his edict. It's happened before."

"Only in matters that affect the spiritual life of Bajor."

"This doesn't?" Jekko snorted. "It affects everyone on this planet, if they go to services or not! Kai Meressa won't let it pass without comment."

Keeve's lips thinned. "The Kai . . . As much as I hate to say it, but I'm afraid she is in no position to oppose Vedek Arin. Her sickness grows worse, and the shock of the attacks has done little to aid her recovery."

"She's not with the Prophets yet," Jekko insisted. "Where there is life, there is hope."

"I hope you're right." He put a hand on Jekko's shoulder. "In the meantime, I need you to stay here after I depart. I'm putting you in charge of all the remaining Keeve clan holdings on the planet. I want you to be my eyes and ears . . ."

Jekko found himself nodding. "All right."

"This isn't the end of this, you understand me?" Keeve looked up into the sky and frowned. "This isn't the end at all. There's much worse to come."

"They're coming!"

Hadlo didn't recognize the voice of the woman, but the raw panic of the cry was plain. In the corridors of the old cargo lighter, women and children in desert robes, men in penitent's rags, and clerics in blues and yellows all mixed together in a screaming, frantic mass. The old priest had to use violence to get through their numbers, shoving them aside to make his way forward.

He fell hard as the ship rocked again with another impact, the metallic decking biting into his knees. There was a child's scream and the wet snap of bone as a young boy broke a limb behind him. Hadlo did not stop to minister to him; there were matters of far greater import to deal with. He went on, adrenaline driving him, making his old muscles tight with pain.

Hellish light spilled in through the grimy portholes in the ceiling of the corridor, beyond them the sight of twisting, writhing hurricanes of yellow-gold energy. They were still inside the sector of space the crewmen called the Badlands, but the constant plasmatic storms had provided poor cover for the Oralians. In the hectic flight from Cardassia, they had not had the luxury of choosing the best men to ferry them. Two ships had been destroyed by the storms in the first day, streams of glowing fire consuming them when they ventured too close. The planetoids Hadlo had been told would serve the Oralians as a hiding place turned out to be barren and airless rocks, warrens of stone that had no functioning life support, no shielding from the constant flood of radiation that bathed everything in the Badlands.

It had been Hadlo's choice to stay on the ships, in the ragged flotilla of transports that were all they could muster. *His choice*—just as it had been his choice to leave countless adherents to the faith behind when the ships had been filled. The cleric saw their faces in the people around him, when he closed his eyes, every night in his dreams. He saw them through the portholes, watching as the last ship lifted off, leaving them to the mercy of a military that had named all of them dissidents and terrorists.

Hadlo pushed on, batting away hands that grabbed at his robes, ignoring the pleading cries. The compartment was just a little farther away.

Red light blazed through the windows and tore a scream from the refugees. He glanced up and saw dying energies falling back on themselves, consuming the gunmetal cylinders of the big bulk tanker; there had been at least seven hundred Oralians on board that ship.

The cleric couldn't see the vessels that had fired the killing shots, and he tore himself away, moving again, pushing and snarling at the living tide around him. At last he was at the hatch and he forced it open. Hadlo closed the door behind him and sank to the floor just as another blast buffeted the lighter.

He dragged himself into the chair before the communications console, his hands shaking. *How did they find us?* The question rolled through his mind. *The Badlands are an uncharted wilderness . . . This cannot be chance . . .* The answer brought a sour taste to his mouth. *Betrayal, then! Someone sold our lives for their own! Of course!* One of the ship crews perhaps, or an Oralian who had fallen from the Way and lost faith.

Hadlo tried to work the controls, but his hands were shaking. In his nostrils there was the stink of ashes and blood, and he felt a sudden rasping tightness around his feet and ankles. He did not dare look down for fear of seeing the vipers coiling around him. "The vision!" he cried. The dream granted to him by the Orb was returning again.

Reality hazed and flowed like rain across a windowpane. *Rough caresses over his legs and bare feet, a touch like old dry parchment. The snakes burying him, ashes and fire and the wind like razors, the screaming hooded faces—*

Hadlo slammed his hands on the console and shouted, "No! Oralius, I beg you! We cannot perish unknown in this place! I must ... I must be heard!" The cleric punched at the controls, fear robbing him of reason. "Bennek! Bennek, do you hear me?" He stabbed at the transmit key. Nothing but snarling static answered him, and the ship howled as more shots struck it. Lights flickered as the power trembled toward darkness.

He dropped to his knees. There would be no worse fate than this one, he realized. To die unrecorded and unre-membered, all that he had done for his faith swept away in a plume of nuclear fire. *I will not die in silence! I must be heard!*

"Oralius ... *Oralius?*" He shouted the name. "Prophets! Do you hear me? Have you all abandoned me? My love is for you both—"

"There are no gods here, Hadlo."

The voice made the cleric jerk back with fear. "W-who?"

Laced with interference, the words hissed from the communicator console. *"It took me a while to find you, Hadlo. But I told you this day would come, do you remember?"*

He scrambled to his feet and threw himself at the port-hole in the wall of the lighter's hull. Outside he saw two shapes moving slowly, circling the vessel: Cardassian war-ships. "Dukat?" Hadlo said the name like a curse.

"You are no more use to Cardassia, priest. Your gods have for-saken you. Your faith will not protect you." Hadlo could almost see the smile.

"No!" He lunged at the console. "The Way is eternal, it cannot be destroyed! You must not do this, Dukat! The path to the fire and the burning cities, this will bring that to pass! I have seen it, I know the future—"

But the signal had already ceased, and outside a salvo of disruptor bolts reached down to tear the freighter apart.

It was a simple memorial, one among hundreds of others. There were funerals taking place every day in a dozen cit-ies, and even as Darrah bent to run his fingers over the arc of Lonnic's headstone, the sounds of ritual chants reached him from across the ornamental gardens. In a moment of open grief, Jas Holza had ordered that part of the keep's grounds be consecrated as a place of rest. Markers had sprouted up overnight, and here in this eastern corner there were places for those who had perished in the reprisal fleet at Ajir. Nearby a woman and a young dark-haired boy stood holding *duranja* lamps in front of the stone etched with Li Tarka's name. The woman was crying, but the look on the boy's face was firm with determination as he laid a prayer paper at the foot of the arch.

Darrah rested his hand on the sun-warmed stone and thought of Lonnic Tomo. *One more loss among so many.* He took a breath, and it shuddered through him.

"Sorry about your friend." Syjin put his hands in his pockets, uncomfortable to be among the dead.

Darrah stood. "Thanks." He took a moment to gather his thoughts. "Why are you here?"

Syjin nodded at another arch. "Paying my respects, like you. The engineer on the *Kylen* used to crew with me." He blew out a breath.

"I didn't bring any papers," Darrah said quietly. "Didn't

come here to see Tomo, really. I want to talk to Osen." He
jerked a thumb at the keep behind them.

"They made him a vedek, I heard."

"Yeah. A lot of priests died when the monastery fell,
Cotor and a lot of others. Arin had Gar pushed up the
ranks to fill the gaps." He sniffed. "But now he's got duties,
what with the monks from Kendra being rehoused at the
keep for the interim . . ."

"And he doesn't have time to talk to an old friend?"

"Yeah." Darrah nodded again. Gar's refusal to even
see the inspector wasn't like him. He thought about that
stormy night again, of Gar's wild claims. It was one more
element of a growing disquiet that hung around the lawman like a cowl of smoke.

Syjin kicked at a loose stone. "Listen, uh, Mace. It's best
you hear this from me before someone else tells you. I
don't want you to get mad or anything, okay?"

Darrah looked up at him and said nothing.

"Karys and the cubs? It was me, okay? She came to me
and she asked me to take them to the colony on Valo II.
I didn't put the idea into her head or anything, but I got
them offplanet."

A flare of anger burned bright and then died just as
quickly. "No. It's all right. I'm glad it was you. You don't
need to be sorry. I feel better knowing it was someone
trustworthy who did it. Thank you."

"Trustworthy." Syjin smiled a little. "That's not a term
many apply to me." The smile faded. "She cried all the
way there, you know. She wasn't doing it out of hate. It's
just . . . I don't think she can take it here anymore, and she's
not the only one. People are leaving in droves." The pilot
sighed. "Look, I'm taking some more folks out in a couple
of days. There's space for you as well, Mace. Just pack a bag
and come. You could patch things up, you're a smart guy.
You could—"

"I can't," Darrah said quietly. "I want to, but I can't." He looked up and out over the city. "I can't leave all this undone, Syjin. Something's wrong here. The more I think about it, the more I'm sure of it."

The pilot gave a bitter laugh. "Sure it's wrong! Bajor's being pulled apart around us. But we're just ordinary men. What can we do but get out while we still can?"

Darrah shook his head. "I'm not going to walk away from this. The attacks, the Cardassians, it's all converging. I can see it in the air. Someone has to follow this as far as it goes."

"Why does it have to be you?"

He shot Syjin a look. "Because who else is going to do it? I can't follow Karys to Valo knowing this is behind me."

"She won't wait forever," said the other man, after a long moment.

"I know." Darrah nodded and looked up into the sky. "But I have a job to do. The truth about what's really going on is buried out there somewhere, and I'm going to bring it to light."

Bennek awoke with a jerk. Beside him, Tima shifted beneath the sheets and mumbled something incoherent. The cleric felt awkward and uncomfortable, as if something in the room had changed without his knowledge. He moved slowly so as not to disturb the sleeping woman. His hand was touching the tab for the lamp when he saw the shape of a man-shadow across from him, in the old wicker chair.

"Don't," said Dukat, barely a breath above a whisper. "You'll wake the Bajoran."

Despite the blood-warm heat inside the enclave blockhouse, Bennek's skin prickled with a sudden chill. "What . . . Why are you in my quarters?" He hissed back, shooting Tima a furtive glance. He felt sick; how long had Dukat been there? Hours? Had he seen them together?

As if he intuited Bennek's train of thought, Dukat's next

words had a smile in them. "She's quite attractive, for an alien. As time passes, I'm finding it easier to understand the allure of their women. Tell me, cleric, should I try it for myself?"

"You won't touch her," Bennek husked, teeth bared.

"No?" There was a soft clink and the shadow moved, helping itself to some of the *kanar* left in a decanter on the table. "Hm. A fair vintage, if somewhat functional."

Bennek eased himself to the edge of the bed. He glanced at the inert lamp, wondering if it would serve him as a weapon if the soldier tried to attack him.

Dukat drained the glass and set it down. "While you have slept, Bennek, while you have dallied here with your masks and scrolls, things have altered. I'm here to tell you about the change in order."

"Change?"

A nod. "Oh, indeed. I'm afraid that Hadlo has gone to join Oralius. He and all the dissidents who fled Cardassia rather than cooperate with the authorities."

The priest felt an odd flutter in his chest. "He's dead . . ."

"They all are. Your church, such as it is, no longer exists beyond the surface of this planet. All that remains of the Oralian Way is now on Bajor, and you are their leader." He paused. "Take a moment, Bennek. I understand this is a lot to process all at once."

The bedsheets bunched in his hands, and Tima murmured again, turning away from him. "You did this."

"Does that matter? All that is important now is your responsibility. To your faith, to your followers, to the pretty sleeping Bajoran, to your own life. If you want any of those things to last to the dawn, then you must understand that."

"You're lying," Bennek whispered.

Dukat leaned forward, and Bennek caught a glitter of light from the man's dark eyes. "Don't be foolish. I've never lied to you, Bennek. I have no need to."

The priest took a shuddering breath. Dukat was telling the truth, it was there in every word he said. Bennek tried to take it all in and gasped. *If it's true . . . If we are all that is left of the Way, then what must I do?* He recalled Hadlo's words in the library, his exhortation to protect the faith at any cost. Finally he looked again at the shadowy figure. "What do you want of me?"

Dukat smiled in the dimness. "The preservation of what you hold balances on that most Cardassian of traits, Bennek. Obedience." He got up slowly. "You have the ear of poor Kai Meressa. Convince her that the defense pact will benefit Bajor. Ensure she does not try to sway the Vedek Assembly toward a veto."

"And if I cannot?"

"Then it will not go well for the last children of Oralius." He turned his back on the assignation and walked quietly toward the door.

"I have your word?" Bennek hissed, and got a nod in return. "But where are you going?"

Dukat hesitated. "Home," he explained. "Central Command has seen fit to reward me with a promotion for my service to the Union." He glanced over his shoulder, his gaze like iron. "But don't worry, priest. This planet interests me. I'll be back."

ONE MONTH AGO

◆ ◆ ◆

2328 (Terran Calendar)

18

"The power that moves through me animates my life," said the Cardassian woman, her hands spread to the dull sky. "It animates the mask of Oralius, to speak her words with my voice—"

The burly, balding man at the base of the *bantaca*'s steps shouted at the top of his lungs. "Take your voice somewhere else!" A growl of approval came from the crowd of Bajorans standing with him. "Go back to your shantytown! The Prophets don't want you here, spoonhead!"

"This is going to ignite," said Proka, from the side of his mouth. "You want me to defuse it?"

Darrah ran a hand through his hair and frowned. "No. If we cap this here today, they'll just blow off steam somewhere else, maybe when we're not around. Let it play out." The chief inspector kept close to the parked police flyers, his eyes ranging over the handful of Watch officers that had been assigned to keep order across the City Oval. *Not enough,* he told himself. *There's never enough of us.*

"At least we don't have to stand side by side with Cardie troopers," Proka hissed, picking up on his commander's thoughts. "I'm so sick of that 'Cardassian citizen, Cardassian jurisdiction' crap."

Darrah nodded and said nothing. *What am I doing here?* He asked himself. He had a small but clean office back in the precinct that he hardly used; instead he was out on the street, ghosting the foot patrols and the airborne units like he did every day. His men liked to say that Darrah Mace was "hands-on," but there was more to it than that. He was driven. "Can't stem the tide from behind a desk," he said aloud.

"Boss?" said Proka.

Darrah indicated the bald man. "We got anything on mouthy over there?"

The senior constable nodded, reading from a padd. "Couple of alert flags, suspected involvement with the Circle. Nothing we can prove, though. Cardassians pulled him for allegedly making trouble out at the enclave, but nothing came of it. I think that's where he might have lost the finger."

He looked and saw that, indeed, the bald Bajoran had no index finger on his right hand. "Huh. No wonder he's pissed at them."

"That's why he's here with his friends. Cardassians don't give a damn about the Oralians, which makes them a soft target."

"And to the Circle, a Cardassian is a Cardassian is a Cardassian." The activist group, under its more grandiose title of Alliance for Global Unity, had grown from a minor impediment to a thorn in the Militia's side over the last five years— a matter not helped by the fact that many Militia officers quietly sympathized with the militant isolationists.

There were maybe a dozen of the Oralians at the foot of the spire, holding one of their interminable recitations. Darrah scanned their faces, noticing that there were a couple of Bajorans among the Cardassians, swaddled in the pastel-colored robes. He still found it strange to imagine that a Bajoran could find any meaning in an alien religion, but the choice wasn't for anyone else to make for them, despite what the Circle's propaganda leaflets said.

The woman was trying to go on. "Oralius is the Way of love," she was saying. "Her path parallels that of your Prophets, can you not see that?"

It was the opening the bald man wanted. "I'll tell you what I see, offworlder! I see you masked fools here in my city, trying to take us from the side of the Prophets!" The crowd grumbled in agreement. "It's your kind who are turning Bajor into a ghetto!" He waved his hand toward the mountains. "Who was it that made me lose my job at the ore works, when they came and bought out the mines to strip them bare? Cardassians! Who is raping our lands, paying off the greedy with your damned technology? Cardassians!" The man stepped forward, shooting a look at the police presence, clearly gauging his chances. "We have to listen to the newsfeeds telling us that our Cardassian friends are keeping the Tzenkethi at bay from that snake's nest of yours on Derna, but what is really going on? Our ministers are selling out our world to Cardassia and tightening the noose around our necks!"

"The followers of the Way have nothing to do with the Cardassian Union anymore," said the priest, her voice taking on an angry tone. "If you cannot see past the color of my skin to that fact, then nothing I can say will convince you otherwise!"

The man laughed harshly. "Then we agree on something!"

"Get ready," Darrah said quietly. This scene had played out so many times, he could predict the moment the flashpoint would come with uncanny accuracy. The bitter thought made him sullen. Confrontations like this one were repeated all over Bajor; they had become a matter of everyday life, surges in the slow-burning discontent that underscored everything. *Five years,* Darrah thought, *five years and no reprisal of any note as payment in kind for the attacks. Is it any wonder that everyone is still angry, still searching for somewhere to direct the anger?*

The man stabbed a finger at the Bajorans in Oralian robes. "And you! You're the worst, willingly giving yourselves over to them." He glared at the priest. "You're polluting the faith of our people, indoctrinating our kind!"

"It's not like that at all," argued one of the converts.

"Be quiet!" roared the man. "You're traitors to the Celestial Temple!" He reached for a pocket, and his hand returned with a blunt club; behind him the crowd came forward.

"Now," Darrah snapped, and Proka and his men reacted with a clatter of drawn phasers.

"Step back!" barked the constable, a pickup in his communicator amplifying his voice through the public address speakers on the parked flyers.

Jeers and catcalls erupted among the mass of people as Darrah stepped up to where the Cardassian woman stood, a pistol in his hand. He took a curl of her robes and pulled her toward him. She smelled of dust and the odd, metallic sweat of her species. "You need to take your acolytes and go," he snapped.

"We have a right to be here," she retorted. "The First Minister—"

"Right now," Darrah growled, "unless Oralius wants more martyrs."

She saw the iron-hard glare in his eyes and nodded, retreating back toward the rest of the hooded group.

"You see?" shouted the bald man, and he spat. "You see? Even the City Watch are against us!" He shook a fist in Darrah's face. "Are you bought and paid for too, lawman? Is that your job?"

A hot flare of resentment shot through Darrah, and without warning he smashed the butt of his phaser down on the bridge of the bald man's nose. It broke with a wet crack, and the protester went to his knees, a fan of blood gushing over his lips. "My job?" Darrah snarled. "You don't know a damn thing about it."

Dukat found the look of profound irritation on the senior officer's face quite amusing. "Jagul Kell. Here you are."

"It's *Gul* Dukat now, isn't it?" Kell retorted, crossing the room. "Get out of my chair, Gul."

"Of course." Dukat stood up and stepped away from the ornate desk. It was the same one Kell had used in the Dahkur embassy; in fact, almost everything in the jagul's duty office was the same; doubtless the man had given orders to transfer all the trappings of his rank and pomposity to the naval base here on the Derna moon the moment it had been completed.

Kell's irritation diminished as he took his rightful position. Dukat had deliberately come to the man's chamber unannounced and taken his seat just to rattle his former commander; Kell was overly fond of making a performance out of his superiority, and if he could not assert his control over a meeting at the very start, it made him petulant and uncomfortable. Dukat's amusement at scoring points on the man waned quickly, however; it was, in the end, a worthless exercise.

Kell eyed him. "I have a briefing in a few minutes. Whatever you want had better be something you can tell me quickly."

Setting his agenda before I have even spoken, thought Dukat. *He's the same fool he was the day we set foot on Bajor.*

"I noted your deployment to this sector with the *Vandir,*" Kell continued, giving him the smallest amount of attention he could. "I believe you have your assignments from Central Command already. Do you need some approval from me?"

Dukat shook his head. "Actually, Jagul, I am here to

inform you of additional mission objectives in my assignment here at Derna Base." The name made his lip curl. The facility on Derna was hardly worthy of the name; it was less an outpost than a series of revetments and temporary docks that ships could use between sorties. He imagined that more of the facility's functions were turned toward the covert needs of the Obsidian Order than the Union's navy.

"And those objectives are?" Kell demanded.

"Twofold. Firstly, to impress upon you Command's desire to annex Bajor ... something that in ten years you have yet to achieve."

Kell's eyes flashed with anger. "You share that responsibility with me, Dukat. Let us not forget whose plan it was that brought us to this state of affairs."

"I provided you with an opportunity, Jagul. Command feels you have not fully exploited it."

"Command is light-years away," grated the other man. "Things here are more complex than they might appear from an office on Cardassia Prime."

"No doubt," Dukat allowed. "Nevertheless, I am here to impress upon you that occupation must be formalized, and soon. If not, then other men may have to take your posting here." He gestured around at the opulent office.

The jagul folded his arms, seething quietly. "And the second objective?"

"It appears that the United Federation of Planets has taken an interest in the situation on Bajor. They are considering open political opposition to our presence in the sector."

Kell snorted. "The Federation? Toothless, posturing fools, all of them. Let them bray and talk about sanctions and their stern displeasure."

"It would be unwise to underestimate Starfleet."

The other man glared at him from behind the desk. "I am ranking officer here, and it will be my choice to decide what is and is not *wise."* He gave Dukat a sharp wave of the hand. "You may tell Command that you have delivered your messages. Now get out of my office and return to your duties."

Dukat nodded, letting the jibe roll off him. "I intend to do exactly that."

The Xepolite transport touched down on the apron at Korto starport with a sound that was somewhere between the noise of a dying bovine and a case of cutlery thrown down a staircase. The ungainly ship, little more than a collection of cargo pods mated to a drive module, sagged on its landing gear and shed a cloud of rust fragments. The main hatch dilated in fits and starts until finally it was wide enough for the ship's owner and his most recent passengers to disembark. The captain, like his vessel, was grubby but quite quick, and he followed the two Bajoran women down the egress ramp.

"So, here we are, home sweet home," he sniffed, fishing a patched padd from his pocket. "And as such, if you would be so kind?"

"Thanks for the ride, Hetman Foroe," the older female answered him, the one with the severe face and the shoulder-length blond hair. She seemed to do most of the talking, while the other one, with the large, nervous mouth and black, stringy plaits, hovered nearby. Over the course of their journey, he'd attempted to fathom the dimensions of the relationship between the two Bajorans with little success. *Sisters? Lovers?* He couldn't find a pattern that fitted. Still, his curiosity about them was fading with the prospect of money changing hands. The blond woman tapped a code into the padd, releasing the second half of Foroe's fee, and with that their transaction was complete.

"My pleasure," he said, examining the string of digits. When he looked up from the padd, they were walking away with their bags over their shoulders. "Hey," he said, jogging to catch up. "Now the business part is behind us, I'm curious—"

"No, we don't want a drink with you," said the older woman. *What was she called? Al-something? Ally? Alo?*

"Alla," said the hetman, recalling her name. "I wouldn't dream of it. No, it's just that I was wondering about something." He glanced at the dark-haired one. *Her name is Wenna, isn't it?* "The thing is, most of the Bajorans I deal with are trying to get away from their home planet these days, what with the Cardassians and the unrest and all. But you two came all the way back here from a perfectly nice colony on Draygo. Why is that?"

"Our aunt is sick," said Wenna abruptly. "We're going to Relliketh to look after her."

"Oh." Foroe wasn't convinced, but he had other prospects to pursue at the other end of the port. His contact would be waiting for him, and if he didn't get there in time, the load he expected to be smuggling to Prophet's Landing would be gone. "Well, I hope she gets well soon. And if you ever need a ride back to Draygo—"

Alla cut him off with a withering glare. "Oh, we'll call you, count on it."

As soon as the Xepolite was out of earshot, the older woman turned and shot her companion a look. "What have I told you?"

"Did I do something wrong?"

She frowned and flicked straw-colored hair from her eyes. "Don't volunteer information. It's a sure sign of an amateur working from a prepared legend. He didn't need to know we were going to Relliketh. The bit about the aunt was enough."

"I'm sorry, Lieutenant—"

She shoved the other woman up against the wall of a

hangar. "What did you just say?" she hissed. "Did you just call me *Lieutenant?*" She mimed the shape of a pistol at her head. *"Zap.* You just got us both killed. If someone heard you slip like that, we're blown, the mission is over."

"Sorry. I'm sorry," said the dark-haired woman, and she rubbed at the ridges on her nose. "This is all new to me. It's not what I expected. I'm just an analyst—"

The blond woman slapped the hand away. "Stop that," she said, and stepped back. "Look. You're here for two reasons. First, because you're the best available expert in xeno-anthropology and Bajoran cultural studies, and second, because that cute Welsh accent of yours is, by some quirk of interplanetary linguistics, not too dissimilar to the way they speak down in the southeastern provinces. While you are here, *you are Jonor Wenna,* you understand me? Because Lieutenant Junior Grade Gwen Jones doesn't exist right now. She'll stay that way until we're done here."

"Yes," said Gwen, gathering herself. "Hello. My name's Wenna. I'm from Relliketh—" She stopped. "Right. Sorry. Don't volunteer information."

"Better."

The dark-haired girl studied the other woman. "And what about Lieutenant Alynna Nechayev of Starfleet Intelligence? Where is she?"

"My name is Alla," said Alynna. "I don't know this Nechayev woman you're talking about." There was a weariness in her words. "She must be some kind of ghost."

From the ramp of his ship in the neighboring hangar, Syjin watched the two women walk off and cocked his head, wondering. *The shorter one is pretty, in a rural kind of way. The other one, though, too much like hard work. I know the type.*

The loading chief, a large dark man named Wule, crossed over to him, wiping grease from his fingers. "Ho," he called. "That's the last one off. You're clear to lift once Traffic Control gives you the go."

Syjin nodded. "Thanks. I just hope the Cardassians don't decide to stop and search me again. That's why I hardly ever come back here these days . . ." He shook his head. "Every time I return to Bajor it's like . . . like I'm visiting a sick old friend, and he's closer to death each time."

"It's what things have come to," Wule agreed. "Not like the old days. I can't remember the last time I saw you lift empty."

"Not empty for long," Syjin insisted. "I got a gig. I'm picking up some cargo."

"Coming back here with it?"

"As a matter of fact, I am." He smiled briefly. "Don't sweat it, I've got a little something for you, if you smooth the way with customs for me."

"What?" Wule eyed him.

"Agnam loaf. I know you love it."

The dock chief nodded eagerly. "Say no more. Just don't get jumped by the spoonheads when you come back, though. They catch you with proscribed goods on board and you'll be disappeared . . ."

"It's food, not particle cannons," mocked the pilot. "Hardly worth spacing me over."

Wule gave him a grave look. "Don't be so sure, my friend, don't be so sure." He paused at the threshold. "Where's the rendezvous? You know the Cardies have upped their patrols out past Pullock."

Syjin nodded, running through his preflight checks. "I heard. That's why I'm going to be nowhere near the Badlands." Wule threw him a salute, and the hatch slammed closed behind him.

The destination for the rendezvous with his Ferengi contact had been chosen at random and transmitted on an encrypted channel. Grek, the lop-eared little troll, had a cargo of some of the best rare edibles this side of the Orion sector, and Syjin had buyers all over Bajor ready to purchase them. Although it was bad for everything else, at least in this case the Cardassian presence was good for making such trades scarce, and therefore more lucrative.

He glanced at the navigator matrix and punched in the coordinates. Grek would be waiting for him in orbit around a gas giant, in some nondescript, uninhabited system called Ajir.

They walked for a while, out of the port and into the city proper beyond. Gwen Jones had to rein herself in, stop herself from gawking like a sightseer. Outwardly, she played the part of a Bajoran girl from the south with somewhere to go, something to do. Inside, Jones wanted to stop and look at everything. She had been studying the Bajoran culture for some time, and it fascinated her. Not in a million years had she expected to be plucked from her predictable work at the Office of Cultural Analysis and thrown directly into a covert surveillance mission, with only a taciturn field operative like Nechayev for company.

But now she was here, on Bajor, seeing in the flesh all the things that she had read about in reports and purloined pieces of alien literature. She wanted to stop, to take a tram to the *bantaca* or visit a temple, to try real *hasperat* or go to the parks and see the mirror lakes . . .

"Eyes front," said Nechayev quietly. "Quit staring. This isn't a field trip."

Jones nodded. It was anything but that. From what her briefing had told her, the Federation had been conducting clandestine cultural observation of Bajor for many years, dating back to just before the outbreak of border skirmishes between the UFP and the Cardassian Union. It was only in recent times, with the shift in the political axis between independent Bajor and the expansionist Union,

that the Federation Security Council had decided to take
a closer look at what was taking place in the B'hava'el system. More Cardassian ships meant it was harder to insert
passive probes to monitor the circumstances there. What
was needed was "human intelligence," or, as Nechayev
had described it, "eyes on the ground." Jones didn't know
the full extent of things—her clearance level wasn't that
high—but she'd picked up a few hints from her mission
orders. She knew that Bajoran exiles on Valo II and other
colonies were agitating for intervention on Bajor, and that
Starfleet had to be giving the idea serious consideration or
else she and Nechayev would not have been here; but the
interstellar political climate was complex, and as time went
on, there seemed less and less chance that the Federation
would become openly involved.

Nechayev halted at an empty tram stop and made a
show of looking at the timetable. "We're not being followed," she told her. "And three Cardassian skimmers
passed us on the way without even giving us a look. I think
we're clean."

"What now?" Jones asked.

"Now we locate our contact, and we get the data we
need."

"Do you have a name?"

Nechayev nodded. "Jekko Tybe."

"You look well." As soon as Mace said it, he felt awkward.
The hiss of subspace interference whispered around his
precinct office for the second of delay it took the signal to
reach the Valo II relay.

Karys gave a rueful smile. *"I wish I could say the same
thing about you, Mace. You look tired."*

"It's just work," he said, and regretted it instantly.

"It usually is," she replied. *"So. What do you want?"*

"I had some time," Mace lied.

"*Time?*" she repeated. "*All civilian subspace communications traffic into B'hava'el has slowed to almost nothing. I hear the Cardassians are blocking all but the military channels.*"

He nodded. "And they screen everything else. It's part of the security program, looking for sedition or alien infiltrators." Mace nodded at the screen. "But I have some pull."

"*You're abusing your authority to appropriate airtime to call your family,*" she replied. "*Does that count as seditious?*"

"Damned if I care." He sighed. "I just . . ." He wanted to tell her that he had beaten a man down and it didn't bother him one bit, that suddenly all he wanted was to see the only good things in his life and make sure they were still there; but he kept that closed off. "I wanted to check in with you, see how Nell and 'Jin are doing."

She saw the lie but she didn't call him on it. "*Nell's met a boy. He's polite. Bajin has been very brotherly. He thinks I don't know that he threatened all kinds of trouble if Nell's heart gets broken.*"

A smile crossed his face. "You tell them I love them."

"*Every day,*" she told him. "*They miss you. And so do I.*"

The last words brought him up short. "You do? I thought the divorce put an end to that kind of thing. I just thought you would have, you know . . ." He trailed off.

"*Found someone else?*" Karys shook her head. "*It's funny, isn't it? When we talk now, we just talk. We don't fight. And all it took was for me to fly a dozen light-years away from you.*"

He nodded slowly. "Best thing that's ever happened to our relationship." He sighed. "Come on, Karys, we were killing each other here. The distance stopped us tearing ourselves apart."

She was silent for a while. "*I still think about the day of the attacks. Standing by the broken windows, wondering if you were all right.*"

"I'll say I'm sorry again, if it will help." He blew out a breath. "I felt the same. I felt like my life had been ripped away from me."

Karys leaned closer to the screen. *"You can come here. You should come here, before it's too late, before the trickle becomes a flood."*

"What do you mean?"

"More people are arriving each week, Mace. The colony used to be a few hundred thousand, now it's ballooned to twice that. Life's not easy here . . ." She sighed again. *"But it is a kind of freedom. Come and see."*

He shook his head. "I can't. If I leave now, this city will fall apart. They look to me, Karys. Proka and the others, they look to me. I have to hold it together, and for Lonnic's sake and Jarel's and everyone else's, I have to make things right."

"You don't. You could just leave tomorrow. You could walk away, Mace, walk away and let it burn."

"You know me," he whispered, "you know who I am. You know I *can't.*"

"What I know is that I don't want my children to grow up with a dead father." She reached for the disconnect key. *"Be safe, Mace."*

The screen went dark.

Darrah lost track of time as he stared at the inert monitor, turning Karys's words over and over in his mind.

Stay or go. It seemed like such an easy choice.

Finally, there was a rattle as his door slid open and Proka came into his office, his expression grim.

"Boss, there's been trouble at the Oralian camp."

Darrah glanced at him. "So deal with it."

"Bennek raised the alarm. He wants to speak to you, and you only."

He sighed. "What kind of trouble?"

"Someone tried to firebomb it again. Couple of minor injuries, no fatalities."

The chief inspector got out of his chair. "What does he think that I can do about it?" Proka began to speak, but Darrah cut him off with a wave of the hand. "No, no. Don't say anything. I know the answer."

The two men marched out to the landing pads and took the first fast flyer, out over the city limits and into the plainsland.

19

Kotan Pa'Dar heard his name called as he crossed the docking annex. He had developed a manner of walking, whenever his duties forced him to visit Derna, in which he kept his head down and made as little eye contact with the soldiers and officers there as possible. The last thing he expected was to be waylaid heading back to his shuttle.

But the voice put him off his stride; it could be only one man, someone he hadn't expected to see again. He turned to find Skrain Dukat studying him, the gul gauging him with all the warmth he might have shown to something he had scraped off his boot. There was no sign of the man that had befriended him aboard the *Kornaire* all those years ago. That intense, inquisitive young soldier was gone and in his place was someone that embodied the very model of a Cardassian officer. Arrogant and disdainful, striding about the galaxy as if it were his property.

"Kotan Pa'Dar," Dukat repeated. "You are still here." He said it as if the fact amazed him.

"Gul Dukat," he replied. "I wasn't aware you had returned to Bajor."

Dukat's gaze took in Pa'Dar's ochre-colored tunic and the administrator's tabs running along the edges of the seams. He smirked, as if in response to some private joke. "It seems you've had a change of vocation since we last met."

Irritation ticked at a nerve in Pa'Dar's eye, but he said nothing, only nodding.

The officer came closer. "What happened to your promising career as a scientist?" He reached out and fingered the tabs. "These are the grades of an administrator, a politician."

"I . . . I found a calling that better suited my skill set." Pa'Dar's skin darkened. He refused to allow Dukat to slight him over his difference in circumstances.

"Ah," allowed Dukat, "and here I was, wondering if your family had finally pressured you into dropping your dalliance with the sciences, at long last." He shook his head slightly. "They did so dislike the choices you made, didn't they?" He smiled briefly. "Odd, though. I would have thought you would have returned to Cardassia. Certainly there your family would have made far more . . . interesting options open to you."

"I have duties here."

"On Derna?" Dukat asked lightly.

"On Bajor," Pa'Dar said, his tone hardening. "I am assisting in the administration of the enclave in the Tozhat region."

"A civilian, in such a role? I'm surprised Kell permitted that."

Pa'Dar's gaze dropped. "As you noted, my family does have some influence."

Dukat laughed coldly. "And what have you achieved in Tozhat? Do the Bajorans there appreciate the softer hand of a civilian over a soldier?"

"I worked to show a compassionate aspect to the Cardassian-Bajoran alliance, if that is what you mean, yes," Pa'Dar bristled. "Someone has to."

"Alliance." Dukat picked out the word and mocked it. "That term is an empty vessel, and you're a fool if you think otherwise. The notion of such a thing is pointless."

He shook his head. "I saw you walking there and I wondered how much you had changed, Kotan. I'm beginning to think that you have, but not for the better."

"I look at you and I think the same." His reply was clipped.

When the gul spoke again, the air between them chilled. "Don't make the mistake of getting too close to the aliens. They don't need friends, Pa'Dar. They need masters, and when Bajor formally becomes a client world of the Cardassian Union, it will be our duty to take on that responsibility. For their good, as much as ours."

"Only Cardassia knows what is best for Bajor, is that what you are saying?"

"Of course," said Dukat, as if any other suggestion was idiotic. "It will only be by the Union's benevolence that Bajor can advance. Otherwise, they will remain stagnant." He cast a glance at the crescent of Bajor, huge in Derna's sky. "The evidence is all too clear. A decade Cardassia has been here, and what has been done? The lethargy of these aliens is like a taint, infecting all who come to this world." He shook his head. "But that time has passed."

He's talking about an invasion. The insight hit Pa'Dar like a splash of icy water. "Dukat," he said, the words bubbling up from inside him, coming from a place that he had tried to seal away, tried to deny. "I know what you've done to these people. I've seen the edges of it, I am not blind. The stranglehold Cardassia has placed around Bajor's throat, the Tzenkethi and the threats—"

"Be very careful of what you say next," the gul warned. "Don't say something you will regret . . . something that might force me to make an unfavorable choice. You are far from home, Kotan. Remember that."

The cascade of accusation he was about to unleash stalled in his throat, and Pa'Dar fell silent for a long moment, a sudden awareness of how distant the protection of his family was from him. Finally, he summoned some courage to answer back to the other man. "You and I, Dukat, have nothing more to discuss. Perhaps once I thought I knew who you are, but I see now that all we have are viewpoints in stark opposition."

Dukat's voice dropped to a hush. "I am genuinely saddened to learn you feel that way, Pa'Dar. As a nod, then, to our former friendship, I will tell you this. Don't place yourself in conflict with me. You won't win." He turned away. "Go back to Bajor, back to Tozhat, and smile your smiles to the natives. You'll see how much coin that earns you when we take this world for ourselves."

Pa'Dar tried to find a way to respond, but nothing came. He glanced around him and saw nothing but soldiers, men in black shining armor, moving on errands and toward missions he had no influence upon.

The police flyer settled to the ground, thrusters throwing out a wave of rust-colored dirt as the motors died. Darrah Mace stepped down from the hatch and caught a breath of the dusty air, the moisture draining instantly from his mouth. Out here, in the middle of the plains where B'hava'el beat down from a cloudless sky, the heat was a heavy blanket. Darrah tugged at his collar.

The Oralians coming out from the shanty made little trails of ruddy dust as they walked. The dull, unkempt earth beneath their feet was sun-bleached and eternally dry. Nothing had grown out here for years, not since the attacks; one of the plasma bolts dropped on Korto had gone wide and scored a huge black oval in the grasslands, killing every plant that thrived there. In the aftermath the ground had remained dead, as if it were cursed. No one had wanted it. No one but the Oralians, who had nowhere else to go.

Darrah glanced over his shoulder to the west. The Cardassian enclave was visible at this distance, a large low construct of dark metals and thermoconcrete, extending ever closer to the outskirts of Korto. He hadn't been inside the walls of the cordoned community, not since the changes that had come after First Minister Lale's reelection. Kubus Oak's aggressive lobbying had pushed through the laws that now made Cardassian-owned land de facto Cardassian sovereign territory, and no amount of demonstrations or civil disobedience courtesy of the Circle had stopped it from happening. *Every enclave an embassy,* he thought, *every embassy a place for them to do whatever they want to.*

And those laws had seen an end to the Oralian presence in the enclaves as well. The walled zones were designated for use by Cardassian military, trading and civilian concerns only; theological groups were not accommodated. Darrah walked toward the approaching figures and the ragged collection of old bubbletents and ramshackle buildings behind them. The Oralian Way lived on charity now, on handouts from the Bajoran church and the smallest subsistence grants from Cardassia Prime. He sighed. *These people, they're dying out by the ticks of the clock.*

"Chief Inspector Darrah," said the woman leading the greeting party. She rolled back her threadbare blue hood and gave him a nod. "Thank you for coming."

Darrah returned the gesture. "Tima." He pushed away the moment of disquiet he always felt at seeing a Bajoran dressed in the robes of an alien faith. "It's been a while since we last spoke." His eyes were drawn to her right ear; it was bare of any adornment.

"Three years," she agreed. "At the great wake for the kai."

A memory flashed in Darrah's thoughts. *Three years? Has it only been three? It seems like forever.* He recalled Tima's face on that day, when all of Korto became hushed in memorial for Kai Meressa's passing, her sorrow bright and shining. The wall of silence that hung over the city, the views on the streetscreens of the kai's funeral procession, moving in solemn lockstep down the Avenue of Lights in Ashalla.

Three years Meressa has been gone, and still no one has taken her place. But then again, Darrah thought of Vedek Arin and took some comfort that the irresolute priest from Kendra hadn't ascended to that sacred high office. Bajor's Vedek Assembly was still divided over the kai's replacement, over the Oralians, over everything, and the schism in the clergy spilled over into the lives of ordinary Bajorans. It was difficult to seek truth and solace at temple when the priests within it had no consensus of their own.

"This way," said Tima, leading Darrah and Proka back toward the grubby little settlement. Bennek was waiting for them at the edge, and at a respectful distance other Oralians watched from beneath their hoods, naked suspicion in their gazes.

The Cardassian bowed slightly. "Before we discuss this, I want to show you first what was done." Bennek took them toward a hut built out of an old cargo pod. The wind changed, and Darrah smelled rotting vegetation and the tang of ashes.

"You're limping," said Proka, gesturing at the cleric's leg, which he favored as they walked.

"It's nothing," Bennek replied. "I was burned when I ran to put out the flames. I'll heal."

"Should you be walking on it?" asked the constable.

"This is more important," he replied, and pulled open the door of the pod.

A cloud of dirty white haze rolled out from the inside of the container, and Darrah covered his mouth with his hand at the stink of it. Inside he glimpsed mounds of blackened matter, some of it still weeping smoke where it smoldered. He stifled a cough. "What's this?"

"This," said Tima, "was all the food we had stockpiled from the donations we have been given. Surplus from the *katterpod* farms in the valley, loaves of *mapa* bread given to us by the monks from Korto. All destroyed."

"They came out of the night, as they always do," said Bennek wearily. "They threw crude firebombs, and they deliberately targeted the food stores."

"Did you see anything?" asked Proka, holding up his tricorder to record any statements. "Can you describe them?"

"The same as every other time." Tima turned bitter. "Clad all in black, faces covered." She spat and pointed at the distant enclave. "It's the Cardassians!"

Bennek frowned at her outburst. "We don't know that—"

"It is!" Tima yelled, her anger breaking out. "They want to starve us to death! They hate the Way!"

Darrah held up his hands to silence her. "Calm down. Throwing accusations around without any proof will do none of us any good." He sighed. "One thing at a time. How are you going to feed your people?"

The cleric sagged, as if the weight of the question was too much for him. "I . . . do not know. I will find a way." He sighed. "We have so many here now. Almost all of the pilgrim groups remaining on Bajor have come to this place, so that we have safety in our numbers."

Darrah nodded. After the Oralians were evicted from the Cardassian enclaves, shantytowns like this one had sprung up all across the planet; but many of them had been suddenly abandoned, or fallen victim to mysterious fires. He studied Bennek and found himself wondering exactly how many followers of the Way were left.

"How are you going to keep us safe?" Tima demanded. "Or do we have to take the law into our own hands?"

"Let's not start down that road," said Proka sharply. "We'll investigate this."

"Like you did the last time, or the time before that?" she said bitterly. "Have you ever been able to find a culprit? Or is it that you don't want to?"

"Tima, that's enough!" Bennek broke in. "These are honorable men, and they're doing the best they can."

"But it's not enough," Darrah admitted. "She's right, Bennek. No witnesses, no leads, no suspects. And with the unrest in the city, I can't afford to leave men out here to guard you." He frowned. "I'm sorry. I wish I could give you guarantees, but these are dark times and people are angry, they're frustrated."

Proka nodded grimly. "They're lashing out at anything and everything."

"Everything?" Bennek leaned back, resting on his uninjured leg. "Why, then, does it seem that it's only the children of Oralius who are being attacked?" He shook his head. "Have any temples of the Prophets been set alight? Have any priests of your faith been murdered, Chief Inspector? Can you tell me what I must do to stop it?" He gestured toward Tima. "Is she correct? Must we shed blood ourselves?"

Darrah gave him a hard look and responded with his own questions. "Is that what you want to do, Bennek? Have you been making plans to do those very things?"

The cleric jerked as if he had been struck. "Of course not! The Way is a religion of peace . . ." He faltered for a moment, as if remembering something. "Peace," he repeated. "Violence is anathema to Oralius."

"There are rumors that you think differently now," said Darrah, earning him a sharp look from Proka. "I'll tell you this, even if some think I'm tipping our hand to do it. On the streets, there's talk that desperation is driving you toward a holy war. A religious coup, with Oralius unseating the Prophets here in Korto District."

Shock paled the Cardassian's gray face. "That is insanity! That we would strike at those who have given us succor when our own world turned us out. . . . The very idea sickens me!" He wobbled as he stepped forward. "Look around! Do you see the hungry men and women, the children and the lost ones, come to huddle together?"

Darrah found his eyes drawn to the hooded Oralians all around them, all silent and afraid.

"Can you see a holy army here?" cried Bennek. "We barely hold on to life, Darrah Mace! We have no strength to take it from others!" He sagged back, the outburst having drained him. The cleric's injuries had clearly hurt him more than he had been willing to admit.

Darrah glanced at Proka, fighting off the despair that threatened to settle on him. "Let's go. There's nothing else we can do here."

Dukat paged through the padd, musing as his crew worked quietly at their bridge stations. The report displayed the current deployments and flight operations status for every Cardassian ship in the Bajor Sector, and it made for interesting reading. Getting the information out of Kell had been difficult, and now he had it in his hands, he saw why. The jagul had been remiss, allowing too many ships to be placed too far out from the primary objective, which was Bajor herself. *A tighter noose is required,* he told himself, making notes on redeployment orders. He halted, halfway through. *Of course, whatever orders I give, Kell can countermand on a whim. It would be like him to do that, just to spite me.* Dukat sighed. *What games are being played at Central Command that allow that fool to remain at his post here?* He knew the answer; like so much of Cardassia's infrastructure, the military was rife with nepotism and partiality, and the Kell name held much sway. *Ten years. Ten years he has been here and still the flow of commerce from Bajor is a trickle. Still people on the homeworld are going hungry.* A hard edge of memory cut into him as he thought of Athra, and of the son he had never seen. *Never again,* he vowed. *Never again—*

"Gul?" Dal Tunol turned from her station. "Signal from

the orbital picket. There's a ship moving out of the authorized transit corridors, refusing to answer hails. I'm getting no read from its transponder."

Dukat raised an eyebrow. "Some criminal attempting to circumvent the customs net," he offered. "Can't these Bajorans keep control of their own airspace?"

"There's a Militia vessel in the area," said his first officer. "We can let them deal with it."

He put down the padd. "No. Let's show the locals how to do the job properly." Dukat stood up. "Put us under power, Tunol. We'll consider it a drill." *And I need a distraction to amuse me.*

"Complying," she replied.

The decks hummed slightly as the cruiser's impulse engines came online, and on the main viewscreen Dukat saw the view shift as Bajor's surface dropped away. "Tactical. What's the target?"

"A bulk freighter," came the reply from the gunnery station. "Configuration matches a Xepolite class six transport."

Tunol snorted. "I thought all those ships had been withdrawn from service. Hardly a fitting challenge for a *Galor*-class cruiser."

"No accurate sensor read on internal structure or life signs," said the gunner. "They have a detection mask in place."

Dukat watched the scanners and saw the energy distribution peaking. "That appears to be a power surge. Our friend here thinks he can run."

Tunol placed her finger to a communicator bead in her ear. "Gul, the Bajorans are signaling. They want us to stand down from the pursuit."

"I'm sure they do." Dukat nodded at the gunner. "Put a shot across the Xepolite's bow." Over the keening of a disruptor blast, he turned to Tunol. "I suppose we should follow the letter of the law and warn them."

She nodded and opened a channel. "Xepolite freighter,

this is the Cardassian Union warship *Vandir*. Cut power and stand to, or the next shots won't miss."

Dukat smiled approvingly. "Very succinct, Dal."

"Vessel is slowing," said the gunnery officer, with a hint of disappointment.

"Target his engines," continued the gul. "Burn them off."

"Sir, he is complying," began Tunol.

"That's correct," said Dukat, "but Xepolites are a change-able sort. Let's make sure he doesn't have second thoughts."

On the screen, disruptor bolts ripped into the freighter's warp pylons and cleanly severed the engine nacelles.

"I'm tired of drifting here in orbit while Kell ignores us." Dukat dropped the padd on his chair, his concerns for-gotten for the moment. "I'm going to lead the boarding party. You have the ship, Dal."

They waited for the two-bell tram and climbed up to the top deck as it clattered through the streets of Korto. Jones did as Nechayev told her, taking the vacant seat at the front, while Nechayev placed herself farther down and to the right. She had a good view there; she could keep the rookie in sight and still observe the rest of the passengers without making it obvious. Not that there were a lot of them. At this time of day, the tram was only a third full, and mostly with the elderly going out to temple.

When the man tapped her on the arm, she clamped down on her unease like a vise. "Pardon me," he said, "do you know if this route crosses the Edar Bridge?"

She shook her head. "I don't usually ride the tram."

He nodded. "It's a better day to walk, don't you think?"

The trigger phrase. Nechayev turned slightly so she could see him. "These are new shoes. I'd prefer to sit."

The other man smirked. "Who is it who comes up with these codes?" He offered his hand. "I'm Jekko."

She ignored it. "You were supposed to make contact

with her." She nodded at Jones, who threw her a confused look in return.

"No, I was supposed to make contact with you. She's the analyst, yes? You're the agent."

"Perhaps she's the agent, and she's just good at pretending to be a civilian."

Jekko's smirk turned cynical. "Somehow I don't think so." He glanced around. "So. Where's your starship, Starfleet?"

"Very far from here." Nechayev glanced out the window, as if she were bored. "We're here because Keeve Falor reached out through back channels to the Federation Council. He said you'd have something to show us."

Jekko bristled at her tone. "Isn't a covert military buildup of Cardassian troops on Bajor enough to stir your interest? It's not just ships in orbit or the outpost on Derna. We have intelligence on stockpiles of weapons, combat vehicles, strategic matériel."

"That's your assertion?" said Nechayev. "We know about the starships. Ground forces, that's a different matter. How exactly do you suggest that the Cardassians could move an invasion force onto Bajor without the general population becoming aware of it?" She shook her head. "Keeve's claims need a lot of backing up, if Starfleet is going to take them seriously."

The bridge of the freighter was as far from the clean, steely lines of the *Vandir*'s command deck as it was possible to be. The smell of stale food hung in the air along the cramped cylindrical bay, and the walls were a riot of bare cables where every inch of cosmetic paneling had been removed. The flight crew were on their knees, hands behind their heads, the four of them covered by a watchful gil with a phaser rifle. The captain—although the greasy little humanoid barely deserved such a title—stood, trembling slightly, with one of Dukat's men holding a gun at his head.

The gul folded his arms. "I'm becoming bored," he announced. "I thought you and your rusting scow might make an interesting diversion, but that's waning." He plucked at a bit of broken panel. "This ship is a mess. I'm disgusted by it."

The Xepolite blinked, although his right eye was swelling shut; the injury had come from some small utterance the armed officer had taken exception to.

"Are you going to tell me why you broke from the spacelanes and tried to run for deep space, Hetman . . .?"

"Foroe," husked the alien. "Uh, sir," he added nervously.

"Well?"

"It was just a helm malfunction, like I told you," he said thickly. "I was going to fix the problem——"

Dukat nodded and the officer with the gun smacked Foroe in the side of the head, staggering him. "You don't seem to be listening to me, Hetman. I said I was getting bored. Bored with you, bored with this filthy ship, bored with hearing the same lies." He stepped closer to the other man. "My men are searching all the decks, you do realize that? When they find whatever it is you are smuggling, you'll be prosecuted not only for that crime but also for obstruction of justice. Under the weight of Cardassian law, that's a very severe punishment."

"We're in Bajoran space, you can't——"

Another nod, and Foroe was struck silent again. "Look around, Hetman. Do you really think this sector belongs to Bajor anymore?"

The Xepolite's shoulders sank, and Dukat knew that it was almost over. *In a moment, he will either beg for mercy or offer me a bribe.*

"Look," Foroe said in a low voice, "can't we work out something here, captain to captain?"

Any reply Dukat was going to make was cut off by a chime from his comcuff. He tapped the bracelet. "Report."

"Sir, this is Glinn Orloc. I'm in the secondary engineering spaces near the keel."

Foroe failed to conceal the shock on his face, and Dukat smiled thinly. "What have you found, Glinn?"

"Sir, there's a large concealed compartment, shielded with kelbonite. I have at least forty Bajorans of various ages down here."

"Slaves?" Dukat said mildly.

"They're refugees!" spat one of the bridge crew, and he was clubbed down for his outburst.

Dukat gave Foroe a measuring stare. "Your manifest says nothing about passengers, Hetman. That's a very serious violation."

Foroe's voice took on a pleading tone. "They're just civilians, that's all. They can't afford the exit permits to go offplanet. The security restrictions the Bajoran ministry have put in place are too strict."

Dukat nodded. The limitation of unfettered movement by Bajorans had increased with Kubus Oak's introduction of several "security acts," creating a rise in incidents of people-smuggling. He studied the Xepolite; the hetman was doubtless earning a fine percentage in latinum for his part in this particular operation.

"Civilians," repeated the gul. "Perhaps. Or perhaps they're cell members working with the Circle or Tzenkethi interests, did that occur to you?" He loomed over the smaller man. "Or are *you* working with the Tzenkethi? Is that why you tried to run?"

Foroe stared at the deck. "I . . . I panicked."

Dukat raised his communicator to his lips. "And now you're going to answer for your spinelessness."

The Xepolite's hand shot out and grabbed Dukat's wrist. "Wait, no!" He cried out as the gun struck him again and he fell to the deck. "Wait," he said, biting out the words. "Please! Look, I have information. I know something!"

The Cardassian crouched down until he was eye to eye

with the freighter captain. "What could you possibly know that would be of interest to me?"

Foroe blinked back pain. "Passengers. Two Bajoran women, brought them from Draygo, they were bunked on the second tier." He blinked. "There was something suspicious about them. I heard them talking during the trip. Something about Keeve Falor."

Dukat stood up. "Really? And why should the name of a dissident exile be any concern of mine?" He waved him away. "Get him out of my sight." Foroe shouted and protested all the way out of the room and down the corridor, his cries echoing and growing ever more strident. Dukat circled the bridge, thinking.

"Draygo," said the armed officer. "That's not a Bajoran colony."

"Foroe thought he had something there," Dukat mused. "He genuinely believed it—it was clear on his face." He paused. "Perhaps we should see. Our people do have a reputation for thoroughness to uphold, after all."

The tram rolled into the long tunnel that passed under the City Oval, and Jekko shifted seats to sit next to Nechayev. His intonation was terse. "Listen to me, offworlder. The Cardassians are *already* occupying Bajor, it's just a matter of visibility. You don't see any tanks on the street corners, but believe me, the influence of those snake-faced aliens is everywhere. Every minister in the Chamber who might have stood against them has either fled to exile like Keeve, been threatened into silence, or bought out with money and promises. Lale is only a figurehead now, it's Kubus Oak and his people who have the power, and they're in the pockets of the Cardassians. Every day they're bringing in more 'cultural advisers' and 'contractors' to the enclaves. It's a silent invasion, and once that silence breaks it will shift the balance of power in this sector. Does your Federation want that?"

"Keep your voice down," snapped Nechayev. "Listen to me, because I'm not going to waste time explaining it twice. Starfleet cannot intervene on Bajor without good cause or a formal request from someone in the Bajoran government."

"Keeve Falor—"

"Is an exile on Valo II. His word's not enough. I need indisputable proof to show my superiors before we can even *think* about becoming involved."

Jekko was silent for a moment. "You want proof? I'll take you to the enclave outside the city and you can see it for yourself."

Glinn Orloc stepped out of the cramped cabin and offered the tricorder to his commanding officer. "There is an anomaly, sir."

Dukat glanced at the technician from the *Vandir*'s scientific division still working at the corners of the room with a sensor wand. "Explain."

"A very faint trace of a cellular masking agent on one of the bunks."

"Purpose?"

"The compound can camouflage the DNA profile of the user. It's enough to fool a cursory scan. I've heard the Obsidian Order uses such things to insert spies in alien populations after they've been physically altered to resemble natives."

"Which suggests there are two women down on the planet who only *appear* to be Bajoran," said the gul.

Orloc nodded. "It would seem so."

20

Darrah Mace crossed the atrium inside the entrance to the Naghai Keep and saw the group of priests entering one of the halls, the mutter of their conversation and the snapping of their wooden sandals echoing around him. A familiar face caught his eye and without thinking he called out a name. "Osen!"

Vedek Gar and his party halted, turning to face him. Darrah regretted the outburst immediately; the clerics gave him withering looks and he was reminded of his childhood, of the times when he was called to account at the temple school for a youthful imprudence. There was a moment when he thought Gar would just ignore him, but then a smile snapped on across the other man's face and he crossed to the middle of the stone floor. "Mace," he said with a nod. "Are you well? We haven't spoken in so long."

He nodded. "Yeah . . ." Suddenly he wasn't sure what to say.

"Things have been so difficult recently," Gar continued. "There's so much to do." He glanced at the other monks. "A lot of concerns."

"I'm sure, uh, Vedek." The title seemed strange when he tried to connect it to his old friend; but then, these days Gar was not the person he used to be. The passionate, witty cleric had changed, like so many things, in the wake of the attacks. Darrah had tried many times to place where the shift in their friendship had occurred, and it all came back to the night of the storm. *Osen's face, lit with panic.* He searched the expression of the man in front of him and couldn't see any remnant of that moment. Darrah had never spoken a word of Gar's wild accusations that night, and Gar had never mentioned it again. *Is that why our friendship has faded? Because I'm a reminder of that?*

As much as Darrah didn't want to admit it, the distance between the two old friends had become a chasm yawning between them. Darrah wished he'd said nothing, just let Gar walk on past and not notice him. Once upon a time they had been so easy in each other's company, but now they were like strangers.

"I understand you were called to the Oralian encampment?" The vedek studied him. "Is Bennek well? I'm bringing him and some of his followers to the keep for a prayer meeting tonight."

"There was some vandalism," explained Darrah. "Ever since the Oralians were ejected by their fellow Cardassians, they've become targets for everyone who resents the Union presence."

Gar shook his head. "How terrible. I hope there were no fatalities."

"None." Darrah licked his lips, finding it hard to keep a focus on the moment. He tried to change tack. "Vedek . . . *Osen.*" He sighed. "Perhaps we should meet, talk. Just you and me, like we used to?" The priest started to speak, but Darrah talked over him. "I haven't been to temple in a long time, not since Karys left." It was hard for him to admit it, and he felt the color rising in his cheeks. "I'm thinking I could use a little guidance."

Gar patted him on the arm. "You should see a prylar," he replied with a static smile.

"We've known each other since we were kids." He felt cold, redundant. "You're my priest and my friend, Osen."

"But not anymore, Mace." His fingers touched the ornamental metal ring fastening his robes across his chest that designated his ranking in the clergy. "My position means my time has turned to other, larger matters these days. I can't minister to just one man. Bajor's course is troubled, and it is important for me and the Vedek Assembly to keep a close hand on the helm." He flashed the smile again. "You understand that, don't you? We all have our duties, our sacrifices to make." Gar was moving away from him. "I'm sorry I can't help you."

"When you took your vows, I told you that the worst thing about the priesthood was the politics of the clergy." Darrah threw the words after him. "Do you remember what you said to me?"

Gar looked back. "I don't recall." He seemed almost condescending.

"You said that part didn't matter. That individual faith was the most important thing."

Gar made an amused noise. "Well. Times and attitudes change, Mace." He bowed slightly. "Be well."

The cluster of clerics entered the hall and the door closed, leaving Darrah alone in the sudden silence of the atrium.

Nothing could survive in the Tasak system. A few balls of rock, their atmospheres long since ripped away, and a couple of sterile gas giants orbited around the roiling red mass of the temperamental flare star, keeping their distance. Tasak was a wildly unpredictable solar formation, sometimes going for months without a grumble, other times spitting out promontories of gaseous plasma and frequencies of hard radiation roaring across the interstellar wavebands. Any form of life that had the temerity to evolve on one of Tasak's satellites was mercilessly bombarded by punishing storms of energy; and any ships that passed too near without resilient shields would find their crews poisoned.

All the highly trafficked spacelanes in the Bajor sector gave Tasak a wide berth, but in spite of its lethality—in fact, *because* of it—the system had become an unofficial way-point for ships engaged in less than legal endeavors.

Syjin had his courier concealed in the shadow of a shepherd moon orbiting Tasak VII, having taken great care to make sure the mass of the nickel-iron rock was between him and the star. He was working carefully at the warp field modulation controls, editing the engine output to make it fluctuate far beyond the programmed safety limits.

Like hiding a lit match in a bonfire. It was a tricky business, but if executed correctly, he would be able to make the ship's ion trail vanish into the mess of radiation that blanketed the local area. It would then be a simple matter of setting off once again, safe in the knowledge that anyone tracking him would lose his trace and never be able to pick it up again. He'd be free and clear to head for Ajir and his rendezvous. The Bajoran pilot had done this several times in the past, but it never failed to rattle his nerves. The cockpit space of the little transport ship smelled sweaty from Syjin's perspiration; it was hard to do the job with one eye on the warp matrix display and another on the sensors, watching for the first blush of hard gammas from a sudden radiation surge.

He was on the verge of completion when the scanner beeped, startling him so much he swore a gutter curse. Syjin glared at the screen. "What now?" he said aloud.

On the monitor there was a return from something close to Tasak VII. Not a radiation surge. *A starship.* It was moving quickly, under power. The configuration wasn't one he recognized instantly. The pilot's heart rate jumped. If it was Tzenkethi or Cardassian, if he was caught here by one of them, there would be nothing to stop him from being atomized and his remains would never be found. Another gruesome benefit of Tasak's seething pool of radiation.

He began the restart sequence for the engines as a second beep sounded, this time from the communications system. Syjin blinked and gingerly answered the hail. "Uh. Hello?"

A clipped voice responded over a static-laced channel. *"Unidentified vessel, this is the Federation starship* Gettysburg. *We have detected energy fluctuations in your warp core. Are you experiencing difficulties? We stand ready to assist you, should you require it."*

"Starfleet?" Syjin gaped. "What are you doing out here?" He asked the question without thinking.

The concise, tight diction sounded like a Vulcan's. *"We are engaged on a mapping mission. Do you require assistance?"*

A grin split Syjin's features. A Federation starship, this deep into the Bajor sector, plotting stars? Syjin's career had taught him how to both present and detect falsehoods, and he knew a poor one when he heard it. It wasn't unknown for Starfleet to have vessels out in the deeps, conducting other so-called "mapping missions" and taking note of Cardassian ship movements. The ongoing cold war between the Union and the Federation was well known to every commercial pilot in the sector. He muted the communicator and thought aloud. "What are they *really* doing here? Huh. Do I actually want to know?"

"Unidentified vessel, please state your designation and planet of origin."

He shook his head. "No, I don't think I'm going to be doing that." It was embarrassing, in a darkly comic sort of way. Syjin wasn't supposed to be here, but then, neither was the *Gettysburg.* The pilot toggled the channel open again. "We're fine," he said, "we're all fine here . . ." He trailed off, feeling awkward. "How are you?"

There was a pause. *"We are also . . . fine."*

The warp matrix modifications were complete, and Syjin slipped into his acceleration couch and brought the engines to power. "Great," he replied. "Well, uh, good-bye, then!" Before anything else could happen he let his ship drop away from the shepherd moon and pushed it to warp three. In twelve hours he'd be at Ajir, where Grek and his new cargo would be waiting for him.

On the scanner the *Gettysburg* receded into the clutter of Tasak's radiation backwash. "If you didn't see me, I didn't see you," he declared.

In his chambers, Jas Holza listened to the law officer deliver his report with only half an ear. Darrah Mace was a capable man, if a little too dogged for his own good. He was reliable. The minister studied him and wondered if that had been where he had made his mistakes. *I don't have enough reliable men. Or perhaps it is because I am not a reliable man.* Jas reached for the glass of springwine and drained it in a gulp. The drink burned warmly in his gullet, but the taste faded fast. He was losing his appreciation for this particular vintage.

"You've no leads on the matter of the Oralians, then?" Jas asked, breaking into the middle of Darrah's statement. "Nothing at all?"

The chief inspector shook his head. "They have no security out there, Minister. If I had a few more men . . . Perhaps if you could request that the Militia send some officers to me on assignment from one of the other districts . . ."

Jas sniffed. "Work with what you have, Darrah. Coldri and his staff have adopted a bunker mentality in recent months. They won't be relaxing that anytime soon."

The lawman chewed his lip, and Jas imagined what he might be thinking. *No surprise there, considering the way that the Militia is continually being marginalized.* Only a few days ago, Jas had been informed in minutes from the Chamber of Ministers that Kubus Oak had accepted Cardassian military escorts for his Bajoran cargo vessels, instead of the more usual Militia-crewed ships. And then there were the accusations in the media that Jaro Essa had been involved in the creation of a plan for a military coup; Jaro was protesting his innocence, and no concrete evidence had been uncovered as yet, but the claim trailed him in everything he did. Coldri had already distanced himself from the ambitious young officer, and several newsfeeds—those that Kubus seemed to have an indirect investment in—were stirring up public disenchantment. Rumor had it that Jaro was going to join Keeve Falor and the thousands of others who had gone into voluntary exile offplanet. *A fate I may soon share myself.*

He looked up and realized that he hadn't been listening. "Pardon me, Inspector, my attention wandered. Please repeat yourself." Jas poured another generous glass of springwine.

"I said, sir, that the incidents of civil unrest within the city limits are being dealt with, but the situation isn't improving."

Jas waved a hand at him. "You want stricter powers for arrest and sentencing? Very well. You have them. Do what is required. I want my city held firm." He sipped from the glass. "That is the least I must have . . ."

"Minister, with all due respect, locking people up and harsher policing won't solve this problem. The people need to know that they are being heard." Darrah stepped closer to Jas's desk. "The situation is fragile. People are falling into the old *D'jarra* divisions. The high-caste citizens are afraid, the low-castes think they're being sold out. Perhaps, if you could make a statement, sir, something visible."

"No, I must concentrate on the important matters." Jas shook his head. "Lonnic was always so much better at navigating these kinds of problems for me," he added as an afterthought.

Darrah frowned. "Minister, what's more important than your city?"

The lawman's tone made him bristle. "I don't presume to expect a *Ke'lora* to understand the issues that occupy my days!" Anger came from nowhere, hot and potent. "Do you think that if I had the power to do more, I would not? I am at my limits!" Just as quickly, the rage abated. "I'm empty. I have nothing with which to fight."

"Sir—" began Darrah.

Jas indicated the door with his glass, ignoring him. "Thank you for your report, Chief Inspector. Your input is appreciated, but I'm afraid I must cut this short. I have a meeting in Ashalla tonight. I have . . . I have to prepare."

He drained the glass, hardly noticing the man leave. Jas's sullen mood took full hold. *Another crisis meeting in the Chamber of Ministers,* he mused, *another crisis to go with this crisis and that crisis, over and over. Our freedoms cut away, another piece of meat flensed from the carcass of the governing edicts of the Republics . . .*

Jas examined the glass, seeing himself like the empty vessel, filling with dread as easily as he filled it with wine. His hands trembled a little. Kubus Oak would be waiting for him in Ashalla, as he had been every other time; and on this occasion, just as before, the man would take another piece of him. With the Cardassian influence he had behind him strengthened, the influence Kubus had for so long kept concealed, the minister from Qui'al was consolidating his power base. Talk abounded among the junior politicians that Lale would not seek reelection after his second term concluded and that it would be Kubus in the First Minister's place. Jas tried to recall the time when he had wanted that role for himself, but now it seemed like some childish fancy. The Jas clan's small power was waning as Kubus bought out its holdings, diminishing Jas's authority with each passing month. *How did I come to this?*

"Soon there will be nothing left but these old walls." He rocked back in his chair and spoke to the keep itself. "This alone is ceded to me by my birthright, with no question of its being taken from me." In the old times, in the era of the First Republic, Kubus would have led an army to the gates of the keep and battered them down, then murdered Holza and his family and made himself city-lord. Thousands of years later, things were so much more civilized. "Today," Jas grumbled, "today he will cut me with paper and strangle me with lines of influence. Bleed my money. Kill me without killing me."

Jas listed slightly as he got up and walked to the nearest wall, rubbing his fingers down it. "Old friends," he told the stones, "if nothing else, I have at least learned an important truth. I am a coward. And I am afraid I may be forced to abandon you."

Dukat glanced up and tapped the intercom panel at the sound of the chime. "This is the gul."

Tunol was uncharacteristically hesitant in her reply. *"Sir, someone has just transported aboard."*

"From Bajor?"

"I'm . . . not quite sure. The carrier wave was phase-scrambled."

That piece of information was all that he needed. Dukat's lips twisted. "Send them to my duty room."

"She's already on her way, sir."

Dukat's grimace turned to hard granite, and he turned the padds on his desk facedown, pausing only to flick a spot of dust from the dull metal of his armor.

The door to his chamber hissed open, and Rhan Ico stood outside, flanked by two troopers. She dismissed them without a word and entered the room. Dukat couldn't be sure which he found more irritating: that she entered without his permission or that the two gils obeyed her without question.

"Thank you for receiving me, Gul Dukat." Ico took a chair and smiled thinly.

Dukat noticed that the automatic security subroutines built into the consoles of his duty office had not reacted to her presence; normally, if a member of the Ministry of Science, a civilian, walked into the chambers of a ranking military officer, each one would go blank to conceal data outside her purview. Instead, every screen remained active, silently showing Dukat just how high Ico's clearance went.

He was in no mood for games. "What do you want, Ico?" Dukat was brusque and distrustful.

She frowned slightly, as if disappointed that he wasn't about to engage in the usual rounds of wordplay and dissembling. "I'm aware of the contents of your mission orders," Ico said without further preamble. "It seems that, once more, we share common goals."

Dukat's eyes narrowed. "However true you may think that is, I don't intend to repeat past mistakes with you."

"On the contrary," she countered, "our last association was a great success."

"For you, perhaps. Tell me, how many more of those pretty baubles have you purloined since then?"

Ico spoke as if Dukat had said nothing. "I know what you are looking for."

"A way to terminate you and all your kind?"

She sniffed, smiling slightly, and Dukat chided himself for allowing her to draw from him that flash of annoyance. "The passengers," she went on, "from the Xepolite transport."

"Ah," said Dukat, returning a cold, feral smile of his own. "Thank you for confirming my suspicions that there are agents on board the *Vandir* reporting to the Obsidian Order."

Ico laughed. It was a short, unlovely sound. "I have heard it said that organization has operatives on *every* ship in the Union fleet, from the lowliest fuel tender to the proudest dreadnought." She cocked her head. "But to continue. The masking compound? It is of Federation origin, a tool utilized by Starfleet Intelligence."

Dukat schooled his expression carefully. *Starfleet agents posing as Bajorans, on-planet at a critical juncture such as this one.* It was a worst-case scenario brought to life.

"Clearly, they must be dealt with as soon as possible," Ico went on.

Dukat kept himself in check, resisting the urge to immediately call an alert and begin an aggressive search. "Why are you telling me this? I'd imagine you much prefer to keep the kudos from such a capture to yourself."

She inclined her head. "A number of reasons. You're quite intelligent for a military officer, Dukat. You would have come to the same conclusions in due time. There are matters that I have currently in hand that require the majority of my attention. And, of course, Jagul Kell's lamentably short-sighted self-interest. He's quite incapable of managing such a situation. I think it would be best if he remained uninformed about this development for the time being."

"You want me and my men to do your work for you?"

She smiled coolly. "Isn't that always the way?"

He wanted to punch that smile down her throat. "I don't need your help."

"Don't be foolish," she warned. "I'm giving you a gift."

"And what do you want in return?"

Ico got to her feet. "Why, the same thing that you do, Skrain. A triumphant Cardassia, and a compliant Bajor." She tapped a control on her comcuff and vanished in the haze of a transporter beam.

The evening had drawn into night as they left the great hall of the keep, the Bajoran clerics and the party of Oralians walking side by side without really mingling. Vedek Gar had led the meeting with a reading from Yalar's New

Insights, choosing a parable that Bennek had considered a somewhat uninspired work, while in turn the Cardassian cleric had performed a recitation with Tima, a piece telling the story of the Birth of the Fourth Fate. Even from behind his mask, Bennek had not been able to miss the cold expressions directed toward the woman by some of the Bajoran priests. *I wonder, do they disapprove because of her adherence to the Way, or because she is my lover?* He imagined he would never know for sure. Tima glanced at him and gave a wan smile, concealing a multitude of subtle signals. *She feels the same way that I do; where once we were greeted as honored brothers and sisters, now we have become unwelcome. Oralius has lost purchase on her birthworld, and the same will happen on Bajor, I see it coming.*

"Would you join me on the balcony?" asked Gar. "The night is warm. I will have refreshments brought to us."

Bennek nodded. "I would like that." He followed the Bajoran out of the stained-glass doors, and a light breeze pulled at his robes. The Oralian gathered them in his hands and took the proffered seat at the stone table under the stars. The sky was scattered with light cloud and patches of darkness. "I am sorry that Vedek Arin was not able to be here tonight," he continued.

"He's in Kiessa," said Gar lightly. "Matters of the church. I'm sure you understand."

Tima shot Bennek another look. Before the flyer had arrived at the camp to bring them to the Naghai Keep, she had predicted that Arin would not be present. The man had been slowly aligning himself with the interests of Kubus Oak over the past few months. It was no secret that Kubus's interests were in concert with the Union's, and there was no place for the Oralians there. *Vedek Gar is the only ally we have now,* he reflected, feeling bleak.

A servant brought hot *deka* tea and a plate of *veklava;* the sight of the food brought a sour taste to Bennek's lips as he thought of the burned-out storehouse in the camp, the *katterpod*s and bread all ruined.

Gar poured the tea and cupped the stone mug in his hands, savoring the woody smell. "Bennek, I am glad you came here. I know about your recent problems, about the firebombing and the intimidation. I know you must find it troubling to venture from the safety of your settlement."

"Such as it is," said Tima.

"Your people are embattled, my friend," he continued. "And it pains me to think that the Way may die out." Gar shook his head sadly. "Your numbers have diminished, and they continue to do so, yes? I have heard that many have left the Way and renounced their faith."

Bennek stiffened. *How does he know about that? I have kept that sordid fact a closely guarded secret!* But it was true. On some level the cleric could understand the men and women who fled the camps and gave up their church so that they could eat again, be free again, be considered *Cardassian* again. "This is a troubling time for the children of Oralius," he admitted. "But she grants us the Way, and she will show us a path through adversity."

Gar leaned forward. "Perhaps she already has."

"I do not follow you."

"Perhaps you should," said the other priest. "We have often spoken of how your worship of Oralius and our devotion to the Prophets are but two sides of the same coin. There are those on Bajor who have come to feel your faith is like an unwanted tenant, that its presence will somehow dilute the veneration of the Celestial Temple." His gaze passed over Tima, and the implication was clear; as one of the handful of Bajoran Oralians, she embodied that concern. "We both know that is untrue, but how can we convince the people otherwise?"

Bennek's blood ran cold. "Do you want us to leave Bajor?"

Gar smiled and shook his head again. "No, no, you misunderstand. I do not suggest you leave us, my brother. I suggest you *join* us."

Tima blinked, confused. "Bennek, what does he mean?"

He gasped. "You want the Way to merge with the faith of the Prophets?" The thought of such a thing made the Oralian's heart tighten in his chest. "Give up our identity?"

"You would not be giving it up," Gar said mildly. "It would be a confluence, an assimilation. The Way could come under the auspices of the Bajoran church, and your people would be protected by us." His fingers knitted. "A coming together, Bennek. The Prophets can offer so much to you."

For an instant, he wavered on the cusp of the proposal, the pressures and the great weight of his responsibilities bearing down on him; the temptation to release it all, to let someone else take up the stewardship of the Way, was strong.

And then he heard Dukat's words once again, the memory of them hard and cold in his thoughts. *All that is important now is your responsibility.* Bennek's hands tightened into claws. Hadlo had died trying to keep the Oralian Way from being destroyed by the faithless, and on that night five years ago, Bennek had followed in his footsteps, selling his honor to keep the Way alive. His mentor had asked for sacrifices, and Bennek had made them. But this? What the vedek was suggesting was no less than to accept the slow death of his faith, that which Bennek had struggled to hold off year after agonizing year.

Tima was staring at him, her eyes wide and shimmering with fear. He gave her a nod, reaching inside himself to find the wellspring of devotion he knew lay there. "No," he replied, with shaky defiance. "I see that you mean well, my brother, and I thank you for your offer, but the answer is and will always be no. Whatever adversity threatens to engulf us, the children of Oralius must not flinch from it. This is our path." He took a breath, and found a certainty that he had thought long forgotten. "This is the Way."

Conflicted emotions crossed Vedek Gar's face; Bennek thought he saw anger there, along with sadness and regret. Finally, the other priest nodded. "I did not expect you to agree, my friend. I hope that my words instead spurred you to remember how much your faith means to you." He sipped the tea. "That you elect to forge on despite your hardships, that shows the strength of will needed to stay true to your beliefs." Gar paused, and when he spoke again the warmth in his voice was absent. "But I must warn you that Cardassia will not suffer your presence, even here on Bajor, without question. Soon you may find yourself faced with a terrible choice."

"The Detapa Council believe Oralius is dead within the Union," Bennek replied, "but all they have done is cut her to the core of her most staunch followers, driven her underground. The Way will survive." He got to his feet, and Tima followed. "And whatever choice I must make, I will do it in the name of my faith."

21

The skimmer hummed over the scrubland, keeping in the lee of the dry riverbed. The Bajoran man with the shaven head and the hard eyes steered with quick, economical movements on the yoke. Every light inside the vehicle had been doused, and he was using a night visor to find his way. Gwen Jones found her attention kept falling back to him. He wasn't like Nechayev; Jekko lacked her caustic manner and instead, he had a kind of workmanlike quality to him, a sort of grim determination. He was the first real Bajoran she had ever met, and he wasn't at all what she expected.

In the backseat, Nechayev had her gear pack open, and she was working at the tricorder inside it. Without looking, the woman reached up and passed Jones a small pistol. Jones took the phaser and weighed it in her hand. It was set on heavy stun, and she pocketed the weapon, hoping she wouldn't need to use it.

She glanced out of the window at the blur of the landscape flashing past. Bright light from Bajor's multiple moons gave her clear sight for some distance. In the blue-white illumination the scrubland looked sterile and unwelcoming.

"A decade ago this was all farms," Jekko answered her unspoken question. "*Katterpods* mostly, and a few *kava* orchards."

"What happened?"

"The Cardassians," he said, as if that were enough explanation on its own. He talked without looking away from the job of steering. "Bought up a lot of the land through trade blinds, mostly through the Kubus clan. Got it cheap too, no surprise when it was their fault the place was drying up. See the enclave? The spoonheads sank wells there and drew off the water table, made all the farms in the surroundings fail. Folks out here were happy to take the money and go. Didn't like living next to offworlders anyway."

"Didn't someone complain?"

"Probably. And those that did got paid like the rest, or else they're still out here somewhere, buried in the dirt."

"That's horrible," Jones grimaced.

Jekko drew back the throttle, slowing them to a halt. He shot her a look. "Horrible?" He smiled grimly. "Let me take a guess. This sort of thing is all a bit new to you, isn't it?"

She colored. "It is, yes. I'm not really a field agent, I'm just an analyst—"

"She's here to make sure I don't get caught out by eating with the wrong fork," Nechayev broke in as the skimmer settled to the ground. "So. What now?"

Jekko retracted the canopy, letting the warm night rush in. "We walk from here."

The Bajoran pulled a camouflage net from a compartment in the skimmer and concealed the craft in a tumbledown barn. Jones saw evidence of building foundations all around, the overgrown remnants of a dirt track; the place was likely the site of one of the farms Jekko had mentioned. She turned around and saw the enclave in the near distance, a walled settlement capped with the glassy mushrooms of habitat domes. She could just about make out the red glow of sensor pods around the walls. "How are we going to get in there?"

Nechayev beckoned her to follow the Bajoran into a dusty cutting and there, beneath tinder-dry bushes, was the oval mouth of a tunnel. "Drainage conduits from the old farm complexes," he explained, levering off a metal grille. "Cardassians just built onto them, used the existing infrastructure. If you know where to look, there's a couple of places inside the walls where the new building marries up with the old. We can get in that way."

"You're sure?" Jones asked.

He nodded. "Some data was slipped my way, from a contact in the Korto City Watch. The chief inspector and I go way back."

"Can you trust him?" Nechayev asked.

Jekko shot her a hard look. "More than I trust you."

"But you haven't actually been inside the enclave?"

"No. They haven't been open to Bajorans, not for a long time, not for anyone · without an armed escort from the Union military. For security." He added the last words with hard sarcasm.

"They'll have sensors covering any entry points," Nechayev snapped. "The Cardassians aren't stupid."

"No, but they are arrogant, and arrogance breeds overconfidence." Jekko nodded. "We've never used this way in. But I'm betting your Starfleet hardware will be able to bypass any scanners."

The agent glanced at her tricorder. "We'll see." Nechayev drew her weapon and entered the conduit.

Jones followed. "Watch your head," Jekko told the women. "It's a long walk, so stay alert and make sure you don't step in any barrowbug nests."

"What the hell are barrowbugs?" Nechayev's voice drifted back from the darkness.

Jones gave an involuntary shiver. "Like cockroaches," she said, "but as big as your fist, and they spit acidic venom."

Nechayev swore under her breath, and Jekko waved Jones inside. "After you."

In the dark of the drainage conduits it was difficult to reckon the passage of time, and the repetitive scrape-thud of their footsteps made it even worse. Nechayev concentrated on the glowing display of her tricorder, using the device to scan the tunnels on the go, automatically forming a route map they could use for their egress. Just as he had in the skimmer, Jekko moved with confidence, turning at junctions and crossing over pipeway intersections, never once hesitating or stopping to refer to the faded glyphs on the curved walls. *This guy is good.* She grudgingly admired the Bajoran's tradecraft. *He's committed the entire route to memory.*

With Jones's warning in mind, Nechayev gave a wide berth to the masses of yellowed cottony fibers that clung to the underside of inspection grids and the stone ceiling. At the edges of her vision, she saw spade-shaped things scuttling around them in the halo of her tricorder's dim light and grimaced.

After what seemed like hours, Jekko halted and whispered a single word. "Here."

There were a series of steps cut into the crumbling thermoconcrete, and Nechayev looked up to see faint light filtering through a hexagonal hatch over their heads. She flicked the tricorder over to passive scan, and a smear of color appeared on the display. "There's an isoscanner," she said quietly. "Detects thermal footprints from a living being over a certain size, or metallic masses like scout drones or snoopers." She flipped open the emitter matrix panel on her phaser and dialed back the power output.

"Can you deactivate it?" asked Jones, shifting from foot to foot.

"Not a chance," she replied. "Monitors would register the loss of coverage and the alarms would be screaming ten seconds later. No, this needs a different approach." She stepped behind Jekko and used the man as a prop to steady her arm. "Shield your eyes."

"You're going to shoot it? But didn't you just say—"

"I have the sensor's aperture ratio from the tricorder. I'm going to blind it." She pressed the firing stud, and a lance of orange light reached up and brushed the Cardassian device. "Now, fast!" snapped the agent. "We have less than twenty seconds before the thing cycles and resets itself!"

Jekko was the last one up, and Jones bit down a protest as the big man placed a thick-fingered hand beneath her backside and propelled her up the ladder, shoving her through the hatch. The Bajoran threw himself out of the hole in the floor, and Nechayev forced the duranium hatch back into place, a heartbeat before the sensor pod gave a clicking beep.

"Apologies," said Jekko quietly. "You were moving too slowly."

Jones said nothing and brushed at the film of dust over her clothes. Her heart was hammering in her chest and her palms were sweaty. She was afraid to draw her weapon for fear it would slip through her fingers. "Where are we?" she asked.

"Storage blockhouse," Nechayev replied, glancing around the darkened space of the interior. On either side of them were high racks of skeletal blue metal, each one laden with containers. The air was dry and smelled of ozone.

Circular labels were visible on every storage unit box. Jones peered closely at one of them, frowning. Her grasp of written Cardassian wasn't that good. "I think these are . . . machine spares?"

Jekko levered the top off and used a penlight to look inside. "You think so?" He reached in and pulled out a phase-compression rifle. "No power cores installed. These are brand-new, never been fired."

"There are hundreds of those containers," Jones muttered. "How many guns is that?"

"A lot," said Nechayev, giving Jekko a dour glance. She picked and opened crates at random, coming across caches of sonic grenades and inserts for body armor.

Jones found a rack of oval metal clamps that she couldn't identify. "What are these?"

Jekko took one from her hand and held it up. "Pintle brackets. They slot into sockets on the flatbeds of skimmers so that you can mount weapons on them. A few of these, some heavy phaser rifles, and you can turn any civilian airtruck into an infantry fighting vehicle." He shot Nechayev a look. "Very useful for an invading army."

But the agent wasn't paying attention. She had moved into the center of the broad storage chamber, to a series of low, wide shapes that crouched close to the floor. In the dimness, Jones couldn't make out what they were. Perhaps they were more lines of containers packed close together. The ozone odor was stronger here, and with it came the scent of lubricants.

Nechayev reached down to take the end of a plastic sheath that hung loose over the object. With a jerk of her wrist, she pulled it up and away to reveal what was underneath.

Jones let out a gasp of fright as she realized she was staring into the black maw of an energy cannon.

"Grav-tank," said Nechayev, instantly recognizing the lethal scarab-like form of the Cardassian machine's hull, *"Janad*-class. Main armament: single spiral-wave disruptor cannon. Secondary weapons: stun-field emitters and phaser turrets." She ran her hand over the sloping hull plates. "Reactive armor. Shock bumpers. It's been configured for urban pacification." Nechayev's mind caught up with her, and she panned the tricorder over the vehicle.

Jones walked around the tank, pointing wordlessly off into the darkness. There were dozens more shapes beneath sheets of heavy plastic. "How did they get them here?"

"In pieces, probably." Nechayev gave a humorless chuckle. "In boxes labeled 'tractor parts' and 'baby milk.' "

"And this is only one blockhouse," said Jekko. "There are dozens of similar buildings in every enclave on Bajor." He was pale with shock. "Fire's sake, we never thought there would be things like this . . ." He stared at the inert war machine. "An entire armored division, right outside the gates of the city. Just waiting for the right moment." Abruptly, the Bajoran shook off his surprise and glared at the Starfleet officer. "Is this proof enough for your Federation, Alla, or whatever your real name is? Tanks and guns, ready to be used?"

Nechayev nodded. "I think so."

The light was so powerful that Jones was instantly blinded the moment it fell on her. She cried out and her hands flew to her face, clawing at needles of pain in her eyes.

"Stay where you are!" barked a voice. "Do not move!"

Cardassians! What Jones had thought was fear was swept aside in a tide of even more intense terror. She was rooted to the spot, her thoughts racing away in a rush of panic. *They've found us I'm captured I'll be left behind tortured beaten raped killed thousands of light-years from home—*

She reached out toward the blurry man-shape in black armor. "Please . . ."

"I said, do not move!"

Her vision cleared enough to see the guard aim his pistol at her head.

◆ ◆ ◆

Jekko threw himself over the turret of the tank and down onto the Cardassian glinn, and the beam went wide, screeching through the air. He was briefly aware of the dark-haired girl screaming, collapsing; then the alien was at his throat and choking the life from him. Jekko yanked the Cardassian toward him and butted him hard across the nose, the Bajoran's head snapping the cartilage where he struck.

The impact made his head ring and the glinn dropped away, moaning.

"Gwen!" shouted the other woman, racing to the side of her companion.

Gwen. At least I know the name of one of them. "Is she dead?"

"Not yet." The reply was a snarl. The one who called herself Alla pulled her friend to her feet. Gwen was barely conscious, her right cheek discolored from the nimbus of a near hit from the phaser shot.

Klaxons began to wail. *Scanners must have registered the weapon discharge.* He took a step toward them and nodded toward the hatch in the floor. "Get her out of here. You have what is needed. Take it and go." The overhead lights set in the ceiling snapped on one after another, banishing the shadows. Suddenly they were exposed, pinned by the stark illumination.

"He . . . he's coming with us," groaned Gwen.

Jekko ignored her and pressed an isolinear chip into the other woman's hand. "This is your escape route. I have a warp-capable courier at the starport in Korto. Use it and get out of Bajoran space. Go to your people, show them what's happening here."

"I will," the agent promised. "Thank you."

"He's coming with us," Gwen repeated weakly.

Jekko bent down and scooped up the unconscious Cardassian's phaser, turning his back on the women. Farther down the length of the blockhouse a door slid open and more armed guards came running.

He took careful aim and started firing.

Everything passed in a blur of pain and hazy images. Jones's right side felt like it was on fire, every nerve across the bare skin of her face throbbing with waves of burning pain. She couldn't see properly, just indistinct forms and blobs of dark and light.

"Damn it, girl, keep moving!" Nechayev's breath was hot and close in her ear, and she could feel the whipcord muscle of the intelligence operative where the woman was pressed against her, supporting Jones's sluggish flesh. "One foot in front of the other, come on!"

The grumble of stone on stone threaded down the tunnel behind them, and Jones tasted acrid dust in her mouth. "I hear thunder," she slurred.

"Grenades," was the curt reply. "They're sweeping through the tunnels after us, blasting as they go. Trying to flush us out."

"Oh." The information was washed away in another wave of agony. "Jekko?" Just working the muscles of her face was painful, and tears streamed down her cheeks. "Where?"

Nechayev's answer was forlorn. "He covered for us. Held them off." She swallowed hard and took a deep breath. "The man bought us time. We owe him not to waste a second of it."

Jones nodded brokenly. Up ahead, she could make out the tunnel entrance as a circle of fainter shadow.

"Report," demanded Dukat, crossing the *Vandir*'s bridge to the communications station.

"Alert from the Korto Enclave, sir," said the glinn.

"Details of an intrusion into one of the staging areas by three unidentified Bajorans."

A nerve in Dukat's jaw rippled. "Show me," he growled, throwing a look in Tunol's direction. "Those facilities are supposed to be secure."

"They couldn't have beamed in," offered the woman. "Any transporters would have been blocked by the inhibitor screen."

Still images drawn from a security drone appeared on the main viewscreen. Dukat saw a Cardassian at the feet of a bald male Bajoran and two more females, one supporting another. Part of a tank was visible in the corner of the frame. "They can't be allowed to speak of what they've seen," said the gul.

"The male intruder was terminated on-site," continued the communications officer as a grainy representation of the bald man appeared. "The two female intruders are currently unaccounted for. Search is ongoing."

Tunol skimmed the report on a padd. "Apparently, they entered the complex through the old agricultural infrastructure."

Dukat's eyes narrowed. "Two females," he repeated. "Enhance that image. I want to see their faces."

The glinn obeyed, and Dukat found himself looking at two Bajoran women, one fierce in aspect, the other lolling in her arms, apparently injured. *It's them.* The certainty of it struck him immediately.

"Sir." Tunol approached him, seeing the same thing. "Do you think that—"

"They match the Xepolite's description of the women he brought from Draygo," he snapped. "Contact detention and have him make a formal identification to confirm it." Dukat turned and strode toward the turbolift. "In the meantime, I want a cutter and a security detachment ready to depart for Korto City by the time I get to the shuttlebay."

"This alert is on the wideband, Gul," Tunoł added. "Every security operative on the planet, Cardassian and Bajoran, will know their faces in a matter of hours. Is it necessary for you to take a personal involvement in this?"

He paused at the door. "If Ico locates these females first, they will vanish as if they never existed." Dukat shook his head. "I won't allow that to happen."

Darrah Mace lolled in his chair, hovering on the edge of a shallow doze. An untouched cup of spiced *deka* tea on his desk had gone cold, and out beyond the shuttered glass enclosure of his office the precinct was quiet. He had lost track of time; his days seemed to do that more often than not. Sometimes Darrah would look up and realize that he hadn't left the building for a week, sleeping in his office or up in the bunk room for the shift staff. He didn't enjoy going home anymore. The house was too big for one person, and he rattled around inside it whenever he was there; but then, he couldn't bring himself to think about selling it. Even after the divorce, that seemed like admitting defeat. At the precinct there was always life and clamor. He could rest around that; he needed the noise and commotion to center himself. The silence of empty rooms kept him awake at night.

His back was tense and he got up, stretching. Motion caught his eye outside, and he opened the door. Myda and Proka were standing around a monitor console, download-ing a priority report onto padds. "What's this?"

Myda nodded. "A security alert from the Cardassian enclave."

Darrah grimaced. "Let me guess. Some kid sprayed 'Spoonheads Go Home' on the walls again?"

"It's a bit more serious than that, boss." Proka's tone brought him up short. "Several fatalities. One intruder dead at the scene, two fugitives unaccounted for."

Darrah pushed forward. Suddenly he was wide-awake. "Let me see."

"They're claiming three people broke into the enclave," Myda explained, "killed a bunch of Cardassians, and tried to blow up some civilians. 'Suspected Tzenkethi or Circle agents,' it says here."

"A man and two women," added Proka, passing Darrah a padd. "I was about to run a facial match with the criminal records database and the citizen register, see if we can pull some identities."

Darrah tapped the keypad, and the image of the male suspect appeared before him. His blood ran cold. *Jekko?* His old friend's face stared up at him, slack in death; the image had clearly been captured only moments after he had been killed. "When . . ." He heard his own voice as if it was coming from miles away. "When did this happen?"

"Within the last hour," said Myda. "This is going out to every precinct on the planet." She sniffed. "As if we don't have a big enough caseload."

Proka was watching his commander carefully. "Sir? What do you want us to do with this? It's a priority alert, immediate attention required."

"If the other intruders, the women, are mobile, it's likely they'd be heading straight here," noted Myda. "They get into the city, they could disappear."

The inspector's knuckles were white around the padd. "I need to . . . I need to look at this," he managed. "Don't move on it until I give you the word."

"Sir?" said Myda, but he was walking away,

Darrah went back into his office and dropped into the chair. *Jekko is dead.* The image was burned in his mind. A good, trustworthy man with a keen wit, the kind of man you wanted guarding your back, cold and dead in some Cardassian morgue. His fist bunched and he slammed it on his desk, knocking over the cup.

"Boss." Proka was at the door, holding it open. "We got a problem?"

For a second, Darrah considered sending him away, but then he beckoned him in: "Come here, Mig, and close that behind you."

Proka did as he was told. "I saw the look on your face. You know the man."

"Like he was family." Darrah's voice caught. "I can't believe it. He always seemed fireproof, always surviving the worst through basic training and out on the street . . ."

"He was one of us?"

A nod. "He was my partner when we were Watchmen." A pained smile crossed his lips. "He would always joke and rub the scars under his stubble. 'I'm too vulgar to die,' he would say. 'Prophets won't take a man as crude as me for fear of dirtying the Celestial Temple.' He said that's why they kept him alive." Darrah's expression hardened. "And now he's dead, shot for breaking into a Cardassian enclave."

"They said he was trying to plant a bomb."

"That's shit!" Darrah was on his feet, enraged. "Jekko Tybe is not a terrorist! I've known the man for twenty years, on my mother's grave I'd swear that!"

"Jekko?" Proka repeated. "I know that name. Didn't he run Keeve Falor's security before the minister went to Valo?" He shook his head. "Boss, when the Cardies find that out, they'll sing it from the rooftops. They've already got a shuttle on the way down from orbit with a sweep squad aboard."

Darrah stared at the pictures of the women who had fled. "I don't know these two." A decision formed in his mind. "Get me anything you can on them. If anyone is going to know what happened to him, they will."

"If the Cardassians find them first, they'll be gone like they never existed."

He nodded grimly, his mind racing, the grief and anger

at his friend's death put aside as he fell into the familiar mode of investigation. "Myda's right, if they're running, they'll run to Korto."

Proka returned the nod. "I could make Jekko's files get lost for a while."

"Do that," he ordered, working the computer on his desk. "I think I might know where they're going. Keeve Falor still owns some interests on Bajor, and one of them is a storage hangar out at the port." He turned the screen so Proka could read it. "There's a ship there right now."

"You think that's their escape route?" The constable frowned. "You're making a bit of a leap there, boss." He studied the monitor. "The *Kaska,* a light courier . . ."

Darrah grabbed his holster and strapped it on. "Kaska was the name of Tybe's mother." He made for the door and felt Proka's hand on his shoulder.

"You sure you want to get in the middle of this? The Cardies will shoot first and not even bother with questions later."

"My friend is dead," he growled, "and I don't know about you, Migdal, but I'm sick of letting the Cardassians get what they want."

Tima climbed out of the airtruck's cab and took a breath of the dockland air. She could hear the gentle slosh of the river beyond the warehouses, and the night was pleasantly cooler down here, more so than the heights of the hill district. She thought about Bennek, angry and troubled after his conversation with Vedek Gar. Tima was shocked by the Bajoran priest's words to her lover, and in turn she saw how much they had affected Bennek. He should have been with them now, helping Tima and the others to pick up the supplies to replace those lost in the firebombing; instead he was in a skimmer racing back to the encampment, withdrawn and sullen. She knew his moods; it was best to let him be alone with his brooding, let him take his own time.

Urad, the thin youth who had been driving the airtruck, stepped out with her. Three more Oralians followed behind. "Couldn't we have just come back in the morning?" He seemed to enjoy complaining about everything, his gray hands flapping like birds in front of him. "Why do we have to get the food now?"

Tima glanced at him as three figures in hooded docker's coveralls emerged from the storehouse. "So that the children will not awaken tomorrow and be told that there is no food for their breakfast. We can go back, if you'd like to be the one to tell them and their parents."

Urad grumbled under his breath and stepped forward to meet the dockers, pulling back the sleeves of his robes. "Let's get this done quickly, then," he said, nodding to the hooded men. "Hello. Vedek Gar sent us to—"

The dockworker on the right brought up his fist, and there was a gun in it. Yellow light flashed, illuminating the area all around them, and Urad was thrown back by the force of the blast, rebounding off the airtruck.

"Oralian filth," spat a voice. "You're poisoning Bajor! Get off our planet!"

Tima screamed as more streaks of fire lashed out, each of the men panning beam weapons back and forth across the thermoconcrete dock. Two more of her fellow Oralians were hit, the Cardassians dropping into heaps, wisps of sweet-smelling smoke curling from ragged tears in their pastel robes. She grabbed at the front of the vehicle, fingers scrambling over the surface toward the door. Tima saw one of Urad's friends clawing his way into the cab; then a bolt of the sun ripped into her and she spun away, crashing to the ground.

Life ebbed from her in pulses. Dimly, she was aware of the airtruck humming to life, jetting away under the hand of a panicked driver. The hooded men came closer, and one aimed at the fleeing vehicle.

The one who had fired first shook his head. "No," he said. "We need a witness. Let him run."

The other man nodded and raised his wrist to his lips, speaking into a device there. "Reporting," he said. "Assignment complete."

Blood bubbled in Tima's throat and she spat it out in a reflexive cough.

"This one's still alive," said the third.

The man who had fired first knelt by her side, bringing his face close to hers. In the moonlight, she saw not the smooth lines and ridged nose of a Bajoran but the deep-set eyes and lined flesh of a Cardassian countenance. Her eyes widened in surprise.

He reached for her, and Tima's world ended.

"Preliminary identity sweep has been completed, sir." Glinn Orloc raised his voice to speak over the hum of the cutter's impulse engines. "Nothing on the male as yet, but you were correct about the women. Hetman Foroe gave a positive identification of them as his passengers. Customs logs from Traffic Control list them as Nechen Alla and Jonor Wenna, agricultural technicians from a settlement in Hedrikspool province."

"Doubtless those are cover identities." Dukat nodded. "Anything else?"

Orloc continued. "We've intercepted a report from the City Watch. A skimmer with two females on board entered Korto from the plainslands at high speed, refusing to follow traffic codes."

"The Bajorans have been given a suitable pretext for the alert?"

"Yes, Gul. The fugitives have been classed as terrorist suspects."

"Good. Inform the men to employ whatever level of force is required, but make sure they know I want the women alive."

Orloc saluted and Dukat looked away. Outside, below the cutter's hull, the sprawl of Korto's metropolis glowed against the dark of Bajor's landscape.

Nechayev ditched the vehicle near a public park and hauled Jones onto the first tram they could find. She changed direction twice before taking the route to the starport, all the time working hard to maintain her outward air of calm and control while her heart was hammering against the inside of her rib cage. Jones was muted, the bandage and the antishock drugs from the skimmer's medical kit turning her into a pale ghost of her normal self. The lateness of the hour worked in their favor; there were fewer people around, so Nechayev had a better view of who might or might not be following them. They avoided Militia patrols and groups of Cardassians who seemed to be out on the town. It was only three hours since they had left Jekko behind, and yet it felt like forever, a drawn-out night without hope of a dawn.

The Bajoran's isolinear chip got them through the entry grid and onto the port grounds. The sliver of plastic had a glyph on it, and Nechayev nudged Jones from her daze, waving it under her nose. "What does this say?" she demanded.

"Kaska," she replied. "It's a girl's name."

"Or a ship's?"

"Sure," Jones slurred. "Why not? Can we sit down? The medication is wearing off."

Nechayev pulled her toward a hangar. "Soon." Inside there was a dart-shaped vessel crouching on spindly landing skids. The same glyph was painted on the side, and it looked ready to throw itself into the air at a moment's notice. "Soon," she repeated, leaving Jones at the foot of the boarding ramp as she crept aboard, her phaser drawn.

Nechayev was halfway across the compact cockpit of the *Kaska* when she realized she wasn't alone. She whirled to find a Bajoran man in a dark brown overcoat holding a weapon on her.

"Korto City Watch," he explained. "Drop your weapon and put your hands on your head. You're under arrest."

22

The last of the containers shimmered into solidity inside the cramped cargo bay. Syjin levered the top off the battered drum and ran a sensor wand over the sealed packets inside.

"Well?" Grek's pinched voice grated from the communicator bead in his ear. *"The unlock code, if it's not too much trouble."*

"Just a moment," insisted the Bajoran. "I'd like to check my merchandise first."

"You don't trust me?" The Ferengi sounded genuinely hurt. *"After all the goodwill between us, after every deal we've done and all the profit we have made throughout our lucrative relationship?"*

"Yeah," Syjin said, "and mostly because of what you did on Quatal III."

Grek gave a nasal snarl. *"How long are you going to keep beating me with that? I told you it wasn't my fault those Mantickian olives were spoiled! I was as much a victim as you."*

"But it didn't stop you taking my money, did it? Now shut up and let me finish checking the load." The Ferengi reduced his grumbling to a background mumble, and Syjin completed the sweep. He frowned at the results. "I thought you said this *agnam* loaf was vintage?"

Grek let out another explosive noise of exasperation. *"Oh, are you going to give me a hard time over this cargo now?"*

"This is two years old. I wanted five years, the proper mature stuff."

There was a moment of silence from the other end of the channel. Syjin glanced out of the viewport in the hull to where a crab-shaped transport drifted alongside his vessel in close orbit over Ajir IX. *"It's just as good,"* Grek insisted. *"There's been a shortage of the fungal cultures used in the dough due to an infestation of gree worms, and—"*

"All right, all right." Syjin shook his head. "I'll take it." He drew a padd from his pocket and keyed in a code string. "There. Funds have been transferred."

The inevitable blast of invective came seconds later. *"You deal-breaking wretch! You've cheated me! This is a quarter less than what we agreed upon!"*

"You deliver what you promised, you get paid the full amount. I'm taking a *discount*." He loved using that word in Grek's company; the reflexive reaction of disgust it created in the alien always amused him.

But Grek's usual spitting and frothing was strangely absent. Syjin went to the window again and saw his vessel shifting, puffs of reaction mass jetting from the maneuvering thrusters as it turned toward one of the gas giant's moons.

"Fine," came the reply. *"A chore doing business with you, as always. Grek out."*

Syjin's brow furrowed. That wasn't like the Ferengi at all, to simply roll over and agree without even trying to haggle; and he sounded distracted, as if something else had caught his attention. The Bajoran bounded up to the cockpit of his ship and toggled his sensors up to maximum, afraid that the Ferengi was about to cut and run, perhaps that there were privateers in the area that Grek's larger and more powerful scanners had detected. But they were alone in the Ajir system.

As he watched, Grek's vessel drifted away, closing on

one of the moons of the gas giant. "What are you doing, you ugly little swindler?" Syjin asked aloud. He narrowed the focus of his sensors to sweep the barren moon, and the display flickered with a constellation of bright returns. Duranium alloy fragments were scattered across the surface of the satellite. "Wreckage," he realized. The Ferengi's crew must have spotted the debris while the deal was taking place. That would explain Grek's sudden loss of interest in his trade; he could smell salvage.

Syjin shot a look at his full cargo compartment, and then back at the sensor display. It was definitely starship-grade metals, probably with enough scrap value alone to double the latinum he'd get from the exotic foods. The Bajoran reached for the gear locker that contained his environmental suit. "No harm in taking a look, I suppose," he said to the air.

Darrah used contact strips from his belt dispenser to secure the two women to seats in the *Kaska*'s cockpit and then went to the courier's emergency kit, sifting through it for some pain medication for the dark-haired one.

"If you take us in, we'll be killed," said the blond woman. "You realize that?"

Darrah gave her friend a dose from the hypospray, and the woman's color returned. She mumbled a thank-you.

"How did you know we were going to be here?" she tried again. The older one had a tone to her words that made it clear she was used to being in control of situations like this.

He leaned against the control console and folded his arms. "Nechen Alla and Jonor Wenna. From Hedrikspool." He shook his head slowly. "The duty commander from the Jalanda City Watch is a friend of mine. Do you want to know what he said to me when I asked him to look up those names in his citizen registry?" He let the question hang. "Yes, in answer to your question, yes, I know what will happen to you if I take you in. The thing is, I figured out where you were going and pretty soon the Cardassians will figure it out too. I put a couple of things in place to slow them down, but they'll be here, and I'll turn over two terrorists to them, and you'll never be seen again. Unless you give me a reason not to do that."

Something shifted behind the eyes of the one who called herself Alla. She was measuring her circumstances, he could see the to-and-fro of it in her face. *Weighing her options. I'd do the same in her place.*

But it was the other one who spoke. "We're not terrorists," she said. "We're here to help you."

Darrah wanted to keep a rein on himself, but the words slipped out before he could stop them. "Like you helped Jekko Tybe?" He tossed the padd with a flick of his wrist and it landed in her lap. Jekko's death-pale face stared back up at her, and she flinched. "Did you kill him?"

"No."

"Is that what you did?" His voice rose. "Did you force him to get you into the enclave and then throw him to the Cardassians when your plan fell apart?"

"No!" she insisted. "It was his idea—"

"Shut up!" spat the other woman. "Don't say another damn word!"

Darrah crossed the room in two quick steps and grabbed the blond woman by the chin. "Then you talk to me!" he growled. "He was my friend. One of the few men I'd be willing to put my life on the line for. Tonight I find out he's dead and you were there with him. So you're going to tell me what happened, or we are going to sit here until the Cardassians arrive."

The dark-haired one was staring at the rank sigils on his collar. "You're the chief inspector," she said. "Jekko's friend. His source inside the Korto police."

The other woman looked at him. "You leaked him the documents about the enclave."

Darrah blinked, suddenly caught off guard. "What does that have to do with anything?"

"How do you think we got in there?" she retorted. "Jekko used the intelligence you gave him."

In all the turmoil, the thought hadn't even occurred to Darrah, but now it did and he didn't know how to respond. *I just left some files open, that was all. Jekko said it would help. It would help them keep an eye on the Cardassians.* But nothing more had been said of it; time had passed, and Darrah had thought no more about it. *I gave him the way in. Prophets, am I partly to blame for his death?*

The blond woman saw the train of thought on his face. "What did you think he was going to do with the files, Chief Inspector? Frame them and put them on a wall? He was trying to stop the Cardassian Union from engulfing your planet."

Her words snapped him out of his reverie. "'Your planet'?" he repeated. "Don't you mean *our* planet?" Darrah grabbed his police-issue tricorder from his belt and toggled the device to a scene-of-crime forensic scan mode. Taking the woman's chin in his hand again, he ran the sensor head over her skull. The DNA scan was in the green, but the bone structure readings were off. He released her. "You've been surgically altered."

Both of them remained silent. He put the tricorder away and crossed to the canopy, shooting a look toward the hangar's open doors. There was no sign of movement out in the predawn light.

"Who are you working for?" Darrah sat in a chair and studied the pair. "You're not Bajoran. You're not Tzenkethi, that's a certainty."

The blonde sniffed. "The Tzenkethi Coalition doesn't have any interest in Bajor. They never have."

"There's a memorial at the City Oval with four hundred and ninety-two names on it that says different," he retorted.

"What would you say if I told you the government on Ab-Tzenketh was as shocked by that attack as you were?"

Darrah's lip curled. "I'd say you were misinformed."

She smiled without humor. "The . . . people I work for, they've fought the Tzenkethi on overt and covert battlefields. And what happened on that day, that's not what the Tzenkethi do."

He shook his head. "You can't know that for sure."

"We do," she told him, leaning forward with an absolute certainty in her eyes. "We know because we've broken one of the key Tzenkethi code ciphers. And let me tell you, on that day they were panicking like all hell had broken loose."

"The Cardassians told us—" Darrah started to explain, but then the words he said registered with him and he fell silent.

"Now you're getting it." She nodded. "The Tzenkethi didn't order that attack. They lost contact with that ship hours before it happened. I've seen the communications transcripts."

He wanted to ask the question that burned in his mind, but he pushed it aside. "You're Federation, aren't you?" He got no reply. "If that's true, if you knew that, why didn't your Starfleet tell us?"

"If that information became public knowledge, what would happen? The marauder was totally obliterated by the Cardassians, wasn't it? Nothing left there that could be used as proof either way. And all it would mean was that the Tzenkethi would know their communications had been compromised, and my people would lose that advantage."

"Then who did it?" he snarled, his cheeks hot with anger.

The blond woman gave him a level look. "You already know the answer."

Syjin set the transporter to beam him down to a point at the edge of the debris field, and he felt the shift in gravity instantly. The small moon curved away from him in every direction, and where the surface was a mottled white stone to his right and left, in front of him it was churned up into a blue-gray powder. He glanced up into a sky dominated by the cloudy orange mass of Ajir IX, trying to visualize the final moments of the craft that had come to rest here. *It would have had to have been close to the moon,* he reasoned. *It suffered some kind of damage, got snared by the lunar gravity, and augured straight into the surface, shedding pieces of itself all the way down.* The angle of the collision had been a steep one. Bits of hull metal were deposited all around a giant divot cut from the surface.

He walked on in a loping bounce, the sound of his own breathing resonating around the inside of his helmet. Without an atmosphere to act on the wreckage, there was no corrosion or weathering. All the pieces were perfectly preserved in the hard vacuum. At the edge of his vision, Syjin thought he saw something that could have been a corpse and he shuddered. He'd seen more than enough vacuum-desiccated cadavers in his life as it was.

A large slab of duranium that appeared to be a piece of outer hull was lying half buried in the sand. On an impulse he couldn't really explain, Syjin tucked his fingers under it and turned it over. In the moon's low gravity it was easy for him to shift the door-sized piece of metal, and it fell lazily back to the ground. There was pennant etched into the duranium in blue paint, a symbol like an inverted fork with circular tines. Syjin knew it well; many times he had been forced to make a quick getaway from ships bearing the sigil of the Bajoran Space Guard.

The shiver down his spine returned. *I'm disturbing the dead.* Suddenly, the idea of looting the wreck made him feel sick inside. This was a Bajoran grave, not the remains of some nondescript alien from a world he'd never even heard of. *This place is probably teeming with angry boryhas.*

Shadows moved up ahead and he jumped, startled; but these were not vengeful phantoms. Three figures with the wide-faced helmets characteristic of Ferengi spacesuits approached him, and through the glass bowl of his headgear Syjin saw Grek's sneering, snaggletoothed expression.

"What are you doing down here?" demanded the trader. *"You got a good deal out of me, isn't that enough? Take your ship and go!"*

"Did you know this was here?"

The Ferengi shook his head. *"Of course not. If I knew there was salvage in this system, do you think I'd have brought you anywhere near it?"* He grunted. *"I picked this place at random."*

"Grek, this is a Bajoran naval starship," Syjin retorted, gesturing around. The moment he said the words aloud, something registered in his thoughts. *Lost Space Guard ships . . .*

"No," insisted the alien, *"this is mine."* He clapped his gloved hands together. *"Under the auspices of the Ferengi Salvage Code, I'm claiming this wreckage as my own. I don't think you're in any position to contest that."* Grek nodded left and right to the other crewmen with him, who each had disruptor pistols holstered at their waists.

But Syjin wasn't listening. He looked around. *The reprisal fleet from five years ago . . . Could this be one of those vessels?* His thoughts raced. The final fate of the *Clarion,* the *Glyhrond,* and the scouts had never been determined, and ships sent to search for their remains had come up empty. Syjin recalled the announcement by First Minister Lale, stating that even with the help of Jagul Kell's cruisers, the four lost starships had not been recovered.

"What do you think you're going to do, anyway?" Grek swaggered forward, his boots crunching on pieces of bridge console half-covered by the sand. The sound drew Syjin's attention to something buried there and his eyes widened. *"Even if you dumped that load you just took off me, you still wouldn't have room for any of this!"* The Ferengi grinned. *"I'm gonna take it all!"*

"No," said Syjin, "you're not." He flicked his hand and the palm phaser he kept concealed in the suit's wrist pocket dropped into his grip.

Grek's faceplate fogged as he shouted. *"You're pulling a gun on me? What? After all we've been through together?"* He shook his head ruefully. *"Oh, Syjin. And I said such nice things about you to the boys here, didn't I?"*

The heads of the other two crewmen bobbed in agreement, hands hovering over their holsters.

"Syjin, I said, Syjin almost has the lobes to be a Ferengi, I said! As close to one of us as a Bajoran could get! And this is what comes in return?" He sighed theatrically. *"I thought we were friends!"*

The statement brought a sneer to the Bajoran's lips. "What's the twenty-first Rule of Acquisition?"

"Never place friendship above profit," said one of the other Ferengi, with rote diction.

"All right, not friends, then, but fellow businessmen," Grek admitted. *"Look, put down the weapon. There's enough here for everyone."*

"I only want one thing," Syjin replied, "and you're standing on it."

Grek jerked back in shock and glanced down. Gingerly, he dragged a cylindrical object out of the sand. *"What is this? Looks like a memory core . . ."*

"Log recorder," said Syjin. It wasn't something he liked to talk about, but the pilot had earned the money to buy his own ship by working the recovery docks on Andros, and he knew a flight recorder when he saw one. Those days still came back to him on dark, lonely nights, scrapping dead ships and stripping them for parts. "Give it to me."

"*Give?*" Grek said the word like a curse. "*And what do I get?*"

"I won't put a hole in your e-suit."

"*Oh. Well. That's a fair trade.*" The Ferengi tossed the device toward him and it sailed slowly to land at his feet.

Syjin gathered it up with his free hand and backed away.

"*Look*"—Grek took a step toward him—"*let's not let this minor difference of opinion sour things between us, eh? I've got a line on a consignment of live* porwiggies *coming into the sector next month, and you know they're good eating.*"

The Bajoran shook his head. "I think we're done, you and I. And if there's an iota of empathy in you, Grek, you'll light out of here and leave the dead to rest."

The Ferengi snorted. "*Yeah, sure. I'll get right on that.*" The other crewmen laughed nasally.

For a moment, Syjin thought about shooting Grek anyway, but what good would it have done him? He was only one man, and Grek had a crew of ten on his scow. He couldn't stop them from looting the crash site, but the recorder—that would be important. Without another word, he tapped the recall key on his glove and the transporter took hold of him.

Aboard his ship, Syjin secured the memory core and programmed a speed course for Bajor.

The flames had taken hold by the time Proka got there. Emergency flyers were hovering around the roof of the night market temple, shooting puffs of fire retardants into the plume of black smoke, but they were barely keeping the inferno contained. He pushed through the people flooding outside over the steps—merchants and civilians, women and men, monks and ranjens. They were dirty with soot and were coughing. Green-uniformed medical techs moved among them with breather cylinders and hyposprays.

He grabbed the arm of a passing constable. "Casualties?"

"Eight dead," she replied. "There's a dozen or so more unaccounted for."

Proka swore under his breath. "You were here? You saw what happened?"

The woman nodded gravely. Her face was pallid beneath the patina of smoke dirt on her cheeks. "My shift just finished and I was coming up to the temple for the dawn mass . . ." She stifled a cough and spat out a blob of black spittle. "They get a lot of folks here for that." Behind them, the burning building gave a cracking thud, and a jet of orange fire shot out into the sky as something collapsed inside.

"They only just finished rebuilding this place . . ." Proka said to himself.

The constable nodded. "I was coming up the street and I heard shouting. There were a bunch of people calling out, making noise. I picked up the pace, and when I got there I saw what the fuss was all about. There were Oralians, three of them in those funny robes they wear."

"What were they doing?"

"Shouting out slogans, chanting. They were deliberately goading the people coming to worship, sir. Disrespecting the Prophets."

Proka glared at the burning church and the injured people streaming away from it. "How did that turn into this?" He stabbed a finger at the building.

"Firebombs," said the woman. "Just as I thought someone was going to start trading punches, they all pulled out these little glass balls and threw them." She mimed a fireball with her hands. "I don't know what they had in them. They went up like lightning. Everyone panicked and broke. I got pinned in the crowd and the temple went up like tinder."

"What happened to the Oralians?" he demanded.

She led him toward an alley between some of the shuttered market stalls. "They went down there." The constable gestured around. "You see? There's no security monitor coverage in this area. They must have known that."

Proka shone a torch down the alley. It was a dead end, terminating in a sheer wall with no other means of exit.

"They kept yelling about Bajor," she said. "They said that the Prophets were phantoms, that Oralius was the only true way."

Shouting drew the attention of the law officers. A man with ash all over his clothes was bellowing at the top of his voice. "You! You there!" he screamed. "How could you let this happen? Those Oralian freaks, they did this! Aren't you going to do something? Round them up!" A chorus of angry agreement joined him from several of the other people. "Make them pay for this!"

"We're going to do all we can—" Proka began, but no one was listening. A mob was forming right in front of him, jeering for rough justice.

Ico studied the active map of Bajor and considered the implementation of the endgame. Assets that she had spent the last decade cultivating and positioning were being called into action all across the world, triggered like an avalanche started by a handful of pebbles. In a small way, she had been loath to move to the active phase of the destabilization. The intricate construct of influence and subterfuge she had made was one of her finest pieces of work; she sat back and admired it in the same way one might consider a delicate piece of glass sculpture, so elegant but at the same time so fragile. It was music written and ready to be played, a great piece of theater waiting for one single shattering performance.

That was part of what thrilled Rhan so much about the work: the danger inherent in it, the challenge of keeping so many shifting alliances on the field of play, the insight and totality of dedication required to bring a world to the brink of collapse.

She recalled the words of a Terran—perhaps one of their philosophers or a strategist, she couldn't recall which— who had said that all civilizations existed on the brink of barbarism, only a few days away from brutality and violence. Cardassia Prime had balanced on that knife edge for so long it had become a way of life for them, but fat and complacent Bajor knew nothing of that; it amused Ico to think that her work had taken these aliens to the same place. *And now we'll see how the play unfolds. The set is dressed, the actors in their roles. The curtain rises.*

She examined the map. In Relliketh, a woman whose gambling debts made her vulnerable had closed a sensor window over the Bajoran polar ice cap; a priest in Jo'Kala was taking poison rather than have the identity of his lover revealed to the world; churches were on fire in Hathon, Ashalla, and Korto; the minister for Qui'al was turning a blind eye to troop movements outside his city; unmarked containers were being unloaded from a Son'a transport ship in Tempasa; a Militia commander in Janir had come home to find his wife in the arms of another man.

And there were dozens of others, all small fragmentary dramas that she had engineered, that had no relation to one another on the surface. But beneath, they all pulled upon strings that brought pressures to bear on Bajor.

The screen chimed, and a report made itself known to her. She smiled to herself and tapped a control. Ico spoke into a communicator. "Dukat."

The gul's voice was loaded with irritation. *"This is a secure military channel."*

She ignored the comment. "The Federation spies have

been traced to the Korto starport. I thought you might like to know."

"How can you be certain of that?" he growled.

"I have assets in place," she said languidly, watching the motion of the players on her map. Jekko Tybe's face and his personal records scrolled over an inset screen, revealing his life, his associations, his connections. "That's all you need to be aware of." Ico reached for the disconnect key. "And quickly, Dukat, quickly. I'm sure you don't want to let them slip through your fingers."

Gwen Jones pulled against the restraints, but no matter how she moved, the plastic strips chafed against her wrists. She felt queasy, and not so much from the shock and the effects of the drugs in her system, but from the mounting fear that time was running out for her. She kept darting looks out of the *Kaska*'s canopy, afraid that each time she did, she would see Cardassian soldiers swarming across the thermoconcrete apron toward the hangar.

Nechayev was trying to reason with the Bajoran lawman, who paced back and forth across the small cockpit like a caged animal. "Listen to me," she was saying, "every minute we stay here is a minute more we could have used to put distance between us and the Cardassians. We have to get out, report what we've learned. Don't you get it? We are Bajor's only chance!"

The man rounded on her. "So I let you go, then what? Starfleet rides in with a battle fleet and rescues my planet from the Cardassian Union? I let you go, and you make this madness stop?"

"Yes." Nechayev's falsehood was instinctual and automatic. Jones saw it, and so did the Bajoran.

"You're lying to me," he snarled. "You're telling me what I want to hear." He turned away from them. "You think I don't know? I've been a police officer my entire life, I've faced down liars of every stripe!" He shook his head. "Everyone lies. 'It's not my fault, I'm innocent, I didn't do it, it was the other guy . . .'" The lawman turned back and shouted, "I'm sick of the lies! I'm drowning in them!"

"Then help me expose them!" retorted Nechayev. "Because if you don't, the Cardassians will take us and turn us into two more fabrications, terrorists and murderers. They'll do the same thing to Jekko, and then they'll do it to you!" She rocked forward, pulling at the chair. "You have to trust us, damnit!"

He sat heavily. "Give me one good reason why I should."

Jones licked dry lips. "Because your friend did." The man turned to study her. "Jekko knew what was at stake. He trusted us. He gave up his life so that we could take what we saw and get away." She took a shuddering breath, wincing at the pain in her cheek. "I didn't really know him, but you did. You know what kind of man he was better than either of us, so you tell me. Would he have put his trust in us, died for us, if it hadn't been worthwhile?"

The Bajoran was silent for a long moment before he spoke again. "My name is Darrah Mace. I've spent the last ten years watching everything that is important to me slip away, moment by moment. My wife and children. My friends, my work. Bajor . . ." His words dropped to a whisper. "And no matter what I do, I can't stop it. None of us can."

"We have to try," said Nechayev.

"You think the Federation can help us?"

"I don't know," she admitted, and for the first time Jones felt that she was seeing the real Alynna Nechayev. "But I promise you I will do whatever I can to make sure that they do."

Motion caught Jones's eye, and she jerked around in the chair. "Make a choice, Mace," she said. Skimmers were crossing the runways, converging on the hangar. "We've got company."

Darrah shot to his feet and with two quick motions . they were free of the restraints. Nechayev threw herself over to the pilot's console and pressed the isolinear chip Jekko had gave her into a data slot. The vessel came alive, engines humming to power.

"Unless you want to come with us, you'd better step out." She nodded at the drop ramp.

Jones slipped into the copilot's chair and ran through a sequence of preflight checks; the *Kaska* wasn't too different from the Starfleet shuttlecraft she'd trained on. "They'll be here in less than two minutes," she reported, watching the approach of the Cardassian ground vehicles. "We have to go *now.*"

Nechayev reached out and snatched Darrah's tricorder from his belt, tapping in a string of numbers. "You trusted us and now I'm going to trust you. This is an authentication code and a subspace radio frequency. There's a ship in this sector, the *Gettysburg.* They'll be monitoring that channel."

He took back the tricorder and nodded. "If I learn anything, I'll contact you." Darrah turned and opened the hatch. "Good luck—"

Nechayev never let him finish his sentence. Her hand struck out and she grabbed his phaser before he could stop her. A pulse of light enveloped him and he crumpled backward, tumbling down the drop ramp to land in a heap on the hangar floor below.

"You shot him!" Jones cried.

Nechayev tossed the phaser after him and sealed the hatch. "Just a stun." She jumped into the pilot's chair and eased the *Kaska* off the landing skids and out of the open hangar doors. "Shields up," she ordered, and Jones complied, just in time to prevent a cascade of phaser shots from burning into the forward hull.

"But you shot him," Jones repeated.

"If I hadn't, the Cardassians would have known he let us go. This way, he just looks like he was unlucky." They were moving down the apron now, picking up speed. "Honestly, I did him a favor."

More beam fire thudded off the deflectors. "How are we going to get out of this?" Jones demanded. "Those Cardassians are contacting their ships in orbit right now. They'll intercept us the second we break atmosphere."

Nechayev pushed the throttle forward, and the courier leapt into the lightening sky, crashing seconds later through the sound barrier with the twin thunders of a supercompressed shock wave. "Jekko had some tricks up his sleeve." She smiled, and jerked her thumb at a compartment in the rear. "See that? I noticed it as soon as I got on board."

Jones looked and saw a cracked white spheroid with battered blue components at either end. It was wired into the main power bus, but it seemed out of place. "I don't know what that is."

"Romulan cloaking device, the kind they used to use in the mid–23rd century," she explained, "probably salvaged from an old bird-of-prey."

Jones gaped. "We're pinning our escape on an antique piece of Romulan salvage?"

Nechayev gave a gallows–humor smile. "Well, as we're all being truthful with each other, I should tell you that this courier's practically a museum piece as well." She shrugged. "I rate our chances of making our rendezvous at less than forty percent."

Dukat stood over the unconscious form of the Bajoran law officer and his fists tightened. He wanted to haul the man off the ground and beat an answer out of him.

"Do you know him, sir?" Orloc asked.

The gul ignored the question and pushed the glinn out of his way. "Wake him up," he snarled. "Find out what he knows! Now!" Dukat strode out of the hangar to the line of hovering skimmers. He slapped at his comcuff. "Tunol! Status?"

The reply he got stoked his annoyance even higher. *"Sir, sensors have lost contact with the target vessel. There was an energy surge in low orbit and then it just vanished."*

"Ships don't vanish, Dal," he barked. "They cloaked. Recalibrate sensors and get me a trail. I want it this very second!" He cut the signal before she could reply, but a heartbeat later the communicator signaled an incoming message. "Dukat," he growled.

"Oh, Skrain." Ico's voice was cold. *"I am so disappointed in you."*

23

Outside the shack the encampment used as its infirmary the congregation gathered and muttered darkly. Bennek could hear them through the thin metal walls—not things they were saying, not the words that they used, but the sense of them. The mood of the Oralians was one of fear and confusion, and it hung over the ragged settlement like a waiting storm.

The airtruck was out by the perimeter, the engine still idling and the cab door hanging wide open. The driver was a youth the cleric remembered as being from Culat, and he sat on one of the collapsible metal-framed canvas beds, weeping. Bennek and a woman named Seren, who had been a nurse before she had found the Way, were the only others in the hut.

Between choking sobs and gasps of air, the young man parceled out his story in broken pieces. The docks, the three men. The guns. Urad's execution. The others, lost and likely dead. And Tima. *Tima . . .*

Bennek expected a sudden torrent of emotion to flood over him, but there was nothing. He felt numb all over, disconnected from the moment. He tried to remember Tima's face, the scent of her skin, but it fell away from him, memory denying him. The youth kept speaking, but the cleric heard nothing. His focus slipped away as he tried to enclose the thought in his mind. *Tima is dead. Tima is dead.* But they were just words, meaningless words.

"Who would do this?" Seren demanded, her voice strident and furious. "Why would the Bajorans strike at us? We have always shown them honor and respect!" She spat on the dirt floor. "Why have they turned against us?" The nurse glared at Bennek. "That vedek, Gar . . . He must have done this, he must have sent the killers!"

Bennek shook his head, but she didn't acknowledge his silent denial.

"Th-they called us filth," stuttered the boy. "I was so afraid. I had to run . . . but the others . . ." He choked off his own words with a moan of guilt.

"You did the right thing," insisted the nurse. "If you hadn't come back to warn us, we would never have known this was coming." She turned to Bennek. "We must be ready, they'll try again!"

Bennek got to his feet, his balance lost, lurching. He tried to breathe, but the air in the hut was suddenly stifling. The cleric pushed away and out into the morning. The Oralians outside parted before him, their uncertainty plain upon their faces. He was aware of Seren following him out, her voice cracking as she repeated the boy's words. A wave of shock radiated out around him as the congregation assimilated the horror of it, and in moments that disbelief re-formed into fury. Bennek glanced around and saw it igniting in the faces of his people, but still he could feel nothing himself. He clutched at his chest. The priest felt as if he were hollowed out, every emotion and moment of life inside cored from his being. *Tima is dead. Tima is dead.*

"Are we going to tolerate this?" Seren was shouting. "We are forced out here to live on the charity of others, and then these scum attack us at our very weakest? They burn down our homes, try to starve us, and we do nothing!"

Bennek heard her words and shook his head again, but

it was a feeble gesture and it went unnoticed. Too late he saw it: the followers of the Way had been pushed as far as they were going to go. Oralius and her peace were no longer enough for them.

"We have to strike back!" said the nurse, and a chorus of assent went with her cry. "Fight for the Way, defend ourselves!"

The cleric searched for some parable, something from the Recitations to rally them away from anger, but like everything else, like Tima, that had suddenly been taken from him. Bennek's hand came to his face, and he felt wetness on his cheeks.

He heard his name being called. The youth was behind him, screaming and pointing into the distance. They turned as one to see the lights approaching the encampment from the direction of the city—skimmers and flyers, dozens of them aimed directly at the Oralian settlement.

Bennek walked to the perimeter, to the bare patches of earth haloing the encampment. Dozens of men and women dismounted from the vehicles, all of them Bajorans, all of them mirroring the same hard need for retribution as his congregation. Many of them carried makeshift weapons, cudgels, and stunners. From the lead skimmer came a trio of figures in the robes of the church of the Prophets. Bennek saw Vedek Arin at the head of them, the Bajoran's eyes flinty.

"What do you want?" demanded Seren, and the Oralians snarled and growled in her support. "Come to finish off the rest of us?"

The cleric searched the faces of the new arrivals, looking for men in docker's overalls, and found none; instead he saw hate on every face, the burning need for someone to blame, to find an outlet for a mass of stored-up hurts and lingering affronts.

Some of the Bajorans shouted out hard words in reply

to the nurse, but Arin silenced them with a sharp wave of his hand. He glared at the Oralians. "Bennek," he grated, "why have your people done this to us? After all the hospitality Bajor showed to the children of Oralius, in the name of the Prophets, *why?*"

It was the last thing he expected to hear, and the cleric was bewildered. "What are you talking about? What did we do? What did *you* do, Arin? You murdered our people!" And then, in that instant, as the words left his mouth the hollow inside him filled with a pure, burning sorrow so powerful he could barely contain it. "Tima is dead!" he moaned. "My followers have been slaughtered!"

Arin shook his head, and Bennek wanted to weep. "I know nothing of that," retorted the vedek. "The temples, Bennek! In Korto and Ashalla and elsewhere, your people have attacked our places of worship, setting them afire!" The Bajoran mob reacted to the words, violence bubbling below the surface of their every breath and movement.

"Are you insane?" demanded Seren. "Our people are all *here,* Vedek! Starving and sick because of what your kind has done to us!"

Arin ignored her outburst. "Bennek, listen to me. If you have any shred of integrity, you will do as I say. Submit to my custody, bring your people with us back to the city and answer for this crime. Do this now, or else I will not be responsible for what takes place."

Seren pushed past Bennek. "Your custody? What does that mean? We won't willingly chain ourselves for you. What law are you invoking, what proof do you have—"

"Seren, be silent," Bennek snapped.

The vedek's face flushed crimson. "This a matter above the legality of men. This is a matter of the holy temple! You must submit, or else you will—" Arin's voice was silenced as a fist-sized stone shot out from the lines of the Oralians and struck the Bajoran priest on the temple. The impact dropped Arin to the dirt, a livid wound leaking blood down his face.

Bennek turned and saw the young driver shouting out his hate, and he knew who had thrown the missile. Around him the Oralians erupted into a sudden hostility born of desperation; in turn the Bajorans cut loose and surged forward, the attack on Arin giving them the reason they needed to abandon the last vestiges of civility and retaliate.

The cleric stumbled back toward the encampment as the two groups collided with a clatter of violence. Stones and fire rained down toward him, scattering across the dull earth. Something impacted him hard across the small of the back and he stumbled forward, tripping over the ropes of a bubble-tent and falling to his knees. The confrontation was raging all around. He crawled, trying to drag himself from the melee, and every action was punctuated by a single thought. *Tima is dead.*

Hands grabbed his arms and pulled at his sleeves. He looked up and saw the young man. "You have to run!" he cried; there was no sign in his eyes of an understanding that it was his moment of insanity that had started this madness. "For Fate's sake, you have to go!" The young man thrust a leather bag into his hands, and Bennek felt familiar shapes through the soft hide. "Keep them safe! But go, just go!"

The youth propelled him to his feet, out toward the far edge of the camp. Some animal reaction was triggered, and Bennek ran into the wilderness, heedless and out of control, clutching the bag to his chest.

The Bajoran politician attempted to conceal his discomfort at the two armored glinns who escorted him into the room, but he made a poor job of it. Ico inclined her head, and the soldiers gave her a curt nod and retreated from the chamber, sealing the security door behind them. She smiled. "It's so good of you to come at this early hour. I know it's a long trip to Dahkur."

Kubus Oak recovered a little of his poise and nodded. "Nonsense. It's never an unpleasant task to be in your company, Rhan."

Ico studied him as Kubus tried to hide the fact that he was glancing around the woman's office like a trapped animal searching for an exit. *Does he think I brought him here to terminate him, perhaps? How amusing.* The man's false front of cool affability was slipping around the edges. Ico had made sure that Qui'al was isolated from some of the more incendiary activities she had set in motion today, but still the city-state's leader could not have been ignorant of what was going on elsewhere on his homeworld. She decided not to speak, and steepled her fingers over her desk instead, watching him steadily.

After a few moments of silence, Kubus couldn't resist his natural compulsion to fill the silence and gestured toward the animated situation map on the wallscreen. "That word . . ." He peered at a disk of Cardassian characters. *"Terok.* I've seen it several times on your documentation. What does it mean?"

"Your grasp of our language is improving, Oak. Well done." She gave him an indolent nod, a teacher praising her student. "I suppose it will harm nothing to tell you." Ico stood and rounded the desk. "It is a unique designation for your world. The Central Command generates one for every planet that joins the Union as a colony, client, or . . . associate. In our classified documentation, we refer to Bajor as Planetary Ident: Terok." She smiled again. "Do you see how much I trust you? If any other Bajoran knew that information, I would be forced to sanction them." That she made the comment so casually was enough to make the man pale slightly. Ico moved to hover next to him, in front of the moving play of her great game.

"I . . . am flattered," he managed. "If I might ask, why did you demand my presence?"

"I don't make demands, Oak," she said lightly. "I only *request* or *suggest*. Demands are made by those who have left themselves with no other options."

He looked at her, and this close to him, she could make out the thin sheen of sweat on his face. Finally, the questions that must have been boiling up inside him since the moment he left Qui'al bubbled to the surface. "Rhan, what is going on?" He pointed at the map. "Civil unrest and reports of violence in a dozen cities. People going missing. Confusion and disorder."

Her manner grew colder. "Perhaps I didn't make it clear enough to you. You were told that certain conditions would need to be brought into being, correct?"

Kubus nodded woodenly. "And I've helped you establish some of them. But this . . ." He sighed. "There's much more going on than I was aware of."

She laughed. "Of course there is." Ico saw the momentary look of betrayal on his face. "Oh, dear Oak. Are you upset that you were not given the full dimensions of our strategy? Please understand, it was not an attempt to slight you." She wandered away. "I was keeping you focused. Safe, in a way."

His lip trembled; he was as disturbed as she had ever seen him. "Safe?" Kubus replied, his voice rising slightly. "Safe from the knowledge that you would burn churches or land legions of troops under cover of darkness?"

"Are those things important?" she asked him. "The operation moves forward, and it will benefit Bajor as much as it does Cardassia in the long run. You know that." Ico sighed. "But never forget that we move at Cardassian behest, not Bajoran. We all have parts to play."

"I would have preferred to be better informed," he said tightly.

"As would we all." Ico's reply was airy. She shook her head. "I don't understand your reticence. There was none of this a decade ago when I first came to you with the offer of partnership. And before that, in your many dealings with Cardassia on a trade footing, you never once showed this level of reserve."

"Things change," he managed.

"They do," she agreed, "and I always work to ensure that they change in ways that benefit me." Ico crossed back to him and ran a gray hand over his cheek. The Bajoran's skin was pleasantly warm. "Haven't we always told you that your role would be one of the most important in shaping Bajor's future? And this day's work is a necessary step toward it."

She sensed the change in him; all Kubus had needed was a little stroking to keep him centered.

"Lale has shown some recalcitrant behavior in recent weeks," he noted. "I don't think he wants to leave the First Ministry."

"What Lale Usbor wants is of little interest to Cardassia," Ico said, with more bluntness than she intended. Covering her tiny lapse, she spoke on. "But this is a delicate time, Oak. We enter the final act, but it has become complicated by some outside interference."

"I don't know what you mean."

A nod. "And that is why I brought you here today, so that you will know." She inclined her head. "Those fools in the United Federation of Planets are taking an undue interest. Rest assured that the Union has gambits in place to retard their meddling, but it is important that in the next few days your fellow members of the Chamber of Ministers—the ones of weaker character, that is—do not panic and run to the Federation."

Kubus nodded slowly. "That would be a mistake."

She released another smile. "It pleases me to see that you and I are still so close in our intentions."

"I'll keep the other ministers in line." The man's confidence returned at full force now that he was back on more familiar ground.

"You've done well to date," Ico noted, "although I have had some concerns regarding your control over the actions of Jas Holza."

"Holza?" Kubus mocked. "He's a spent force, too weak to defy me. He'll tow the line or else run to Valo with Keeve Falor and the rest of the exiles. Either way, he's not an issue." He bowed slightly and stepped back. "I'll . . . take my leave, then?"

Ico came close to him and touched him again. "No," she husked, "I think not. Perhaps, Oak, perhaps I will make a demand of you."

She relished the moment of fear in his eyes as her hands strayed to the buttons on his shirt. *Today will be a busy one*, Ico told herself. *I can justify myself this one little diversion before I return to it.*

Darrah Mace sipped the cup of water and swallowed hard, trying to keep the fluid in his gullet. The echoing resonance of the phaser stun would be lingering for a good while yet. By rights, he should have taken some time to lie down, to let his body relax and gather itself; the Cardassians had other ideas, however. They woke him using harsh chemical stimulants and held him for an hour in the hangar, recording everything he said about the escaped fugitives.

At one point, one of the alien soldiers asked him if he was trembling because of a delayed reaction to the stun blast. He lied and said yes. He couldn't bring himself to tell them it was rage that had wound him so tightly that he wanted to rip the throats out of every one of them. Everything the blond woman said was there at the front of his thoughts, hard as diamond. It took every bit of Darrah's self-control to say nothing, to play dumb.

Eventually, they released him. By that time, most of the other Cardassians in the pursuit group were gone anyway, summoned away by their commander. *Dukat,* Darrah told himself. *It was him.* The gul appeared to have problems of his own, nursing his own fury at being denied the Starfleet women. Dukat ignored Darrah and let his junior officers supervise the interrogation. He could feel the disdain oozing from the Cardassian. *He didn't even recognize me. I was just another Bajoran, just another impediment.*

"Are you all right, sir?" asked Myda.

He glanced up, coming back to the present. "I'm okay." Darrah had returned to the precinct to find the usual controlled chaos of the place strangely absent. The station house was almost empty, with desks left untidy and monitors still ticking over. "Where is everyone?"

"Gone," she said wearily. "We had to activate every officer in the city. You saw it on the streets. It's out of control."

Darrah nodded grimly. Korto was slipping into lawlessness and anarchy. The roads were choked with terrified people trying to flee, angry people looking for a fight, and criminals using the cover of unrest to loot and pillage. "You contacted the command precinct in Ashalla?" She nodded. "You told them what's happening here?"

"I sent a priority alert," she explained, sitting down on the desk next to him. "Asked for emergency support units. But they told me there was no one to send." Myda sighed. "This is happening all over Bajor, sir. We're on our own."

"Kosst," Darrah swore quietly. "How are we supposed to keep this together?"

"It gets worse," said the woman. "Our people are dropping off the grid. No answer on comms."

Darrah sagged in the chair and listened to the odd quiet of the precinct house, the faint clicks and beeps of the unattended computers. A law officer not responding to signals from home base was usually a sign that they were incapacitated, or worse—but he had a creeping feeling that a lot of the men going dark were abandoning their posts. *Can I blame them? If you knew how widespread this was, what man wouldn't want to look to the safety of his own instead of protecting strangers?* A bleak smile touched his lips in a moment of self-recognition.

He looked at the woman. "Why are you still here, Myda?"

She understood the question. "My family will be okay, sir. I have a job to do."

Darrah let out a bleak chuckle. "I used to think that." He waved her away. "Go on, get going. Make sure they're safe."

Myda shook her head. "I won't. I'll make them safe by keeping a lid on this. Out there I'm just one more person. In here, I can make a difference."

Darrah got to his feet. "For the sake of the Prophets, I hope so."

She followed him to the dispatch console. "It's a pity you didn't get to the port in time to stop those fugitives," said Myda. "Maybe they had something to do with all this."

"Maybe," he said flatly. On some level, he was still trying to assimilate what the women had told him. He grimaced as he realized he didn't even know their names. The lawman took the tricorder from his belt and studied the data string the operative had entered there. The Cardassian who had held him hadn't recognized what it represented.

"You have something there, sir?" asked Myda.

"Damned if I know," he admitted. Something else was bothering him, along with the hundreds of other issues pressing into his thoughts: *How had the Cardassians known that they would be at the port, at that hangar?* He felt a cold sensation creep through his gut. *Is that why they let me go? Because Dukat or one of the others is monitoring the precinct? That must be it . . .*

"Mace!" They both turned toward the sound of his name, and the lawman's face clouded as he recognized a familiar figure scrambling over the duty officer's desk. He was dragging a heavy pack with him.

"Syjin? What are you doing back here?"

The pilot came over, his usual breezy manner gone. "Never mind that," he snapped. "I have to talk to you, right now."

"In case you haven't noticed, Bajor's falling apart all around us," Myda retorted. "And this area is off-limits to civilians."

Darrah waved her away. "It's okay, Myda." He shot Syjin a look. "You said you were getting out. It's a mistake coming back to Bajor. People are taking any ship they can find to get offworld."

"I didn't land at the port," the pilot explained, speaking rapidly. "My bird is still in low orbit. I beamed down." He held up the pack. "You need to see this, Mace, and right now." Syjin shot Myda a look. "In private, I'd say."

Darrah frowned and beckoned his friend toward his office. "In here, then."

Syjin closed the door and dropped the bag on his desk. "Take a look."

Inside was a battered cylindrical data module, the kind the Space Guard fitted as a redundant memory core aboard their ships. Darrah leaned in and read the identity plate fused to the dense metal. One word made his breath catch in his throat. *"Clarion?* That was the ship—"

The pilot nodded. "The ship that Lonnic Tomo was aboard. One of the lost reprisal fleet."

The lawman ran his hands over the surface. It was undamaged. He started looking for output ports. "Where did you find this?"

"The Ajir system, a clump of dead planets off the main trade lanes. Look, that's not important. What is important is that this thing is still in one piece. Whatever happened to the *Clarion* and the rest of those ships, it's in here." He tapped it with a finger. "I tried to connect it up to my bird's mainframe, but I couldn't get into the logs. I need a more powerful machine and someone with the clearance to get access . . ." He looked at Darrah and trailed off.

"And you figured a police officer would be just right?" Darrah studied the unit. The Starfleet woman's words echoed again. *You already know the answer.* He thought about the attack, about Lonnic and the ships that had never come home. "The truth is in here," he breathed. "Fire's sake, Syjin. Do you understand what you've found?"

He shook his head. "Not really, Mace. That's why I brought it to you, because you're smarter than me. You always know the right thing to do."

Darrah reached for a connector cable and then halted. "If the Cardassians are monitoring the precinct's data-streams, they'll know the moment I hook this up."

"What do they have to do with this?" Syjin asked.

Darrah ignored the question and studied the device for a long moment; then he got to his feet and put it back in the pack. "Come on. We can't do this here. We have to use an isolated system, one with no connection to the planetary data network."

"Where are we going to find something like that?"

Darrah grabbed his coat and weapon. "I know where."

The image was blurred slightly by the motion of movement in the second it was captured, but light-intensification subroutines built into the viewscreen had cleaned up the sillhouette enough for any observer to be certain of what they were seeing. "A *Janad*-class tank," said Nechayev. "All it was missing was a crew and the will to use it."

Across the *Gettysburg*'s briefing room, at the far end of the conference table, the young lieutenant with the serious expression gave a low gasp. "Oy. They're loaded for bear."

The Vulcan woman to Nechayev's right nodded. "An accurate estimation, Lieutenant Gold, if overly colloquial." She glanced at Nechayev. "You are certain that the vehicles were ready for deployment?"

"There's no doubt in my mind, Commander. And let's not forget, my report covers only one enclave location. There's a dozen on Bajor, each potentially concealing similar weapons stores." She paused and winced, rubbing her eyes.

Captain Jameson, who had remained largely silent during her debriefing, leaned in. "Lieutenant, are you all right?"

"I'm fine, sir," she lied. "Fine" was actually quite a long way from how she felt right now, and there had been a moment out there in the black aboard the *Kaska* when Nechayev had thought she would never feel anything again.

Jekko's courier, its systems finally overwhelmed by the enormous power drain placed on them by the vintage cloaking device, had finally given out. The cascade shutdown had wrecked everything, fusing the systems and terminating life support. Nechayev and Jones climbed into the decrepit emergency environmental suits in the ship's locker and waited for the ice to start forming. Jones slipped into unconsciousness first, as the cold, hard stars wheeled around them. Nechayv tried to stay awake, clutching her phaser in numb fingers, but she followed the other woman into blackness as hypothermia reached in and took hold.

The *Gettysburg* had found them soon after, as Commander T'Vel had told her, homing in on Nechayev's encrypted recovery beacon. The *Kaska* was in the starship's shuttlebay, a few decks below them, being picked over by the engineering crew. Nechayev felt a flicker of guilt; the little vessel had killed itself saving their lives, and it deserved a more noble fate.

"Are you sure you don't want to return to sickbay?" said Jameson. "We can resume this at a later time."

Sickbay. She'd woken up on the biobed gasping for air and panicking, dreaming of snakes. Jones was still down there, sleeping off her recovery. "No, sir," she said firmly, shaking her head. "Captain, with all due respect, this can't wait for a later time. We have to act now."

Jameson and T'Vel exchanged glances. As an operative for Starfleet Intelligence, Nechayev was used to the idea that there would be information that she was not privy to. The concept of "need to know" was integral to being a good operative. As such, she'd learned to recognize when her superiors were holding something back. Nechayev glanced around the room; as well as the captain and his executive officer, she was flanked by Gold and *Gettysburg*'s chief of security, an Andorian female named sh'Sena. She hadn't had the opportunity to get to know them beyond the most cursory of conversations; in her experience, starship crews tended to be tight-knit groups who didn't exactly *resent* the presence of an intelligence operative on temporary assignment to their vessel, but they didn't welcome it either. Of them all, sh'Sena was the only one Nechayev had spent any time with, mostly during the mission preparations before she and Jones had been inserted on Draygo. The Andorian's mood read wrongly to Nechayev's trained eye. *Something has happened. While we were undercover, something happened.*

She turned back to Jameson. "What's changed, sir?"

The captain folded his arms. "Tell me your mission objective, Lieutenant."

"Covert assessment of the political situation on Bajor." She reeled it off automatically. "Primary mission goal: make contact with a local asset in the employ of Bajoran exile Keeve Falor, evaluate all available intelligence, and exfiltrate." She sighed, ignoring for a moment that the planned

silent departure from Bajor had mutated into a headlong
race with Cardassian guns chasing them all the way.

"And what was the purpose of that mission?"

"We were sent in there to answer a question." Her tone
stiffened. "Is the Cardassian Union going to forcibly annex
the planet Bajor?" She jerked her thumb at the still image
of the tank. "Well, sir? You tell me."

"I'd say the answer is clear," Jameson replied. "And the
next question becomes, what are we going to do about it?"

Nechayev read the reply in his eyes and she went cold.
"Nothing."

The captain nodded. "That's right. Starfleet wants us to
stand back and maintain a safe distance. We're to observe and
conduct signals intelligence for the moment, but no more."

Nechayev blinked and leaned forward. "Sir, I'm not sure
if you understand the gravity of the situation. I was down
there, I felt the mood of the people. They're on a knife
edge." She shook her head. "Captain, a man died so I could
bring this information out safely! He gave up his life without hesitation because he thought we were going to help his
world." The agent tapped the tabletop. "We have a window
of opportunity here. Bajor is one step away from governmental collapse, and the Cardassians are giving them a push!
We can stop that, but we have to move on it right away!"

"Without a direct mandate from the Federation Council, we're not going back in," Jameson said flatly.

Nechayev was the veteran of a dozen clandestine missions. She was highly trained, one of the best field agents in
the division. She understood that dispassion was an important factor in maintaining the clinical distance required to
be a covert operative. And yet, as she sat and listened to
the *Gettysburg*'s commander cut off the last hope for Bajor,
something inside her snapped. "I can't accept that," she
retorted. "Those people are in clear and present danger.
We can't just walk away!" The outburst surprised everyone,

Nechayev included. *It's Gwen; all her wide-eyed naïveté has rubbed off on me.*

"But we will," said T'Vel, "because we must." The Vulcan glanced at Jameson, seeking permission, and he nodded. She continued. "Starfleet Intelligence has discovered that the Cardassian Union is operating a concealed listening post *within* Federation space, from a moon in the Delavi system. To use your term, Lieutenant Nechayev, that outpost represents a clear and present danger to the hundreds of Starfleet vessels and colonies that operate within its detection range."

"Command is drawing up an assault plan as we speak," added sh'Sena. "Once in place, we'll take the outpost and neutralize it."

"But in the meantime we have to keep our hands free of the Bajor Sector," said Jameson. "The Cardassians know we're sniffing around. If they think we're coming into the area in force, they'll go dark. You know how they work; the Delavi outpost will be abandoned and they'll set up somewhere else, somewhere we *don't* know about."

"Starfleet will lose the opportunity for the intelligence coup of the decade," said the Andorian. "Delavi is the keystone for the Union's surveillance operations in the Federation."

Nechayev nodded slowly. "So we let Bajor get swamped by Cardassia so we don't tip our hand, is that it?"

"Bajor isn't a part of the Federation," noted Gold. "I don't think anyone here believes it's a good situation, but we have to fight our own battles. Nobody in the Bajoran government has asked for our help. As much as I hate to say it, this is a matter of internal alien politics."

"David's right," said Jameson. "Delavi is a threat to Federation stability, here and now. Bajor . . ." He sighed. "Bajor is a problem for another day. We're spread too thin out here to do otherwise."

"Captain—" began Nechayev.

Jameson shot her a look. "The matter is closed, Lieutenant. For better or worse, the Bajorans are on their own."

"This way," said Darrah, leading Syjin down the ornate corridors of the Naghai Keep. "Don't lag behind."

"I'm coming, don't panic," said the pilot. "I'm just admiring the sights, you know? People like me don't usually get invited into the ancestral home of the Minister for Korto District."

They reached the heavy nyawood door to the great library and Darrah shouldered it open. "Just don't steal anything." He strode inside, and Syjin followed him in.

The pilot tilted his head back to take in the multiple levels of the chamber. "Ooh. Look at that." He clicked his teeth appreciatively. "All those books. I didn't think there were that many in the world."

Darrah beckoned him toward a console set in a six-sided stone table in the center of the chamber. "Stop acting like a tourist and get over here. It's not like you're a big reader anyway."

Syjin walked over, his dusty boots tapping across the marble. "Well, if they have pictures . . ."

"Be quiet!" Darrah growled, removing the memory core from the bag.

"I still don't understand why you brought us here," Syjin frowned. "Seems like a lot of trouble to read some files."

Darrah worked the crystalline keyboard. "This is a stand-alone library computer. No connections to anything outside the walls of the keep, which means there's no path of entry for any data-mining software or surveillance programs. Right now, this console is the equivalent of a locked room." He drew a fistful of glowing optical cables from the bag and connected them to the battered piece of hardware. "Plug these into the interface socket there, behind the wooden edging."

Syjin flipped open the finely tooled panels and locked the connectors home. "Done."

Darrah placed his hands flat on the panel. "All right. Let's take a look. See what we have."

"Take a look at what, Darrah?" Both men glanced up, startled. Two levels above their heads, in the racks of scrolls from the Second Republic era, Vedek Gar leaned over the handrail and watched them warily. The cleric moved to a wrought-iron spiral staircase and made his way down, talking as he descended. "What are you doing here? Haven't you seen what's going on out in the city?"

Darrah had automatically drawn his pistol, but he didn't holster it again straightaway. "I've seen," he replied. "Believe me, I've seen it."

"Syjin?" Gar continued. "Is that you? Prophets, you haven't changed a bit."

"Uh, Vedek," managed the pilot. "Hello."

Gar exited at their level and approached. "You have a weapon there, Mace. Are you expecting trouble?"

"I'm always expecting trouble," he said cautiously. "Part of my job."

The priest glanced at the memory core. "So. I repeat my question. Take a look at what?" He reached for the device. "This?"

Darrah interposed himself between Gar and the memory core. "I'm going to use the library computer. It won't take long."

There was a moment of awkward silence. "Do you want me to leave?" Gar asked. "Oh. It's private, is it? Something you don't want to share with an old friend?"

Darrah's tone cooled. "Didn't you tell me you couldn't afford to be that anymore, *Vedek?*" He put emphasis on the title. "You said you were too busy for that kind of thing."

Gar frowned. "I'm sorry if I offended you. That wasn't my intention." He reached out his hands and touched Darrah on one shoulder, and Syjin on the other. "Recent years have put a great distance between us, haven't they? But on a day like today, we need to be close again." He shook his head. "Bajor needs our strength."

"Mace, let's just do this," said Syjin. "We're wasting time."

Darrah holstered his gun and activated the console. "All right."

A data pane appeared as the ornate machine linked to the data storage device, a holographic screen shimmering into being above the stone table. The cleric gasped as he read the information presented there. "The *Clarion?* This is from the warship *Clarion?*" He shot a look at Syjin. "You found this in space? Where?"

"Ajir IX," said the pilot. "There was wreckage all over the surface of a moon. It was pure accident that I happened to be there." He grimaced. "Probably nothing left now, not after the Ferengi got to it."

"Ferengi?"

He nodded. "A nasty little scumdrinker called Grek. But at least I got this away from him."

Gar smiled. "We have the Prophets to thank for guiding you, Syjin. You've done their work by bringing this recording home."

Darrah worked the console, filtering through layers of stored information. "There's some corruption, but it's still readable. I think I can play back the feed from the *Clarion*'s bridge monitors . . ."

The holographic sphere trembled and became a portal into events five years in the past. The display showed the command deck of the Space Guard warship, the crew moving on errands of duty. Beneath the main image, smaller data panels showed environmental information, sensor readings, power curves. Syjin leaned closer. "Systems all seem okay," he noted. "When was this?"

"I spooled back to a few minutes before the recording stops," explained Darrah.

Gar pointed at a figure who wasn't sporting the same gray uniforms as the *Clarion*'s bridge crew. "That's Lonnic Tomo."

Her voice issued out of a hidden speaker, laced with static, but still clearly the woman they knew. *"We have nothing but circumstantial evidence that the Tzenkethi were even involved!"*

Darrah ignored the stab of emotion that came from seeing his friend alive and well once again. He steeled himself, knowing what would come next.

They listened in silence to the voices of the dead. *"Sensor sweep complete. I can confirm the presence of volatile stocks aboard the alien vessel, sir. Refined triceron, military grade."*

"They found the Tzenkethi," said the priest.

Syjin waved a hand at Darrah. "This part we know. They located the marauder and engaged it. But what happened then?"

Darrah moved the recording along in skips; they saw the engagement in fast-forward, the battle unfolding in blinks of motion. The destruction of the scouts, the fighting between the assault ships and the marauder.

Syjin's hand stabbed out. "There! Stop it there!" He pointed at a time index. "Play that."

Voices crackled through the halls of the library. *"New contacts, bearing two-one-seven mark seven!"*

"More Tzenkethi?"

"No. Cardassian. A pair of light cruisers. They're closing . . ."

None of the men spoke as they watched the Cardassian ship commit murder; first the biogenic weapons were transported aboard the Tzenkethi craft, then the same horrific tactic employed on the *Glyhrond* and the *Clarion*.

Darrah's blood rumbled in his ears, and for a moment he felt as if he was going to throw up.

They saw the deaths unfold. *"Get the shields back up now!"*

"Bioweapons . . . They're beaming them in all over the ship! Deflector shields are inoperative!"

"What did they do?" Syjin gasped. "What did they do?"

"They killed them all," Darrah said in a low voice, leaden with disgust and revulsion. Gar, his face a mask of static shock, reached out to stop the playback, but Darrah shook his head. "No. There's more. We owe it to them to hear everything." On the screen, among the dead and the dying, Lonnic threw herself over to the communications console and tried to speak.

Darrah saw a change come over her face, a terrible acceptance that her end was only moments away. She stiffened. *"This is Lonnic Tomo aboard the Bajoran Space Guard warship* Clarion," she began. *"We are under attack by Cardassian vessels. They have already . . . killed the crew of the* Glyhrond *and a Tzenkethi marauder, and—"*

With that, she died and slumped to the decking. The replay went on, showing no movement, recording only silence.

"That's not what was broadcast," Syjin grated. "The last message from the fleet they played on the newsfeeds, after they went missing, it was different . . . They changed it!"

Darrah nodded. "To hide the Cardassian involvement. To stop us from knowing who really used that marauder to attack us five years ago."

Gar blinked. "What are you suggesting?"

The lawman glared at the priest. "I'm not suggesting anything! You saw the same thing we did, Osen! There never was a Tzenkethi threat! The Cardassians engineered a lie for us to fall for, and we did. . . ." He shook his head. "Prophets save us, but we did."

"Clearly, this is a most serious revelation," Gar spoke carefully, moderating his words. "But we can't afford to act emotionally. We must be rational."

"Rational?" Syjin bleated. "How can you be so cold-blooded?"

"I am not!" Gar retorted hotly. "But what do you propose to do with this information? Where will you take it? What if *it* is the lie, something created by the Tzenkethi or the Federation to discredit—"

Darrah silenced him with a gesture, ripping the cables out of the connector sockets and stuffing the memory core into the bag again. "You're right. He's right. We can't do anything with this. We have to give it to someone who *can* use it, keep it safe."

"There are deep reliquaries beneath the Kendra Monastery," Gar said quickly. "Many places where it could be concealed."

Syjin shook his head. "We can't hide this! We have to use it!"

"The Chamber of Ministers in Ashalla," said Darrah. "We take it to them. Show them all what we have seen. They won't be able to deny it, Lale and Kubus and all the other Union sympathizers."

"How will you get in?" demanded Gar.

Darrah gathered up the bag. "Jas Holza is there. I can get to him."

Gar called after them. "Jas? He's nothing! He won't lift a finger to go against the majority!"

"He will hear me out," Darrah replied. "For Lonnic's sake, I know he will listen."

24

Syjin angled the police flyer into the sky and pushed the throttle to maximum. A thin rain was starting to fall, and it streamed off the canopy as the pilot guided them upward. "I'll get over the clouds, get some altitude."

Darrah watched Korto fade away as the thin white haze enveloped them. In a way, he was willing it to happen, for the city to be covered so that he wouldn't have to see the blemishes of fires and rolling chaos in the streets. There was a riot of garbled communications overlapping across the Militia bandwidths. Darrah skipped down the channels and found nothing conclusive; only one fractured, static-laced report stood out. "Did you hear that?" he asked.

Syjin shook his head. "Something about Cardassians." Sunlight flooded the cockpit as they burst out of the cloud layer.

"Troops. I thought I heard him say 'Cardassian troops.'" The inspector rubbed his face with his hand. "It's starting."

"We'll make it to Ashalla," Syjin assured him. "We've got just enough fuel for the trip."

Both men fell silent. Minutes passed and neither uttered a word, the two friends looking inward, trying to take stock of the terrible things they had learned. Finally, Syjin let out a sigh. "Mace?" When Darrah didn't answer, the other man gave him a sideways look. "Mace? Look . . . I have to say this, because it's eating me up inside."

"Say what?"

"Those logs . . . I just can't help thinking about what Gar said."

The priest had decided to remain in Korto; he had promised to get to Vedek Arin and pass on the revelation from the *Clarion*'s data core to the senior cleric. Darrah eyed the pilot. "What are you talking about? You saw Lonnic, you saw the bioweapons! You saw it, for fire's sake! With your own eyes."

"Did I?" Syjin replied. "I mean, I just can't help thinking, what if that was a fake? Something engineered by the Circle or the Federation or the Tzenkethi, who knows? What if it was left there and I was meant to find it? Maybe . . . maybe Grek led me there deliberately! He could be in on it."

"No," Darrah insisted. "Those log recorders are tamperproof. A subspace signal, that can be manipulated, but that memory core is unalterable. That playback, that was what happened."

"Can you be sure of that?" Syjin insisted. "Do you really believe that I found that unit because the Prophets wanted me to?" He snorted. "I haven't seen the inside of a temple since I was a boy! I'm hardly the best choice!"

Darrah turned in his seat. "It doesn't matter how or why! Why can't you accept the evidence of your own eyes?"

"Why can't you deny it?" came the reply. "You're the lawman, you're the one who distrusts everything. It could be fake! How is that idea any less likely than yours, that the Cardassians have been fomenting a conspiracy with men in our own government?"

"Because I'm certain!" Darrah roared. "More certain than I have been about anything in my life!" He glared at the pilot. "I've seen more lies than any man should . . . and I know the truth when I find it."

Syjin sagged against his flight restraints. "I hope you're right. Because if you're wrong, we've both thrown our lives away."

Darrah shook his head and rested his hand on the pack. "We get this to Jas, and he'll make sure that Coldri and the others see the recording."

"Jas Holza," said Syjin coldly. "Everyone knows he's weak. What makes you think you can trust him not to fold and give it to Kubus or the spoonheads?"

Darrah felt the shape of the device beneath his fingertips. "He won't, he needs this. He needs what it represents. A chance to redeem himself."

An alert signal blared, lighting a proximity warning glyph on the console. Syjin jerked as if he had been struck. "We've got company. An orbital cutter, dropping down from the ionosphere."

Darrah looked out the window. He could make out a shape above, a dark dart with a thin white contrail. "Cardassian?"

"What do you think?" the pilot said snidely.

"How did they find us?" Darrah demanded.

"Right now, that doesn't matter—" Syjin's words turned into a yelp of pain as a searing white bar of light crossed the nose of the police flyer. The aircraft bucked and groaned as a string of emergency lights flashed on. "Warning shot?"

"No." Darrah was grim. "His aim was off. He's too eager. If he'd waited a second longer, we'd be atoms."

Syjin gripped the control yoke and wrenched it back and forth. The blue sky beyond the canopy spun lazily, gravity tugging at them. "They cooked off the steering canards on the nose," he reported through gritted teeth. "We're losing height." Another beam flashed through the portside windows, and the flyer resonated as if it had been struck by a huge hammer. Syjin's console became a field of red warnings. "Ah," he muttered. "My mistake. We're not losing height. We're crashing." The nose of the aircraft began an inexorable drop, falling below the horizon.

"Can you put us down safely?" Darrah called.

The pilot released his straps, tossing them aside. "Not a chance. He's coming back for another pass. We'll be scrap iron before we hit the cloud layer."

"What are we going to do?"

Syjin reached out and grabbed the pack from him. "Well, I'm going to do this." The pilot's hand ducked into his jacket, and Darrah heard an answering beep; then with a glitter of light he dematerialized, leaving the lawman alone in the plummeting flyer.

He exploded with rage and shouted at the sky. "Syjin, you son of a whore, don't leave me to die!" Darrah struggled out of his straps, ignoring the sun-flash off the Cardassian cutter as it turned to bring its guns to bear. He threw himself toward the hatch. "I'll haunt you the rest of your living days, you cowardly little—"

Syjin's face split with a grin as the column of golden radiance grew dense and formed into the shape of a man. Darrah stumbled forward out of the transporter alcove, saw him, and yelled. "Bastard!"

The punch came wild and hit the pilot in the jaw, throwing him to the deck. His head rang like a struck gong and he spat. "That's a fine way to thank a man who just saved your life!"

Darrah shook off his moment of disorientation, glancing around the cramped interior space. "Where are we?"

"My ship," said Syjin, gingerly probing the side of his jaw. "In orbit. Sorry about giving you a fright back there, but my transporter's a basic model. It can't manage more than one person at a time. If I'd brought us both up at once, there's no telling what might have happened." He sighed. "Honestly, I'm surprised the damn thing worked. Every time I use it I think I'm going to end up scattered to the solar winds."

Darrah grabbed the strap of the pack and Syjin caught the other end; they engaged in a brief tug-of-war. "Let go," snapped the lawman. "Reset the coordinates for Ashalla and beam me down."

The pilot couldn't believe what he was hearing. He sighed. Police officers. They gave new meaning to the word "dogged." "Did you miss all the shooting, exploding, crashing stuff just now?" Syjin pulled at the pack. "Think, Mace, think! They knew where to find us! They must be tracking you, or me, or this thing! If they were waiting for us in the air, don't you think they might be waiting for you in Ashalla as well? You won't get within a hecapate of the Chamber of Ministers." He saw the comprehension on the other man's face, and Darrah let go of the bag.

"If we can't get to Jas, then we're stymied." Darrah crossed to the command deck and sat in the copilot's chair. "I'm willing to bet there's an alert going out for us right this minute." He snorted. "Not that there's anyone paying attention."

Syjin nodded. "In this chaos they'll be able to disappear us, and no one will ever know." He took his chair, commencing the ship's warm-up sequence. "We show our faces on Bajor, we're dead men. We have to get away." The pilot blew out a breath. "There's that free ride to Valo I promised you. Offer's still valid."

But Darrah shook his head, drawing his tricorder from his belt. "No. I've got a better idea."

It took all of Dukat's self-control not to throw the padd in the face of Glinn Orloc, right there on the bridge of the

Vandir. His carefully directed plans to seek out and capture the Starfleet spies had disintegrated around him at the final moment, and now there was nothing. No leads, not a single direction to take that might turn him back on their trail. After beaming back from Korto empty-handed, he ignored Kell's increasingly strident communiqués from Derna and took the *Vandir* out beyond Bajor's orbit, opening up the sensors to search for the cloaked ship; but the zone around the planet was dirty with energy signatures from the large, slow troopships moving down from the lunar base, and the other cruisers that were taking up positions over the major cities, in case a punitive bombardment was needed to push along the collapse. Any ion trail or energy residue would be lost in the clutter, like one single voice subsumed inside the rattle of a hurricane.

Bajor was falling, graceless and slow, and Skrain Dukat should have been there to see it. Instead, he was sifting through empty space searching for a ship that had already escaped.

"Nothing," he growled, referring to the contents of Orloc's report. "The finest vessel the Union has to offer, and we can find nothing?" He glared at Tunol, demanding an answer when he knew there was none she could give; but the officer had a wary look on her face, as if she had something to tell him that would irritate him further. "Speak, Dal!" He barked. "If you have something to say, spit it out!"

She licked her lips. "Incoming signal, sir. Source is, ah, encrypted."

"Ico," he spat, his ire rising a notch. "Put the witch on." The woman's face shimmered into being on the viewscreen. Her ever-present, insufferable smile was in place. Dukat wondered how much it would take to dislodge that infuriating mien, and privately hoped that one day he would have the chance to find out. He spoke before she

had a chance to open her mouth. "What do you want?" demanded the gul. "I'm still trying to clean up your mess."

Ico took the barb in good humor and dismissed it. *"This is becoming a very interesting day, Dukat,"* she said conversationally. *"Opportunities, some taken, some missed. And now something unusual."* The woman smiled, as if in reference to some private joke. *"Acts of the past return to haunt us. Like Ajir."*

He stiffened at the mention of the star system. "Get to the point, if you can. Or is there something in the Obsidian Order's training that makes all its lackeys pedantic and verbose?"

Ico's pallid lips thinned. *"Such effrontery. And after I contacted you with a gift. How rude you are."*

Dukat turned away. "This is another waste of my time. Tunol, cut the channel."

"That would be a grave mistake," Ico grated, and for the first time there was annoyance in her tone.

Dukat halted his first officer with a wave of the hand, and inclined his head, waiting.

When Ico spoke again, all the usual artifice in her tone was gone. *"It seems you were not as thorough at Ajir as you reported, Dukat. Materials from the Bajoran ships survived their destruction, including a memory core. I don't believe I need to express the concern that will result if the data on that device is broadcast."*

Dukat's muscles bunched under the sleeves of his armored tunic. A dozen questions immediately assailed him, but the most important pushed through to the front of his thoughts. "Where?"

"I believe it is aboard a Bajoran light freighter running under this transponder ident." A code string bloomed in the corner of the screen, and Tunol set to work on it. *"They're doubtless going to make an attempt to flee the system. Perhaps, Gul, you might be able to redeem yourself by catching this one."*

"How did you come across this information?" he demanded. "What's your source, Ico?"

She didn't answer him. *"It would be unwise for you to fail twice in one day, Dukat."* The viewscreen went dark.

He grimaced and looked away. None of the junior officers would meet his gaze.

"Sir?" Tunol beckoned him from the sensor console. "The transponder code checks out. A ship with that ident is registered at Korto starport. Traffic Control logs it as entering Bajoran space several hours ago."

"Where is it now?"

She worked the panel, bringing up a tactical plot of the B'hava'el system. A white square flashed, moving slowly out from the orbit of Bajor along the plane of the ecliptic. "Here. At full impulse, we can be on them in ten metrics."

"I grow tired of being at her beck and call," Dukat said in a low voice. "She's trying to diminish me in the eyes of my crew."

Tunol inclined her head. "With respect, sir, the only order valued by the crew of the *Vandir* is that which comes from you."

Dukat allowed a small smile. "Then my order is given. Obliterate that ship."

Darrah Mace was careful to double- and then triple-check the data as he input the code string into the communications grid. He glanced at the tricorder again, selecting the correct subspace frequency.

"If you're thinking about wide-banding that recording, you can forget it," Syjin informed him. "This old bird doesn't have that kind of capability."

"I'm not doing that," he replied. "I'm . . . I'm calling in a debt."

"That's a Federation code," said the pilot, with alarm. "Is there something you're not telling me, Mace?"

"Plenty," Darrah replied, "so just concentrate on the flying. When can we go to warp?"

"Soon," came the answer. "Just after we clear the belt." The words were barely out of his mouth when an alert chimed on Syjin's panel. He groaned. "Didn't we just do this once already?"

"Cardassians!" Darrah saw the sensor screen react. "A *Galor*-class cruiser, closing fast. We're no match for a ship of that tonnage."

"No, really?" Syjin mocked. "Do you think?"

"It's the *Vandir*," noted the lawman. "Huh. That's Gul Dukat's command."

"A friend of yours?"

Darrah shook his head. "Not even close."

Syjin sneered. "Well, I make it a rule never to have more than one ship blown out from under me on a given day." He poured more power to the impulse drive, and the ship surged forward. "Let's play a game."

Out beyond the canopy, Darrah saw a wall of glittering dust racing toward them: the Denorios Belt, a ring of charged energetic plasma that existed out beyond the orbit of Bajor. "What are you doing?" he asked, in the most reasonable tone he could manage. "I know I'm not a starship pilot like you, but isn't the belt, to put it mildly, extremely dangerous?"

"That's one way of thinking of it, yes," Syjin replied. His fingers danced over the helm controls as disruptor blasts arced past them. "But less dangerous than a *Galor*-class starship."

"You're sure about that?"

Syjin shrugged. "Not really."

They plunged into the belt at maximum speed, with the *Vandir* close behind. The cruiser was surprisingly nimble, vectoring hard to dodge around pockets of rippling gaseous energy that Syjin avoided with ease. Darrah kept silent, watching his friend do what he did best—fly by pure instinct. Syjin's face was oddly placid, except for the occasional smile. He was actually *enjoying* this; without the fetters of gravity and atmosphere, ship and pilot moved in perfect step, dancing rather than flying.

Behind them, *Vandir* came on, the deflectors of Dukat's warship flaring as it forced its way through clusters of energized neutrinos that would have sent the smaller Bajoran ship tumbling.

"He's still on us," Darrah said as the shuddering, spinning turns became more forceful. His throat was dry.

"I know," Syjin replied calmly. "Careful, now. This is going to get rough." He smiled. "Well, *rougher.*"

They took a hit, and then another. A panel behind them crashed and broke apart. Over their heads, a conduit ruptured and a puff of hot gas emerged, spitting and dying away as automatic sealants activated. They were rolling and bouncing, up and down, back and forth. It was all Darrah could do to cling to the restraints of his chair. "This isn't like before," he managed, between gritted teeth. "This is worse."

"Just hold on," Syjin told him.

Gul Dukat appeared to have other ideas; the disruptor barrage was finding their range, zeroing in.

"I'm looking for something," continued the pilot.

"What, the Celestial Temple?" As boys, Prylar Yilb had taught them that the belt, visible from Bajor with the naked eye during the solstice, was fabled in myth as the place where the Prophets made their home. Darrah had never really believed that, not in a literal manner, but suddenly he was wondering. Were his gods going to reach out and smite the Cardassian ship snapping at their heels?

Syjin read his mind. "The Prophets help those who help themselves." He grinned as a telltale flashed on his console. The pilot turned the ship and aimed it like an arrow. "My

father was a pilot, my grandfather, and his before him ...
And the tricks get lost sometimes, but other times they get
passed on." A rumble echoed through the ship, and a sudden acceleration took them. "Hold on," Syjin called, strain-
ing to say the words. "I found us a boost!"

With a blink of energy discharge, the Bajoran ship
skipped out of the Denorios Belt, cast like a stone thrown
out over a lake. The *Vandir* was still chasing them, but it fell
behind, slipping off the close-range proximity scope.

Eventually the speed bled away and the velocity-
distorted stars became more regular as they settled into
normal warp flight. Darrah gingerly got out of his chair.
"What was that, the hand of god?"

"You could call it that," Syjin said, wiping a film of
sweat from his brow. "Actually, that was a tachyon eddy.
The old Republic solar sailors used to use them to propel
themselves to other star systems, back before we had light-
speed drives." He mimed a sail with the blade of his hand.
"Like a coastal wind pushing a yacht."

"I thought that was a spacer myth," Darrah replied. "A
bar-stool story for the elderly crocks who can't see to fly
anymore."

Syjin shot him a grin. "Now you know different. In
the old eras, they used to make a sacrament to the Prophets before they crossed the belt, so maybe you were right.
About the 'hand of god' thing."

Something caught Darrah's eye and he bent to examine
the engineering panel. "I don't think so. Not unless they
want to call us back to the Celestial Temple pretty soon."

"What's wrong?" Syjin vaulted out of his seat.

There, on the console, the system status display showed
a rupture running the entire length of the ship's port drive
nacelle. "We're bleeding plasma." Darrah frowned. "Must be
from one of those disruptor hits."

Syjin grimaced. "Speed's dropping. We'll be bounced

out of warp and stuck on impulse, light-years from anywhere," he spat. "It'll take years on sublight to reach the nearest planet! We'll starve first!"

Darrah shook his head and tapped the long-range sensor display. "No, we won't." The *Vandir* was still following them. "Dukat's going to solve that problem for us."

"Give me that again," said Jameson, turning in his chair to look across the bridge at Ensign Muhle.

The *Gettysburg*'s Tiburonian communications officer nodded, one hand pressing a transceiver to his large ear. "Confirming, sir. Signal prefix identified as mission code for Lieutenant Alynna Nechayev."

The captain glanced at the woman in question. "You have an explanation, Lieutenant?"

"Yes, sir," she replied, aware that all eyes on the bridge were on her. "Before we escaped Bajor, I managed to . . . cultivate a new intelligence asset. The man who aided our flight, a local law enforcement officer named Darrah Mace."

"You coerced a Bajoran into becoming a Federation operative without consulting your operational commander?" T'Vel said coldly. "A very risky action."

"It seemed like a good idea at the time," she replied curtly. "I thought he might have access to information that could be useful." Nechayev sighed. "That was before we decided to abandon Bajor to the Cardassians, of course."

Jameson frowned at the comment. "Gold," he called, nodding to the other officer. "Passive sensors, please. What do we have at the coordinates the signal originated from?"

"Working," said the lieutenant. "Here we go. One Bajoran ship at impulse, fluctuating power levels. Can't get a life sign reading at this range."

"Anything else?"

Gold widened the search area. "Oh boy. That's a yes,

Captain. Another contact, reads as a Cardassian cruiser. He's coming at them like he's hungry."

"Position?"

"Close to the Federation border," Gold replied.

T'Vel raised an eyebrow. "But not close enough for a sanctioned intervention."

Nechayev rounded on the Vulcan. "That's a distress call, Commander! Sent specifically to this ship!" *To me*, she added silently. "Are you suggesting we ignore it?"

"I am suggesting nothing," said the woman, unruffled by the lieutenant's words. "In this matter, any involvement is wholly at the discretion of the ship's captain."

Jameson sat quietly in his chair, his hands knitted before him, staring at the stars on the viewscreen.

The *Vandir* arrived and brought hell with it. Bright spears of glowing energy reached out to pierce the ship, and the vessel was bathed in a crackling glow.

Inside, Darrah and Syjin were thrown about as the shields fluttered. "You have any weapons on this thing?" demanded the lawman.

"A laser cluster on the nose, if it still works," Syjin replied, clinging to his console. "That'd only irritate them, I think."

"We have to stay out off their disruptor arc." Darrah did his best to help at the copilot's station. "Keep agile."

"Easier said than done." Another blast slammed into them, and sparking electrical shorts crawled across the deck plates. "We're losing deflectors. He gets a direct hit on us and we're not even going to have time to feel it."

"Aft shields at twenty percent." Darrah worked the console. "I'm transferring power from the forward array."

Gravity had been the first thing to go, and the inside of the cockpit was a mess of floating dust, pieces of stale food, and sundry other bits of debris. Syjin threw himself out of his seat and pivoted to land neatly at the engineering station. "Hold it together, Mace, just for a moment." The ship hummed as another bolt kissed the dorsal shields. "Bah. No call for surrender? This Dukat's got no class at all."

"No argument there," Darrah grated, pulling the ship this way and that. He lacked the skill of his friend, but the threat of imminent death made any man a fast learner. But he couldn't escape the feeling that the *Vandir* was toying with them, bracketing the Bajoran ship with beam-fire, herding them into a kill zone.

"Still," Syjin said, a laugh in his voice. "This is exciting, isn't it?" The pilot worked frantically to divert precious energy from non-critical systems to the shields.

"What?" Darrah couldn't believe his ears.

"We used to play space battles as kids, didn't we? You and me and Osen, behind that big old *kava* tree outside the docker dormitories—"

The next bolt that hit them punched through the weakening shields like they were vapor. The disruptor beam sheared off the starboard nacelle entirely and released superheated plasma back into the ship, letting it unfold in a wild, uncontrolled reaction. Seeking the path of least resistance, it cracked up through the hull and touched a power conduit. Systems all over the ship exploded like bombs, including the engineering console. The detonation overpressure punctured Darrah's eardrums, and in horrifying silence he saw Syjin pinwheel around the cabin to collide with the far bulkhead. The pilot was blown across the room, a ragged doll trailing streamers of blood that coiled away in zero gravity.

He forgot the controls and screamed his friend's name, floundering after him through the acrid and choking air. Syjin kept drifting away from him, still turning gently, as if he didn't want Darrah to see his ruined face.

Lights were going out all around him, and suddenly

the air felt thick and greasy, hard to push down into his lungs. Darrah kept reaching for his friend, fingers sweeping and missing at the cuff of his blood-soaked jacket. Behind him, a black pack drifted across the cockpit, the mass of the object inside carrying it on an aimless course.

"Confirm motion-kill," noted Orloc. "Target has lost power. Life support has failed." He looked up at Dukat. "I can send men aboard, sir, or bring it into the bay."

"New contact," said Tunol. "Dropping from warp, closing on intercept vector."

Dukat shot her an angry look; he was a breath away from giving the final order to fire. "Identify it," he scowled.

"Federation," she said, with a lilt of surprise. "A light cruiser."

"They're hailing us," reported a glinn. "Shall I respond?"

"Of course not," Dukat snapped. "They've got no jurisdiction here, no matter how close to their borders they say we are. Starfleet can watch me dispatch this annoyance and then complain to our backs as we return to Bajor."

"They might attack," warned Orloc.

"That ship's not a match for us," Dukat began, but a look from Tunol brought him up short. "What?" he hissed.

"Three more vessels of the same class approaching. They must have been hiding in the warp signature of the one we detected." She licked her lips. "Gul, we can't oppose four—"

"Come about!" he snarled, silencing her, angry that he would be denied the chance to defy Starfleet to its face. "Orloc! Load a seeker munition into the aft tube and program the Bajoran's silhouette into the warhead. Fire when ready."

"Coming about," Tunol reported. "Course?"

"Bajor." Dukat spat the word back at her. "Maximum warp. We are done with this fool's errand."

From behind him, Orloc called out. "Seeker away and running."

"They're taking the bluff," said Nechayev. "The Cardassians are moving off."

"Good," replied Jameson. "If he didn't, we'd be stuck here going head to head with nothing but sensor phantoms for backup." It had been the captain's idea to manipulate *Gettysburg*'s warp signature to produce a series of echoes; to a cursory scanner sweep, they would seem like a flotilla of identical starships.

"The Bajoran ship's coming apart at the seams," reported Gold. "Scanning. I'm reading one life-form on board."

"The Cardassian ship has ignored all hails—" Muhle started to speak, but T'Vel's strident tones broke over him.

"Cardassian is firing." She was clipped and firm. "Seeker missile."

Jameson shot Nechayev a hard look. They were running at Red Alert status, ready to meet any attack with equal force; the *Gettysburg*'s crew had crossed swords with the Cardassian Union on more than one occasion. "Are we the target?"

"Negative!" replied Gold. "He's going to warp, and the seeker's homing straight in on the Bajoran!"

"Captain," Nechayev pressed. "We have to get that man out of there."

He didn't respond to her. "Lieutenant Gold, are you certain? Are we the seeker's target?"

"No, sir," said the officer. "It's entering terminal phase now, ten seconds to impact. Nine. Eight—"

Jameson nodded to T'Vel, and the Vulcan gave the order. "Lower the shields. Transporter room?"

"Ready, Commander." Nechayev heard Gwen Jones's voice on the other end of the intercom.

"Lock on and energize."

◆ ◆ ◆

By rights, Jones should have still been in sickbay, but she was going stir-crazy in the starship's medical center and when the alert condition sounded, she took the opportunity to assist the *Gettysburg*'s crew at their stations; and besides, it would help if the first face Darrah saw was a familiar one.

Across from her in the transporter room, Lieutenant Commander sh'Sena and a Bolian ensign named Jolev were poised with their phasers drawn, with Nurse Tepper standing nearby with a medical kit. The Andorian, it seemed, was willing to take no chances.

"Transporter room?" T'Vel's crisp tones cracked over the intercom.

"Ready, Commander." The technician at the console gave her a thumbs-up sign.

"Lock on and energize."

"Energizing," reported the operator, shifting the slider pads on the panel. A human shape accreted in the blue-white halo of the transporter effect, and Jones stifled a gasp as Darrah Mace's face came into being. His expression was one of pain and shock.

The beaming process concluded, and Darrah collapsed to the floor. Jones rushed to his side, with Tepper at her heels. The nurse popped a hypospray at the Bajoran's neck, waving a medical tricorder at him.

A strong odor of burnt plastic radiated from the man, and he coughed harshly. He blinked and focused on Jones, gulping down air. "You?" Blood leaked in thin trails from both his ears.

"It's me," she confirmed.

He pushed Tepper away, trying to get to his feet, wobbling where he stood. "The pack . . ." He croaked. "Where's the pack?"

"I don't understand," said Jones, reaching for him.

He didn't seem to hear a word she was saying. "All in the core," he muttered, losing his balance. "The core. In the ship. Syjin . . ."

"The ship's been destroyed," said the technician. "We barely yanked him out in time."

"No," Darrah gurgled, coughing up thin bile. "Prophets, no! They all died . . . They all died for it . . ." He clutched at Jones's sleeve, flailing. The Bajoran tried to say something else, but his words became a hollow gasp and he buckled.

Tepper snapped her tricorder closed. "He's badly injured. Beam us directly to sickbay."

Jones watched the man shimmer and vanish. On her hands where she had touched him there was soot and dark, arterial blood.

Eventually, when the muscles in his legs became rigid with cramp and his lungs felt like they were flooded with acid, Bennek stopped running. He hid in the alleyways, burying himself among the wreckage and the abandoned debris of a city that was tearing itself to pieces.

The fear inside him was a kind of terror he had never encountered before. It was a certainty, a complete and utter awareness of one fact: the entire metropolis was geared to destroy him. Every living being he saw, every figure he encountered, all of them wanted Bennek dead.

The Bajorans, running and shouting, some praying and others fighting among themselves for food, for a vehicle, for old hurts given freedom by the anarchy; the Militia, who moved not as policemen did on Cardassia, with boldness inspired from fear of their badges, but skulking in the shadows as Bennek did, afraid for their lives; and the Cardassians, insect-sharp in their black armor, stalking the streets with copper rifles in their grip and armed skimmers preceding them.

Speakers on the skimmers and the few streetscreens that

still worked were broadcasting the same loop of careful speech, a string of platitudes recorded by Lale Usbor calling for calm across the planet and assuring the people that their Cardassian friends were here to help restore peace.

On occasions, as he moved from building to building through the rainy morning, Bennek saw Union soldiers panning tricorders around the streets, the devices bringing them through masses of displaced citizens to groups of swaddled figures hiding in disguise. *Oralians.* Without ceremony or comment, the troopers took Bennek's brethren out of sight of the Bajorans and phasered them down, using high-energy blasts to disintegrate the bodies. They didn't offer them the chance to recant.

The first time, he wept, clutching the leather bag to his chest and rocking in the wet darkness. The second time he just watched, and the time after that, and the time after that.

It took all day to reach the hill district on foot, and then an hour or two more before he was at the ornamental gardens and through to the Naghai Keep. Bennek didn't pause to wonder where the Militia guards had gone; he could hear the humming of skimmers following him up the hill. The sound pressed him on, buoying his aching legs as a swimmer would move on a wave crest. Into the keep, and the corridors beyond. Searching. Searching.

Panic built in his chest, a heavy knot of it like a vise being slowly tightened more and more until his ribs would crack. "What if he is not here?" Bennek asked the question aloud, and it echoed down the corridors. "Oralius save me, but what if he is not here?"

The cleric had gambled it all on this one thing, on the single hope that he would find the man he needed in the Naghai Keep. If he was wrong, then his failure would be total. "Am I the last?" he asked the air. "Am I the last one to walk the Way?"

He turned a corner and his pulse raced. He knew this place: the quarters that the priests of the Celestial Temple had taken after the destruction of the monastery at Kendra. If he was here, it would be in one of these rooms.

He crossed up and down the corridor, finally halting outside a door. "Gar! Gar!" It was hard to speak without gasping. "Are you in there? For Fate's sake, open the door!"

When the latch released, he threw himself at the door and fell inside. The vedek was there, watching him with cool, wary eyes. Words spilled out of Bennek's mouth, babbling gratitude to find his fellow cleric still here, still alive. Gar seemed to find his questions and his appearance here strangely at odds. It was almost as if the Bajoran wasn't aware of the madness enveloping his world. The vedek gave him water and, finally, the panic began to subside. It had been in him so long that the Oralian had almost forgotten what the absence of it felt like.

Gar eyed him. "Why are you here? You must know the keep won't offer you any sanctuary."

Bennek almost cried out in shock. "You would turn me out?"

"I mean that this place won't protect you."

The reality of those words hit him like hammers. The skimmers—they had been so close behind. The soldiers—even now they were likely tracing his steps through the gardens, into the keep, toward the central tower . . . They would find him. It was inevitable. That made this choice all the more important.

Gar seemed to sense the understanding within the other cleric and spoke with gentle care, encouraging him to remember his faith, to take strength from it. Bennek wanted to, so very badly he wanted to, but he saw his beloved Tima's face in his mind's eye, and thought of the dead in the streets. He was afraid he would break down and weep like a child.

The skimmers were outside. He could hear the noise of their engines. Bennek looked up and asked for help. "Can you hide me? Please?"

When Gar shook his head, he felt as if darkness had swallowed him whole. *Denied? He wants to let me die?* Panic returned, swamping him in its embrace. For one moment he longed for the numb nothingness he had felt after learning of Tima's death. And there, in her memory, he found something close to strength.

"I'm sure even Oralius knows that no man can be strong every day," said the Bajoran.

"But now I have to be," Bennek told him, and drew out the contents of the bag he carried. A tiny gasp of sadness escaped him when he saw that the recitation mask he held was damaged, but he pressed on, reaching in again to reveal the nested tube of precious *brangwa*-hide scrolls. He tried and failed to keep his hands from trembling. A choice was made, and words formed on his lips. *I am going to die.* He knew it as clearly as he knew the sun would set and rise again. *Just as Hadlo did, just as Tima and all my brothers and sisters. But Oralius will survive. She must.* "You cannot hide me, I was wrong to ask it of you. I will leave this place, but in the name of our twin faiths, I ask you to do this for me, Osen. Conceal them. Hide the mask and the scrolls from the soldiers and promise me you will never reveal their location as long as you live, not until the soul of Cardassia grows strong again, not until the Voice of Oralius is ready to be heard once more. Tell me you will do this. Swear it!"

The Bajoran looked down at the burden Bennek placed in his hands. Outside, he could hear the approach of Cardassian boots across the wooden floors of the keep. Bennek felt tears blurring his vision. "In the name of your Prophets, *swear it!*"

And then Gar Osen did something odd. He smiled. Not in the warm manner of a friend greeting another friend, or the comradeship of distaff cousins, but in the cold way a victor would take pleasure from the groveling surrender of an enemy.

The door to the chamber shattered under a heavy boot and banged open. Bennek reeled back into the room and fell against a chair. His eyes darted around, seeking another exit, but there was only a barred window and they were eight stories high.

A glinn and a pair of low-ranked garresh entered. The enlisted troopers were bored and annoyed with the detail they had drawn, but the glinn looked confused. He was waving a combat tricorder about and frowning.

"Is there a problem, Glinn?" asked Gar, without even a hint of fear.

"We're tasked to recover all Oralian dissidents for processing," said the officer. He pointed at Bennek. "This is one of them. But my readings are wrong."

"How so?" Gar made it sound like this was some parlor puzzle game. Bennek was frozen at his side, too afraid to speak or to move. The two garresh had their guns aimed squarely at his chest.

The glinn pointed the tricorder at the Bajoran. "I'm getting five Cardassian biosigns in this room, not four." The young officer blinked. "You're not—"

"Lubak Five. Tul One. Karda Nine." Gar said the words with a flat, slightly irritated sigh, moving the mask and the scrolls to his right hand. "Authenticate."

The officer was so surprised to hear a Cardassian code issue from the mouth of the cleric that he input the string into his tricorder without really thinking about it. He read something off the screen and his gray skin whitened. "Forgive me, Agent," he began. "We were not aware that the Order was operating in this zone."

Bennek finally regained control of himself, enough to turn and face the other man. "Agent?" he repeated.

He turned to meet the straight-edged push-dagger that had appeared in Gar's left hand. The blade went right through the gap between his ventral ribs and into his heart muscle. Bennek attempted to speak, but all that emerged was a choking rattle. He fell to the floor, hard, first to his knees and then into an untidy heap. His breath came in wheezing, razor-edged gulps. "Osen . . ." He forced the word from his lips in bubbles of bloody foam.

The priest bent and spoke quietly, so only Bennek could hear him. "Osen? He's dead, Bennek. Nothing is left of him. Do you remember the storm, Bennek? The storm?"

He nodded. It was painful.

"He died then. I've been him ever since."

"Who . . ."

The priest smiled again. The man's voice shifted slightly, the pitch rising. "Don't you know me? I'm so upset."

"Pasir!"

The agent smiled and showed him the mask and the scrolls; then, with a callous toss, he threw them into the fire pit. The ancient wood and *brangwa* hide crackled and popped as the flames bit into them. "Oralius is dead, Bennek. Like you."

"No. No." Each word was agony to speak. "Oralius . . . will live. She will . . . return!" He coughed up thick, coppery bile, the darkness clouding in around him. "One day."

But the other man had walked away. "Glinn," he heard the voice say, a voice that sounded exactly like Gar Osen's, "dispose of that."

When the men had gone, he made a face at the patch of dark blood on the wooden floor. He cleaned it with a hand towel, then threw that into the fire along with the ashen remains of the mask and the ridiculous scrolls. The burning animal hide had given the room a musty air, and he opened the window to let it clear.

With care, he recovered a slim black rod from the spine of an old book, which bent in two to reveal a microcommunicator device. He activated it and spoke a code phrase. In a few moments, it vibrated once to show that the connection was secure.

"I'm sorry to bother you," he began, "I know you have a lot to deal with at this juncture."

"Make it quick," said Ico.

First, he gave her the names of the glinn and the two troopers. They had become aware of his deep-cover assignment, and at this stage there could be no possibility of compromise. Ico assured him the men would be dead before nightfall. Then, as he rubbed the pink, dull skin of his face, he told her about the tricorder. "I'm seeing a marked recession in my biometric masking. This will need to be addressed immediately. If it goes on too long, elements of my original physiology will start to reassert themselves."

He heard her sigh. *"That was an expected side effect. The swiftness of the xenoplasty we performed on you had its disadvantages. But it's a minor problem, and it can be corrected. I'll see to it."*

He thought about that night in the storm, when Pasir Letin became a ghost. The face he now owned was on Gar Osen as the flyer dove toward the lake, carrying the priest to a watery grave. He remembered the transporter beam snatching him away, depositing him in the operating theater, and Ico there, smiling at him. Promising him that all the pain would be worth it. Normally, the process of biometric alteration was lengthy and arduous, but they had accomplished it in hours. He recalled one of the Obsidian Order clinicians telling him how his heart had stopped three times during the process, from the sheer agony of having his body remade. "How?" he asked. "How will you see to it?"

"*I'll arrange for you to come to us. We'll spread the treatments over a longer period this time.*" She paused. "*Was that all?*"

He was looking out the window again. "It's really happening today, isn't it?" He felt a twinge of excitement, like a child presented with an ascension gift. "After so long."

"*Indeed.*" He detected the slightest hint of pride in her voice. "*And we have you to thank for setting us on our way. We have begun tracking down the rest of the Orbs. In time we'll have them all, alongside the gift you sent me from Kendra.*"

"The information about the memory core, the Ferengi . . ."

"*Those issues are being addressed at this moment. Don't concern yourself over them.*"

"And the next phase of my assignment?"

"*All in good time.*"

He switched off the device, placed it back in its place of concealment, and then returned to the business of being Gar Osen, vedek of the Temple of the Prophets.

Dukat advanced along the corridors of the Derna outpost, scowling at any man who got in his way, scowling at the walls and the low ceilings, at the rodent-warren of prefabricated tunnels. The facility had Danig Kell's stamp on it—all brute force and bluntness, without a single measure of grace or intelligence. The jagul imagined himself in the mold of the Bajoran city-lords of history, watching from the high castle keep over the people he ruled; and the Derna moon was the highest castle of them all, a pale disk visible in Bajor's sky in the weak morning light. Kell waited up there, impotent and disconnected from the rabble below, from the real potential of Bajor, waiting for the day when Cardassia Prime would name him Prefect, and governor of the planet.

Dukat found the symbolism of the Derna Base to be beneath him. It was not Cardassian enough. Skulking in the near-lifeless craters of a ball of rock? The Union deserved a more impressive seat of power, something that could stand aloof but be forever watching. Something that was Cardassian in its blood and bone. *A new satellite,* he considered, *something stark and barbed, something that would let the Bajorans know their world had changed.* He wanted the aliens to look up into their sky and see a bright new star, and know it was the eye of Cardassia.

The glinns at either side of the hatch snapped to attention, and Dukat dismissed the thought. The door slid open and he entered Jagul Kell's chambers.

He stepped into the middle of an argument, the moment and tension of it still in the air, suspended only by his arrival. Kell turned an acidic glower from Rhan Ico where the woman sat in a wide chair, and trained it on Dukat. For her part, Ico seemed, as ever, to be entirely composed.

"Gul Dukat. You finally see fit to grace me with your presence."

Dukat folded his arms. *If I had but one dagger, which of them would I kill with it?* He allowed himself to enjoy the fantasy of their murders for a brief interval. There was nearly equal loathing in him for the pair of them.

Kell took his silence for the insolence it was and banged his fist on his desk, making the padds on it jump. "You!" he spat. "Both of you! Does this rank mean nothing?" The jagul drummed his fingers on the status tabs of his armor. "Why am I the last to learn of events taking place beneath me? How dare you operate with autonomy! I am in command here, and I will grant you only the freedom that I deem suitable!"

Ico made herself more comfortable and maintained a bland neutrality. Kell took up a padd and threw it at Dukat, who caught it easily. The faces of the two Federation fugitives looked back at him from the screen. "Spies? Why was

I not informed immediately that our operations here could have been compromised?"

"Time was quite short, and circumstances on Bajor became fluid," ventured Ico. "Perhaps the jagul is not aware of the complexity of—"

"I am aware!" he barked. "Despite your best efforts, Ico, I am fully aware!" Kell pointed a finger at Dukat. "Perhaps I would be more forgiving of this lapse if you had not let these females escape alive, free to take all they know to the Federation Council."

Ico made a derisive noise. "I will be the first to admit that this is a failure on the part of the gul, but we must think in terms of damage limitation. What can the Federation do?" She curled her lip. "They will wring their hands. They will have a debate. Then another and another, then shake their heads and do nothing, all the while nursing their guilt at doing so." The woman leaned back in the chair. "It's too late now. Bajor has been ours for years. What we are doing now is bringing that fact into the light. And by the end of the week, we will make it legal, as if it had always been so."

"But this is not the whole scope of your failure, Dukat!" Kell's color darkened. Dukat saw the look in his eyes. He would not back off. Kell was determined to claim blood from the other officer. "The wreckage on Ajir IX? This . . . this memory core?" Dukat glanced at Ico, knowing exactly where the jagul had gotten that fragment of information. "Did you recover it?"

At last he spoke. "The ship carrying the device was destroyed. I gave the order myself."

"That is not what I asked you!" Kell thundered. "Are you certain it was destroyed?"

"I believe so."

"You *believe so?*" Ico mused. "You do not believe that the Federation ship you encountered took it aboard?"

Dukat's jaw hardened, and he made a mental note to commence a security purge of the *Vandir's* crew the moment he returned to his ship. "I do not. We were driven off by superior numbers, but not before the Bajoran ship was destroyed."

Kell was shaking his head. "As much as I wish I could excise you both, I cannot." He placed his hands flat on the desk. "It is a matter of influence and power . . ." His gaze traced over Ico's insipid smile to bear on Dukat. "And my power is over *you*, Gul."

"All I have done was in service to the Cardassian Union," Dukat answered.

"Liar! You are an ambitious renegade, interested only in your own aggrandizement, and I will personally assure that Central Command learns of the catalog of errors that occurred during your posting here!" He banged the table again. "I am to return to Cardassia Prime where I will accept, as is my due, an elevation to the rank of legate." Kell showed his teeth. "Before I do, I give this order! The *Vandir* is hereby reassigned, and you will return to the fleet in disgrace. I will see you ruined, Dukat! Your father's influence will count for nothing, and if there is any justice, your family will share in your ignominy as well!"

"You have no right . . ." Dukat began.

"Accept your punishment, Skrain," Ico said airily. "Show that you are still a Cardassian, underneath the armor."

He was surprised when Kell rounded on the woman. "You are no better!" he spat. "You have stirred up a hornet's nest down there!" He stabbed a finger at the floor, in the direction of Bajor. "Do you think I do not know the spoor of the Obsidian Order's work? You are to blame for staging the attacks on the Bajoran temples and the stirring up of hate toward the Oralians!"

And more that we can only guess at, Dukat added silently. That was the Order's way; if you could see one of their gambits, you could be certain there were ten more that you could not.

"The only difference between Dukat's arrogance and yours is that you have kept your hands clean throughout it all." Kell turned away from her, choking on his anger.

Ico showed the slightest glimmer of annoyance in those dark eyes. "Then I would say that difference is a most profound and important one, Jagul Kell."

Dukat stepped back and considered them both: Kell, rocking with such coiled fury that he might at any moment suffer some sort of spontaneous coronary; and Ico, the icy hate and concealed disdain for all around her coming off in invisible waves. A dark chuckle caught in his throat, and then suddenly he was laughing at them.

"You dare to mock me?" Kell snarled.

"You mock yourselves!" Dukat retorted with venom. "You are fools, both of you. Your vision narrowed to this pathetic game you play, sparring across Bajor as if it were some private arena for your sport?" He shook his head. "In all of this, as this world falls into Cardassia's grasp, what occupies you the most?" He snorted. "Not succor for our hungry masses, but which of you can use me to score points from the other." He turned away. "You have no understanding of what Bajor represents. I knew it five years ago, a decade ago, and it is still true today."

"Bajor belongs to Cardassia because of what I have done," Ico snapped, her mask of calm cracking. "I have set this in motion."

Dukat laughed again. "You have. Like a child putting a flame to tinder, without foresight to see the inferno that will grow from it." He walked toward the door. "Your plans . . . your schemes will ultimately come to nothing." He halted on the threshold. "And do you know why?"

"Oh please, enlighten us," Ico sneered. "I cannot wait to hear sage council from the common son of a minor archon!"

"You think you know the Bajorans. You don't know

them at all." Dukat felt a flash of sudden insight, a moment of hard, sharp self-knowledge. *I know the Bajorans. They are like me. At heart, struggling, fighting, searching for a path, nursing old hates. Seeking vengeance.* He gave the others one last look, and when he spoke it was with such conviction that neither Kell or Ico could find the words to deny him. "History will prove me right, and I will walk on Bajor again. Of that"—Dukat smiled coldly—"you can be certain."

OCCUPATION DAY TWENTY

◆ ◆ ◆

2328 (Terran Calendar)

Epilogue

The darkness opened up for him, just once, a rush of painful white light flooding into his sensorium. Everything about Darrah ached, as if he had been taken at both ends and twisted like wire. Among the blurs there was a face framed with dark hair, a pleasant face with kind eyes.

"Wenna?" Speaking came hard, but he managed it. He tried to raise a hand to touch her face, but he couldn't get it off the bed. She reached down and took it, her smooth skin against his rough, scarred flesh.

"My name's Gwen, actually," she said, in that not-quite-Hedrikspool accent. "Just rest, Mace. You're okay. Everything's going to be fine."

He had been dreaming, or something close to it. Fires, he remembered. The smell of burning. And dry, rough skin being drawn across his body, serpents massing in the dark. He blinked the motes of dream-thought away, concentrating on the woman. Part of her face seemed pinker than the rest, as if she'd been sunburned. He slowly remembered her in the hangar, the burns there from a phaser's near hit. She looked much better. He wanted to tell her that. But something about her was wrong. He couldn't place it.

The hangar—that seemed like only moments ago. Like the ship, like Syjin, like the explosion. Only moments ago.

"How . . . long?" Darrah labored to make the shape of each word.

Gwen's pretty face clouded, and the darkness started to roll back over him. "Just rest," she repeated.

Darrah didn't want to, but the choice was taken from him. He fell away into the black.

He had no sense of intervening time, just disjointed images, sounds, sensations. When all these finally stitched themselves together, he awoke in the medical center of the Starfleet ship, surrounded by busy people in white jackets. They ministered to him for a while and pronounced him well.

A severe-looking Andorian brought him to a bowed room where one wall was a series of portals looking out over the disk of the starship's primary hull, over a cluster of warp nacelles and out to the static blackness of space. The void reminded Darrah a little too much of the darkness that had claimed him, and he sat with his back to it. He didn't understand the shape and meaning of the rank sigils worn by the blue-skinned woman. She told him her name was sh'Sena. She sat across from him with a human male who tried to look friendly, watching. The Andorian dipped her head forward in that way that her species did, so that the antennae rising from her skull were trained upon Darrah, sensing him. She told him this was a debriefing, but he had given enough interrogations in his life to know when he was on the wrong end of one.

After a while, after a few questions too many, he began to get irritable. "I'm tired of giving you answers and getting nothing back," he snapped. "I want you to do some talking now." He pulled at the collar of the nondescript coverall garment they had given him to wear. It was itchy against his flesh, rubbing the dots of scar tissue from the dozens of small lacerations he had suffered aboard Syjin's dying ship. His hand kept falling to the place on his hip where his phaser would have been; they had let him keep only his earring, although it was tarnished and in need of some repair. He pitched forward suddenly, startling the human. "I've told you what happened on Bajor, now what are you going to do about it?"

"That's not up to me," said sh'Sena.

"Then, who is it up to?" he demanded.

A door slid open and another human entered. He was of average height, athletic, but he carried himself with a poise that Darrah noted immediately. The reactions of the other Starfleet officers confirmed it. This was the commander. "I'm Captain Mark Jameson," he explained. "Mr. Darrah, you have to understand the circumstances. Things have moved very quickly."

Mace was about to argue when a horrible thought struck him. He swallowed hard. "How long? How long was I out for?"

Jameson frowned. "By Bajoran reckoning? You were unconscious for twenty days."

A choke of air caught in his throat. *Like only moments ago.* "Where . . . where are we now?"

"Still in the Bajor Sector. We've been monitoring the situation on your home planet, gathering information and tracking signals. As I said, things have moved quickly while you were recovering."

Darrah felt sick. *What does he mean?* He was gripped with sudden terror that Bajor had somehow been destroyed, the planet flashed to atoms by some catastrophe.

"You do deserve answers," said the captain, getting to his feet. The other two officers followed him to the door. "These people will try to give them to you, if they can."

As Jameson and the others left, two women entered the room. *Alla and Wenna. But not.*

"I'm Lieutenant Alynna Nechayev," said the blond woman. "You've already met Gwen Jones." She nodded to the dark-haired girl.

Jones placed a steaming cup in front of him. *"Deka* tea, from the replicators. It's not quite the real thing, but I thought you'd like it."

"Thanks." He sipped the drink; she was correct. Darrah blinked, and rubbed the ridges on his nose with his index finger. "You both look . . . weird without them."

Nechayev spread her hands as she sat. "This is who we really are."

Darrah nodded, but inwardly he doubted the woman would ever really show him that. She wasn't like Jones, all close to the surface. Nechayev was one of those people who sank into their own depths, hiding almost all of themselves.

"How are you feeling?" asked Jones.

"Lost," Darrah said, with a sigh. "Look, isn't it possible for me to claim asylum or something with you people?"

The women exchanged glances. "If you want to, yes," said Jones.

"And then you could do something? Call in Starfleet?"

Nechayev shook her head. "Doesn't work that way. Bajor is an independent world, Mace. We can't just intervene in its affairs."

"But you can come and spy on us?" He blew out a breath, exasperated. "How can you sit back and let the Cardassians invade?"

Jones's face was sad. "We can't stop it, Mace, because it's already happened. Bajor is under Cardassian occupation."

"What? No! They had troops and tanks, but they don't have control—"

"Yes, they do. Two weeks," Nechayev broke in. "It's been two weeks." She shook her head. "Key figures in the Bajoran Chamber of Ministers have officially announced that the unrest on your planet was caused by a terrorist group, the Alliance for Global Unity. They claimed they were working with militants in the Oralian Way to destabilize

Bajor, funded by the Tzenkethi Coalition and the United Federation of Planets."

"Key figures?" he spat. "Lale?"

"Lale Usbor is dead," said Jones. "Murdered by Oralian radicals, so the newsfeeds would have you believe. Minister Kubus Oak is currently acting as interim secretary for planetary affairs."

Jones tapped a keypad set into the tabletop, and a monitor on the wall ran a series of clips from intercepted public broadcasts. Darrah's gut twisted as he saw Kubus being sworn in at the Chamber. His eye was caught by the sight of Jas Holza in the background. The man's face was a rigid, unexpressive mask. He looked beaten and cowed. Of Militia leaders like Coldri Senn and Jaro Essa there was no sign.

"Kubus has officially gone on record as stating that the Cardassian troops on Bajor are 'peacekeepers,'" Nechayev continued. "He says they were invited in to help bring stability to the planet."

"No one will believe that!"

"It doesn't matter," she replied. "The Federation cannot legally become involved in something that has been given official sanction by the Bajoran government."

"Kubus Oak isn't the Bajoran government!" Darrah snapped. "He's a Cardassian puppet!" He was going to say more, but then he saw new footage unfolding on the screen: images from the rebuilding site at the Kendra Monastery. There was Vedek Arin, calling for calm across the planet and endorsing Kubus's stance; but Darrah couldn't look away from the concerned, faithful expression on the man at his side. Vedek Gar's head bobbed in agreement with everything that Arin said.

Syjin's words came back in a rush. *They knew where to find us! They must be tracking you, or me—*

"Or someone told them," he whispered. The import of that thought, that Gar Osen could be a traitor, made him feel sick. *He performed my wedding ceremony. He blessed my children. We are . . . friends.*

And with the thought of Osen, Mace thought of Syjin, the laughing, wild fool torn apart in a welter of blood. He thought of Proka and Myda, still back there on Bajor. Were they still alive? Had they been gunned down in some back alley, named as terrorists after the fact? He held on to the table, feeling dizzy. With a trembling hand, he reached out and sipped at the unpleasant tea.

After a long moment, Nechayev spoke in a low voice. "We can't do anything for your planet now. But there are operations in place. Other people—this ship, even—are taking steps to oppose the Cardassians."

"And what can I do?" he asked in a dead voice. "A lawman without law to enforce. A man without a world."

"You can take asylum within the Federation if you want, like you said," offered Jones. "Or somewhere else."

He nodded woodenly. "Yes. I'll tell you where you can take me."

Jameson wouldn't let Jones accompany them down to the surface of Valo II, so they said their good-byes in the *Gettysburg*'s transporter room. As Darrah and Nechayev materialized in the square of the main settlement, Mace still had Gwen's *D'jarra* earring in his hand, the one she'd used during the mission. The gift was all she had to give him, she explained, a small piece of Bajor for him to carry.

Darrah glanced at the Starfleet officer. "I can take it from here." A group of Bajorans were approaching them.

Nechayev nodded, hesitating with her hand over her communicator badge. "For the record, I wanted to tell you this. The Federation was wrong to let Bajor slip away. We had a chance to intervene and we didn't. Now the Cardassians have a grip there, and they'll coil around it like snakes with prey." She leaned closer, and her voice became conspiratorial. "I will do whatever I can to help your people resist them. Someone has to."

With a nod, the woman stepped away from him, and in a moment he was alone. Darrah glanced around. He'd never visited Valo II, but he knew the place from images and newsfeeds. A small colony on a temperate world, farms and resorts, the kind of place a man might retire to.

None of that applied to the planet he saw around him now. The settlement was overloaded with people, the adobe buildings crowded out by the sprawls of shantytown shacks made from cargo pods and scavenged metals. It was the mirror of the Oralian encampment outside Korto, but here the people peering warily from the flaps of makeshift tents were all Bajorans.

He recognized the man at the head of the greeting party. "Minister Keeve."

Darrah got a shake of the head in return. "Not for a long time. I'm just Keeve Falor now. And we know you, Darrah Mace. We know you well enough."

They shook hands. Mace frowned. "Jekko Tybe was killed," he told the other man, eliciting gasps from some of Keeve's men. "He saved lives by giving up his own."

Keeve was silent for a moment, then nodded. "He spent it well, then. That's like him. A good man. He'll be missed." He beckoned Darrah after him. "Come on, this way. Valo's not the jewel it once was, but there's still room here. Still room for Bajorans."

They walked. Darrah was curious to see that the place was open, without the divides between *D'jarra* castes he had expected. Keeve saw the question in his eyes and nodded. "We're all Bajorans now, Darrah. Soldier, priest, lawman, minister. We need to look to what's common to us, not what sets us apart from one another."

He halted near a shallow river where ragged children were playing and women worked. Even among all this, there was life and community. For what seemed like the first time in years, Darrah felt hope bloom at the sight of the simple ordinariness of it, the sight of life going on despite all the darkness that threatened it. "What can we do?" he husked, turning to face the other man.

"Resist," said Keeve. "Fight the Cardassians at every turn, gather our strength and weaken theirs. Fight for Bajor."

Darrah nodded slowly. "We turned out backs, and look what it brought us. We turned our backs and they took our world from us."

Keeve smiled and pointed. "Not all of it." Three figures were racing up the riverbank toward them: a teenage boy with long hair and wide eyes, a younger girl who was crying with joy, and behind them a woman who made Darrah's heart lift.

His face split in a smile, and for that moment everything he had lost was returned to him.

THE TEROK NOR SAGA
CONTINUES IN
NIGHT OF THE WOLVES

Appendices

The following is a guide to the specific characters, places, and related material in *Day of the Vipers*. Where such an item was mentioned or appeared previously in a movie, episode, or other work of *Star Trek* fiction, its first appearance is cited.

APPENDIX I: BAJOR

Characters

Arin (male) priest, aide to Kai Meressa

Coldri Senn (male) a high-ranking Militia officer

Cotor (male) a senior vedek at the Kendra Monastery

Darrah Bajin (male) eldest child of Darrah Mace and Darrah Karys

Darrah Karys (female) wife of Darrah Mace

Darrah Mace (male) officer of the Korto City Watch

Darrah Nell (female) youngest child of Darrah Mace and Darrah Karys

Els Renora (female) public defender for Korto Justice Department (DS9/"Dax")

Gar Osen (male) priest, resident of Korto District

Jarel (male) an artist, cousin of Darrah Karys

Jaro Essa (male) Militia officer (DS9/"Homecoming")

Jas Holza (male) Korto District administrator and member of the Chamber of Ministers (TNG/"Ensign Ro")

Jekko Tybe (male) adjutant for Minister Keeve Falor, former partner of Darrah Mace

Kalem Apren (male) member of the Chamber of Ministers (DS9/"Shakaar")

Keeve Falor (male) member of the Chamber of Ministers (TNG/"Ensign Ro")

Kored (male) junior officer aboard the Militia Space Guard vessel *Clarion*

Kubus Oak (male) member of the Chamber of Ministers (DS9/"The Collaborator")

Lale Usbor (male) First Minister of Bajor, succeeding Verin Kolek

Li Tarka (male) colonel in the Militia Space Guard; commanding officer of the Militia Space Guard vessel *Clarion;* father of Li Nalas (Li Nalas first appeared in DS9/"The Homecoming")

Lirro (male) duty technician aboard Cemba Station

Lonnic Tomo (female) senior adjutant to Minister Jas Holza

Meressa (female) kai of the Bajoran faith (DS9/"Indiscretion")

Myda (female) officer of the Korto City Watch

Proka Migdal (male) officer of the Korto City Watch (DS9/"Cardassians")

Rifin (male) captain of the scoutship *Eleda*

Rifin Belda (female) wife of the captain of the scoutship *Eleda*

Syjin (male) freelance pilot and courier

Tikka Rillio (female) a childhood bully who made Syjin's life hell

Tima (female) religious novice

Verin Kolek (male) First Minister of Bajor during 2318

Wule (male) dock chief at Korto's starport

Yilb (male) an old priest who taught Darrah Mace, Syjin, and Gar Osen when they were youths

Places

Avenue of Lights: a central boulevard in the city of Ashalla

Ashalla: capital city of Bajor (*DS9/Mission: Gamma, Book One—Twilight*)

Cemba (aka **Cemba Station):** commerce station and civilian spacedock in high orbit over Bajor

Derna: fourth moon of Bajor. (DS9/"Image in the Sand")

Golana: Bajoran interstellar colony (DS9/"Time's Orphan")

Kendra Monastery: main site of theological study in Kendra Province (Kendra Valley first mentioned in DS9/"The Collaborator"; Kendra Province first mentioned in DS9/"Penumbra.")

Korto City: major metropolis on the northern continent of Bajor, situated in the Korto District of Kendra Province on the banks of the Tecyr River, in the plainslands between the Kendra Valley to the northwest and the Sahving Valley to the southeast. Other locations in the city include the Naghai Keep and its ornamental gardens, the Night Market and the Night Market Temple, the precinct house (headquarters of the city police department), the Edar Bridge, the City Oval (where the city's *bantaca* spire is located), the Hill District, the Low-Caste District, the river docks, and the starport. Public transport around the city is by tram.

Naghai Keep: An ancient castle several thousand years old in the Korto City. Ancestral home of the Jas clan, seat of local government for Korto District. The keep is on a hilltop overlooking the city, set in a series of ornamental gardens, with a ring wall surrounding a central cylindrical tower.

Qui'al: city on the northern continent of Bajor, governed by Minister Kubus Oak (The Qui'al Dam is mentioned in DS9/"Destiny.")

Tecyr River: waterway that flows west from the Perikian Mountains toward the sea. Korto City sits on the river a few miles inland. (The Perikian Peninsula was first mentioned in DS9/"The Circle.")

Tilar: Bajoran peninsula (*DS9: Unity*)

Ships

Clarion: Militia Space Guard heavy assault vessel, commanded by Colonel Li Tarka

Eleda: civilian scoutship belonging to the Jas clan, lost in Cardassian space

Glyhrond: Space Guard heavy assault vessel (named after the Bajoran river)

Kaska: civilian light courier belonging to Jekko Tybe

Kylen: civilian scoutship belonging to the Jas clan, part of reprisal fleet

Pajul: civilian scoutship belonging to the Jas clan, part of reprisal fleet

Food & Drink

cela tea: hot brewed beverage (*Worlds of Star Trek: Deep Space Nine, Volume Two—Fragments and Omens*)

copal: ciderlike beverage

deka tea: hot brewed beverage (DS9/"Wrongs Darker than Death or Night")

hasperat: spicy Bajoran dish, wrapped in a flatbread (TNG/ "Preemptive Strike")

jumja: confection made from the sap of the *jumja* tree (DS9/"In the Hands of the Prophets")

Other

Age of Enlightenment: Bajoran equivalent of the Rennaisance era

bell: a benchmark of time, similar to "o'clock," as in two-bells, ten-bells, etc.

Chamber of Ministers (aka **Council of Ministers**): representational body overseeing the governance of Bajor (DS9/"The Homecoming")

City Watch (aka **the Watch**): metropolitan police force, a division of the Militia. Ranks in the Watch include watchman, constable, senior constable, inspector, chief inspector, captain, and major.

Dakeeni manta: sea creature common to the Dakeen coastal region (Dakeen Monastery was first mentioned in DS9/"The Collaborator")

First Minister: elected political world leader of Bajor (DS9/"Shakaar")

fusionstone: ancient building material (*Worlds of Star Trek: Deep Space Nine, Volume Two—Fragments and Omens*)

grass vipers: gray-skinned snakes

hiuna **leaf:** Bajoran tobacco

kellipate: unit of distance, to *linnipates* (DS9/"Progress")

kosst: A swearword or curse derived from Kosst Amojan. (DS9/"The Reckoning") However, the words' original meaning was simply "to be." (DS9/"The Assignment")

linnipate: unit of distance, roughly two or three meters

lugfish: large, slow, and ugly fish

Lupar's Summer Tales: a series of popular folk fables

nyawood: type of wood, similar to mahogany

Orb of Truth: one of the Tears of the Prophets, the first Orb taken by the Cardassians. (*DS9/Mission: Gamma, Book Three—Cathedral*)

porli **fowl:** a chickenlike food animal

Space Guard: space naval forces, a division of the Militia

Tears of the Prophets (aka **Orbs):** mysterious objects that sometimes impart visions or insights upon those who gaze into them (DS9/"Emissary")

tessipate: unit of area, (DS9/"Progress")

Tilar's New Insights: a volume of religious tracts regarding the worship of the Prophets

tyrfox: wily canine predator

Vedek Assembly: council of religious leaders (DS9/"In the Hands of the Prophets")

Yerrin syndrome: an incurable genetic blood disorder

Religious Ranks

The following is a breakdown of known ranks in the Bajoran religion, as established in various episodes of *Star Trek: Deep Space Nine,* in ascending order.

prylar: a monk

ranjen: a monk specializing in theological study

vedek: a high-ranking priest, typically a regional spiritual leader

kai: the world leader of the Bajoran religion

D'jarra *Caste System*

Until recent times the Bajorans had a series of castes called *D'jarra*s. This is a rough order of ranking for the ones that have been established so far.

Ih'valla: artists (above *Te'nari*) (DS9/"Accession")

Te'nari: unknown, but below *Ih'valla* (DS9/"Accession")

Mi'tino: low-ranked merchants and landowners

Va'telo: pilot, sailor, driver, and similar professions

Ke'lora: laborers and lawmen

Imutta: Those who deal with the dead, the "unclean" and lowest-ranking *D'jarra* (DS9/"Accession")

APPENDIX II: CARDASSIA

Characters

Dukat, Athra (female) wife of Skrain Dukat

Dukat, Procal (male) an archon in the Cardassian military justice system; the father of Skrain Dukat. (Note: The elder Dukat is listed in some sources as being a military officer, and in others as a justice of the court. *Day of the Vipers* splits the difference and describes him as a military judge in the Central Command's equivalent of the JAG office. He was first referred to as "the late Justice Procal" in DS9/"The Die Is Cast".)

Dukat, Skrain (male) Cardassian military officer who served under Danig Kell during the formal first contact with Bajor, and eventually became prefect of Bajor during the occupation (DS9/"Emissary"; Dukat's given name was first established in the DS9 novel *A Stitch in Time*.)

Hadlo (male) a senior priest of the Oralian Way

Hekit (male) a jagul in the Cardassian military

Ico, Rhan (female) non-military xenologist

Kell, Danig (male) commander of the starship *Kornaire* in 2318, later promoted to jagul and placed in charge of Bajoran affairs by Central Command. (DS9/"Civil Defense")

Letin, Pasir (male) priest of the Oralian Way

Matrik (male) a glinn serving aboard the *Kornaire* in 2318

Orloc (male) a glinn under Dukat serving aboard the *Vandir* in 2328

Pa'Dar, Kotan (male) non-military scientist assigned to the first contact mission to Bajor. The Pa'Dar family are all politicians and they disapprove of Kotan's dalliance with the sciences. (DS9/"Cardassians")

Seren (female) a follower of the Oralian Way, a former nurse

Tunol (female) Dukat's second-in-command aboard the *Kashai* and later aboard the *Vandir*

Urad (male) a young follower of the Oralian Way

Places

Corvon: a population center on Cardassia Prime

Ingav: a planet annexed by the Cardassian Union in 2301 (*DS9/Section 31: Abyss*)

Tellel Basin: population center on cardassia Prime

Terok: military locational/strategic designation code for the planet Bajor (Terok Nor was established in the DS9 episode "Cardassians" as the original name of the space station that later became Deep Space 9.)

Senmir: population center on Cardassia Prime

Ships

Daikon: starship in service with the Union navy in 2323

Kashai: starship commanded by Skrain Dukat in 2323

Kornaire: *Selek*-class ship commanded by Danig Kell in 2318 (DS9/"Waltz")

Selek class: starship in service with the Union navy, an older-model vessel, not as new as the larger *Galor* class

Vandir: *Galor*-class ship commanded by Skrain Dukat in 2328

Food & Drink

rokat: dried, salted fish jerky; an unpopular dish among naval crews

seafruit: marine animal, analogous to a sea cucumber

taspar **eggs:** tasty when they are boiled, fried, or scrambled; eating them raw is not recommended (TNG/"Chain of Command, Part II")

tefla **broth:** soup of shellfish and vegetables

Other

deca: a measurement of distance, roughly equivalent to a meter

Faces of the Fates: a term for the recitation masks used by the Oralian Way

Galor Banner: the symbol of the Cardasssian Union

***Janad*-class tank:** military urban assault vehicle

jevonite: precious stone (TNG/"Chain of Command, Part II")

metric: a measurement of time, roughly equivalent to a minute

Oralian Way: religion dating back to the First Hebitian civilization on Cardassia Prime, the followers of the Way wear hooded, pastel-colored robes with lines of ornamental beads denoting "rank" within the religion. There are at least four books (or codexes) in the Oralian texts known as the Recitations. (The Hebitian civilization was first mentioned in TNG/"Chain of Command, Part II"; the Oralian Way was established in the DS9 novel *A Stitch in Time*.)

Tethen: a figure from the Oralian religious texts, "the proud man" from the fourth codex of the Recitations.

Military Ranks

The following is a list of Cardassian ranks and their Starfleet analogs. This system borrows from the work of Steven Kenson's unpublished *Iron & Ash* supplement for the *Star Trek* Roleplaying Game from Last Unicorn Games.

garresh: noncommissioned officer

gil: ensign (*Star Trek: Deep Space Nine Technical Manual*)

glinn: lieutenant (TNG/"The Wounded")

dalin: lieutenant commander

dal: commander
gul: captain (TNG/"The Wounded")
jagul: commodore or rear admiral
legate: admiral (DS9/"The Maquis, Part II")

APPENDIX III: MISCELLANEOUS

Characters

Foroe (Xepolite male) owner/operator, or "hetman," of a tramp freighter

Gold, David (human male) Starfleet lieutenant and senior officer on the *U.S.S. Gettysburg* (*Corps of Engineers #1: The Belly of the Beast*)

Grek (Ferengi male) trader and associate of Syjin

Jameson, Mark (human male) captain of the Federation starship *Gettysburg* (TNG/"Too Short a Season")

Jones, Gwen (human female) Starfleet lieutenant junior grade; specialist in Bajoran culture and language

Muhle (Tiburonian male), Starfleet ensign serving as communications officer aboard the *U.S.S. Gettysburg*

Nechayev, Alyanna (human female), Starfleet lieutenant; intelligence operative (TNG/"Chain of Command, Part I")

sh'Sena, Dilat (Andoran *shen*) Starfleet lieutenant, chief of security on the *U.S.S. Gettysburg* (*Corps of Engineers: Turn the Page*. Note: sh'Sena was erroneously named th'Sena in her first appearance.)

T'Vel (Vulcan female) Starfleet commander; executive officer of the *U.S.S. Gettysburg* (*Corps of Engineers: Turn the Page*)

Tepper (human female) Starfleet officer serving as a nurse aboard the *U.S.S. Gettysburg*

Places

Ab-Tzenketh: homeworld of the Tzenkethi Coalition (The Tzenkethi were first mentioned in DS9/"The Adversary")

Delavi III: location of a covert Cardassian listening post (*Corps of Engineers: Turn the Page*)

Talaria: homeworld of the Talarian Republic (TNG/
"Suddenly Human")

Starships & Technology

flyer: generic term for a small aircraft

U.S.S. Gettysburg: Federation starship, *Constellation* class,
commanded by Captain Mark Jameson (TNG/"Too
Short a Season"; the *Gettysburg*'s class was first suggested
in the *Star Trek Encyclopedia.)*

marauder: generic term for a Tzenkethi cruiser

shimmerknife: a small edged weapon with a vibrating
blade

skimmer: generic term for a near-ground hovercraft

Food & Drink

agnam **loaf:** fungal foodstuff that requires several years to
mature for the best taste

methrin **eggs:** tasty when they are boiled, fried, or scrambled

porwiggies: porcine creatures used as food animals

tranya: a beverage originating in the First Federation
(TOS/"The Corbomite Maneuver")

Acknowledgments

I'd like to express my gratitude to the people who helped me find my way across the Final Frontier; top of that list must be Lolita Fatjo, who, in addition to becoming a good friend in later years, saw the determination in me and held open the door to the Star Trek universe.

Respect is also due to Michael Piller and Ron Moore, whose generosity and honesty first convinced me I had a shot at becoming a professional writer; to Joe Menosky, Bryan Fuller, Andre Bormanis, and Michael Taylor, who all gave me sterling advice; and to Brannon Braga, Jeri Taylor, and Robin Burger, who made me look great.

Thanks to Marco Palmieri for bringing me into the prose Trek fold, to Diane Duane, Peter Morwood, Andrew Robinson, Una McCormack, John M. Ford, and all those who set the bar.

And for all the support—both moral and technical—I'd like to thank the following people: Ben Aaronovich, Karen McCreedy, Peter J. Evans, and Jon Chapman, each of whom helped me mold this story in one way or another; Geoff Mandel, for his Star Charts and for my nebula; Steve Kenson, for his work on the unpublished Iron & Ash sourcebook; Alan Kobayashi, Terry Erdmann, Paula M. Block, Michael and Denise Okuda, Debbie Mirek, Dayton Ward, and Kevin Dilmore for their works of reference; my friends

among the crews of the good (and bad!) ships *Endeavour,
Genesis II, Intrepid,* and *Bargazer* for journeys into and out
of adversity; the Friday Nighters, the Enfield Suicide Squad,
the Chappa'ai gang, the Starfury mob, the Tech Crew, and
the Novelscribes.

And last, but never least, much love to Mandy Mills—
half-Vulcan, half-Romulan, all gorgeous.

About the Author

James Swallow is proud to be the only British writer to have worked on a *Star Trek* television series, creating the original story concepts for the *Star Trek Voyager* episodes "One" and "Memorial." His other associations with the *Star Trek* saga include the short stories "Closure," "Ordinary Days," and "The Black Flag" for the anthologies *Distant Shores, The Sky's the Limit,* and *Shards and Shadows,* the script for the video game *Star Trek Invasion,* and over four hundred articles in thirteen different *Star Trek* magazines around the world.

Beyond the final frontier, as well as a nonfiction book (*Dark Eye: The Films of David Fincher*), James also wrote the *Sundowners* series of original steampunk westerns, *Jade Dragon, The Butterfly Effect,* and fiction in the worlds of *Doctor Who* (*Peacemaker, Singularity,* and *Old Soldiers*), *Warhammer 40,000* (*The Flight of the Eisenstein, Faith & Fire, Deus Encarmine,* and *Deus Sanguinius*), *Stargate* (*Halcyon* and *Relativity*) and *2000AD* (*Eclipse, Whiteout,* and *Blood Relative*). His other credits include scripts for video games and audio dramas, including *Battlestar Galactica, Blake's 7,* and *Space 1889.*

James Swallow lives in London, and is currently at work on his next book.

Not sure what to read next?

Visit Pocket Books online at
www.simonsays.com

Reading suggestions for
you and your reading group
New release news
Author appearances
Online chats with your favorite writers
Special offers
Order books online
And much, much more!

THE NEW ADVENTURES OF STAR TREK: DEEP SPACE NINE®

FROM POCKET BOOKS
AVAILABLE WHEREVER BOOKS ARE SOLD
ALSO AVAILABLE AS EBOOKS

www.startrekbooks.com